Daughter of Deceit

BY PATRICIA SPRINKLE

Family Tree Mystery Series
Daughter of Deceit
Sins of the Fathers
Death on the Family Tree

MacLaren Yarbrough Mystery Series
What Are You Wearing to Die?
Guess Who's Coming to Die?
Did You Declare the Corpse?
Who Killed the Queen of Clubs?
When Will the Dead Lady Sing?
Who Let That Killer in the House?
Who Left That Body in the Rain?
Who Invited the Dead Man?
But Why Shoot the Magistrate?
When Did We Lose Harriet?

Shelia Travis Mystery Series

Deadly Secrets on the St. Johns

A Mystery Bred in Buckhead

Death of a Dunwoody Matron

Murder in the Charleston Manner

Murder in Markham

Job's Corner Chronicles

Carley's Song

The Remember Box

Daughter of Deceit

Patricia Sprinkle

HARPER LUXE

An Imprint of HarperCollins*Publishers*

FIRST HARPERLUXE EDITION

HarperLuxe™ is a trademark of HarperCollins Publishers

Library of Congress Cataloging-in-Publication Data is available upon request.

ISBN: 978-0-06-166913-2

08 09 10 11 12 ID/RRD 10 9 8 7 6 5 4 3 2 1

Acknowledgments

Thanks to . . .

Obviously this is a work of fiction, so Winston Holcomb and his military record are entirely fictitious. However, while I never assigned Winnie to any specific heavy-bomber group, I based his military history largely on records from the 376th and the 461st Heavy Bombers Groups of the Fifteenth Air Force. The Fifteenth did bomb the South Synthetic Oil Refinery, Blechhammer, Germany, on November 20, 1944, they did meet heavy flak, and two crews did bail out over Yugoslavia. As I have learned about the bravery of those crews during World War II—the missions they flew, the medals they earned—I have come to greatly admire them. So much so that for our anniversary, my husband gave me *Bomber Missions: Aviation Art of*

World War II by G.E. Patrick Murray, the same coffee table book Tom Murray had in his library.

I am grateful to those who created and continue to maintain web sites for the heavy-bomber groups, and I owe special thanks to Hughes Glantzbert, historian of the 461st Heavy Bombers Group, for steering me toward other information and web sites I needed.

Thanks, too, to Bruce Gamble, formerly of the U.S. Navy and currently a military historian, and to Mary K. Howle, attorney and former Air Force Captain, for pointing me to other web sites and sources for military research; to Winter Benedict of Atlanta's High Museum of Art, for researching current prices for Monet paintings; and to Patricia Browning, long-time resident of Buckhead, who read the manuscript to be sure I fairly represented her neighborhood. The accuracy of the book is due to them. Any inaccuracies are my own.

Making books is a cooperative effort, so once again I have to thank my agent, Nancy Yost; my editor, Sarah Durand; and my publicist, Danielle Bartlett. They are the invisible faces behind these pages. Finally, as always, I thank my patient husband, Bob, who recognizes that writing is not a profession, it is an obsession.

Primary Characters

Katharine Murray

Tom Murray, her husband

Posey Buiton, Tom's sister

Hollis Buiton, Posey's youngest daughter

Bara Holcomb Weidenauer, Atlanta socialite

Foley Weidenauer, Bara's second husband

Carlene Morris, Foley's mistress

Payne Branwell Anderson, Bara's daughter by her first marriage

Ann Rose Anderson, Payne's mother-in-law

Winston "Winnie" Holcomb, Bara's father (deceased)

Nettie Payne Holcomb, Bara's mother (deceased)

Scotty and Eloise Payne, Bara's maternal uncle and his wife

Murdoch Payne, Scotty's daughter

Rita Louise Phipps, old friend of Bara's mother
Kenny Todd, computer genius and friend of Katharine's son, Jon
Maria Ortiz, Bara's friend

Daughter of Deceit

Chapter 1

Monday

Bara Holcomb Weidenauer was on a mission to save her life. She sped through Buckhead on a hot August Monday, headed for the storage unit where she had sent her father's things after he died. Winnie had had a habit of tucking stray fifties and hundreds into desk and dresser drawers until he needed them. She desperately hoped she could find a few. Her husband had frozen her bank accounts and credit cards, and her cash was almost gone.

She groped for her father's silver flask in the glove compartment of her navy Jaguar. "A little something to steady my nerves," she explained. She unscrewed the top with one hand in a practiced motion and held the flask up, waiting for objections.

She got none.

She was alone in the car.

In fact, Bara was alone on the street—a rarity at that hour in Buckhead. Mornings in that privileged Atlanta community, where massive houses sit on acres of tree-shaded lawns, usually feature a parade of maids and lawn service trucks, delivery vans, and women heading to aerobics, meetings, and children's activities.

Taking her privacy as a sign—for Bara seldom took a drink when someone else could see her—she gulped down two big swigs of Wild Turkey's *Rare Breed*. That's what her husband kept under his bathroom sink. She felt no guilt about stealing Foley's bourbon. He owed her.

She didn't really like the taste of alcohol, but had learned young to appreciate the way it relaxed strictures her mother had imprinted on her brain: *Be sweet, now. Pull down your skirt. Wear a hat, honey— your skin turns so dark in the sun. Don't let profanity pass your lips. Don't stride so—ladies glide like swans. Don't be rowdy—nobody wants to marry a tomboy.*

Bara lifted the flask to toast the invisible presence who hovered at her shoulder, as impossible to please in death as in life. "I *was* a tomboy, Mama, but two people still wanted to marry me. Foul-mouthed losers, both of them, but they asked to marry me. Fool that I was, I let them."

Linking Ray Branwell and Foley Weidenauer in one thought required a large, fortifying gulp. The whiskey blazed down her throat but settled like a water balloon in her stomach. It never landed as easy as it went down. Her mother's disapproval accompanied every swallow.

She kept one eye on the rearview mirror as she drove out what she thought of as the back door to Buckhead. West on West Pace's Ferry Road where the governor's mansion, up near Peachtree, was by no means the largest house on the street. Left onto Moore's Mill and past several miles of houses that were smaller, but still beyond the means of most Atlanta residents. Across a railroad bridge far too short to prepare one for the sudden change to seedy strip malls, light industry, and a sewage treatment plant. Foley had no idea where Bara was hiding Winnie's papers. Bara had no intention of letting him find out.

She pulled into the parking lot, took one more short swallow, and continued her defense to an invisible jury. "I need a pick-me-up this morning. If I don't find some money, I don't know what I'm going to do."

She left the flask in the glove compartment. Bara didn't carry whiskey in her purse. She was no drunk.

Heat rose in waves from the parking lot asphalt. Atlanta's morning temperature was eighty-five and rising. "Why did I put on long sleeves and silk?" she muttered, pulling her shirt from her body to let in some air. Because she hadn't been thinking clearly. She hadn't been thinking clearly since Winnie died.

As she unlocked the door to her unit, she protested, "I know it's been four months, Mama. I know I need to go through all this. I would have, if Foley hadn't demanded that divorce almost immediately. Fighting him has taken every bit of strength I've got."

She stepped into the dim, chilly unit separated from others by thick concrete walls. A sob caught in her throat as she saw the big leather chair and desk Winnie had used at home. A whiff of his scent glossed the musty air. He could have simply stepped out for a moment. His mahogany bedroom chest stood with its back to a wall, still full of clothes she could not bear to discard. Shoulder-high stacks of boxes contained the contents of his library: books, awards, trophies, and knickknacks. Other boxes held files from his downtown office—files without which Foley couldn't carry out all of his diabolical plan. Had Bara had a premonition of what he was going to do? Was that why she had seized and hidden all Winnie's files immediately after his death? She was pleased to think she had been at least that smart.

"Pass 'GO' and collect two hundred dollars," she muttered hopefully as she sank into Winnie's chair. To appease her mother's pious spirit, she added, "Fervently do we hope, devoutly do we pray."

As she pulled out the bottom drawer, she had to overcome a surge of guilt. Her father's desks had been off-limits when she and her brother, Art, were small. "I need groceries," she whispered to Winnie's memory. "I will not beg Foley for milk money."

An old manila envelope lay on top. Bulky, it was faded to a dull gold—the kind of place Winnie might have stuffed cash and forgotten it. When she shook it, it rattled. The tape that once sealed the flap was brittle, provided no resistance when she slid a finger under it. Inside, she felt plastic, paper, and round hard disks. She sank into Winnie's chair and dumped the contents onto the top of the desk. Out fell old driver's licenses, political campaign buttons, and masses of yellowed newspaper clippings. Among them were all her report cards and letters to Winnie.

No money.

Disappointed, she was about to shove everything back in when she felt something hard lodged in the bottom. She shook the envelope again. Out tumbled a chain holding a thick silver locket shaped like a heart. She held it to her breast, trying to capture a memory.

She had been small, and it had thumped heavy against her dress. Had she worn it, or merely held it against her? She could not remember.

Had it been Nettie's? Had her mother ever been sentimental enough to carry her husband's picture around her neck? Bara would like to open it, but her gnawed nails were too short to slip between the halves, and she had no thin blade with her. She put it back in the envelope with the rest of the junk, to examine at home.

She returned to the drawer and flipped through three ledgers that had been under the envelope. She found nothing. She set them aside and took out a wooden cigar box. Had she finally hit pay dirt?

Instead, a pile of beribboned medals brought back a memory of startling clarity:

She was sitting on her daddy's lap with her legs dangling down his while he opened the wooden box. She could feel the soft/hard place where his artificial leg connected to the stump. The smell of sweet tobacco filled her nostrils as Winnie lifted the medals out one by one. She clapped with delight as he held them to catch the sun. She reached for one bright star.

The memory ended, as many of her childhood memories did, with unhappiness. Her mother had caught them poring over the medals and put a stop to their game. "Bara, come wash your hands. It's almost time for lunch. Winston, put those things out of the reach of small hands and curious minds." Nettie Payne Holcomb had a genius for taking light and laughter out of life.

Not like Winnie, who loved to laugh. He had whooped when Bara had stomped her small foot at the president of the C&S Bank and insisted, "He is Winston Arthur Holcomb Senior. He is not Winnie. Winnie is a stuffed bear!"

Her daddy had laughed and thrown her high in the air, then he'd explained, "My friends call me Winnie, for Winston."

"May I call you Winnie too?"

"Sure. Call me Winnie."

Her mother hadn't liked it. Nettie always called him Winston. But she had failed to make Bara call him Daddy after that. By the time Bara was ten, she was also calling her mother Nettie—but only in the privacy of her own thoughts and with selected friends.

The next time Bara had asked about the "ribbons and stars," though, Winnie had said, "Your mother asked me to put them away." She had never seen them again. Wherever he had kept them while she was growing up, he must have put them back in his desk drawer when he moved into a condo two years before he died.

In the dusty storage unit she rocked gently in the butter-soft chair that smelled of Winnie and sifted through the medals, her pleasure mingled with regret. There was the gold star she remembered, Purple Hearts she had thought cute—having no idea of what it cost to earn one.

She wished Winnie had told her what his medals were for. He had been a hero in World War II, had returned from Italy with one leg. Why had he always refused to talk about what he'd done in the war?

In addition to Winnie's medals, she found a Bronze Star with her brother's name on it, sent by the U.S. Army after it was too late for Art to wear it. Her big brother had not always been kind, and their mother clearly preferred him, but Bara had loved him. She deeply regretted that his remains lay in an unidentified grave somewhere in the jungles of Vietnam.

She lifted the tail of her shirt and polished the star before replacing it in the box. Then she rummaged all the way to the bottom of the cigar box, hoping Winnie had stashed money there. She unearthed a small envelope, blank and sealed.

It was heavy. Coins? Winnie never saved coins. He emptied his pockets into any handy receptacle when he changed clothes. Her mother endlessly complained, "You are putting temptation into the way of the maids."

He would drop the coins into used coffee cups or empty vases and retort, "They are welcome to any change they find. I will not walk around with that weight."

Maids. The thought of maids made Bara tremble with rage. She wouldn't be in the mess she was in except for a maid named Carlene.

From the beginning Bara had not liked her. She was not only blond, curvy, and sly, she was sullen and insubordinate to Bara and Deva, Bara's housekeeper. When Deva had reported that Carlene was more apt to stroke the silver than polish it, Bara had said, "So fire her."

"I did, but she complained to Mr. Foley. He told me to give her another chance."

Bara had shrugged. "One more month." She had kicked herself a thousand times since.

When Deva had caught Carlene trying on Bara's clothes, she had fetched Bara. Carlene saw her mistress in the mirror and smirked. "Your shoes are too big for me."

Bara had fired her at once.

That led to a huge row with Foley. Six months later, Carlene was wearing sapphires and spending time with Foley in downtown bars. Bara was searching frantically for cash in a concrete storage unit.

She took a deep breath and clenched her fists. She would not cry. She made it a matter of pride. She might kill Foley, but he would not make her cry.

What was in the blank envelope?

She opened it and dumped another Purple Heart and a set of dog tags onto her palm. Her eyes blurred as she read the name: WINSTON ARTHUR BRANWELL. Her son's tags and medal, sealed away and shoved down under all the other medals as if they were too much for Winnie to bear.

Pain burrowed deep and clutched her. "Oh, Win!" Tears she would not shed for Foley fell for Win. They spotted her red silk shirt like drops of blood. She had known Win was too fragile to make a good soldier, had begged him not to listen when Foley called him a sissy and taunted him with the heroism of his uncle and grandfather. But one day Foley's taunts goaded Win into a rage so fierce that he had enlisted before he'd cooled down. Bara would never forgive Foley for that. Never.

Win had been killed in Baghdad the week before Christmas. His loss was still a raw gash in his mother's soul. When the news had come, she'd had to be sedated for weeks. Winnie must have intercepted the medals and stored them with his own. Oh, Win! Winnie!

She had borne too much that year. Clutching Win's medals close to her heart, she flung her head down on her bony knees and had a major meltdown.

A thump somewhere in the building reminded her she was not alone. She inhaled deeply through her nostrils and pressed her lips together, the way her mother had taught her. *A lady never cries in public.* She dried her tears, then replaced Win's medals in the cigar box and set it beside her on the floor. Desperately she shook each ledger. Finally she had her reward: a couple of fifties fluttered onto her lap. That was enough for the moment. She had lost her zest for the search.

She powdered her face to remove traces of tears, and dabbed on lipstick with a shaky hand. She replaced the ledgers in the desk drawer, but carried the cigar box and old envelope to the car with her. She might as well run by a grocery store while she was out and had a little change in her pocket.

She entered the Publix warily. Bara had never bought groceries until two months ago, when Foley had fired their staff. She had never realized how many choices buying food entailed. Bewildered, she roamed the store amid towers of stuff she didn't want or need. She couldn't make even minor decisions. Bananas or cantaloupe? Pork chops or chicken? In frustration, she piled her cart with everything.

What a relief to finally reach the aisle for beer and wine. She didn't like wine, but put three bottles of cheap red in her cart. Red wine was supposed to be good for your heart—or was it your stomach? It was healthy, anyway. Probably full of vitamins.

At the register, she found she had more than depleted her newfound wealth. Flushed with shame, she randomly selected items to abandon and fled to her car. She headed home with more food than one woman needed, almost nothing in her purse, and a barbed wire of grief piercing her heart.

Chapter 2

Fifteen minutes later, Katharine Murray stepped off her shaded veranda and hoped the morning would not be her last.

Riding with her sister-in-law was risky at the best of times. That morning, Posey was tootling up her drive in a new red convertible that looked no bigger than a bumper car, and although Atlanta was eighty-five in the shade, Posey had the top down. In large sunglasses, her bright hair wrapped in a white scarf, she looked like an aging Hollywood star—except that nobody used the word "aging" in the presence of Posey Buiton.

"Do you like it?" she called. "Wrens brought it home yesterday as a surprise birthday present. I've got the air conditioner on, but I couldn't bear to leave the top up on my first day. Okay?" Without waiting for an answer, she waved a gold chiffon scarf. "I brought this for your hair. It will look good with your coloring."

Posey Buiton might be flighty about some things, but she had a faultless eye for clothes. The scarf was a perfect complement to Katharine's auburn hair, copper shirt, and creamy slacks.

Katharine wanted to say, "Thanks, but I've decided to stay home," but a voice in her head reminded her, *Be nice! You called Posey for a ride and she gave up an aerobics class to drive you.* Was that her mother's voice or her own conscience? It was hard to tell them apart at times.

Ignoring every shred of common sense she possessed, Katharine lowered herself into the passenger seat. The car had plenty of legroom if you didn't mind sitting on your tailbone.

"Wrens spoils you rotten," she said, tying on the scarf. "You both know your birthday isn't for another month. By then he'll have forgotten this was supposed to be your present."

"And don't you remind him." Posey stroked the dashboard. "Isn't it gorgeous? You ought to ask Tom to buy you one." The car leaped down the drive and Posey slammed on brakes halfway to the street. "Sorry. I haven't gotten the feel of the pedals yet."

Katharine resigned herself to the next fifteen minutes, glad their drive would not take them outside the residential part of Buckhead—streets where Posey had grown up. Katharine had scarcely comforted herself with that thought when Posey flew out of the drive without braking and barely missed the back bumper of a passing navy Jag.

"Sorry. I was looking for my turn signal." Posey didn't sound the least bit dismayed. She peered after the Jag. "Wasn't that Bara Weidenauer? Bless her heart, she is going through so much right now. Have you heard about Foley's latest little trick?"

Katharine shook her head. "I don't know them very well."

"You know her daughter, Payne, Lolly's roommate. She married Hamilton Anderson."

Nobody but Posey Buiton would have named three daughters Laura, Mary, and Hollis and insisted on calling them Lolly, Molly, and Holly. So far only the youngest had rebelled and insisted on being called by her full name.

"Only slightly." Katharine didn't point out that she'd had little reason to keep track of her nieces' college roommates—she'd had children of her own to raise.

"You were at their wedding, " Posey persisted.

Katharine's chief memory of the extravaganza Bara Weidenauer had flung for her daughter was of the receiving line, where the tall dark groom stood beside his lovely but quiet bride while her mother, in a sparkling silver dress, outshone them both. Not intentionally, but because wherever Bara was, she lit up the room. "We sat on the groom's side," Katharine told Posey. "Ann Rose and Jeffers put us on the list."

The Anderson men had been the pediatricians of choice in Buckhead for half a century. Hamilton Anderson took care of Posey's grandchildren. Hamilton's father, Jeffers, had taken care of Posey's three daughters and Tom and Katharine's children, Susan and Jon. Jeffers's widowed father, Oscar, had cared for Posey and Tom when they were small. But Katharine's primary connection to the family was that Ann Rose Anderson, Jeffers's wife and Hamilton's mother, was one of her best friends, in spite of being twenty years her elder. Katharine and Posey were headed to Ann Rose's that very morning for a meeting to discuss adult illiteracy in Atlanta.

"Speaking of Jeffers," Posey executed a turn without finding her signals and waved at the driver who blew his horn behind her, "didn't I hear that he and Oscar have gone on a world cruise or something out in the Far East?"

"Not exactly. They're spending several months on a medical ship that stops in ports and takes care of destitute people."

Posey grimaced. "Lord only knows what germs they'll pick up."

"They're doctors. They know about germs. What were you going to say about Payne?"

"She is worried sick about her mother. I am, too. I don't know if Bara can survive."

Bara hadn't noticed the convertible shooting out of the Murrays' drive. She'd been taking another slug of bourbon. "I've had a bad shock," she excused herself, "and whiskey is good for shock. Those blasted medals. The Holcomb family has done far more than enough for our country. What has the country ever done for us?"

She felt her father's grip on her shoulder as soon as she voiced that heresy. Winston Arthur Holcomb Sr. had remained a strong supporter of John F. Kennedy's sentiments long after Kennedy was shot.

"But Winnie," she protested as she reached her own street, "we couldn't all be like you."

How old had she been when she realized she would never play football at Georgia Tech, never become a war hero? When did she give up her dream of becoming an architect and a partner in Holcomb & Associates? At what age had she finally agreed with Nettie that she could not grow up to be just like Winnie?

As the Jag purred up the long hill to the stucco mansion she called home, Bara demanded of the universe, "How did my life go so flat-out wrong?"

She slammed on the brakes barely in time to avoid crashing into the garage door. That would have been disastrous. She had no funds to repair it, and Foley's lawyer . . .

She would not think about Foley or his lawyer.

She would not think about her own lawyer, either. Poor Uncle Scotty knew practically nothing about divorce. His specialty was golf. When he wasn't on the links, he handled accounts for a few condominium associations. She suspected he didn't do that very well. Still, her mother's only brother was all she could afford at the moment, and she had to have a lawyer in this mess.

She took another gulp of whiskey as she fumbled for the door opener, had to press the button twice before the door began to rise. She pulled slowly into the four-car garage, turned off the engine, and laid her head on the wheel. "It wasn't supposed to be like this."

She lifted her head to study her face in the flask, a reflection as distorted as her life. "I was programmed from birth for marriage and good works," she told it somberly. She ticked off the accomplishments of sixty-two years on her fingers. "Debut, Randolph-Macon, marriage to Ray, two kids, all those fund-raising shindigs, then Foley, my own private roller coaster to hell." She flung back her head and took a swallow that choked her. "Dammit, Mama," she roared, "between us, we have wasted my life. And what do I have to show for it? Nothing!"

She blearily contemplated the white door in front of her hood and wondered whether she had enough energy to carry in the groceries.

Two months before, Deva would have bought the groceries and brought them home, but Bara had come home one day to discover that Foley had dismissed her entire staff—some of whom had been with her for twenty years. Instead, he had hired a weekly cleaning crew and a lawn service.

"Like a museum or something," Bara had stormed.

"We're only keeping the place in shape to sell," he had said coldly.

"I'm never going to sell. And who's going to do the cooking and laundry?"

"For those, my dear, you are on your own."

Since then, Bara had subsisted on yogurt, cereal, fruit, and TV dinners. She had ruined several good garments before she'd discovered care instructions on those little tags sewn in seams. Recently she had noticed, to her dismay, how much Publix charged for milk and detergent.

"I bought too many groceries," she lamented, resting her forehead on the steering wheel. "Too many groceries, too much house."

It had been big for four people. For one, it was enormous.

"Not one, two," she reminded herself. "Foley's in the basement. I've got a rat in my basement, Mama. That's what happens when you marry one. You know what he said yesterday? He wants me to sell my car!" She clutched the wheel of her beloved Jag. Why didn't somebody come to rescue her from so much pain?

"I'm going under, Winnie!" she cried. "I can't hold out much longer."

She took two long swallows from the flask. To forget. But she couldn't.

Even after months of therapy, she still woke some nights weeping because she had killed her daddy.

Chapter 3

The air filled with the theme from *The Lone Ranger.*

It took a couple of seconds for Bara to realize the music was not the soundtrack to her thoughts, but rather, her new cell phone's ring tone. As she grabbed her black leather purse and pawed through it, she smiled. She and Chip had chosen the ring tone together. "It goes bump-a-bump," he had announced with satisfaction. Her three-year-old grandson was the one person in the world who could still make her smile.

The phone was buried deep in her purse, eluding her shaking fingers. "Blasted nuisance," she muttered as she searched. "Never would have gotten the danged thing if Payne hadn't insisted. I sure named her right. The girl can be a royal pain."

She pulled out the phone and flipped it open without looking to see who the caller was.

"Bara?" It was her cousin, Murdoch Payne, Uncle Scotty's only child.

Bara scowled. Next to Foley, Murdoch was her least favorite person on earth. In order to reach the phone in the Jag, Murdoch's voice had needed to travel from her house to a satellite thousands of miles above the earth and back to a very small target. Couldn't it have gotten sidetracked along the way?

"You didn't forget the literacy meeting at Ann Rose Anderson's this morning, did you?" Murdoch sounded exactly like her Aunt Nettie used to: *Oh, Bara, what have you done now?*

Bara huffed. Of course she had forgotten the meeting. Who wouldn't, with the shock of finding those medals? If she had remembered, she needn't have gone to the grocery store until later. Ann Rose was serving lunch.

"I didn't forget, I'm running a little behind."

"It's already ten forty. If you aren't here in five minutes, we're going to be late."

Murdoch lived in a small white house on the unfashionable fringe of Buckhead. The street hadn't even been in Buckhead when Murdoch's family had moved there, but Buckhead was oozing in all directions as developers coopted the name. Winnie used to predict that all of metropolitan Atlanta would eventually be in either Buckhead or its equally prestigious neighbor, Vinings.

"I'm coming," Bara snapped.

Murdoch gave another righteous huff. "You'd better hurry."

Some people claimed that Murdoch, eight years younger than Bara, was a saint. Hadn't she given up her job and condo to move back in with her father after her mother's dementia got so bad they'd had to put Eloise in a nursing home? Every time Bara heard about "Saint Murdoch," she had to clench her teeth to keep from pointing out that Murdoch had hated her job and had never liked the one-bedroom condo that was all she could afford after she lost most of her money in the technology bubble—convinced, with her usual stubbornness, that she knew more about investing than her broker. Murdoch had been delighted to move back home and devote herself to travel and genealogy while Uncle Scotty spent his days happily serving a few clients, playing countless rounds of golf, and dropping in once a day to visit Eloise—who often had no idea who he was, but thought him charming.

Bara sometimes wondered if Murdoch and Uncle Scotty were aware that she knew they lived comfortably because Eloise's teacher's pension was supplemented by income from a generous trust fund Winnie had set up to take care of his wife's brother and his family, after Scotty climbed into the saddle of his father's successful law firm and rode it to the brink of bankruptcy. If so, they never mentioned the fact. Murdoch often publicly praised her daddy for paying the bills so she could use her money for frequent trips and genealogy books.

How ironic, Bara thought, that Winnie supported Murdoch, Uncle Scotty, and Eloise, when he could not support his own daughter. Not yet. He had left his estate divided between Bara and Payne with a special trust fund for little Chip, but Foley—

She would not think of Foley. Why further ruin her day?

She shook the flask instead, to see if there was more whiskey in it.

"Bara? Are you still there?" Murdoch demanded.

Bara blinked. She had forgotten she was talking to Murdoch. Murdoch was so easy to forget.

"I'll be there in a jiff." She hiccupped and tried to conceal it with a cough. "The world won't end if we're a few minutes late."

"Get here as soon as you can." Murdoch hung up with another righteous huff.

Bara took a defiant slug before she reached for the door handle. As soon as she emptied the trunk and stopped to powder her nose, the *William Tell Overture* again filled her car. She punched the button and shouted to Murdoch, "Keep your britches on! I'm coming!"

It wasn't Murdoch, it was Payne. Murdoch must have called her, because Payne sounded like she was edging her way barefoot across a field of shattered crystal. "Hey, Mama, it's me. What you doing?"

"Sitting in my garage trying to get off the damned phone so I can carry my groceries into the house and go pick up Murdoch for an imbecilic meeting."

"You've been drinking, haven't you? You never swear unless you've been drinking. Were you drinking and driving?"

"You are getting downright neurotic on that subject. I am not driving. I told you, I'm sitting in the garage. I took a couple of swallows sitting right here, to steady my nerves before going to pick up Murdoch. And I'm swearing because I've got to take her to a meeting. I have been to enough meetings in my lifetime to qualify for a Congressional Medal for meeting goers. I wouldn't go, except Ann Rose twisted my arm so hard she nearly broke it. But I would never have promised if I'd known I'd have to drive Murdoch. You know she makes me think of fingernails on blackboards. I can't talk now, I'm running late. I had to go get groceries. There wasn't a bite to eat in the house. Now I have to carry the dratted things in before the meeting or my frozen foods will melt."

"You carry in your groceries and I'll come pick you up. I don't want you driving. I'll be there as soon as I tear Chip away from his sandbox."

Normally Bara would have been delighted to see Chip, but Payne's tone enraged her. "I'm fine to drive, Miss Prissypants. And I've got to go. I'm late."

She punched the button to end the call. Almost immediately the phone rang again. That time she checked the name. Maria Ortiz. She pressed the button to disconnect. Maria was one friend Bara was avoiding at the moment. "I can't talk right now," she apologized to the air. "I've got to get to that blasted meeting." She wasn't too drunk to feel a pang of regret. Maria deserved better of her. But Maria also expected too much.

Down in the basement, Foley Weidenauer heard the garage door open while he was shaving. Foley shaved with a blade. His beard was heavy, like the rest of him. He was a bear of a man–tall and burly. He held the razor poised while he waited for the garage door to go down. As soon as Bara slammed the door to the house—Bara always slammed doors, as if she had a grudge against them for standing between her and wherever she wanted to go—he would go upstairs and try once again to make her see reason. She would not win this battle. Foley was determined she wouldn't, if he had to camp in the basement for a year. His lawyer had advised him not to move out of the house. They didn't want her claiming he had abandoned it.

Foley was confident he had everything on his side. Not only power and money—although neither Bara nor either of their attorneys had any idea how much he had stashed in offshore accounts, and were only beginning to learn how little he had left where she could get to it. He also had one weapon she could not match: time. He was fifteen years younger than she, forty-seven his last birthday. In his prime. He could wait her out. He would not live in that basement forever.

He inhaled and wrinkled his nose. Even with two dehumidifiers going, the place smelled musty, like the cheap apartments he and his mother used to live in. There had been a lot of apartments, because they kept getting kicked out for the friends she brought home. Foley was ten before he had discovered the nature of her relationship with those friends—one of whom, forever nameless, had been his father. He had been eleven when Social Services took him away. He'd had to scrabble and fight his way through school and into decent society because of that woman. He would not permit another woman to hold him back now.

He leaned forward and frowned to see a new gray hair in the thick pelt that covered his head. He jerked it out and flung it into the toilet. His hair was as dark as it had been when he was twenty. He intended to keep it that way as long as possible. When he inhaled and pulled in his abs, Carlene said he had the figure of a man of thirty.

Carlene had the figure . . .

He permitted himself a moment's leisure to mentally scan every curve of her body. Soft. Delectable. Not like Bara, the dried-up old prune. He had another twenty-five good years left. He intended to spend them with somebody who would pleasure and admire him, not constantly carp and compare him to her daddy.

But where was Bara? He opened the door of the bathroom and listened intently.

When old Connor Payne, Bara's maternal grandfather, had built the house and installed basement living quarters for his servants, he hadn't worried about whether they would feel the damp or be bothered by noises above them. The way the wooden floors creaked, a listener in the basement could track the movements of anybody on the first floor.

Hearing nothing, Foley left the basement by its outside entrance and hurried around to the garage. Bara was sitting in her Jag.

"I want to talk to you," he called through the closed window.

She reversed into the turnaround so fast that he had to jump out of the way to avoid being hit by the side mirror. Foley glared until the Jag was out of sight.

She hadn't bothered to close the garage door. He checked the door into the house and found it unlocked, the security system unarmed. Again. The woman still counted on servants to protect her house. Anybody could come in and steal everything they had. Anybody could come in and hide in a closet, rape and murder her when she returned. Anybody could come in . . .

Foley smiled.

Chapter 4

Jeffers and Ann Rose Anderson lived with Jeffers's father, Oscar, in a magnificent brick home atop a gentle hill, surrounded by acres of landscaped lawn and a high brick wall. Oscar's wife had inherited the house from her father—a scion of a family endowed with old money. When Oscar's wife had died the year Jeffers finished med school and married Ann Rose, Oscar had suggested that the newlyweds join him in the big house until they found something they liked better. They had lived together amicably for forty years.

That morning, the drive was full of cars, so the only place Posey could park was down near the wall. Posey didn't mind. She went to aerobics twice a day. Katharine didn't. The house was nearly a block away, uphill. As she panted in Posey's wake, she hoped she would live long enough to reach one final glass of water.

"Don't you dare leave me alone with Ann Rose," Posey warned as they approached the front steps. "She intimidates me. She's so . . . so erudite. I mean, look at all those trips she takes. She never travels simply to relax and shop. She comes back with lectures." Posey's idea of a perfect vacation was two weeks on tropical beaches at five-star resorts with a cold drink close at hand, gift shops within easy strolling distance, and a spa off the pool. Katharine had never figured out how Posey and Tom, growing up in the same house, had turned out so different. Tom adored trips where he came back more educated than he left. So did Katharine.

That was only one thing she and Ann Rose had in common. Another was that neither had grown up in Buckhead, although both their mothers had been born and bred there. Katharine had grown up in Miami, where her father taught at the University of Miami School of Law. Ann Rose grew up in Mississippi, and had met Jeffers in New Orleans while she was getting her masters in English and he was at Tulane med school. Like Katharine, Ann Rose had come to Buckhead as a bride.

A third thing they shared was a firm conviction that wealth was not a measure of personal value, but a trust from God to be used for the good of others. They had often worked together in hands-on projects in Atlanta's poorer neighborhoods, and both belonged to organizations that lobbied the recalcitrant Georgia legislature to remember that children matter as much as highways. But Katharine felt that Ann Rose's priorities were clearer than her own. Ann Rose might live in a spacious home filled with antiquities her husband's mother's family had accumulated over several generations, but she had taught in an inner-city high school until her recent retirement, and she personally dressed and lived simply and had never spent much time in beauty parlors or spas. She had always been comfortable with her sturdy body and prematurely white hair. Her one extravagance was travel, and her lectures were widely requested by women's clubs and churches.

"When does the woman sleep?" Posey demanded "Now remember, if she calls for volunteers and you see me about to raise my hand, grab me."

"She's looking for people who *want* to tutor, not people who have been shanghaied. All you have to do is listen to what she has to say, then we can eat and leave."

"Yeah, but you know how impressionable I am." Posey patted frothy curls that created the impression of a blue-eyed bimbo, unless you got a good look at the shrewdness in those eyes. "I might volunteer if she makes a really great speech."

"You're about as impressionable as stainless steel," Katharine told her, "but stick with me, baby, and you won't get hurt. You're just along for the ride."

Posey reached for the doorknob. "Isn't that what you said before that trip where I almost got shot?"

By the time Katharine got her glass of water, the meeting was about to begin. Posey motioned her to a chair she had saved at the back of several rows set in the large front hall and whispered, "If I fall asleep, prop me behind that suit of armor over yonder."

Aerobics and social events, not good works, were Posey's forte. She and Wrens attended black-tie functions for many good causes and contributed generously, but Posey was at the meeting about adult illiteracy only because Katharine was currently without a car. Hers had been wrecked several weeks earlier. Since Tom represented his company in Washington most weeks and only came home on weekends, she had been using his Lexus, but that week, he was working in Atlanta. She had realized during breakfast that she'd need a ride to the meeting, and her fingers had dialed Posey's number out of habit. As she settled into her chair, she reflected that a new car might be essential for her health.

As Ann Rose was beginning her PowerPoint presentation, the front door opened and the scent of bourbon flowed into the hall. Katharine and Posey looked back to see Bara Weidenauer swaying in the doorway. "Lordy," Posey breathed. "Is she drinking again?"

As always when Bara made an entrance, the room fell silent. The woman's long, strong face wasn't beautiful, but she was striking: tall and slender with arresting dark eyes, a mass of once-black curls that were now silver, and eccentricities that kept Atlanta talking. Hostesses dreaded what Bara's blunt tongue might say in their homes, but they invariably invited her. Parties were remembered and talked about if Bara had been there. Committees were never dull if she chaired them. Events that she orchestrated raised more money than others in the city. Her father, Winnie Holcomb, had been a mover and shaker in a city that loves to be moved and shaken, and in the realm of volunteer work, Bara was as unorthodox and effective as her dad.

She raised one hand in apology. "Sorry I'm late. I had to run by Publix for a few things. Oh, drat, I forgot to take them out of the car. Do you reckon they'll be okay?" She flapped one hand in Ann Rose's direction. "Never mind. Go on with what you were saying. Sorry I'm late."

Whispers of surprise rippled the room. Katharine heard ". . . drunk?" ". . . buying groceries?" She wondered which of the two the women found more shocking.

Ann Rose, who was seldom ruffled, asked, "Do you have anything that needs to go in the freezer or refrigerator?"

"They ought to be all right for a couple of hours."

Ann Rose raised her voice slightly. "Katharine, since you're near the door, would you ask Francie to have someone bring in Bara's groceries and store them properly until she's ready to leave? Bara, give Katharine your keys. I believe there's a seat here on the couch."

Two women obligingly shifted to make space for a third in the center. Katharine took the keys and headed in search of Ann Rose's cook. Ann Rose resumed her speech.

The kitchen bustled with caterers in gray uniforms with white aprons, preparing dainty sandwiches and finger foods under Francie's stern eye. Francie—who had run the Anderson kitchen since Jeffers was a boy and who insisted that the Anderson staff wear soft peach uniforms ("more friendly" she called it)—accepted the commission as if it were nothing out of the ordinary. "Bara don't know a thing about groceries. I'll take care of them."

As Katharine rejoined the group, Posey leaned over and whispered, "Did you know there are grown people in Atlanta who don't know how to read? I'll fill you in later." Katharine would be interested to hear what Posey absorbed. That ought to give Ann Rose a baseline for the least somebody could retain.

Ten minutes later, the doorbell rang twice, an urgent summons. Katharine rose to answer, but reached the door in a dead heat with a peach-clad maid. The maid opened the door, then stepped back to let Katharine welcome the newcomers.

Katharine found Murdoch Payne about to press the bell a third time. Behind her stood Payne Anderson wearing an anxious expression and the casual seersucker shorts and T-shirt of a young mother who had been forced to run out when she'd planned to be home all day.

No stranger seeing the two women on the doorstep would guess they were cousins. Payne at thirty looked a lot like her mother used to: tall and striking, with smooth olive skin, perfect brows above dark eyes, and short silky curls the color of polished ebony.

Murdoch looked like a large mouse in a tan pantsuit and comfortable shoes.

Payne spoke in a low, anxious voice. "Did Mama get here safely?"

Katharine nodded, but before she could speak, Murdoch sidled into the hall and announced, "Bara forgot to pick me up, after I'd called!"

Katharine had never liked Murdoch much. They had served together on a couple of committees, and the woman screeched when she got excited. She also took forever to make up her mind about minor decisions, driving other members of the committee wild with pointless discussion; yet, if she were in charge of anything, she would make impulsive, unwise decisions that left messes for others to clear up.

She took the first empty chair she came to—which happened to be the one Katharine had just vacated—and dropped her purse on the floor with an indignant clunk! Since she didn't look before she dropped it, she squarely bombed the half-full glass Katharine had left beside her chair. Water flowed under Katharine's purse and across the hardwood floor.

The same maid who had opened the door hurried forward with towels to sop up the mess. Murdoch ignored her and continued her lament. She didn't bother to lower her voice, being one of those women who presume their distress is the concern of the world. "I'm sorry to be so late, but Bara forgot to come get me." She glared at her cousin. Bara ignored her.

Payne apologized for them both. "I'm sorry we interrupted the program."

Ann Rose smiled her forgiveness, but Rita Louise Phipps—a frail elderly woman in a wing chair—gave Payne a formidable frown. She had been the close friend of Payne's grandmother, Nettie Holcomb. For five decades Rita Louise, Nettie, and Katharine's aunt, Sara Claire Everanes, had formed a triumvirate that arbitrated Buckhead's manners and monitored its social gates. Posey used to refer to them as "the scariest women in town." As the only survivor of the triumvirate and the widow of an Episcopal priest, Rita Louise presided over any gathering like a queen. She lived with one maid in a condominium high above Peachtree Street, where, Posey pointed out, she could look down on everybody else.

Rita Louise had used her money and influence to insure her husband a pulpit in Atlanta for his entire ministry, but it was his own humility and ability to speak truth in love that had guaranteed that Father John was revered and loved. His widow was revered and feared.

That morning, Rita Louise sat with her gnarled hands resting on a silver-headed cane, swollen joints covered by emeralds and diamonds. Her silver-gray shirtwaist and matching cardigan had been in style forty years before and would be in style forty years thence, as would the double strand of pearls that circled her throat. Her long, slender feet, encased in gray flats, were crossed at the ankles. Her silver hair, confined in the French twist she had worn all her adult life, looked ready for a tiara.

Posey had been known to ponder whether she ever combed out her hair completely, or whether bugs might nest in its recesses. That remark, fortunately, had never reached Rita Louise.

The only discordant note that morning was Rita Louise's too-bright lipstick. Katharine, having helped her mother and two elderly aunts dress for social occasions for years, suspected Rita Louise's eyesight wasn't what it used to be. Her vinegary disposition certainly was. Her eyebrows—not simply silver but strongly penciled charcoal gray—drew together. "Get yourselves settled so Ann Rose can go on with her program."

"I can't stay. I have Chip in the car." Payne clutched Katharine's arm and drew her toward the door. "Does Mama seem to be okay?"

Katharine glanced toward the couch near the window, where Bara's neighbors on both sides were hunched as far as they could get into the fat arms of the couch, looks of distress on their faces. Payne's gaze followed Katharine's and she caught a quick breath of dismay.

As if drawn by a magnet, Bara looked that way. "You don't have time to tutor anybody."

Payne turned a miserable pink. "I only came to bring Murdoch. Do you want to go home?"

"I just got here. Go on home." Bara waved a hand dismissively.

"You forgot to pick me up," Murdoch repeated.

Bara shifted to show them both a bony shoulder.

Ann Rose, conditioned by years of teaching unruly students, remained unruffled. "If you'd like to stay, Payne . . ."

It was a clear dismissal. "Take care of her," Payne told Katharine softly as she left. One maid let her out the front door and another materialized with a chair for Katharine.

As Ann Rose finished her speech and opened the floor for discussion, the army of caterers silently moved into the dining room across the hall, putting out trays of sandwiches, tarts, and crudités, and crystal pitchers of iced tea with lemon and mint. One opened bottles of chilled wine while another carried in a silver pot of coffee. Peach-clad maids set up card tables and chairs in the far end of the hall and covered them with soft green cloths and small vases of flowers. Katharine had seen that the den and library were already full of tables when she carried back Bara's keys. Posey was right. A woman who could invite fifty women into her home, give a lecture, and then serve them a sit-down luncheon was formidable.

Having eaten a light breakfast, Katharine was more than ready for lunch. Being at the back of the crowd, she looked forward to being at the head of the line.

"Katharine?" Ann Rose called. "Since you're back there already, will you be so kind as to pour coffee?"

Katharine grabbed a tiny crabmeat-and-cream-cheese sandwich and swallowed it in two bites before taking her position behind the silver service.

Murdoch, who had managed to secure the position Katharine had hoped for, held out a porcelain cup and nodded toward the pot Katharine held. "That set is almost as nice as a tea set we have in our family. It was a gift from Dolley and James Madison to one of our ancestors. Did you know that?"

"No, I didn't." Katharine handed back her cup and looked toward the woman next in line.

Murdoch, however, wasn't finished. Ignoring the line building up behind her, she gushed, "Oh, yes.

It's Revere silver, and a beautiful set. I used to go to Grandmother's after school every afternoon until Mama finished at her school and could come get me, and I loved picturing Dolley Payne Madison touching every piece. It's engraved 'To George and Ellen Payne from Dolley and James Madison on the Occasion of Their Twenty-fifth Anniversary.' I haven't yet established exactly who George was or how he was related to us, but Dolley was a Payne before she married, so she must have been related to us, as well. I may have proof by next week. I'm flying to Boston Thursday night for a mini-reunion weekend at my college, then I'll spend several days looking at documents I can't get online. I've also traced one branch of our family to the *Mayflower*, and if I can find the money"— she gave a self-conscious little laugh to show she was joking, for who in that group ever had to worry about money?—"I want to go to England in October for a genealogy conference, and then visit the village I think we originally came from. Didn't I hear that you are interested in genealogy too?"

Not that interested.

Katharine didn't say it, because she recognized the snide remark for what it was: not the truth, but a desire to put Murdoch down. She said lightly, "I've only begun to wet my toes in the genealogy ocean.

Until I get in deeper, I have no idea how far I'll want to go."

But I won't bore other people with it, she vowed. She looked pointedly at the woman behind Murdoch. "May I give you some coffee?"

"I'll catch you later," Murdoch promised as she reluctantly moved away.

Chapter 5

After a busy twenty minutes Katharine was relieved by Francie, Ann Rose's cook. "Go on and get yourself a plate. I'll take over here." Katharine gratefully handed over the coffeepot and piled a plate with vegetables, small sandwiches, and tiny muffins. She added two petite éclairs and a couple of pecan tarts, claimed a glass of iced tea, and roamed the house looking for a seat. All the chairs were full except for the best seat in the conservatory.

"Sorry. We're saving this for Rita Louise," a woman at the table apologized. Katharine didn't mind. The conservatory—filled with tropical plants and Oscar Anderson's sizable orchid collection—was so warm and humid, she preferred another room.

In the living room, she found Rita Louise with Bara. The old woman sat rigid with propriety in the chair next to the couch, without plate or cup. She wore the expression Katharine would have expected to see on the face of a determined martyr—or the wardress of a women's prison. Clearly, she intended to guard Bara during lunch to be sure she did nothing outrageous. The women made a stark contrast: Rita Louise the pale ice of a gray winter's day and Bara, in red silk, a vivid fire. Bara had moved to the end of the couch and had laid her head back against the cushions with her eyes closed. Was she paying any attention to what Rita Louise was saying? Rita Louise was saying it with force and indignation.

Katharine, hesitating to interrupt, heard, "Nettie promised me that lamp! My aunt was great friends with Louis Tiffany's family."

Bara spoke without opening her eyes. "Nana left it to me, not Mother."

Rita Louise gave a small huff of impatience. "Your grandmother was very unfair to your poor mother at the end. Nettie deserved better." She looked up and noticed Katharine hovering nearby. "Did you want something, dear?"

"Hello, Miss Rita Louise. They're saving a place for you in the conservatory. May I sit here?" Rita Louise was past eighty, and ought not miss a meal. Besides, if Bara was still a bit under the weather after lunch, Katharine would offer to drive her home. Bara might think her presumptuous, but Bara's house was in walking distance of her own. And while the neighborhood's lack of sidewalks could make walking a bit dicey during rush hour, Katharine was sure she'd be safe enough at one thirty—safer than driving home with Posey.

Rita Louise rose. "Thank you, dear." Her nod conveyed gratitude both for the information and for Katharine's rescue. "Eat something, Bara," she urged as she departed.

Bara didn't move.

Katharine was grateful to find that the whiskey fumes had mostly evaporated. "Are you all right?" she asked, seating herself in the vacated chair. It was scarcely warm from Rita Louise's tenure. The woman was far too civilized to generate body heat.

Bara opened one eye to see who the intruder was, then closed it again. "I'm not real well this morning. Had a shock earlier today and it hasn't worn off." Her voice was the deep, husky drawl Katharine associated with too much whiskey and too many cigarettes, yet until that morning, she had never known Bara to smoke or drink.

"Could I get you some coffee and a few snacks?"

Bara considered the matter with closed eyes. "Coffee would be good. Black. I'm not hungry."

She ought to be, Katharine thought. Once thin, she was now gaunt. The bones of her wrists and ankles were downright skeletal. Yet she must have had some cosmetic surgery recently, because the skin of her neck was smooth, her jawline as sharp as it had been at forty, and her eyes had that wide look plastic surgeons seem to think is natural.

Katharine set her plate and cup on the glass-topped coffee table, left her purse to reserve her chair, and headed back to the dining room. She returned to find that Posey had claimed her seat, rosy with indignation. "You forgot your promise, Katharine," Posey complained as soon as Katharine was in earshot. "Ann Rose backed me into a corner and made me agree to teach a woman to read. It's all your fault."

"It'll do you good." Bara hauled herself erect and reached for the cup Katharine offered with an offhand "Thanks."

Exactly as if I were one of the maids, Katharine thought as she sat on the couch. She knew it was petty to resent Bara's casual acceptance of her service, but she had missed the mark when she'd told Posey she and Bara were only slightly acquainted. She was utterly beneath Bara's social radar.

Posey, who had been born in the same circle as Bara, transferred her glare to the older woman. "Easy for you to say. First I have to get trained, and then, what if my pupil doesn't learn? It'll all be my fault because I'm a bad teacher."

"It won't kill you to try." Bara drank the hot black coffee greedily. "The training is only one weekend. After that you tutor an hour a week. Do something for somebody else, Pose." She reached over and took one of Katharine's éclairs from the plate on the coffee table. Katharine was astonished to see that her nails were chewed and ragged, the polish chipped. Bara was usually exquisitely groomed.

She was also surprised that Bara had absorbed so much of Ann Rose's presentation. "Are you going to tutor?"

"Not right now. I'm a little busy at the moment. My dearly beloved husband has been giving me all sorts of grief, and I have to sort that out before I do much else. You've heard what he's trying to do, haven't you?"

"I have," said Posey, at the same moment Katharine said, "No, I haven't."

Bara was more than willing to share her troubles.

"Oh, hon!" she moaned dramatically to Katharine, "my daddy was scarcely in his grave before Foley announced he wants to divorce me, take half of every blessed thing I own, and spend it on my former maid."

She began to shake. Her tremors grew so violent that Posey put a hand on her shoulder and urged, "Take deep, easy breaths. Inhale. Exhale. That's right. Now another. Inhale. Exhale."

Gradually Bara calmed. "Sorry about that. Hits me all of a sudden sometimes."

"Who is your lawyer?" Posey demanded.

"Uncle Scotty."

"Scotty? He doesn't know a thing about divorce, and he's not tough enough. Why didn't you use Mason?" Mason Benefield was the Buckhead divorce lawyer of choice.

"Mason is representing Foley, and Uncle Scotty's giving me a good deal. Foley has frozen all my bank accounts and charge cards, so I had to take what I could afford. It's a real mess." Bara rubbed her ravaged face with one hand. "On top of all that, I found a cigar box this morning full of war medals among some of Winnie's things. He must have kept the box hidden in his desk drawer, because I hadn't ever seen Art's medal or . . . or Win's." She took another deep breath and exhaled through rounded lips. "Finding them plumb knocked me for a loop."

Katharine and Posey exchanged a look, but neither came up with anything to say. To Katharine, finding medals seemed insignificant beside everything else

Bara was facing, but she knew from recent experience that sometimes it is the small things that push you over the edge. And she had never held in her hands a medal her son had earned by giving his life.

Bara gave a harsh laugh. "I'd better hide the medals from Foley, hadn't I? Or he'll want half of them, to add to his horde of stolen goods." She picked up her cup and took a quick, nervous swig.

"He can't have your medals," Posey objected. "They have nothing to do with him, not even Win's. You had Win long before you married Foley."

Bara reached over to Posey's plate and extracted a tiny éclair. "I had my house long before I married Foley too, but he wants that." She bit into the éclair as if she wished it were some portion of Foley's anatomy.

"Why don't you get the medals framed for your wall?" Posey suggested. "You could leave them at the framer's for ages. Foley need never know you've found them."

Bara finished the éclair, purloined Katharine's corn muffin, and spoke in a muffin-muffled voice. "Might get them framed for Chip. He's only three, but one day he might appreciate them. I don't know what most of them are for, though. Not much point in giving a kid medals if he doesn't know who got what for doing which. Or which for doing what.

Whatever." She drained her cup and peered down into it. "I'm out of coffee."

Aunt Sara Claire used to couch requests as statements like that. It's what children learn when they are raised with servants or doting aunts who wait on them. Katharine went to refill Bara's cup. While she was at it, she filled another plate. Might as well insure that she and Posey got something to eat.

She came back to find Posey saying, "Katharine knows a lot about genealogy. She can find out about your medals, no problem."

"Oh, really?" The way Bara was staring at her, Katharine had the feeling it was the first time the woman had really looked at her in the years they had been acquainted. Her gaze was that of somebody inspecting a museum exhibit that had turned out to be more interesting than expected.

Katharine, who had auburn hair and the temper to go with it, felt her face flush. Twenty-five years in Buckhead and she was still, to the core of the inner social circle, nothing more than Tom's wife, Posey's sister-in-law, and Sara Claire's niece?

"I don't know a thing about medals," she said tersely, "and I'm just beginning to learn about genealogy. Here. I brought you some food to go with your coffee." She set the plate and hot coffee before Bara.

"I'm not hungry." Bara demolished a crabmeat sandwich in two bites.

Posey finished a strawberry dipped in white chocolate and wiped her hands on her napkin. "Don't be modest, Katharine. Look how you figured out about that family down on Bayard Island last month."

"Where's Bayard Island?" Bara ate a second sandwich.

"Between Jekyll and Savannah." Posey launched into a long and greatly embellished account of what had happened when Katharine and a friend went down to investigate whether a grave belonged to the friend's grandfather. "Katharine figured out all sorts of stuff about the family, going all the way back to the Civil War," Posey concluded.

While Posey talked, Bara steadily continued eating the food Katharine had brought. At the same time, she was considering Katharine with thoughtful eyes. A writer describing Bara's expressions might have used phrases like "dawning realization" and "new respect." Katharine was caught between being flattered by the woman's unwonted attention and resenting it.

Bara is very important, dear, her Aunt Sarah Claire reminded her. *She comes from two of the wealthiest, most influential families in Atlanta.* Katharine had long ago accepted that her relatives, though dead, persisted in hovering around her in what the Bible calls "a cloud of witnesses," providing a running commentary on her life.

But she's only a human being, her father insisted. *No point in holding her in awe.* Her father had been a great believer in the equal value of all people.

And for twenty-five years she has treated me like a ghost and looked right past me, Katharine silently agreed.

That's not fair, dear. She remembered your name at Payne's wedding, her mother chided.

Katharine tuned in to Posey and Bara to find Posey describing some research Katharine and Dr. Florence Gadney had done on the Internet.

Bara interrupted mid-sentence. "I've never been much interested in family history. Murdoch takes care of all that. She's a nut about genealogy. She's even traced Winnie's family, and he had nothing to do with her. Don't let her get to talking about it, or you'll never get away." She took a sip of coffee and grimaced. "Stuff's gone cold on me."

Katharine refused to rise to that bait a second time.

Cultivate compassion, dear, her mother reminded her. *She is a human being, after all. Don't dismiss her because she's rich.*

Katharine sat like a rock.

Posey—who clearly expected Katharine to fetch more coffee—gave her a surprised look and rose to get it. While she was gone, Bara confided, "Murdoch nearly wet her pants last year when she found out one of our ancestors came over on the *Mayflower*. Heck! Simple logic could have told her that any family, who's been in this country since the 1800s, ought to be able to trace somebody back to the *Mayflower*. Those people bred like rabbits. But to hear Murdoch go on about it, you'd think our ancestor was the captain. I figure he was probably a stowaway." She threw back her head and laughed, a raucous sound that earned her several curious stares.

After a minute's silence, she added, "I do wish I could identify those medals, though. Winnie had them all crammed together in that old cigar box. Purple Hearts and Art's Bronze Star are the only ones I recognize. Do you think you could figure out what they were earned for?"

"No," said Katharine. "I don't know a thing about military medals."

"Sure she could." Posey handed Bara her coffee and gave Katharine the encouraging look of a mother whose child has been asked to play the piano.

"I don't—" Katharine began.

Bara interrupted again. "I really like your idea of framing them for Chip, Katharine."

As Katharine recalled it, Posey had suggested framing the medals and Bara had had the idea of framing them for Chip.

Bara consumed a cucumber sandwich and chased it with a swig of black coffee. "I want Chip to grow up knowing what kind of man his great-granddaddy Holcomb was. You'll help me, won't you, Katharine? For Chip? Don't make me ask Murdoch, *please.*"

"Don't ask Murdoch what?"

They hadn't noticed Murdoch and Rita Louise approaching.

Posey stood and offered Rita Louise her chair.

"Nothing important," said Bara.

Posey didn't mind explaining. "We're talking about Bara framing her daddy's military medals for little Chip. I think it's a great idea. Katharine has offered to help her identify what he earned each one for."

Katharine opened her mouth to protest, but Rita Louise was first to the mark. "Oh, my dear!" she objected. "That was so long ago! Surely you have enough on your plate to worry about right now."

"Besides, I really don't know a thing about—" Katharine had gotten that far in her refusal when two things stopped her. One was the look Bara gave her: that of a drowning woman clutching a slender plank in a dark and desperate ocean. The second was the realization that she had greatly enjoyed the research part of two genealogy investigations she'd been involved in that summer.

She hadn't enjoyed *all* the investigating, of course. Parts had been downright dangerous. But how much danger could be involved in investigating military medals?

"I can try to find out something about them," she capitulated, "but I'm not sure I can succeed."

"Of course you can," Bara encouraged her. "You are an intelligent woman." Katharine had no time to preen, for Bara immediately added, "Tom Murray would never have married an unintelligent one." She returned to the subject of the medals. "I might hang them on my own wall for a while. Maybe they'll inspire me to get my act together again."

"Did you ever have your act together?" Murdoch may have tried to make it sound like a tease, but the question had a spine of spite.

Bara jutted out her chin. "I most certainly did. Back in nursery school, before you were born. I knew exactly who I was and what I was going to be. I had Miss Collins. I'll bet you did, too, Posey."

Posey nodded. "So did my girls. That woman taught until she was older than God."

"I had Miss Collins too," Murdoch chimed in, "but what did she have to do with you having your act together, Bara?"

"One day she asked us to go around the circle and tell what we wanted to be when we grew up. I was the first to answer, because I knew exactly what I wanted to be. You know what I said? 'A daddy.' It had never occurred to me I had to grow up to be a mommy. Real shame, too. I've made a mess of it. But Mama wasn't much of a role model."

"Don't talk about Aunt Nettie like that!" Murdoch protested as Rita Louse drew herself up like a porcupine preparing to strike.

"Your mother was notable for her devotion to others *and* her common sense," she said in an icy tone.

Bara grimaced. "The only sense Mama ever had was the good sense to marry Winnie, and the only thing she was notable for was belonging to every organization in Atlanta devoted to good works. I never imagined I'd grow up to be just like her. Lordy, I hate good works, don't you? I mean, do those folks really want our help? I keep thinking if we gave them the money we spend on balls and fancy fund-raisers, they could help themselves. Have you ever stopped to ask what percentage of money given to help the poor winds up buying booze for charity do's or paying salaries for middle-class do-gooders?"

Rita Louise pulled herself to her feet. "You are clearly under the weather, dear. I advise you to go home and sleep it off. Posey, would you see if my car is at the door?"

Posey came back to offer her an arm, and Rita Louise stumped off with her head high.

Bara watched until she was gone, then lifted a leg and ruefully inspected her red flat. "I seem to have inserted foot into mouth up to knee. What made me bait that poor woman? But if Mama had let me grow up to be an architect—" She broke off with a self-deprecating laugh. "I'd probably have messed that up, too." She leaned over and clutched Katharine's hand. "You cannot know how grateful I'll be if you can help me identify those medals."

Katharine felt a twinge of the compassion her mother had spent a lifetime trying to teach. "I can try, but I'm not promising anything."

"Wouldn't matter if you did," Posey grumbled as she resumed her chair. "You promised not to leave me alone with Ann Rose, and look what happened. Next thing I know, you're over there pouring coffee, and I'm getting coerced into teaching somebody to read. Never trust a do-gooder. They're too easily sidetracked by another good deed. Are you ready to go?"

Katharine remembered the good deed she had originally come to perform. "Do you want me to drive you home, Bara? I could walk home from there. I don't live far from you."

Bara struggled to her feet. "I am fine. Besides, I have to take Murdoch, or she'll never let me hear the end of it."

"I'll get another ride."

Katharine couldn't blame Murdoch for looking nervous.

"You blamed me in front of everybody for not coming to get you. I'll jolly well take you home." Bara caught her cousin firmly by the elbow and steered her out. At the arch, she called over her shoulder, "I'll bring the medals over later so you can get to work on them."

Chapter 6

When the others had gone, Katharine frowned at her sister-in-law. "Why'd you force me to tell her I'll identify those medals? What if I can't?"

"Tit for tat. If I have to tutor, you have to identify medals. Besides, like she told me, it won't kill you to try. Now let's get out of here before Ann Rose catches me and starts asking when I'm fixing to take that training."

"You think she's okay to drive?" Posey asked a couple of minutes later, shading her eyes to watch Bara's Jag roar down the drive and make a fast left between the high brick pillars.

"I don't know, but she wasn't going to let us tell her she wasn't. Let's pray she doesn't hurt herself or somebody else before she gets home."

Walking downhill was faster than coming up, but hotter. Katharine was glad to reach the little car, and hoped Posey would hurry home. Instead, as soon as she started the engine, Posey inquired, "Do you mind if we tool around a little? I haven't gotten to drive it hardly at all. I'll be very careful," she added, seeing Katharine's expression, "and I'll tell you more about Bara's troubles."

Katharine tied the chiffon scarf around her hair. "I don't mind riding around for a little while, but I don't need to gossip."

Posey—who garnered information like jewels, at aerobics classes, spas, and the beauty parlor—sputtered with indignation. "I don't gossip! I simply share my heartfelt concern for other people. Poor Bara needs all the concern we can give her right now. You know what-all she's already been through this past year, right? Her son killed in Iraq before Christmas, then right after Easter, her daddy—well, you know the mess about how he died."

Winnie Holcomb had plunged from the balcony of the penthouse he'd moved into after giving Payne and Hamilton his house. Atlanta had been doubly shocked by his death. Winnie was widely beloved. He had also designed the tower he lived in, and Holcomb & Associates had set a high standard in Atlanta for architectural safety. Their parapets were higher, their railings more closely spaced than any others in the city.

"He must have been pushed," Buckhead had insisted.

"His deadbolt was locked and his security system armed," the police reported.

"Do you suppose he jumped?" people began to whisper.

"How could he climb over a chest-high parapet with that artificial leg?" Winnie's staunchest supporters retorted.

Before anybody had satisfactorily answered those questions, even more shocking discoveries emerged. The autopsy revealed that Winnie had been dead before he hit the ground. A bullet was found in the remains of his skull, but no gun had ever been found.

For weeks, Atlanta was rife with speculation. Had somebody managed to come into Winnie's penthouse, kill him, lock the deadbolt, and arm the security system on the way out without being detected by cameras in the elevator or stairwell? Or had Winnie climbed on the parapet and blown out his own brains, then dropped the gun as he fell?

Proponents of the first camp drew diagrams to show how a person could stand in the elevator and avoid the camera. Proponents of the second camp were divided between those who believed the suicide gun had been picked up by somebody on the street and those who believed it was still lodged high in one of the trees ringing the condo. Four months later, the mystery remained.

Katharine said soberly, "I've heard several people say he adored his grandson, and Win's death unhinged his mind."

"It could have. It certainly sent Bara into a tailspin. She had a complete breakdown. And then Winnie died—but you haven't heard what Foley has done most recently?" Posey's voice rose in astonishment.

"Only what she told us today. I told you, I don't know the Weidenauers that well."

Posey set out to educate her. "Bara's family on both sides has been here forever. One of her many-great-grandfathers was mayor, back in the mid-nineteenth century, when the town was called Terminus."

Katharine nodded. " 'Regarded as a brash nonentity south of Marietta, never expected to be anything more important than the place where railroads came together.' That's more or less a direct quote from your brother."

"I'm surprised Tom hasn't given you the whole history of the Paynes and the Holcombs, then. Their history is Atlanta's history. Both sides of the family made a lot of money after the war, one in lumber and the other in cotton. Connor Payne, Bara's granddaddy, ran for governor back when Nettie was in college. He lost, but he got the Buckhead vote, and Harold Holcomb, Winnie's father, ran his campaign. They were real good friends. My mother used to say that Winnie's marriage to Nettie was arranged before they were even born."

"Surely not!" Katharine knew that several Buckhead couples had grown up together, but she had presumed they'd chosen each other in spite of that.

Posey was far more practical. "They could have decided to marry other people if they'd wanted to, but it united the fortunes and kept the money from outsiders."

"Outsiders like me?" Katharine teased.

"You aren't an outsider. Your mother grew up in Buckhead, so you belong here, whether you like it or not."

"But Tom wouldn't have married me if I didn't?"

"Tom would have married you if you'd been born on Mars. He came home from the party where he met you and said, 'Okay, Pose, there might be one woman I could stand to spend the rest of my life with.' He'd sworn he was going to be a confirmed bachelor if all women were like me. But getting back to Bara and Winnie—"

"I know about Winnie. 'Football hero, war hero, outstanding architect, and founder of Holcomb & Associates, which has designed and built a number of the skyscrapers that grace our lovely skyline.' That's not Tom, that's too many banquet introductions to count. But Winnie's dead. Can we move beyond the past and get to the present?"

"In a minute. Did you ever know Winnie's son, Winston Arthur Junior? Of course you didn't. He was killed before you came. Not to speak ill of the dead, but Art was a lot like Nettie—stuffy, rigid, self-righteous. I think he must have been a disappointment to Winnie, although I never heard him say so, but Nettie adored him. The light of Winnie's life was Bara, who was five years younger. She—you weren't here when she was in high school, were you?"

"I wasn't born until she was in high school."

"I wasn't hardly born, either." Posey conveniently forgot the five years she had on Katharine. "But I was fascinated by her. She was a track star, president of a lot of clubs, and always up to pranks. She also wore dreamy clothes. I thought her utterly glamorous and wanted to grow up to be exactly like her. Once she started Randolph-Macon, though, she went off the rails. Started smoking and drinking and did wild, zany things. One night she danced in her slip in a downtown fountain. Mama said they were fixing to put the picture in the paper until Winnie called Ralph McGill and got him to pull it. Another night she sideswiped the governor's limo, drag racing down Peachtree. And when she got arrested for driving under the influence, she wound up teaching the entire lockup a series of bawdy songs."

"Are those stories true?"

"Absolutely. Daddy was the lawyer Winnie sent to bail her out of jail. He said she wouldn't leave until the prisoners got the harmony right."

"That's weird. I heard the drag-racing story back when I first joined the Junior League, but at a small dinner party at Aunt Sara Claire's one evening, I mentioned it and Aunt Sara Claire said, 'Don't believe those ridiculous lies, dear. Bara would never have gotten into the Junior League if they were true.'"

"Pooh," was Posey's inelegant reply. "Bara got into the Junior League the same way anybody else in Atlanta does, including you: because of her mother. And every one of the stories is true, no matter how much Sara Claire and Rita Louise tried to whitewash them for Nettie's sake."

Katharine remembered more of that long-ago conversation. "Father John and Rita Louise were at dinner that night, and Rita Louise said, 'I always thought Bara got into difficulties because she lost her grandmother her freshman year of college. Except for Winston, Viola Payne was the only person in the world who could exert any control over that girl.' But Father John frowned at both of them and said—pretty sternly, for him— 'Perhaps that was because Viola was the only person besides Winston who ever showed that child any love.' Do you think he could have been right?"

"How should I know? Like I said, I was a mere infant when she was growing up. But I do know Bara stopped drinking after she married Ray Branwell."

"For love?"

Posey's laugh held little mirth. "For self-preservation, is more like it. Ray was the heir to a restaurant-chain fortune, but very wild. He drank a lot, got into public brawls, and my mother used to wonder if he beat her. Mama claimed Bara would never have married him if her mother hadn't disapproved of him so strongly. But for whatever reason, Bara stopped drinking soon after Payne was born, and settled down."

"Settled down?" During Katharine's years in Buckhead, Bara's excesses had provided constant fodder for conversation. Her clothes were brighter, her vacations more daring, her conversation spicier than Buckhead was accustomed to. Her most flamboyant excess had been her steamy romance with Foley Weidenauer six months after Ray Branwell died. Their escapades had furnished the *Atlanta Journal-Constitution* with "Peach Buzz" tidbits for two months before the couple flew to Greece and married. Bara had been forty-seven, Foley, thirty-two. Her children were fifteen and twelve.

Posey went on sharing her heartfelt concern for Bara.

"All this mess with Foley is what has started her drinking again. It's a dadgum shame she ever married him in the first place, and let him worm his way into Holcomb and Associates. Nobody knows who his people are, but anybody could tell when he first got to town that he wasn't raised right. His manners have improved a lot since he married Bara."

Katharine, whose parents had firmly preached the equality of all people and had declined to raise their daughter by society's restricted definition of a lady, felt pity for the man. "Wasn't he a CPA? I thought that's why Winnie hired him." At the time of the Weidenauer marriage Katharine had been busy raising two children and keeping house while Tom traveled, but she had absorbed that much.

"Maybe so," Posey sounded dubious, "but the board would never have considered Foley for chief financial officer a few years ago if he hadn't been Winnie's son-in-law. God only knows why they made him CEO after Winnie died, but Wrens says Foley's strength is knowing how to charm the socks off people in high places."

"Has he done anything worse than ask for a divorce, take a mistress, and get himself made CEO of Holcomb and Associates? I mean, that's bad enough, but you sound like he has single-handedly introduced bubonic plague to the city."

"He just about has. Apparently, even before Winnie's death, Foley had been chatting up an Arab conglomerate that's interested in buying the firm. A couple of weeks ago they made him an offer, but in order to get the votes to sell, he needs Winnie's shares. Winnie's lawyer informed Foley that Winnie left those shares exclusively to Bara, so Foley informed Bara that she can either give him those shares, or they will have to sell both houses and most of their investments to give him all he's entitled to."

"Can he do that?"

"Wrens says he can. When they got married, Bara was stupid enough to put Foley's name on the titles to both her Buckhead house and her Lake Rabun house, and she let him mingle their bank accounts and investment portfolios—which means all of that is now legally common property, and Foley is entitled to half of it. Bara would have to sell a lot more than their Buckhead house to give Foley half of everything they own. If he can manage to get Winnie's shares put into the mix, she could well lose everything else. Wouldn't you think she would have insisted on a prenuptial agreement? But no, she was crazy in love." Posey's drawl deepened in disgust.

"I never thought about a prenuptial when I got married."

"Neither did I, but we were kids, starting out. Bara was in her forties when she married Foley, with two big houses and pots of money she had inherited from both sets of grandparents, her mother, and Ray. The worst thing Foley has done so far, besides parade his bimbo all over town, is tie up their bank accounts and put a freeze on the credit cards. Bara is practically destitute."

"Destitute? She drives a Jag and lives in an humongous house."

"But she had those things before this mess started. She couldn't sell them if she wanted to, until the divorce is settled." Posey slammed on her brakes at a red light. "Sorry. I was going a little faster than I realized."

Katharine had to wait for lunch to settle back into her stomach before she asked, "Would her shares in the firm be an equal exchange for half of all the rest?" She had no idea how much Bara's shares in Holcomb & Associates were worth, but big houses on Lake Rabun were worth small fortunes, and a house about the same size as Bara's in Buckhead had recently listed for seventeen million dollars. Housing woes that had afflicted the rest of the country scarcely made a ripple in the sale or purchase of houses that size.

"It doesn't matter what's worth what." Posey sounded like she was reminding a sixth grader that two plus two equals four. "Bara's daddy founded that company and her granddaddy Payne built both houses. Her granddaddy Payne gave Bara the Buckhead house when she married Ray, so they could raise their children there, and her mother left her the lake house when she died. Foley's only been married to her for fifteen years. Both houses and the business ought to be hers."

A car across the intersection moved. Posey took out her rage at Foley by gunning her engine and leaping forward. Brakes squealed. Two very expensive pieces of machinery nearly collided. The other driver shook his fist.

"Watch where you're going," Posey shouted at the other driver as she roared by.

"He was making a left on the arrow." Katharine hoped her heart rate would eventually revert to normal. "Our light hadn't changed."

Posey slapped one cheek in chagrin. "Oh, drat! I forgot that arrow. It didn't used to be there." She waved an apology at the other driver, but he had already disappeared—probably to vent his anger on another hapless motorist.

"The arrow has been there for years," Katharine reminded her.

"I told you, I'm getting used to the car. I can't think about everything at once."

"Then think about driving."

Posey sulked for several minutes, but she was seldom miffed for long. "By the way," she said, as if they were in the middle of an amicable conversation, "don't tell Hollis I was with you today. I told her I was lunching with friends, but I didn't say who, because her car's in the shop, and if she had known I was coming over to your place, she'd have wanted to ride over with me and work all morning. But I'd told Molly to take her to the club for lunch. I think she needs to get out a little." Like many Buckhead matrons, Posey regarded the Cherokee Town Club as an extension of her own dining room. "Hollis looks a little peaky to me," she continued. "I hope she's not working too hard on your house."

Katharine's home had been vandalized in June. Since then, Hollis had been using her brand-new degree in fabrics and textiles from the Savannah College of Art and Design to help restore it. They'd been moving at a steady pace until Hollis had gotten shot the month before, during a weekend at Jekyll Island—a memory that still made Katharine shudder, for she had invited her niece on the trip. She had been doing all she could in intervening weeks to help Hollis take it easy.

"I don't think she's overworking," she reassured Posey, "but she's working me like a slave. Don't tell her I've been with *you*, or she'll wonder why I wasn't home figuring out where all the new pictures go. She is determined to have the place finished before the party."

Posey gave a huff of bafflement. "I cannot imagine why you decided to have a party for a hundred people this month, with Hollis still recuperating and everything you still have to do."

"It's a hundred and fifty people, and I offered to give the party before Hollis was hurt. I thought it would give us a deadline to work toward. It was Hollis who insisted that we not call it off. She is sure we can be ready."

Posey sighed. "You are both crazy as loons."

Hollis was normal enough, in Katharine's opinion— she simply danced to a different drum. Her tall blond sisters had gone to colleges their mother approved of, married men Posey liked, borne children she adored, and were now devoting their lives to a routine of children's sports and standard young-mother activities, while occasionally mentioning that when the children were a little older, they might go back to work. The fact that Hollis preferred a sandwich at her aunt's kitchen table while poring over fabric swatches to lunch with her sisters at the club was only one of the traits that drove her mother straight up the nearest wall. Hollis's tendency to bring home men with blue hair and multiple piercings was also high on Posey's list of complaints.

Katharine, on the other hand, was very fond of Hollis, the only one of Posey's children who was small and dark like her uncle Tom and her cousin Susan, and who had brilliant ideas for remaking the Murray home. "You're going to be astonished at how proud you are of Hollis one day," she said, adding, "if we live so long," as Posey slammed on brakes to avoid rear-ending a yellow Cadillac driven by a white-haired woman who had come to a complete stop before turning right.

"Let's enjoy the ride and not talk for a while," Katharine begged.

Chapter 7

Bara arrived home to find a silver Mercedes convertible in the circle near her front door and a red Miata on the apron beside the garage, where her servants used to park. The Mercedes belonged to Uncle Scotty. She tried to remember if in some moment of weakness she had invited him and somebody else over. She doubted it. She hadn't been feeling too sociable lately, or flush enough to lay out money for food and liquor. Besides, who would cook and serve?

Her head was beginning to throb. She needed a drink. But the only thing she had left was gin, and she needed it for her breakfast Bloody Marys. Tomato juice and lime were so good for you, and Bara had been making Bloody Marys with gin instead of vodka since college—she preferred them that way.

Oh, joy, she remembered. *I got wine at the grocery store.* But when she popped the trunk, her groceries had been stolen! No, Ann Rose's cook had taken them. "Blast it," she moaned.

The box of medals and old envelope were still in the trunk, but she'd get them later. Right now, she wanted a drink.

Quietly, so Uncle Scotty wouldn't hear, she grabbed a tumbler, unlocked the deadbolt to the basement, and tiptoed down the stairs, wrinkling her nose at the mustiness. She crept toward the bathroom Foley was using and extracted a bottle of bourbon from his stash under the sink. She filled her tumbler, downed half of it, and decided to take the bottle with her. Foley wouldn't notice for a while. A Scotch drinker, he only bought bourbon for guests, and he wasn't likely to entertain but one guest in the basement. Carlene didn't deserve *Rare Breed.*

Upstairs Bara left the bottle in the kitchen and made her way through the recesses of the house. "Uncle Scotty?" she called. "Are you here?"

"I'm here." He was in the front of the house, standing with his hands in his pockets, looking around the spacious foyer and elegant rooms with a wistful expression. "How are you, shug?" He gave her a kiss.

At eighty-six, Scotty Payne had shrunk until he was almost her own height, but he was still a handsome man, with crisp gray curls and a ruddy complexion. He looked hopefully at her glass, but she wouldn't have offered him a drink if she'd had any to offer. She didn't intend for him to stay that long.

"How did you get in? And who is driving the Miata parked out back?"

He jingled his key ring. "I still have my old front-door key from when I used to live here. We didn't see a Miata."

"We?" Bara looked around.

"Hey," Murdoch called from the dining room. "I was looking at the Dolley Payne Madison tea set before I go to Boston. I ought to know something more about it by this time next week." She sounded as excited as if she were off on a Star Trek expedition to discover worlds where no man had ever gone before. Or woman.

Bara ignored her. "What did you want?" she asked Scotty. "Have you got good news?"

"Sorry, hon, I don't. But I'm going to need some money on your account. I can't work for free, you know, as much as I'd like to. I've got bills to pay." By which he meant greens fees, bar bills, and his tailor.

"I can't pay you any more until you get me some money. You know I can't lay my hands on cash right now."

"You've got your father's shares. Sell some of them."

"Who are you working for? Those shares are what this whole thing is about right now."

"This thing is about a divorce," he said bluntly. "I don't care if you sell the shares to Foley or to Santa Claus, I need to get paid. I have expenses, you know."

"If you would get them to drop those ridiculous ideas about Winnie's estate, I'd have plenty."

He shook his head. "No can do. They do have a point, you know. It's hardly fair for you to get half of Winnie's estate and Foley to get nothing."

"You are nuts! Who are you working for?" she asked again.

He peered around the hall, moved over to a table and peered at the painting over it. "Is that my grandmother's Monet? I'll bet it would fetch a pretty penny."

"It's part of the inventory of the contents of the house. Besides, Nana left it to me. I wouldn't sell it."

He looked around the lavishly furnished house. "So what isn't part of the inventory?"

"Not much, according to Foley."

"Not the tea set!" Murdoch called from the dining room in indignation.

Bara didn't bother to raise her voice, since Murdoch could obviously hear her. "No, Nana's will stipulated I was to pass it to my daughter, if I had one. I've told Foley and his lawyer, but I don't know if they've absorbed that fact. I ought to go ahead and give it to Payne, to get it out of the house. But everything else here, we both had appraised. Not that our appraisals always agree."

"What did they value the Monet at?" Scotty peered at the dreamy water scene.

Bara hesitated, but she might as well tell him. It wouldn't be a secret once Foley took her to court. "My appraiser said it could go for as much as fifteen million. Some sell for more, but he thinks that's a fair value for this one. Foley's man evaluated it higher, of course. Foley's getting high appraisals on everything I want to keep."

Murdoch's shoes clattered on the marble floor. "Fifteen million *dollars?*" She peered up at the painting. "Nana paid that much for a painting?"

"It was her mother's, and has increased considerably in value since my grandmother bought it." Scotty's voice was bitter with envy.

Bara used to feel guilty that her grandmother Payne had given her three family treasures while Scotty and Murdoch got stocks and cash. Even if they had invested wisely—which they hadn't—the sum Nana had left them in lieu of the tea set, the painting, and her Tiffany lamp would not have kept pace with the increase in value of the painting alone. Still, Bara doubted whether either of them would have kept the painting long enough for it to appreciate much. The tea set was all Murdoch valued, and Scotty was not sentimental.

"It should have all been mine," Scotty grumbled. "The house, the painting, all of it. I was the older son. Nettie was taken care of by Winnie."

"Granddaddy offered you the house when he decided to downsize," Bara reminded him. "You told him it was too big and expensive to run, so since Ray and I were getting married, he gave it to us."

"He should have sold it and given me the money," Scotty insisted. "You and Ray didn't need all this space. If you and Foley sell, I'm tempted to sue you for at least half of what you get for it." Before Bara could reply, he returned to his earlier question. "Isn't there anything you could sell right now, that's not on the inventory?"

"Nothing but a few necklaces Foley gave me. He claimed he wouldn't take them back because they were given in love," Bara grimaced in distaste, "but the truth is, he didn't want anybody finding out how cheap he is. I could sell them, I guess, but all together they aren't worth as much as Mama's pearls—and Foley had no scruples about putting them on the list."

She was talking to air. Scotty had gone into the dining room and was examining the silver teapot. "This set certainly ought to have come down to me. You aren't even a Payne."

"Nana left it to me as her oldest granddaughter."

"You were always her favorite," Murdoch complained.

"Nettie should have gotten it, at least." Scotty peered at the hallmark on the bottom.

"Mother and Nana had quarreled about something. You'd know more about that than I would." Bara hoped her uncle would tell her what he knew. She had always wondered why her grandmother had cut Nettie out of what she privately called the silver service succession.

Scotty didn't rise to the bait. Instead he put down the teapot and examined the inscription on the tray. "Murdoch would appreciate it a lot more than you do."

"I sure would," Murdoch agreed.

"Nana wanted me to have it, the Monet, and the lamp. She left them to me by name, remember? 'To my beloved Bara Holcomb I leave . . .'" Bara had memorized the words, held them to her heart in the bleak weeks after her grandmother's death. *My beloved Bara.* Even Winnie had never called her *beloved.*

Scotty was examining the bottom of the creamer. "It should have come to me. Mama probably made up that 'oldest granddaughter' bit so she could do what she wanted to with the set. That means you can sell it or give it to us if you want to. It's worth a pretty penny, I'll bet."

"It's not mine to sell," Bara insisted. "It is to go to Payne."

Scotty remained unconvinced. "Payne wasn't even born when Mama gave you that set. You were still in college when Mama died. Murdoch cares a lot more about that sort of thing than you or Payne, either one. Sell it to Murdoch. Then you can pay me what you owe."

Murdoch looked willing to write a check on the spot, but Bara dashed her hopes. "Murdoch couldn't afford to pay me anything like what it's worth, and you both know it. Still," she added to her cousin, "if you paid room and board, your daddy wouldn't be so hard up."

"That's none of your business." Murdoch flounced out to the front hall. "Come on, Daddy."

Scotty set the creamer down and murmured, "Listen, if you want to sell this thing on the QT, I've got somebody who could get you a good price. More than Murdoch could pay, that's for sure."

Bara sighed. Scotty and her mother had looked a lot alike, but inside they had been made of different fiber. Nettie had been rigidly righteous and proud of it. Scotty was softer and superficially easier to like, but had the morals of a cuckoo.

"I told you. It will go to Payne. It has been handed down for hundreds of years."

"Come on. If it disappeared now, who'd know it wasn't stolen? Like I said, I've got somebody who would make you a good price."

"Go home." She rubbed her throbbing temples. "I can't deal with this right now." She was developing a two-drink headache, and the bottle in the kitchen was calling her name.

Scotty paused at the arch to the hall. "I'm not a public defender, hon. I can't keep working for free."

"You're not working at all. If you'd do what I've already paid you for, you'd get me out of this mess and we'd both have enough to live on."

His laugh was short and brutal. "Face facts, sweetie. Foley holds all the cards in this divorce. He has supported you for years."

"He has not! I've paid most of the household bills our entire marriage."

"Stupid you. But if we fight him, you know Mason. He'll get Foley everything you've got." At the front door he delivered an ultimatum. "I need a check by next week. Okay?"

She didn't bother to reply. They both knew the answer to that.

He was halfway down the steps when she remembered something. "I want your key to this house."

Scotty laughed and kept walking.

She locked the door after him and dragged a chair to prop under the knob. A nap. That's what she needed. Another drink and a long nap.

A stealthy sound upstairs caught her ear. It must be whoever had come in the Miata. She probably hadn't put on the security system when she left the house. She never could remember to punch all those little buttons.

"Hello?" she called up the stairs. "I know you're up there. I heard you. Come on down, right this minute." Perhaps she should have been nervous, but she was too tired. Besides, what burglar would park on the drive and remain upstairs while she and Scotty quarreled? There was a back staircase leading to the kitchen.

She crept up the curving marble staircase, listening intently. The silence was too pregnant to be empty. She could feel somebody listening as intently as she.

She still carried her shoulder bag, so she reached for her cell phone and was punching 911 when somebody spoke above her. "Who are you calling?"

Bara looked up to see Carlene Morris beside the ebony newel post Granddaddy Payne had been so proud of. "It's me," Carlene said with a simper. "Foley sent me to get a few things."

Fluffy gold hair flowed over a cotton top that showed off high little breasts and left her midriff bare. Her skirt barely covered the minimum. Everywhere else her skin was an unwrinkled, golden tan. Something long and bright dangled from one hand.

"How did you get in?" Bara demanded, climbing a few steps.

Carlene shrugged. "I still have my key to the back door from when I worked here. Nobody asked for it back." She descended a couple of steps and peered down at the foyer. "What was it you said was worth fifteen million dollars?"

Bara didn't answer the question. She had recognized what Carlene held, and was enraged. "Those necklaces are mine!"

Carlene shrugged. "Foley bought them. Now he wants me to have them." She smiled the satisfied smile of a young woman on the make who has found a generous middle-aged lover.

"They aren't his to give. Put them down and get out of this house. Do you hear me? Get out!"

Carlene came down toward her, swinging the jewelry insolently. Bara saw that in addition to the necklaces, she carried Grandmother Payne's diamond tiara, the one Granddaddy had bought prematurely for her to wear as First Lady of Georgia. Foley must have given that slut the combination to Bara's safe!

Bara stepped aside to let Carlene pass, then gripped a banister with one hand and a handful of hair in the other. She twisted the silky strands around her fingers and tugged hard.

Carlene screamed and writhed.

Bara tugged a second time. "Drop it!" she commanded. "Drop all of it!" When Carlene hesitated, she tugged again.

Carlene dropped the jewelry with a stream of sewer language.

Bara let go and shoved her shoulder. "Go on," she said. "Get out. He deserves you. You speak the same language: gutter-raised filth."

Carlene stumbled down the steps and ran to the front door. She yanked the chair away from the knob and shouted, "You are crazy. I'm telling Foley, and he's going to get you committed. You are downright crazy!" She wasn't so pretty with her face red and her mascara streaked with tears.

Bara threw back her head and laughed. "You haven't seen crazy yet. If I ever catch you in this house again, I will strangle you with my bare hands. That is not an idle threat."

As she locked the door again she remembered Carlene's key. Did the whole world have keys to the house? She'd gotten Foley's back—that was one thing Uncle Scotty had accomplished—but Uncle Scotty still had his, Murdoch probably had one from when she used to come to Nana's after school, and Carlene had one. How many other servants had taken keys when they left? For all she knew, all of Nana's living servants still had keys as well.

Bara checked outside doors to be sure they were locked, rammed chairs under each knob, and armed the security system with furious fingers. Feeling marginally more secure, she stomped to the library, flung her purse on a chair, and headed for the desk telephone. "I'm going to change every lock in this blessed house!"

She stood helpless with the phone in her hands. She could not afford to change her locks.

The receiver beeped a muted busy signal, announcing she had voice messages. She might as well check them, then she'd have that drink and take a nap.

She'd had three callers.

Ann Rose said, "You forgot your groceries. Call me when you get home and Francie will bring them over."

Payne said, "Hi, Mom. Just checking in to be sure you are okay."

Maria Ortiz cried, "*¡Querida!*" *My dear!* "Are you all right? I hope you are simply on one of your fabulous trips, but I have not seen you for two weeks, and I am worried. Call me."

Bara's hand hovered over the button to call Maria back, but she slammed her fist on the desk and hung up the phone.

In the kitchen, she filled a tumbler to the brim, tossed back half of it, refilled the glass, and carried both glass and bottle as she climbed three flights to the attic. She searched dim corners until she found a box labeled COLLEGE STUFF. The box was covered with dust, the sealing tape gold and brittle. Inside, wrapped in felt pennants that used to decorate her dorm room, she found a silver gun. Winnie had bought it for her when she was in college and had insisted on teaching her how to use it. She had carried it faithfully until she married Ray, but had soon realized that with his volatile temper, she was in more danger with a gun than without one. For years it had been hidden in the attic.

She lifted it out and sighted along the barrel with a desperate whisper. "How did I get to this place?"

She found bullets for the gun in the bottom of the box and loaded it as Winnie had taught her. She carried it downstairs, then stood uncertain what to do with it. Should she carry it in her purse? Didn't you need a permit nowadays to carry a gun? Where did you get a permit? Were the bullets still good? Did they wear out with age?

By then she had drunk three glasses of whiskey and was weary beyond endurance. "I'll think about all that later." She laid the gun on the dining-room table, strode to the powder room and took two pills to make her sleep, downing them with whiskey.

She returned to the hall and stood frowning at the Monet. "I really ought to increase the insurance on that thing," she muttered, then gave an unfunny laugh. "With what? But I ought to at least take it to the storage unit until this mess is over."

She stared at the misty scene and knew she couldn't bear to take it down. It had hung there as long as she could remember. She and Nana used to stand and admire it together.

"Putting it in storage would be like losing Nana all over again!" she cried.

But she wouldn't put it past Foley to steal it—or send Carlene to do it.

"Slut! What am I going to do?"

The pain was a physical thing, racking her whole body. She collapsed into a chair in the foyer and sobbed.

Gradually the whiskey and pills began to take effect. The Monet was another thing she would think about later. At the moment, all she wanted to do was fling herself down on the leather sofa in the den and get some sleep.

Chapter 8

Posey pulled into Katharine's drive and brightened to see the black Lexus parked at the front walk. "Tom's home early!" She obviously thought he was inside pouring wine for a romantic afternoon tryst.

Posey seemed convinced that Katharine and Tom spent the few hours they had together each week making passionate love, feeding each other frosted grapes, and giving full body massages. Katharine suspected that Posey—married to a large, comfortable man who looked like his passion meter never rose above two on a ten-point scale—projected on her brother and his wife all her own romantic fantasies.

More experienced in what her husband considered romantic, Katharine eyed the car with a jaundiced eye. Tom never parked outside the garage unless he had to go out again soon. She hurried up the steps, wondering what was wrong.

She nearly stumbled over several large boxes left beside her front door, and bent to read the labels. "Oh, no!" They contained a set of china and a set of silver flatware for twelve, which she and Tom had purchased to replace what had been stolen or smashed. They must have been delivered after Tom got home.

She picked up the box of silver and struggled inside, dreading what he would say if he found out that thousands of dollars' worth of merchandise had been left on their veranda. He had instructed her not to sign permission for deliveries to be left outside when they weren't home. Could she get them inside to her study without him hearing her?

She set down the silver beside her computer desk and went for the china, but the boxes were too heavy for her to lift.

"Tom?" she called as she closed the front door behind her. "Are you here?" She braced herself for his displeasure.

"In the library," he called back. Did he sound a little uneasy, too?

Katharine was so accustomed to silence in the house that another voice was a pleasant change, but not all that she heard was pleasant. From the kitchen came the wails of an unhappy cat. She hurried to open the door and Phebe, the smaller of her two calicos, streaked across the hall and into Tom's library.

"Did you shut the cat in the kitchen?" she demanded at the door of the room.

"Sure. You know I don't want her in here." He carried the squirming cat to the door and dumped her in Katharine's arms.

She carried the cat and followed him back into the library, stroking the irate little animal to calm her. Maybe it was the result of everything she'd been wanting to say to Posey about her driving and hadn't, compounded by anger at the delivery company for dropping heavy, valuable boxes on her doorstep as if they were junk mail, further compounded by her worry that Tom would be angry, but for whatever reason, she opened her mouth and surprised them both.

"If you lived here all the time, you could set boundaries where the cats are concerned, but since you are usually here two days a week and Phebe's here seven, I think that gives her squatter's rights, don't you? She doesn't hurt a thing, she's fully house trained, and she doesn't climb your shelves. She merely likes to sleep on the rug by your fireplace. I think she's come to regard it as her own. So have I."

Katharine loosened her grip, and Phebe leaped from her arms. The cat stalked past Tom with a haughty tail in air and curled herself on the small Oriental.

Tom looked from Katharine to the cat and back again with a startled expression. "I see." He walked over to the shelf and chose a book, held it for a second with his back to her, then started for his desk. He paused by the rug on his way back to his briefcase. "Okay, Phebe, the rug is yours. May I keep rights to the desk?" He stroked her gently and gave Katharine a rueful grin.

She was shocked by the unaccustomed taste of victory.

In his job, Tom was famous for logical reasoning and working out compromises. He was also famous for never speaking without thinking first. Those were some of the things that made him excellent at what he did. At home, though, she had always catered to his preferences. She had believed it was what a good wife did. After all, he had enough conflict to deal with in his job, and was home too seldom to need hassles during the time he was there.

This quick win opened up all sorts of possibilities.

"How was your meeting?" he asked.

She blinked, needing a second to remember where she had been. "Good. Ann Rose got a number of volunteers, including Posey."

"Posey? She went?"

"She drove me—in a new red convertible Wrens bought yesterday for her birthday."

"Her birthday's not until next month."

"I know. She hopes he'll forget the car by then."

Tom looked her up and down. "And you came home in one piece? Amazing."

"There were a couple of times when I figured you'd have to order a coffin, but we survived." Enough banter. "Are you going somewhere?"

He hesitated. She knew that look. Tom hated to disappoint anybody, especially her. "Sorry, hon. I've got real good news and sorta bad news. Which do you want first?"

"The good news isn't anything like a terrific trip that means you are going to be out of town for our party, is it?" She couldn't keep a tremor out of her voice.

"I am committed to be here for the party. I promised. But that's two weeks away. The *bad* news is that some senators are squabbling right now and we're caught in the middle. I need to go up and sort things out. I'll fly back Thursday night and take off Friday so we can have a long weekend to tie up loose ends. And I'll come home the following Thursday, too. I promise. But I do have to go to Washington this week." He went to the shelves to choose another book. Tom never went anywhere without several things to read.

Katharine was so disappointed that her legs wouldn't hold her. She sank into the closest chair and tried to figure out why. She was used to his rhythmic coming and going, had even been disconcerted when he'd announced the past Friday that he would be working in his Atlanta office for a week. Accustomed to setting her own schedule from Monday through Friday, she had mentally checked her calendar and been frustrated because she had several evening engagements that would conflict with the hour he preferred dinner. Used to casual meals, she had inventoried the freezer and found it sadly lacking. She had spent Saturday morning shopping for groceries when she needed to be working on the house.

So why should she feel so let down to hear he was going away?

Because it was awfully easy to get used to having him around.

He came over and sat in the matching chair, misunderstanding her silence. "I've already done everything I was supposed to for the party." He consulted the latest technological gadget he used to keep track of his life.

While he punched tiny buttons, Katharine remembered the day they'd chosen the first leather armchairs, those that had been slashed by the vandals.

"We'll spend long evenings together by the fire when I retire," Tom had promised.

When he'd gotten home and found them ruined, he had gone out immediately to buy new ones. However, while Katharine appreciated his sentiment, she knew good and well that he wasn't likely to retire anytime soon. He wasn't yet fifty, and very good at what he did. His ability to meet with warring parties and bring them to compromise was legendary in Washington, and one of the things Katharine admired about him. It was a rare and precious skill in this contentious world, and one of the reasons he earned enough money to keep his family in the style to which they were accustomed. If the only way he could do what he did best was to be away a lot, she could deal with that. She had. But now that the children were gone, she seemed to miss him more than she had before.

She realized he was listing what he'd done about the party.

". . . and I had Brandi reconfirm with the tent folks this morning. They'll be here early next Friday to set up. She checked with the chairs and tables people, too. They will come Friday around noon. While I was at it,

I had her call and reconfirm the tablecloths and dishes, so you don't need—"

"Dishes!" she yelped. "Drat, I forgot. Our new china is sitting in boxes outside the front door. Apparently it was delivered while I was out."

"It wasn't here when I arrived. I never signed for it, either."

"They must have rung the bell. Didn't you hear it?"

"I ate a quick sandwich on the back patio. But they should have taken it away and left a message." He gave her a penetrating look. "You haven't given blanket permission for them to leave things out there when you aren't here, have you?"

Buoyed by her earlier victory and angry that he was leaving when he'd said he'd be home, she lifted her chin. "Yes, I have. If they leave a message, I have to call to schedule another delivery, then stay home to wait for it. That's too much trouble." When he didn't reply, she added in a gentler tone, "The house is a long way from the street, Tom, and besides, we seldom have deliveries this valuable. Will you carry it in?"

He rose, his lips stiff with disapproval. "Where do you want it?"

"Put it on the kitchen counter. I'll need to wash it before I put it away."

"Can't Rosa wash it? She's coming tomorrow and would be glad to do it." Tom had grown up in a house where the maid did everything. After twenty-five years he was still puzzled by Katharine's casual participation in housekeeping.

"Why are you trying to decide who washes the china when you won't even be here?" she demanded.

He blinked, unaccustomed to attack.

She was instantly contrite. They were grouchy because neither of them wanted this sudden change in their schedule.

She defused the conflict with a laugh. "Rosa *could* do it. She's glad to do anything to get out of cleaning. But you know as well as I do that deftness is not one of her gifts. If anybody breaks a piece, I'd rather it was me. So set it on the counter, muscle man. I'll have time to wash it after you've gone."

She waited in the chair while he carried in the boxes, treasuring up the small sounds he made so she could carry those bits of him through the next few days. He came back consulting the small screen in his palm. "To pick up where we left off, Brandi has confirmed that the dishes are coming Thursday. I'll have Louise call the liquor store from Washington, but they already know what we want, so it shouldn't be any problem. I had Brandi call Elna, too, to see if she needed any help with the food. She says it's under control. My jobs are done—plus a couple of yours." He didn't even sound smug about it. Tom was competent, but seldom smug. He also didn't mention their brief quarrel. Neither did she.

"Good for you."

While he fetched his keys from the kitchen, she wondered what it would be like to have a Frank or Johnny she could tell with an airy wave, "Please take care of all the petty details of my life so I can deal with the big stuff."

He came back and picked up his briefcase. "I need to hit the road. My flight leaves at three." He kept clothes in his Arlington condo, so packing was mostly a matter of changing reading materials. He pulled her to her feet and close to him. "I'll miss you. Hold down the fort."

He draped one arm over her shoulders and she walked him to the car. She was determined not to let her disappointment show, had vowed years before never to send him away thinking she was sad or mad. Life was too fragile for that. "You forgot to tell me the good news," she reminded him.

He gave her a squeeze. "I wondered if you'd remember to ask. I have to go to China in September, and can clear my schedule to stay an extra two weeks. Would you like to come?"

Delight rose in her like a winged bird. "China? Could we see Jon?" Their son had graduated from Emory in May and left almost immediately for two years in one of China's northern provinces, where he was teaching English. Katharine missed him terribly, especially since Susan was already in New York working for a brokerage firm.

Tom nodded. "We can fly Susan over as well, if she can get away. I told you it was good news. Two weeks *after* my meetings. I promise. I've told the office I'll be on vacation."

"Then go to Washington, do what you have to do, and hurry back."

He gave her a lingering kiss, his lips familiar on hers, then drew back only far enough to murmur, " 'If it were done when 'tis done, then 'twere well it were done quickly.' " He kissed her again.

"Don't be a show-off. But I love you." She gave him a quick kiss on the nose.

"I love you, too. See you Friday." He threw his briefcase in the car. She waved goodbye and headed back to the empty house with a lighter step. China! She hugged herself in excitement. Jon and Susan! And two whole weeks with Tom!

Besides, she reminded herself, it would be a lot easier to get done what she needed to do that week without worrying about bigger meals and time for conversation.

Easier, but lonelier.

Posey phoned ten minutes later. "I am so mad I could spit."

Katharine, who had been mentally touring China, came to earth with alarm. "What happened? Did you have a wreck?"

"I don't have wrecks. But if Tom Murray was standing in front of my car right this minute, I might run him over. He called to ask about my car, and he said he's on his way to the airport. Is he really?"

"He has to go back to Washington for three days."

"When you-all have a hundred and fifty people coming to your house Saturday a week?"

"He'll be back this weekend, and things are pretty much on schedule."

"He ought to be home this week to help you."

"Wrens is home all the time. What does he ever do to help with your parties?"

"That's different. I told Tom to come back home or I'd whop him upside the head."

Katharine felt a flicker of hope in her chest. "Did he agree?"

Posey huffed. "No, he said it's a good thing he's married to you instead of me. He said you have everything under control."

"I do, actually. He's done what he promised to do, and more."

"I still can't believe you'd let him go off when you have all those people coming."

" 'Let' is not the operative word. You know Tom's work."

"He needs a new job."

Some days Katharine was able to deal with friends and relations who thought Tom needed a new job—or that she needed a new husband. Some days she even thought the same thing. At the moment, however, with his kiss still on her lips and China in her future, she wasn't going to let anybody—even Tom's big sister—criticize him and get away with it. "What else could he do that he'd be as good at? Or enjoy as much?"

"Husbands aren't supposed to be gone all the time. It's not normal."

"Get real, Posey. Not everybody has a husband or wife who works in town. The whole global economy is built on people who travel. Executives, sales reps, airline pilots, flight attendants, long-distance truck drivers, folks who do training for their companies, entertainers, professional athletes, politicians—all of them are gone a lot. Not to mention folks in the military and all those people who live at home but work long hours—doctors, lawyers, nurses, firefighters, police officers. If you add in those who work night shifts and those in jail, you discover there are millions of wives—and thousands of husbands—who are often home alone."

She could roll the list off her tongue so glibly because one recent evening when she had felt especially sorry for herself, she had poured herself a gin and tonic, fetched a pen and pad, and enumerated all the other wives who were in her same boat. She might be lonely at times, but she was certainly not alone.

"I'll bet if we had taken a poll in that meeting this morning," she concluded, "we'd have found a lot of wives there whose husbands are gone a lot."

"I could name a few," Posey admitted. "Ann Rose, for instance. And there are some, like Bara, who wish they didn't have a husband around. But I still don't know how you stand it. I don't know why you had to give this party, either. I mean, really! For your yard man's daughter?"

"Anthony is more than a yard man. He's a friend. And he's kept this yard for twenty years. He and Elna deserve to enjoy it. Besides, I've known Patrice since she was five. Can you believe she's getting her Ph.D.?"

"I still think you're a saint to do it. Listen, do you want to come to dinner at the club? Wrens has some stuffy old dinner meeting." Dinner at the club was Posey's invariable method of cheering up herself and others.

"Ha!" Katharine teased. "So you don't have a husband home tonight either." She considered accepting, then came down with a thump.

Tom had taken his car! Busy saying what needed to be said, neither of them had remembered he'd be leaving her without wheels.

She didn't think her metabolism could stand two rides with Posey in one day.

"Not tonight. I have things I need to do. But thanks. You are sweet to offer."

Katharine spoke automatically, her mind on cars. She needed one this week, with all the errands she had to run, a pupil to tutor, and one lunch date. Could she dare buy one without Tom's advice? Could she take a cab and look at some? She had taken a cab recently when her car got towed, and it had cost a fortune. If she had to go to many dealerships, she'd more than pay for a car looking for one.

But she couldn't stay home all week without transportation. Maybe she could reach Tom before he parked his car, tell him to leave his parking ticket in his armrest. If she could get a ride down to the airport, she could take the Lexus from the park-and-ride place, use it while Tom was gone, and pick him up Thursday night. But how could she get to the airport? She didn't have enough cash for a cab. Did they take credit cards? She hadn't ridden in them enough to know. She could take MARTA, but she wasn't going to ask Posey for a ride in afternoon traffic, even to the nearest MARTA station. "How soon will Hollis get her car back?"

"Not until Thursday. She's rented one for tomorrow and Wednesday."

Why hadn't Katharine thought of that?

Because she had never rented a car in her life. Tom rented them.

There is a first time for everything. "Who did she rent from?"

"Enterprise. They came and picked her up. I told her I'd run her over, but she insisted on letting them come. I swear, that child never lets me do a thing for her."

"She accepted a costly college education and the complete overhaul of a four-room apartment, including a small truckload of furniture from Ikea. Maybe this time she valued her life and safety."

"If you're going to be rude, I'm hanging up. Actually, I need to hang up anyway. I'm taking a late

aerobics class to make up the one I missed this morning. If you decide to beat up that brother of mine when
he gets home, give me a call. I'd like to get in a few
thumps myself."

Katharine had barely hung up when Tom called.
"Hon, I'm about to catch my plane, but I left you
without a car."

"I just remembered that, but it's okay. I thought I'd
rent one for the week."

"I should have known you'd have it covered. Have
I ever told you I not only love you, I appreciate your
great mind? Don't ever go all fluffy-dithery dependent
on me. Okay?"

"Not likely."

An hour and a half later she drove through afternoon
traffic in a white Nissan Altima. She liked the car. It
handled well and had plenty of room. She put Altimas
on her list of cars to consider when Tom got back. But
no car could compensate for being out in Atlanta's rush-
hour traffic.

When she got home, she decided to treat herself
to an afternoon swim. In one short day she had lived
through the stress of two rides with Posey, a meeting,
a disturbing conversation with Bara, the disappointment of Tom's leaving, the challenge of renting a car,
and thirty minutes of inch-worming her way down

West Pace's Ferry Road. She deserved a reward. As she pulled on her suit, she couldn't help remembering how Posey got her own car, and the fond, indulgent tone Wrens used when he spoke of her. She asked the little cat curled on her bed, "Do you reckon fluffy-dithery dependent wives are the really intelligent ones?"

Chapter 9

Since Katharine didn't have to cook for Tom, she might as well tackle the new dishes after her swim. "Definitely a bluegrass music job," she said as she selected CDs from the rack in the den. She wasn't talking to herself. The small cat had poked a curious head in the door.

While she washed, Katharine sang along. Phebe jumped onto the countertop and curled up next to the cookie-jar pig. Savant, the big cat, crouched in the door to the utility room, watching the party but not committing to it. Katharine had brought the orphaned cats home with her in July from Bayard Island, and Savant was still ambivalent about his new home.

As she lowered the first plates into the hot suds, memories of special meals the family had eaten on the former china rose to haunt her: Thanksgivings when her parents had been alive, Christmas dinners when the children were small, birthday celebrations with Tom's parents. Her knees buckled as she thought of all that lying in shards in an Atlanta landfill. She grabbed onto the edge of the sink and waited for the grief to ease.

Sudden sadness still swamped her since the break-in. Sometimes she tried to distract herself, but that afternoon she let tears flow while she worked her way through dinner plates, salad plates, bread plates, and saucers. When Atlanta's former Everett Brothers crooned, "What have they done to the old home place? Why did they tear it down?" she broke down and sobbed.

That, of course, was when the doorbell rang.

She checked the clock on the stove. Who dropped in unannounced at five thirty in the afternoon?

She grabbed a dish towel and swiped her eyes before heading for the front door, still holding a soapy cup. Phebe reached the door first and wove a pattern around her ankles as Katharine answered the bell, which had rung for the second time.

Broad rays of late sunlight made it hard to see the face of the woman on her threshold, but Katharine recognized the voice. "Oh dear," said Bara, "is this a bad time? I'd have called, but I didn't have your number."

Katharine sniffed and forbore to mention that Tom was listed in the phone book. "I'm fine. I've been washing dishes. . . ." She held up the cup to prove it.

"That could make any woman break down and cry." Bara held out a small wooden box. "I won't keep you. I ran over to bring you Winnie's medals, plus a couple of my brother's."

The box brought a fresh sting of tears to Katharine's eyes. "My daddy used to buy cigars in boxes exactly like that."

"Back when they could still get cigars from Cuba."

Katharine could now see Bara's face. Her eyes held a matching shadow. "Come in and have a drink," she offered. "I could use some company."

She regretted the impulse immediately. From the eau-de-alcohol that accompanied her, Bara did not need a drink. Besides, that was the first time Bara had ever been in her house, and the place was only half furnished. The upholsterer had promised the furniture for last week but was late.

Katharine had a moment of hope that Bara would turn her down, but she nodded. "I don't usually drink, but today I could use one."

Katharine knew it was silly to feel like she had to defend the half-empty rooms and the ladder in the living room, but sunlight was streaming in the bare front windows and she couldn't keep herself from babbling an explanation. "We had a break-in a few weeks ago, and they slashed all of our upholstered furniture. It's being re-done, so for now, I hope you don't mind sitting in the breakfast room. As you can see, we have no sofas, armchairs, or dining-room chairs, so the breakfast room is the only place *to* sit, except Tom's library."

Bara followed without comment until she saw the array of dishes draining on the countertop. "Are you washing every dish in the house?"

"No, this is new china we bought to replace a set that was smashed. I wanted to wash it before I put it away."

That concluded Bara's interest in porcelain. She sat and stretched out her legs, as relaxed as if she sat at kitchen tables every day of her life. "I like your music. That country twang is so sweet it makes me want to crawl up on somebody's lap and rock."

Katharine listened to identify the performers. "That's Mama and the Aunts. Tom saw them in Washington a few weeks ago and bought me the disk. Do you like bluegrass?"

Bluegrass music seemed an unlikely interest for a sophisticated woman in shoes that cost more than Tom's first-class flight to Washington, but Bara nodded. "It reminds me of a woman from North Georgia who used to take care of me. Maisie would sing while she rocked me. Mother wasn't much on rocking—or singing—but Maisie was a champion at both." She leaned back and seemed lost in memory for a moment—or was she trying to find her way through an alcoholic fog?

At last she confided, "My mother was so prejudiced, she didn't want black servants in her house. A fine Christian woman in many respects, but she had an absolute blind spot where race was concerned." She held out one tanned, skinny arm. "She didn't even like me to go out in the summer sun, I turn so dark." She gave a raspy laugh. "I've sometimes wondered if I am living proof that we brought in at least one ancestor from the woodpile, but you would never get my mama to admit something like that."

Katharine was shocked to receive such personal information on their slight acquaintance, and suspected alcohol had something to do with Bara treating her like a bosom friend. She didn't want the woman sobering up later and ruing all she'd said at the Murrays', so instead of the wine she'd been about to offer, she pulled out a pitcher of tea.

Bara called across the kitchen, "Do you have a little bourbon? I had enough caffeine at lunch."

Katharine hesitated, then capitulated. "Sure." She fetched it from Tom's bar and poured herself a glass of white wine.

Bara seized her glass and downed half of it in one swallow, then reached for the bottle. "May I? I'm really thirsty this afternoon."

Replying more out of good manners than good sense, Katharine said, "Of course. Help yourself. Would you like some cheese and crackers?" She had no idea how long Bara might stay, and she was getting hungry. Besides, maybe the crackers would soak up some of the bourbon.

"That would be great. I haven't had a bite since Ann Rose's."

The simple thing would have been to get up and fix a plate of cheese and crackers. Katharine would never be sure why she asked, "Would you like an omelet and a salad instead? That's what I was planning to fix for supper, since Tom's not here."

"You know how to make an omelet?" Bara couldn't have looked at her with more admiration if she had admitted knowing how to design a rocket to the moon.

"Sure. Nothing to it." Katharine moved to the refrigerator and took out eggs, milk, butter, Swiss cheese, ham, tomatoes, half a Bell pepper, and fresh mushrooms.

Bara joined her at the counter and watched in fascination while Katharine chopped the vegetables and ham and grated the cheese. "We ought to make the salad next," she suggested, feeling like a television chef with Bara watching her every move.

As she took the ingredients out of the fridge, she half expected Bara to volunteer. Instead, Bara seemed to be taking an inventory of her fridge. "How do you decide what to put in here?"

Katharine thought she was joking at first, but the intent way Bara was looking through bottles on the refrigerator door shelves implied she was serious.

"Anything that is perishable—vegetables, milk, eggs, yogurt, cheese, anything I want chilled, like tea or Cokes, and anything labeled 'Refrigerate after opening.'"

Bara picked up a bottle of steak sauce and examined the label. "Where does it say that?"

Katharine took the bottle and looked for the words. Finally she found them in eight-point type on the back. "There."

Bara frowned. "They ought to put a big symbol or something right on the front. What if people miss that little bitty type? They could die."

Katharine smiled. "That's a great idea. Why don't you call somebody in Washington and suggest it?"

"I might." Bara closed the fridge and leaned against the counter. She watched Katharine assemble the salad as if she were preparing a gourmet dish. When

Katharine dropped butter in a pan and whisked the eggs and milk while it melted, Bara was right at her shoulder, following every move.

"How much milk did you put in?"

"Just a tad."

Bara huffed. "That's why I can't cook. Nobody knows how much of anything goes into what they make."

"Figure on a teaspoon per egg," Katharine suggested. "Maybe a little more. Now a dash of salt and pepper, and into the butter it goes."

Katharine put a couple of sourdough rolls into the oven and divided the salad onto two of her new plates. Bosom buddies or not, she would not feed Bara Weidenauer on kitchen dishes.

She was gratified when the omelet folded smoothly instead of falling apart like some did, and browned perfectly. She slid half of the omelet beside each salad, added a roll, and carried the plates to the table. She went back for a couple of her new silver forks and cloth napkins.

Bara drifted over to the table and stared at her plate like the food had magically appeared. "I cannot believe you did that so fast. That's all there is to it?"

"That's all." Katharine filled water glasses and joined her. "I usually ask a blessing. Do you mind?"

"Of course not." Bara bowed her head. "Pray that I don't kill Foley, will you?"

She ate every bite, but accompanied the food with bourbon, not water. When she had finished eating—including a large wedge of the chocolate cake Katharine had made for Tom the night before—she shoved away her cake plate. "That was marvelous. Thank you very much."

She made no move to carry her dishes to the sink.

As Katharine rose to get them off the table, Bara pulled the cigar box toward her. "Shall we look at the medals now? This is one of the few things I have from Winnie." She stroked the lid. "He gave Payne his house and most of the furniture, thank God. I never cared for Mama's taste in furniture, but Payne loves it. All I have are the contents of his offices—downtown and at his condo. I didn't keep any of the furniture, except one desk, one chair, and his bedroom chest, but there's lots and lots of boxes. Someday I need to go through it all, but I can't seem to find the time." She gave her raspy laugh. "Maybe I'll die and let Payne do it."

She tilted the bottle over her glass and stared when nothing came out. "I seem to have finished this bottle."

"I'm sorry. That's all there is." Katharine told herself it was not a lie. That was all there was in that particular bottle. She was not about to open another.

Bara sipped her water. "I am so glad Winnie deeded Payne the house and moved into a condo before he . . . died. Otherwise, the house would be tied up in all this mess. Foley's holding up probate of Winnie's will. Had you heard that?"

Katharine shook her head. She really didn't want to sit through more confidences about Bara's personal life. The woman would never want to lay eyes on her again once she sobered up and reconsidered some of the things she'd shared.

Bara went right on sharing. "He and his lawyer want me to sign an acknowledgment that Foley has a claim to part of Winnie's estate, because we were married for more than ten years and still married when Winnie"—again a pause before the final word— "died."

Katharine stared. "That can't be right. Not if Foley divorces you."

Bara gave a one-shoulder shrug. "I didn't say it was right, I said it's what they are doing. They are trying to apply some law about a survivor's rights to an ex-spouse's pension or something, saying that Foley would be entitled to a hunk of Winnie's money once I die because Winnie's estate is, in a sense, my retirement income. However, he is generously willing to accept a flat sum—an outrageous flat sum—as soon as the will is probated. Uncle Scotty assures me they don't have a leg to stand on, but they're holding up probate, which is all Foley really wants. It's been hard on Payne and Hamilton. They want to use her inheritance to make improvements on the house." She didn't mention her own cash-strapped situation, but Katharine suspected she had it in mind.

"Has Scotty pointed out that Foley might die first?" Katharine asked. "Maybe you could counter-sue for a lump sum based on his pension."

Bara laughed. "I like the way you think. Unfortunately, they've got it all charted out. I'm a little older than he, you know"—she dismissed fifteen years with a wave of one hand—"so the lawyer has devised a complicated actuarial table based on our ages, Foley's opinion of the relative states of our health, and the likely appreciation of the estate's value in coming years. They've come up with an astronomical figure that I owe Foley. Uncle Scotty says it's all bluster, but so far he hasn't gotten me a dime."

Appalled at how avarice had replaced affection in their marriage, Katharine sipped wine and said nothing.

Bara didn't seem to need a response, just a new set of ears. "I won't let him get his greedy hands on Winnie's money. He wants to spend it on that—" She broke off.

"I don't need to be using nasty language in your house, but let me tell you, if your husband ever brings home a sexy maid, you go straight to the bank, take out every penny in your joint accounts, and stash it where he can't find it. I cannot believe I was so dumb."

She reached for the bourbon glass, gave it a disappointed frown, and set it down. "He's not getting my money, though, and he's not getting my house. I'll fight him to my last cent. Granddaddy Payne gave me that house when my first husband and I got married, so we could raise our children there. That put Murdoch's nose permanently out of joint, I can tell you that. But she wasn't but thirteen and didn't need a house. When she got out of college, Granddaddy gave her stocks equal to the value of the house, but she has never stopped harping about the fact that I live in what she calls 'our old family home.'" Bara deepened her voice on the last three words, then she gave her raspy laugh. "It's not our old family home. It's not even old. Granddaddy built it after he got defeated in that gubernatorial election, and Mama and Uncle Scotty were grown by then. I think Granddaddy only built it so he'd have a house grander than the old governor's mansion. The place is hard to heat and the devil to keep—especially now that Foley is pinching pennies like Ebenezer Scrooge—but I'll be damned if he gets it or makes me sell. He cannot have my grandparents' house!" She slammed her fist on the table so hard her fork jumped. "Sorry. I get carried away sometimes when I think about Foley."

She leaned over the table and confided, "I've put Winnie's stuff where he can't find it, though. All his bank statements and lists of investments. I will never know what made me do that, but as soon as Winnie died, even before Foley started making noises about divorce, I called movers and had them pack up everything in Winnie's office downtown and in his condo. I sent his furniture to the Salvation Army and the rest to a storage company, and I paid the movers and the storage fees for a year in cash. What do you reckon made me do that? My guardian angel? In any case, Foley has no idea where the stuff is. It's driving him crazy. I keep the key with me at all times." She patted her flat chest. "And I make sure I'm not followed when I drive there."

She grew thoughtful in another lightning mood swing. "Maybe I shouldn't have been so hasty about giving away Winnie's furniture, though. When Foley finishes with me and I'm standing in West Pace's Ferry Road in my skivvies, I may wish I'd kept a bed and a chair. Blankets and pillows, too. Oh well, maybe the Salvation Army will take me in."

"At least you got your daddy's medals." Katharine thought it was time to channel her thoughts in happier directions.

"Yeah. And his business papers, books, awards and trophies, knickknacks he had on his shelves, things like that." Her voice grew so remote, Katharine suspected she was talking mostly to herself. "When I was little, I used to play in Winnie's library in the evenings while he worked. Sometimes I'd draw, and sometimes I'd play store with foreign money he kept in a wooden box on his bookshelf. Not this box," she patted its lid, "but another box he said was made of olive wood." She stopped with a look of dawning comprehension. "That's where that locket was!" She spoke softly, as if to herself.

To Katharine, she explained, "This morning I found a locket I thought I had seen before, but I couldn't remember when or where. It was in that box, in Winnie's bottom drawer, the only other time I saw it. I opened the drawer one evening while he worked and found the box with the locket. I held the heart up to Winnie's ear and said, 'Listen, Winnie! It's beating.' But he said, 'Let me have that, Bara. It's too valuable to play with. When you get older, I'll give it to you. But you can have the box.' I pitched a fit, of course—it was what I did best—and I think that was when Winnie showed me the medals."

"Probably trying to distract you," Katharine suggested.

"Probably. And I'll bet it was after that night that he filled the smaller box up with coins from around the world and put it on his bookshelf—and forbade Art and me to go into his desk. I had never seen either the locket or the medals again until this morning."

She dumped out the medals and spread them like a rainbow across the table. She placed a Bronze Star at the end. "This and one of the Purple Hearts were my brother's. His name's on the Bronze Star. I didn't bring my son's Purple Heart. I know what it was for." Her voice was bleak as she fiddled with the three Purple Hearts. "I can't believe how cute I thought these hearts were, back when I was a child. I had no idea . . ."

She stopped and stared at them, her eyes shiny with unshed tears. Katharine looked at her helplessly, having no experience with handling a heartbroken drunk.

"They had to suffer. That's what they had to do. Suffer and die. Just like me. I'm suffering, Katharine. And if things don't get better, I'm going to die."

She got up and lurched toward a box of tissues on the counter, blew her nose and dabbed her eyes, then left the wadded tissue beside the box. She lurched back to the table, fell into her chair, and picked up a bright gold star. "This one was my favorite. See the woman in the center, with long hair and a helmet? I had long hair and I wanted to ride a motorcycle when I grew up. I thought she was beautiful." She traced the word VALOR on the medal. "I was too little to know what this word meant. I asked Winnie, and he said, 'Doing something really stupid that people later decide was very brave.' For years I thought *valor* meant *stupidity*."

She continued to finger the medal. "I wonder if Winnie got this when he lost his leg. You knew he had a prosthesis, didn't you?"

"I knew he limped." Katharine spoke cautiously. What should she do with Bara? Call Payne? Drive her home? Put her to bed upstairs? Could she climb stairs?

"It was amputated above the knee, but I don't know why. He never talked about it." She fetched the tissue box and swiped away more tears. "I can see why you were crying when I got here. That music is sad." The CDs had recycled and Mama and the Aunts were singing again.

"I wasn't crying over the music," Katharine confessed. "It was the new dishes."

Bara was willing to abandon memories for a mystery. She gave the gold-rimmed plate before her a bleary look. "You don't like them? They look okay to me."

Katharine decided to talk, hoping time would sober Bara up a bit. "They're fine, but my folks and Tom's had eaten off the old set, and they're all dead now. Maybe I'm silly, but I felt like memories got smashed with the dishes." She stopped, stricken, as she remembered that Bara was likely to lose more than a few dishes.

"*Mrrow*," Savant chided from the utility room. Katharine was pretty sure that was cat for "Plates are plates, for heaven's sake, and it's been two months. Get over it!"

Or was that Aunt Sara Claire's voice in her head?

Bara held up her fork and watched light glint off its handle. "Is this new, too? Did the bums steal your silver?"

"Yes, and we had gotten it from Elizabeth and Duncan Moffatt." Katharine's voice wobbled. "They were good friends of Tom's parents, and they retired to Florida about the time we got married. They gave us their silverware for a wedding present."

"Those old dears? I haven't thought of them in ages. When I was a girl, we used to visit them sometimes. They had such a quaint little house over in Morningside."

The Moffatts had lived in a two-story Tudor-style house with four bedrooms—a larger house than the one Katharine grew up in—but she supposed that if you'd lived in mansions, anything smaller seemed quaint.

Katharine took a deep, ragged breath. "I can't bear to think that somebody has bought Elizabeth's silver at a bargain, with no idea of how special it is."

Bara reached over and covered Katharine's free hand with her own. Her palm was unexpectedly warm and moist. "I know how you feel. When I think of Foley getting his nasty hands on my daddy's business or my granddaddy's houses, I could throttle him!" She clutched Katharine's hand so hard, Katharine winced. Bara didn't notice. "I tell you, Katharine, there are nights when I lie awake having very dark thoughts. If you ever hear that Foley Weidenauer has been beheaded, stabbed through the heart, or hung up by his thumbs in a deep dark dungeon and left to starve, you'll know who did it."

She hauled herself to her feet. "I'd better be going. Have to hang a few cobwebs in my dungeon. Let me know what you find out about the medals."

"I'll drive you," Katharine offered.

"I can drive! You think I'm drunk? I can hold my liquor, just like Winnie." She snatched up her purse and headed for the door. "Thanks for supper. I have lived more than sixty years and never knew how to make an omelet. Live and learn."

Katharine watched her down the drive. The Jaguar moved slowly, but did not weave. She stood for an instant praying for both Bara and anyone she might meet on her way home.

The phone was ringing as she stepped inside. Tom was calling to say he'd arrived safely and was in his place. "What were you doing?"

"About to recycle your bourbon bottle."

"You drank all that?" He was astonished. "You hate bourbon."

"Your sudden absence has driven me to drink." She paused long enough for him to wonder if it was true, then explained, "I had Bara Weidenauer over. She drank it."

"Is she drinking again? I thought she'd given that up."

"Apparently this mess with Foley started her again."

"If she drank all my bourbon, is she passed out on the floor?"

"No, she is driving home as we speak. I'm praying she gets there."

"What did she want? I didn't know you knew Bara well enough to invite her to supper."

"We've never been drinking buddies until today," Katharine agreed, "but she's in bad shape." She filled him in on her evening.

"You aren't thinking she's been given to you, are you?" Tom was well acquainted with Katharine's mother's theory that certain people are given to us by God, to take care of for a season, but he was not a believer. "Don't let her consume you. If she's that needy . . ."

"She won't," Katharine said quickly. "She wasn't given to me by God, she was thrust on me by Posey. I have no trouble distinguishing between the two. Besides, I have a party to get ready for, remember? All I'm going to do is check on these medals for her in my free bits of time. It shouldn't take long, and it might be interesting."

"I have an art book on bomber missions somewhere in the library. Try the fourth shelf from the top at the right. It might have information you can use." Tom had a huge collection of books and an amazing memory for where every one of them was shelved. "It has paintings of some of the planes they flew."

"I'll check it out. Sleep well, hon. You'll be home Friday?"

"Ought to be Thursday evening, with bells on."

"I'll be listening for them."

With a smile she headed to her computer. She could finish the dishes in the morning. She wanted to see what she could find online about military medals.

Her first attempts yielded little. Ancestry.com, which had been so helpful in checking old census records, had few military records as recent as World War II. A simple search for "military medals" yielded a number of companies that wanted to sell her medals. Who knew you could buy a medal? But they had no useful information for Bara. Katharine read a Wikipedia article about the British military medal and an article that said the U.S. had little use for military medals before 1917, because they were reminiscent of European armies and their domination. None of that was any help, either.

By then it was very dark outside, and her house seemed big and empty. She went to look for Tom's book and tucked it under one arm. Reaching down, she scratched Phebe under the chin. "Let's call it a day, little kitty, and go upstairs to read in bed. I can try more sites in the morning. This isn't a matter of life and death."

Or so she thought at the time.

Chapter 10

Tuesday

Determined to finish with Bara's request and get
on with preparations for her party, Katharine
went to her computer right after breakfast.

She got only a blank screen.

"You're not but a month old," she reminded the
computer.

It still wouldn't boot.

She checked the plug, made sure she hadn't left a
disk in the drive, and tried again. Nothing. She stared
at it in frustration. Whom should she call?

"Nobody should let all their children leave home,"
she muttered to Phebe, who was batting at dust motes
in the hall. "You need to keep one at home to maintain
the technology."

She had a heartening thought. Morning in Georgia was evening in China, and any excuse to call Jon was a gift.

She fetched her cell phone, grateful that Tom had ignored her protests and invested in one that let her make international calls without breaking the budget.

"Hey, Mom." He sounded so close. She pressed the phone to her ear. She missed him terribly, but being Jon, he swept away sentiment with a rush of practicality. "Can't talk long. I'm heading out to a class on sword fighting. What's up?"

"Sword fighting?" Katharine pictured him lying on a mat covered with blood. "Are you crazy?"

"It's cool. We don't use real swords yet, just sticks."

Yet?

Katharine bit her tongue. Protests would have no effect. She might as well save her breath for prayer.

"I've got a problem with my new computer. It was fine last night, but today it won't boot. I've tried several times, but get nothing. Is it possible to figure out what's wrong without carrying the whole shebang back to where I bought it?"

"Sounds like it crashed. Call Kenny Todd. He went to Tech, but he hung out with one of my roommates. He's a computer genius and he's still in the area, working for Google. I've got his work number here." He rattled it off. "Tell him I told you to call. He'll fix you up. Now I gotta go." He was gone before she could say goodbye.

She cradled the phone in her hand a few seconds longer, trying to absorb the fact that only seconds ago it had connected her to China. China was the other side of the world, the place you ended up if you dug a hole deep enough. Why had she ever let Jon go so far from home?

As if she could have stopped him. He had jumped at the chance to teach English for a couple of years—although given his own casual approach to the language, Katharine wondered what kind of English his students were learning.

She sent up a prayer for protection from sticks and swords as she dialed the number.

"Hello. This is Kenny Todd." He had such a strong North Georgia twang that he gave the greeting three syllables, lifting the word in the middle, and pronounced his name K*inny Ta-ahhd."*

"I'm Katharine Murray. My son, Jon–"

"Has something happened to Jon?"

She loved him instantly for his concern. "Oh, no, it's my computer. It's new, but it seems to have crashed. I called Jon—he's in China—"

"Yes, ma'am, I know. We e-mail all the time. He seems to be having hisself a fine old time over there on the other side of the world." Listening to his light laugh, she wondered what Jon told his friends that he did not tell his parents.

"He may be," she agreed dubiously, "but meanwhile, I have a dead computer and he says you are a computer genius. Do you think you could possibly come look at it for me and see if you can tell what's the matter? It's practically new, and if I have to take it back, I will, but I'd hate to go to all that trouble if it's merely a little something. I'll be glad to pay whatever you charge."

"No problem. Can it wait until this evening, though? Say around six? I have to work." He said it with the pride of a man holding down his first paying job.

"Six would be great. Do you know where we live?"

"Somewhere up in Buckhead is all I know."

She gave him directions and he repeated them. She hoped he was also writing them down. "I'll see you at six," he promised, and rang off.

Rosa arrived at nine to clean. While she worked, Katharine went out to tutor a child, had lunch with a friend, and got home mid-afternoon, as Hollis was riding in beside a stalwart young man with purple streaks in his bleached hair. "This is Dalton," she greeted her aunt. "We've come to hang your living-room drapery."

Dalton looked at his feet and didn't say a word.

Hollis perched on the piano bench and watched. Dalton climbed the ladder and hung the drapery Hollis had designed and sewn.

"They are marvelous," Katharine said honestly. "I am impressed."

Hollis shrugged, her usual response to a compliment. "Dalton is coming back tomorrow morning to hang your pictures."

"Not tomorrow. Thursday." The words came out like a rusty hinge. Katharine wasn't sure who was more surprised to hear the young man speak, herself or Dalton.

"Thursday," Hollis agreed. "Dalton has to build sets tomorrow. Have you decided where you want all the pictures to go?"

"I'm working on it," Katharine hedged.

"You haven't given it a thought. Admit it, Aunt Kat! You've been lolling around eating bonbons and reading trashy novels again. That's all she does," she added in an aside to Dalton.

He shuffled his feet, obviously uncertain whether to laugh or believe her.

When he'd gone, Hollis said, "He's shy as can be, but sweet, and he's amazing when it comes to building sets. Give the man a hammer and he can work a miracle." She looked around in satisfaction. "As soon as the furniture arrives, that's the downstairs almost finished."

Katharine wished Posey could see her daughter at that moment, cheeks flushed with pride. Hollis looked like she had at three, before she had realized she would never measure up in her mother's eyes to her two big sisters.

One word, however, caught Katharine's attention. "Almost? I thought we *were* done."

"You need some stuff sitting around. Decorative accessories."

When Katharine still didn't respond, Hollis said impatiently, "You know—plates, figurines, little bits of art—stuff like you had before." Hollis encompassed the entire downstairs in one sweep of her arm. "Can you go shopping with me tomorrow?"

Katharine's eyes roamed the room. For an instant she saw it as it used to be, dotted with mementoes from special people and trips she and Tom had taken around the world. She remembered the bright sunny day in Algiers when they had bought the Islamic prayer rug, the rain pounding outside a London antique shop as they chose the Toby jug for the mantelpiece, the wind that had blown them into the Dublin hole-in-the wall where Tom found the Celtic cross of green marble that used to sit on the chest between the front windows.

She had to clear her throat to get rid of a frog. "That stuff, as you so elegantly describe it, either came from friends and relatives or took us twenty-five years to collect. We can't replace it in one day's shopping."

"No, but we need to get something to fill the space until you buy other stuff at your leisure. Otherwise the place is going to look like some model home a developer is trying to sell."

"Let's have a Coke and think that over," Katharine suggested. "You've already been doing too much this afternoon."

When they were seated at the table with Cokes before them, Hollis asked, "So is it okay if I come around eleven tomorrow so we can go shopping? And is it possible to get the painter out this week to change the color in that one upstairs bedroom?" Seeing her aunt's expression, she sighed. "Too bad. It really is the wrong blue, so there's no point in putting up the curtains or the spreads on the beds. They'd clash horribly. And if we close the door, nosy people are going to open it to take a peek. How about locking the door?"

"We'll need the bathroom off that room," Katharine reminded her. "And so what if folks see one bedroom unfinished? The point of the party isn't to show off our house."

"I'd like to have gotten the whole thing done before the party." Hollis had the wistful look of an artist required to display a not-quite-finished painting.

"You and I have both worked as hard as we possibly could. Let's call it a day."

"Can you shop tomorrow afternoon?"

Katharine repressed a groan. She loathed shopping. Still, it would soon be over. "If I can persuade you not to drag me to every gift boutique in town looking for the perfect *stuff.* At the moment, I need to comb my hair. I've got somebody coming over."

Hollis called after her as Katharine headed to the powder room, "Who's coming?" From her too-casual tone, she suspected her aunt of entertaining a string of men while Tom was away.

"A friend of Jon's who went to Tech and apparently knows a lot about computers. His name is Kenny Todd."

"Eeew!"

"You know him?"

"Unfortunately."

Katharine stepped out of the powder room to ask, "This from a woman who dates men with blue hair?"

Hollis looked like she had swallowed an exceptionally sour pickle. "Kenny is a hick from the mountains of North Georgia. I hope you can understand a word he

says. Don't let him track straw all over your carpets."
She drained her Coke with one long swallow. "I'd better
go. I don't want to be here when he arrives."

Too late. The doorbell rang.

Katharine was surprised at Hollis's expression. Was
that dislike? It looked more like panic.

She went to answer with a frown of puzzlement.
Hollis was generally the defender of the poor, outcast,
and downtrodden. She had never, so far as her aunt
could remember, ever made fun of anybody less fortu-
nate than she. What did she know about Kenny Todd
that Katharine didn't?

Chapter 11

Having entertained Jon's friends for years, Katharine knew what to expect: a long, lanky male in cut-off jeans, baggy T-shirt, long hair, and scuffed shoes without socks. None of Jon's friends seemed to own socks.

The young man on her doorstep was not much taller than she, and dressed like a tycoon. He wore khaki slacks with a sharp crease, a white shirt, and a navy blazer with a power tie. His yellow hair was cut so short she could see pink scalp. His brown loafers glowed with polish. Only the red Mustang behind him looked like something that might belong to a friend of Jon's: it dated from Katharine's youth, and even though the state was in the worst drought of the century, the car had been polished until it gleamed.

He stuck out a square hand. "Miz Murray? I am Kenny Todd." His voice sounded like it had on the phone, high and nasal with a mountain twang.

She gazed at him in admiration. "I don't suppose you could give Jon a few lessons in the proper attire for a college graduate, could you?"

"No, ma'am," he said, earnest as an undertaker. "I can't teach Jon a thing. He's way ahead of me."

"Most of the time he looks like he recently survived some natural disaster that ripped his clothes to shreds and wiped out all the barbers."

"Maybe so, but he cleans up real good when he wants to. The rest of the time, I reckon he figures it don't— doesn't matter." His eyes were as blue as the sky and equally serious.

"I reckon he does," she echoed without thinking. Flustered, she stepped back. "Won't you come in?"

He glanced down at the floor of the veranda. "There's a big package here for you. Do you want me to carry it in?"

Katharine stepped out and peered down at the label. "Drat! It's a bookshelf I ordered for Jon's bedroom. I've told them not to leave things without ringing the bell, but it doesn't do any good. I'd appreciate if you'd bring it in and leave it in my study."

The box made him stagger, but he still wiped his feet on the mat even though there had been no rain for weeks. He entered the front hall as if it were paved in gold instead of slate, and followed her to the study. No straw on his shoes, she noted as he set down the box with a *whoof!* of exertion. "That sucker's heavy," he told her. "I'm sorry I'm late. I got caught in traffic. It's pretty bad today."

"It's always bad around here at this time of day."

"Some of your streets could use widening."

She didn't bother to explain that people of wealth prefer old, inconvenient houses and narrow, inconvenient streets. He might ask why, and she had no idea.

He stepped back out into the hall and looked around. "I like your house. And that's a fine piece, there." He had zeroed in on the most valuable piece of furniture they owned, an eighteenth-century table that held Tom's jade collection. She and Tom had fallen in love with the table on a trip to England years before, and had bought it as an investment.

"That jade is practically the only thing left in the house worth having." Hollis spoke from the kitchen door. In black jeans and a black top, with her dark hair and vivid lipstick, she could have passed for a witch.

Kenny was certainly staring at her like she had come in on a broomstick.

She sauntered over next to the table. "Hey, Kenny. I'm Hollis Buiton, Jon's cousin. We've met." She flung down the words like a challenge and seemed poised to run.

Kenny nodded. "I remember. You go to that school down in Savannah, the artsy place. You're looking real good." He sounded so surprised that it was the same as an insult.

It obviously annoyed Hollis. "I graduated from SCAD. Now I'm helping Aunt Kat redecorate her house." If she had hoped to impress Kenny, she was disappointed. He didn't say a word. "The house got broken into back in June," she added. "It was practically destroyed."

Katharine was puzzled. As a rule, Hollis didn't babble.

Kenny replied not to Hollis, but to Katharine. "I'm real sorry to hear that, ma'am." He jerked his head toward Hollis. "Is she living with you while Jon's away?"

Before Katharine could answer, Hollis did. "No. I have my own place. Are you still fooling around with computers?" She made it sound like one step up from underwater basket weaving.

"Working for Google." He pulled down one sleeve of his jacket as if he feared it was too short.

Katharine was intrigued. The two of them bristled like cats spoiling to fight.

Hollis gave a languid wave toward the table. "The jade's only here because it got stolen the weekend before the break-in, so it wasn't here when the second set of burglars arrived. Fortunately, it was recovered."

Kenny asked Katharine. "Why didn't the folks who stole the rest of your stuff take that table? It's extremely valuable." He stroked the top, then said with a slantwise look at Hollis, "A lot more valuable than the jade, actually. But you probably know that."

Hollis waited for Katharine to refute it, but Katharine had to nod. "I know."

Hollis's eyes narrowed to slits. She didn't say a word.

Katharine continued, trying to ease the tension, "I have no idea why the thieves didn't take furniture, but all they seemed to want were smaller valuables and carpets."

Most of the rest they smashed, shattered, or slashed. She didn't bother to say that. Kenny didn't need a recital of her misfortunes. But she felt a sharp pain, as if a crystal shard had pierced her heart. Grief takes you like that—out of nowhere, unexpected.

Kenny stroked the tabletop again. "They sure as shooting must not have known the value of this piece. It's a beauty."

When he bent to look closer at the wood, his profile made Katharine think she had seen him before. "Did I ever run into you over at Jon's?"

"No, ma'am. I would remember. I never forget people, or when and where I've met them." He glanced toward Hollis as he said that. Hollis bent down and picked up an invisible speck on the hall rug.

When Kenny peered through the arch that led to the living room, Katharine automatically explained, "Most of the furniture is away, getting new covers. The people who broke in slashed the upholstery, as well."

Heavens! she chided herself. *Do you have to explain your life to a stranger who's only going to be here an hour? How pathetic is that?*

Kenny spoke cautiously, repeating himself as if determined to say the right thing. "Are your sofas and chairs antiques, too?"

"Oh no, they're plain, garden-variety stuffed furniture."

He gave the room an appraising look. "I'll bet when they get back, this room will be lovely and comfortable." He was so solemn that Katharine wanted to tell him to relax—except it would probably only make him more nervous.

"It doesn't even have the pictures hung or decorative accessories around," Hollis said scathingly. "You don't have any idea how good it's going to look."

He lifted one shoulder in a careless shrug. "Looks good to me."

"Hollis has been helping me redecorate," Katharine told him. "She's very good. She helped me choose the color schemes and she has made all my drapery."

If she hoped that might thaw the ice in the hall, it was a forlorn hope. Kenny looked around as solemnly as if he were a judge at a home show. Hollis watched him, tense as one of the entrants. Kenny pretended to ignore her, but Katharine had the feeling his antennae were tuned in her direction. "Looks like you're doing a pretty good job," he said eventually.

"I'm doing a real good job," Hollis retorted. "Not that you'd know."

He shrugged again. "Probably not."

Whatever it was that crackled between these two young people, it made Katharine uneasy. Hollis might choose weird young men to date, but she was basically sound. What gave her this intense dislike for Kenny?

All Katharine knew about him was that he was the friend of a friend of Jon's, and Jon picked up people the way cats pick up fleas, expansively including them in his circle without bothering to find out much about them. Could she be sure Kenny wouldn't show up with a truck the next time she left the house and steal what the last thieves had left?

Chiding herself for thinking such thoughts about a young man who had come across town in rush hour traffic to help her, she offered, "Would you like a Coke? Hollis and I were having one when you arrived."

He brightened. "That would be real nice. It's hotter than the hinges of—well, it's real hot out there."

Katharine brought all three drinks from the kitchen. She found Kenny and Hollis in the dining room, eyeing each other like enemies waiting for the battle to begin.

"I suppose you know all about that rug?" Hollis demanded.

He knelt and brushed it with his fingers. "It looks like a fine old Aubusson to me, handwoven back when they were still made in France. Is that right?"

Hollis didn't answer. Possibly, Katharine thought, she didn't know. Hollis had been more interested in decorative fabrics and tapestries at SCAD. But Kenny's answer tallied with the information that came with the rug, which Tom had bought a few weeks ago for their anniversary.

Hollis folded her arms over her chest. "I guess you studied them at Tech?" She sounded so snotty that Katharine wanted to swat her.

Kenny gave her a sunny smile. "Why, you know, we have one on the floor of the old shack up home."

This had to stop. "You must like antiques," Katharine told him.

He hadn't realized she was there. Abashed, he stood and brushed his knees. "Not to say like them, ma'am, but I grew up around them. The women in my family all collect them."

Hollis gave a grimace that made Katharine suspect that she, too, was picturing a small white house on a hillside with flea-market antiques flowing across the sagging porch to join a host of broken appliances and junked cars. But would that sort of collector be able to identify a handwoven rug?

She handed him his Coke. With a grateful "Thanks!" he took a long swallow.

"What does your family collect?" she asked, feeling like she was single-handedly pushing a heavy conversation uphill.

Kenny grinned. "It's not the family, only the women. But they collect almost anything you can think of. They started with small stuff—dishes, clocks, things like that? But then they moved up to furniture. By now, it has become a pure-T obsession with them. That's how I recognized the table back there." He gestured with his head. "Having been drug all over the place looking at old furniture, I've picked up a bit of knowledge."

"You'd better not count on knowing enough to buy stuff without getting it appraised," Hollis warned. "I took a class on antique furniture, and people get fooled all the time into thinking they are getting a bargain when they aren't."

He favored her with a look out of the corner of his eye. "I'll give you a call if I'm ever of a mind to buy something."

"Do they sell antiques, too?" Katharine had shopped with friends in antique and secondhand shops in North Georgia. They ranged from broken-down sheds fenced with chicken wire to historic buildings divided into stalls for several dealers. Wouldn't it be odd if one of those shops belonged to Kenny's family? None of them, however, had carried pieces like her table or that rug. Where *had* he learned about quality antiques?

"No, ma'am, they never sell anything. They ship 'em back home and find some place to put 'em. They've brought home so many, Daddy and my uncles had to build places to hold 'em. But not one of my mama's chairs or sofas is any good for sitting on. I wish Mama could see how you've mixed up your antiques with comfortable pieces. I'll bet when you are finished, it will look a lot more realistic, like the furniture is furniture instead of for show."

"Thank you."

Kenny either sensed her embarrassment or felt he'd said too much, for he asked, "Where is that computer you were wanting me to take a look at?"

"Back in the study." She led him across the hall.

As he slid into the desk chair, he bent and said softly, "Why, hey, little kitty. You hiding under there?"

Phebe was a streak of orange and black as she dashed for Tom's library door.

"She doesn't like you," Hollis commented. The word "either" hung in the air.

"She's new to this house," Katharine explained quickly. "Still a little skittish around strangers. That's the computer," she added, feeling foolish since he was sitting in front of it.

Once Kenny touched the computer, he didn't notice anything else. He set his glass on the floor and bent over the keyboard like a concert pianist making the acquaintance of a new instrument.

He looked up in a minute. "Do you mind if I shed my coat and tie?"

"Of course not." Was her son this polite in other people's houses?

He literally rolled up his sleeves before he went to work, revealing muscular forearms covered with a fuzz of light yellow hair. Watching him, Katharine was impressed with the difference between his diffidence in conversation and his confidence in his work. First he made sure the computer was properly assembled.

When he tried to turn it on, she held her breath until they were both sure nothing was going to happen.

"I'd have felt like a fool if it had worked," she admitted.

He laughed. "That's what people always say. Let's see what's inside the CPU." He pulled a small screwdriver from his shirt pocket, opened the box, and began poking and prying inside. "Looks like your motherboard's shot." He began to whistle.

Hollis huffed. "Sound cheerful about it, why don't you?"

Kenny tightened his jaw, but did not rise to the bait.

"But it's almost new," Katharine protested.

"Happens sometimes. It'll still be under warranty, so you could take it back and have them give you another one. But if you like, I've got a motherboard in my car I could install. It would save you time and a bit of trouble."

"That would be great." One thing you learned by living alone was how to make decisions quickly. With all she had to do in the next two weeks, time was more precious than money.

He pushed his chair back. "I'll go get it. I'll be right back."

"Ah'll be rat back," Hollis mimicked his accent when he was out the door.

"What is the matter with you?" Katharine demanded. "He seems nice enough."

"He's a self-righteous prig."

"Can you at least be polite?"

"No." She picked a novel off Katharine's shelves and headed to her Uncle Tom's library. "But I'll stay until he goes. I'll be reading in here. Call if you need me."

That made Katharine more nervous. She went back into the kitchen and switched on the CD player, thinking bluegrass music might warm up the atmosphere, but when Kenny walked back in the hall he stopped and frowned.

"You don't like the music?" Katharine asked.

"It's okay if you want to keep it on, but I like classical, myself."

She cut it off and brought back a magazine to read in the wing chair by her study window while Kenny worked. He didn't ask where Hollis had gone, but her absence seemed to relax him. While his fingers were busy inside the computer, he began to whistle the song they'd just heard on the CD. Katharine lifted her head to listen. "You are the only person I know who can whistle a whole song on key."

He flushed. "Sorry. It's a habit I can't seem to break."

"I like it. Do you sing?"

"No, ma'am. The only musical talent I have is for whistling." He resumed work, but stopped whistling. In a few minutes, he said, "Let's see what she does."

When the computer booted, he linked his hands above his head and stretched.

Katharine smiled. "You are amazing. I'll bet your family's real proud of you."

His chuckle was as sunny as his smile. "Not really. Every one of the men sat me down and suggested I get some training so I can find a real job in case the computer industry goes bust, and they're all waiting for me to show up on the front porch one night admitting I'm starving and need a loan."

Thinking about how she wished Jon were closer, she asked, "Do they live far away?"

"About an hour and a half north of here."

"Is your mother okay about your living in Atlanta?"

"Oh, sure. Mama gets around more than Daddy, so she understood why I might want to live in the city. She told me to do whatever makes me happy. But before I came down here, her sisters gave me all sorts of helpful advice." He ticked them off on his fingers. "Janie said, 'If you ever need a little money, give me a call and I won't tell the others.' Wanda said, 'If you wind up in jail, give me a call. I'll come bail you out and won't tell your folks.' Flossie warned me not to forget my roots, and Bessie told me she is real disappointed, because she had me slated to be a preacher. Can you imagine that? She knows good and well I never planned on being a preacher. All I ever wanted to do was work on computers."

"You did a great job on mine. How much do I owe you?"

"Not a thing. I got that motherboard off a computer I bought for parts, and I've more than made back my investment selling pieces to other folks."

"But your labor?"

"Jon's fed me enough times to pay for that. I'm glad to do his mama a favor, him being out of the country and all. You call me if you have any more trouble, you hear?"

"Thank you. The biggest trouble I'm likely to have tonight is trying to track down a friend's father's military medals. She left a box of them and wants me to see if I can help her figure out what he did to earn them."

What made her say that? Could she possibly care whether a young man she scarcely knew saw her as a woman with interests and abilities of her own, and not simply as Jon Murray's mom?

Kenny lit up like a summer morning. "Military history is something of a hobby of mine. Could I see what medals you've got?"

She fetched Bara's cigar box, vexed with herself. Chances were good that Kenny knew little more about military medals than she did, but he'd spend the next who-knew-how-long trying to track them down. Why hadn't she remembered that giving a computer geek a research subject is like throwing fresh steak to a starving dog?

Chapter 12

S he came back to find pictures of medals on her computer screen. "This is U.S. Military About dot-com," he informed her. "It tells all about various medals and what it takes to earn them, and it has good pictures, too. I've bookmarked the site for you to read later."

He did seem to know his medals. He lifted each from the box as if he and they were old friends. "Here's three Purple Hearts. The folks who earned them either got wounded or killed." Ignoring Katharine's wince, he picked up the Bronze Star. "This one's engraved on the back. See? Was that your friend's dad?" He pointed to the name.

"Her brother. He was killed in Vietnam. One of the Purple Hearts is his, too, but I don't know which one. The rest of the medals belonged to their daddy."

"He must have fought in the Second World War. This one's the Victory Medal they gave to all the folks who served." Kenny showed her a big round disc with a woman's figure on it and the words WORLD WAR II. It hung from a ribbon with a rainbow of colors on each side of a wide red stripe.

"It is certainly bright." Katharine didn't know what else to say.

"And here's an Air Medal, a Presidential Unit Citation, and—whoa! Look at this!" He held up a blue circle with a gold border, golden wings joined by a white star, and the number 15 embroidered between the wings. "It's a Fifteenth Air Force patch. I've never seen one of these." He stroked it between his forefinger and thumb as he explained, "The Fifteenth was made up of heavy-bomber groups stationed in southern Italy during the last eighteen months of the war. Most of the fellows started out in Africa, but once southern Italy was taken, the army established the Fifteenth in the fall of 'forty-three and sent them in."

He continued as if Katharine had objected. "I know we hear more about the Eighth Air Force, but that's because they were stationed in England, where most of the reporters were. My Uncle Vik claims if it hadn't been for the Fifteenth Air Force, our land troops could never have won the war. Their crews flew over enemy territory and blew up communications lines, oil refineries, major roads, and railroad yards—all sorts of infrastructure that Germany needed to win the war. Uncle Buddy agrees. He was in the air force during the first Gulf War, and he's big into air-force history. He says folks make a lot of fuss over the infantry's role in the invasion of Normandy, but they forget that the Fifteenth flew over enemy territory every single day, long before the ground troops got there. The Fifteenth also had a photo unit that flew unarmed over enemy territory, to shoot pictures for the bombers. Can you imagine the courage that took?"

He was so engrossed, he didn't bother to wait for Katharine to nod. "And they had an amazing track record for rescuing air crews shot down in enemy territory. No other air force completed successful escape operations in as many countries."

"Show-off." Hollis drawled from the door to the library.

Kenny turned bright pink. Like Katharine, he seemed to be cursed with blushes that rose anytime he was embarrassed or annoyed.

"He is impressive," Katharine chided her niece. "I didn't know all that. Did you?"

"No," Hollis admitted grudgingly.

"I probably was showing off," Kenny admitted to Katharine, ignoring Hollis, "but military history is in my blood. Up where I was raised, practically every stream and hill was the site of some battle. If you dig much, you're likely to uncover cannonballs and stuff. My granddaddy's got such a big collection of old cannonballs and ammunition in his basement, the county fire department has a plaque on his house saying they will not come in case of fire."

Hollis frowned. "You're putting us on."

"No-siree, it's the gospel truth. He can't get a speck of insurance, either. To hear him brag, you'd think that old collection was something worth having. He's a real military buff. He was in the navy during Vietnam. Daddy and all my uncles, except Vik, served in some branch of the U.S. military."

Hollis curled her lip. "Every man in the family but you?"

Katharine was surprised by her contemptuous tone. Hollis was vehemently opposed to war. Kenny, however, didn't seem bothered. "Yep. Everybody but me. I don't like fighting. I got licked when I fought kids at school. I figure I can do more for my country doing what I do best than shooting at somebody I never had a quarrel with. I can't get real excited about re-enactments, either, but Granddaddy, Daddy, and all my uncles are involved in them. And almost every evening they sit around Granddaddy's house re-hashing battles.

To hear them tell it, if they'd of been the generals, the South would have won. When they aren't talking about the War of Secession, they're talking about World War II, Vietnam, or the Gulf Wars, figuring out how they would have done things different. You can't grow up hearing war talk day and night without some of it sinking in."

The term "War of Secession" wasn't one Katharine used, but she had heard it somewhere recently. While she was trying to remember when or where, Hollis sauntered over and picked up a medal dangling from a blue–and-yellow ribbon. "What's this one? It's real pretty—looks like a sun or something with a bird of some sort in the middle."

"It's an Air Medal. The bird is an eagle with lightning in its talons. You had to fly a certain number of missions to earn one. Twenty-five or thirty, I think." He turned it over and showed them the engraved name: WINSTON ARTHUR HOLCOMB.

"That's not very many," Hollis objected. "Uncle Tom flies that much every few months." She laid the medal down as if it were unimportant.

Kenny cocked one eyebrow. "Does Uncle Tom fly with folks shooting flak up from the ground? And with fighter planes stuck on his tail?"

Katharine gave Hollis a warning look and answered for her. "No, he doesn't, and you're right. That would be a lot of missions to fly under those conditions." She was not about to let World War III break out in her study.

"What's this one?" Hollis lifted a plain blue ribbon framed in gold with raised leaves on it. "It doesn't look like a medal at all."

"It's a Presidential Unit Citation. I'll bet his unit got that for flying some of the Ploesti raids."

Meeting blank stares from the women, he was delighted to elaborate. "Ploesti was a huge oil refinery in Romania. Germany took it over, and by 1943 had it producing something like a million tons of oil a month plus the highest-octane gasoline in Europe. The folks who would later be the Fifteenth Air Force started bombing it around August of 'forty-three, and they bombed that sucker for nearly a year. That earned the whole unit a citation." He set it back on the table.

Katharine picked up the gold star Bara had loved. "What is this one?"

Kenny took it and held it reverently. "Whoa! This is the Medal of Honor, the highest honor the military can bestow. They almost never give one, and when they do, the person has to have done something spectacular. It's so special that even if a private gets one, a general will salute him."

"Or her," Hollis added.

"Or her," he conceded. "Your friend's daddy must have been a hero of major proportions."

Katharine nodded. "So I understand. But researching what he did to earn this many medals could take ages, couldn't it?"

"Not necessarily. They give a citation with every medal. If your friend's daddy kept his medals, he probably kept his citations."

She was delighted it could be that simple. "I'll tell her. Thanks so much."

Getting rid of Kenny wasn't so simple. He was still fingering the Medal of Honor.

"We can actually get the citation for the Medal of Honor online. Back in 1973, Congress decided they ought to collect the citations from all Medal of Honor recipients in one place, and that entire record is now available at www-dot-army-dot-mil. They have the recipients listed by name and the war they fought in." He set down the medal and started typing. "What was his name, again?" In a very short time the printer spat out the results. Kenny handed Katharine the printout with the expression of a puppy presenting a slipper. "Here he is."

Katharine thanked him, but made no move to read the paper. "Thanks. I'll give this to Bara."

Hollis reached for the sheets. "Aren't you even going to read it? Mrs. Weidenauer won't mind." When Katharine hesitated, Hollis began to read aloud.

Holcomb, Winston Arthur (Air Mission). Rank and organization: Captain, U.S. 15th Army Air Corps. Place and date: Blechhammer, Germany, 20 November 1944. For conspicuous gallantry and intrepidity above and beyond the call of duty while serving as pilot of a B–24 aircraft on a heavy-bombardment mission to attack the South Synthetic Oil Refinery at Blechhammer, Germany, 20 November 1944. Before this mission, Captain Holcomb had already completed the required number of missions, but he unhesitatingly volunteered for this assignment. The mission was highly successful, but costly. Twenty-three of the twenty-six planes over the target were hit by flak. The plane which Captain Holcomb was flying was riddled from nose to tail by flak and knocked out of formation. A number of fighters followed it down, blasting it with cannon fire as it descended.

Hollis stopped and complained, "They make this sound like an action movie."

Kenny took the papers from her. "Let me read it if you can't show the proper respect."

"I can show respect." She snatched back the sheets and kept reading.

A cannon shell hit the craft, blowing out the windshield, killing the copilot and wrecking the instruments. Captain Holcomb's left leg was struck above the knee. However, none of the other members of the crew knew how to pilot the plane, so he asked his crew to apply a tourniquet to his leg while he continued to fly.

Again Hollis stopped. "Do you think this is really true?"

"Of course it's true," Kenny declared. "They verify it very carefully."

"Whew!" Hollis took a deep breath before continuing.

The controls failed to respond and 2,000 feet were lost before he succeeded in leveling off. The radio operator informed him that the bomb bay was in flames as a result of the explosion of cannon shells, which had ignited the incendiaries. With a full load of incendiaries in the bomb bay and a considerable gas load in the tanks, the danger of fire enveloping the plane and tanks exploding seemed imminent. When the emergency release lever failed to function, Captain Holcomb gave the order to bail out. Four of five surviving crewmembers left the plane. The waist gunner's parachute, however, was on fire. *He beat out the flames and continued firing at the enemy while Captain Holcomb, thinking only of saving his crewman, continued to fly.*

"He must have been in excruciating pain," Katharine exclaimed.

"At least," Hollis agreed, "but the style still leaves something to be desired."

"Keep reading," Kenny commanded.

The plane was under enemy attack for another half hour before Captain Holcomb lost the fighters. Flying his crippled bomber over peaks as high as 14,000 feet, Captain Holcomb informed the gunner that a crash landing was imminent. He ordered the gunner to take his own parachute and exit the plane, to lighten the load. From the ground, the gunner watched the plane land in a distant upland meadow. When it burst into flames moments later, the gunner believed the captain had perished. Local residents assisted the gunner to return to base, where he reported Captain Holcomb's bravery and death.

Kenny interrupted, surprised. "He died?"

"No," Hollis told him. "It was like Mark Twain— the rumors of his death were greatly exaggerated. I've known this man all my life. Hush and listen!"

Six weeks later, Captain Holcomb rejoined his unit. He stated that he had been pulled from the plane by local residents who informed him he was in Yugoslavia. His wounds were treated by a local nurse, whose family cared for him until he was able to travel, then they assisted him to rejoin Allied forces. Although Captain Holcomb had received excellent care, his leg could not be saved. He returned stateside 15 February 1945.

They stood in silence for several minutes. Katharine had no idea what the others were thinking, but a searing conviction was burning itself into her brain: *The man who endured that flight would never have killed himself.*

That's as far as she had gotten when her thoughts were interrupted by Hollis. "Why have you got these things, Aunt Kat?"

"Bara asked if I could find out what each medal was for."

Hollis rolled her eyes at Kenny. "Aunt Kat takes on some of the dumbest projects. Why couldn't Mrs. Weidenauer do her own research?"

"Your mother volunteered me, so don't ask why I didn't say no. You've lived with Posey all your life. But at least, thanks to Kenny, it won't take as long as I had feared. All I have to do is ask Bara to look through her father's files for citations to go with the other medals, right?"

He nodded.

Hollis slid a glance Kenny's way, then strolled over to the computer. "I see you got it up and working again."

"Yeah. That's what I do." He started to put the medals back in the box, but Katharine touched his hand to stop him.

"What are all the little stars at the bottom?"

"Battle stars awarded to his heavy-bomber group during the war. Do you know what bomber group he was in?"

"No idea."

"If you can find out, you could Google it. A lot of them have Web sites, with pictures and memoirs. Some also list missions they flew, and citations and stars awarded to the whole group. As for the medals, like I said, each one comes with a citation stating what was done to earn it. Tell your friend to look for the citations."

"What if she can't find them?" Hollis made it sound like a test.

Kenny passed. "She could go to www-dot-national archives-dot-gov and click on the veterans pages. They should be able to help her figure out what the medals were for. She'd need to do it herself, though, as next of kin. They don't release those records to just anybody. And they had a fire back in 1973 that destroyed a number of records. Still, they can usually reconstruct a good bit of a man's service record—or a woman's," he added before Hollis could protest, "if the next of kin requests it."

"I'll bet we could get most of the information by searching for Winnie's name." Hollis leaned toward the keyboard.

"Not now," Katharine protested as the hall clock chimed seven.

Kenny verified the time with his watch. "I didn't know it was so late. I ought to be getting home, I reckon."

"I reckon so," Hollis mimicked his accent.

To Katharine's surprise, he grinned. "A little more practice and you might learn to talk right."

Hollis grinned in spite of herself.

"Would you like to stay for supper—both of you?" Until the words were out of her mouth, Katharine hadn't known she was going to utter them. Immediately she regretted the invitation. How pathetic was that, inviting young adults who had millions of interesting things to do to stay and eat with somebody as old as their mothers?

To her surprise, Kenny accepted at once. "If you're sure you don't mind. A home-cooked meal would beat a fast-food hamburger, which is what I eat most nights on my way home."

"I'd like a home-cooked meal for a change, too," said Hollis—as if she couldn't go downstairs any night of the week and eat one that Julia, her mother's cook, had prepared.

"Fine." Katharine tried to conceal her chagrin. What was she going to feed them? This habit she was developing of inviting strangers to dinner on the spur of the moment was getting out of hand. Still, she did have shrimp in the freezer and pasta in the pantry. "Shrimp fettuccine okay with you? With salad and rolls?"

"Sounds great," Kenny told her. "Do you need any help?" He picked up his glass from the floor and looked with dismay at a small puddle left by condensation. He whipped out a clean handkerchief—*a handkerchief?* Hollis asked Katharine silently over his head—and wiped up the water, then drained the glass and held it up. "Shall I set this by the sink?"

"I'll get it," Katharine offered, but he shook his head.

"My mama would have a fit if I let you wait on me."

She led them toward the kitchen, wondering what she'd do with them while she prepared the meal.

Chapter 13

S he had an inspiration.

"Those bookshelves I ordered for Jon's room were delivered this afternoon," she told Hollis. "Kenny put them in my study. Think you all could assemble them?"

"Sure." Kenny flexed his hands like he couldn't wait to get started. "Do you have a couple of screwdrivers?"

Katharine fetched the screwdrivers and abandoned the two of them to the job. "Supper in forty-five minutes."

In the kitchen, she put on water for pasta and shrimp. She was tearing romaine when Kenny joined her. "Do you need any help, ma'am? Hollis says she has the bookshelves under control." His gaze wandered through the bay window, where the afternoon had become a soft, diffused yellow. A couple of butterflies were playing together above the purple buddleia and a sparrow was having an evening bath. "You've got a gorgeous yard."

"Why don't you go walk around a little? You've been cooped up inside all day."

His face lit up. "I'd like that. Living in an apartment, I don't get outdoors much, but my grandma loved flowers, and I used to help her out in the yard."

She waved him toward the door. "Enjoy."

Hollis came into the kitchen a few minutes later, disgusted. "I finally pried the box open, but I think the instructions are translated from Chinese. They don't make a speck of sense." Before Katharine could reply, Hollis glanced out the window. "What is he doing?"

Kenny had his nose buried in a yellow rose.

"A man who loves roses can't be all bad," Katharine told her. She stepped to the door and called, "Kenny? Would you come get a knife and cut a few flowers for the table?"

"I got a knife." He pulled out a pocketknife. "Will daisies and liriope be okay? They look pretty together, and you got some healthy-looking liriope."

"I sure do. It would take over the place if I'd let it. Cut as much as you like."

"Of course he has a *ni-i-ife*," Hollis said under her breath as Katharine rejoined her. "He probably has a plastic pocket liner, too."

"Hollis," Katharine warned.

In a few minutes, Kenny appeared in the doorway carrying a bouquet of yellow and white daisies, purple liriope flowers, long liriope fronds, and a single yellow rose. "That was such a perfect rose, I couldn't resist it," he told Katharine, holding it out. "I'm partial to yellow."

"Did you finish the bookshelf?" he asked Hollis while Katharine put the flowers in water.

She shook her head. "The instructions don't make sense. I think they were badly translated from Chinese."

"You want me to help you?"

"No, Kenny, I do not want you to he'p me. You can't do it, either, unless you understand Chinese. None of the pieces fit."

"I might be able to figure it out," he said mildly. "My family builds houses, so I'm kinda handy with a screwdriver. Besides, I've put together a lot of shelves these past few years."

She thrust a screwdriver at him. "Have a go, then. It's all yours." She wiped her palms on the seat of her pants as if to wipe away all responsibility for the results.

Katharine said quickly, "You don't have to do that. We're going to eat pretty soon."

"This shouldn't take but a few minutes." Kenny headed to the study.

Hollis followed him, and Katharine heard her ask, "Aren't you even going to read the instructions?" Her voice was as icy as the dregs of Coke in the glass on the drain board.

"These things are pretty much all alike." Kenny began to whistle a Chopin prelude. Savant sidled out of the utility room and into the hall. Phebe followed.

Hollis entered the kitchen breathing so heavily, you'd have thought she was related to dragons. Katharine shut the door to the hall and switched on her new CD so Kenny couldn't hear their voices. "What on earth is the matter with you?"

"I can't stand show-offs." Hollis screwed up her face. " 'My family builds houses. I'm kinda handy with a screwdriver.' Hick!"

"That's no excuse for being rude to a guest. I've never seen you like this."

Actually she had. As a child, Hollis could be insufferable to Posey's snootier friends, but only if they were rude to maids, yard men, or others who served them.

When Hollis didn't answer, Katharine demanded, "Where did you meet him, again?" She was grasping at straws, trying to understand.

Hollis did not meet her aunt's eye. "Around. With Jon."

"Well, whatever has been between you is your business, but I don't want blood flowing down my hall. Do you understand? So be sweet."

"Yuck," was Hollis's inelegant reply.

"Make the salad while he's assembling the shelves."

Hollis started slicing tomatoes like she'd rather have Kenny's neck on the cutting board. Katharine tried to remember why she had ever thought this dinner party a good idea.

Kenny knocked hesitantly on the kitchen door. "I'm finished. They look real nice."

When Katharine opened the door, he wrinkled his forehead at the music.

"I'm sorry you don't like bluegrass," she told him. "It keeps me sane when I'm cooking. Besides, this is a really good group, don't you think?"

"It's okay." He sounded cautious, like he didn't want to offend.

"It's better than okay," Hollis blazed. "That group is great. You grew up in the mountains. You ought to learn something about bluegrass so you can recognize good stuff when you hear it."

"I know bluegrass, I just like classical better. You all want to see the shelves?"

Katharine and Hollis followed him to the study. While they examined the shelves, he bent over and picked up Savant, cradling the cat in his arms. An unmistakable purring filled the room.

Katharine stared in astonishment. "You are the only person I know who can hold that cat, and I've never heard him purr."

"Maybe he's partial to short, good-looking men." Kenny tugged the cat's ear and Katharine could have sworn that crusty old cat smiled.

"You like cats?" Hollis sounded like she might be willing to grant Kenny one point in his favor, but he rejected her olive branch.

"Oh, we kep' a few around the barn when I was growin' up, you know?" Kenny bent and put Savant down. Crouching close to the floor, the cat slithered toward the utility room.

Kenny nodded toward the finished set of shelves. "Where was it you wanted them, ma'am?"

Hollis answered before Katharine could. "Upstairs in Jon's room."

"You want to get the other end?" he asked her.

She started toward the shelves with a determined look in her eye, but Katharine stopped her. "She can't. She was shot last month, and she isn't supposed to lift anything yet."

His jaw dropped. "Shot? What the Sam Hill were you doing?"

"I wasn't doing anything," Hollis said sullenly.

"She was trying to defend their beach house from an intruder," Katharine explained. "And she was very brave. She could have been killed."

Kenny shook his head in disbelief. "You all certainly lead exciting lives. Tell me where you want the shelves. I can probably carry them up myself."

Hollis led the way, admonishing him not to hurt the newly painted walls. Katharine was delighted to have a few minutes to herself. She took stock of dinner. At the rate she was going, she wouldn't have food on the table before nine.

When the two young adults trooped back downstairs, she said, "Okay, somebody needs to finish the salad and somebody needs to set the table."

"I'm making the salad," Hollis reminded her, although so far only the tomatoes were chopped.

"I'll set the table," Kenny offered.

"Are we planning to eat down by the pool?" Hollis asked. "The dining room isn't usable and I hate to eat in a kitchen."

Katharine tried to remember the last time she'd seen Hollis eat anywhere else.

She gave the window a dubious look. "Don't you think it's too hot out there?"

"There may be a breeze. Let me check." Kenny stepped outside the kitchen door and went to the far side of the patio, lifting his face to the sky. Hollis fetched a tray and started filling it with pottery plates, stainless-steel utensils, and cloth napkins.

Katharine asked softly. "Now who's trying to show off?" Hollis knew good and well she usually used plastic place mats and paper plates and napkins down by the pool.

Hollis gave her an evil grin and added a round cotton tablecloth and the vase of flowers to the tray.

"It's cooled off some, and there's a little breeze," Kenny announced.

"Good." Katharine ran water into a bowl and handed him a sponge. "You'd better wipe the table before you set it. It hasn't been used lately."

He headed out, whistling.

"What are you trying to prove?" Katharine demanded when he was out of earshot.

"Lighten up, Aunt Kat. He'll probably think using real plates and cloth napkins down by a pool is cool. It's not as if we went out and bought stuff to impress him. We're using what you already have, right?"

"Yes, but . . ."

"You've got it, so use it. It's a party."

Katharine headed to the fridge. If they were going to be festive, she'd serve wine. Maybe a couple of drinks would mellow them into decent dinner companions.

She was setting wine, a pitcher of iced water, and glasses on a tray when Kenny came back. "I'm ready for the dishes. And do you have any citronella candles? The mosquitoes are whining."

"We've got citronella torches. Hollis, show Kenny where they are in the garage."

They fetched the torches and Kenny headed back toward the pool. "Do you need matches?" she called after him.

"I got matches," he called back.

"He was probably a Boy Scout," Hollis said derisively.

"You were a Girl Scout," Katharine reminded her. Hollis had been a particularly zealous scout up through middle school.

Hollis chopped vegetables and didn't reply.

When dinner was ready, Katharine filled one tray with salad, pasta, and shrimp, and called for Kenny to come carry it out. She picked up the tray of wine, glasses, and water, and told Hollis, "Bring the bread." She didn't want to make an issue of it, but she didn't want Hollis carrying anything heavy.

Katharine motioned for them to be seated, but Kenny moved to stand behind her chair. "May I help you, ma'am?"

She ignored Hollis's smirk, slid into her seat, and unfolded her napkin. "I hope you don't mind, Kenny, but we usually pray before we eat."

"We ask a blessing up home," he said easily.

"So why don't you ask it?" Hollis challenged him.

Katharine expected him to decline, but he said, "Sure." He looked out over the lawn with his eyes wide open and said, in the tone of one addressing a friend, "God, this sure is a great evening and a beautiful place. If this dinner tastes half as good as it looks, we will be truly blessed. But even as we enjoy ourselves, we remember that there are those who don't have enough. If there are ways we can help them, please let us know. Amen."

Katharine was touched by the prayer, but she lifted her head to see Hollis wrinkling her nose. Was there no pleasing the child? In high school she had made a faith commitment and stuck with it. She had built houses in Mexico and rocked infant orphans in Romania, had stayed active in church during college when most of her peers slacked off, and was still active. Yet she couldn't look more disgusted with Kenny if he had flung off his clothes and begun some wild, blasphemous rite.

Hollis's disgust turned to smugness when Kenny grew stiff and formal after the prayer, so conscious of minding his manners that Katharine was tempted to beg, "Relax. We aren't giving you a grade."

As she started pouring wine, she looked inquiringly at Hollis to see if she wanted any. Hollis seldom drank wine—not on principle but because she disliked the taste. However, she was being so unpredictable tonight that anything was possible.

Instead of answering her aunt's unspoken query, Hollis said, "Kenny will want water. He doesn't drink."

"Wherever did you hear such a thing?" he demanded. "I'd love some wine, please." Katharine filled the glass a little fuller than she had intended and handed it to him.

Hollis reached for the next glass and, ignoring her aunt's surprise, took a large gulp. "Um—good choice, Aunt Kat." Kenny gave her a sharp look, then bent his head and started buttering his roll. "What?" Hollis demanded. "What?"

"I didn't say a thing." He bit into the roll and chewed slowly.

Hollis took such a big swallow, she choked. Katharine felt like she was watching a bizarre episode of reality TV. She regretted the wine. It didn't seem to be improving things. Why wasn't she eating alone in her kitchen with a good book?

She racked her brain for a subject—any subject— they could discuss without quarreling. "How'd you wind up at Tech, Kenny?"

It was a good choice. He was a born storyteller and didn't mind embellishing the facts to get a laugh. "By the seat of my pants and the help of a saintly woman. Nobody in our family ever went to college. All the men are builders except Uncle Vik, who works on cars. I like cars, so I'd figured on taking a technical degree and going to work with him, especially the computer part. However, my high-school counselor pulled me out of class one day, which liketa scared me to death, wondering exactly which of my infractions of the rules she had found out about." His gaze slid toward Hollis, but she was gazing over the pool as if she were alone at the table, enjoying nature and a solitary meal.

"All the counselor wanted, though, was to tell me she'd noticed I wasn't applying to college. She said with my grades and test scores, she thought I should. We both knew what I'd major in. I've loved computers since I got my first one when I was eight. She recommended Tech and even helped me fill out the application, to make sure I did it right." He gave a self-conscious little laugh. "She made me apply for a Hope scholarship, too, but when I got home and told Daddy, he was madder'n a coon dog that's sat on a hornet's nest. Said our family has never taken charity from the government and wasn't about to start."

"Hope scholarships aren't charity," Hollis protested. "They're the only good thing to come out of the Georgia lottery."

"I know that, but Daddy still felt like it was something he didn't want or need. Granddaddy figured a way around his objections, though. He told Daddy that after all the money our family has spent on lottery tickets over the years without ever winning more'n a few dollars here and there, it was high time we got some good out of our investment. When Daddy looked at it that way, he agreed I could take the scholarship. But I think he still expects me to pay it back someday. And I know he wonders why I'd rather sit in an office, when I could be building houses or fixing cars." His grin was so infectious, Katharine laughed. Even Hollis's lips twitched before she tightened them.

"Does your mother work?" Katharine asked.

Kenny gave a curt nod. "She used to keep books for granddaddy's business. Now she does some singing engagements."

"What kind of music?" Hollis demanded.

"Bluegrass and gospel, mostly," he admitted with a grimace.

Katharine wondered if he was always ashamed of his mother's singing, or only because of what Hollis had said in the kitchen about mountain people and bluegrass music. He looked like he'd rather discuss anything else, but the sense that mothers ought to support each other made Katharine say, "When she is singing sometime, I'd like to come hear her."

She was glad when the meal was finally over. As a fitting end to a nerve-wracking evening, Savant streaked out the front door as she held it for Kenny. Kenny dashed down the drive after him and grabbed the big cat before he reached the street.

"You stay here, kitty." He stroked him as he carried him back. The cat struggled to get free, but gradually grew calm in his arms.

"You can have him if you want." Katharine hoped he'd take her up on it.

"They won't let me keep pets where I live." He tried to put it in her arms, but the cat writhed and bucked. "Is there somewhere I could confine him for you?"

"Put him in the utility room off the kitchen and close the door."

He came back sucking one hand. "Got me," he said cheerfully.

"You'd better watch that," Hollis warned from where she was propped against the doorjamb to Katharine's study. "Cat scratches can fester."

"I'll put something on it. Thanks for a lovely evening, Miz Murray. You are as easy to talk to as Granddaddy said you were."

"I beg your pardon?"

"My granddaddy, Lamar Franklin. He said he keeps running into you at the history center."

Lamar Franklin. A construction worker from the North Georgia mountains with a passion for genealogy and history. She'd run into him twice. Each time he had helped her solve a genealogy problem. The prior month he had seemed to know enormous amounts about Civil War naval history. And he was the one who referred to the Civil War as "the War of Secession."

"I thought you reminded me of somebody." The young man in carefully ironed khaki pants and an oxford-cloth shirt bore little resemblance to the tanned old hippie with his gray ponytail, callused hands, black jeans, in-your-face T-shirts, and scuffed boots, but the profile and the deep blue eyes were the same.

"Yes, ma'am. Folks say we resemble."

"He seems to know a lot about genealogy. I'm amazed at the long words that roll off his tongue." She could have bitten her own tongue. Did that sound condescending?

If so, Kenny didn't seem to notice. He laughed. "They ought to. He practically haunts the history center when he's not working, trying to trace our family back to somebody important. So far the best he's come up with is Daniel Boone, and that's not real certain, but he keeps a-trying. And he's gotten so good at that genealogy stuff, he gets a lot of invitations to talk about it to groups all over the South. Last time I saw him, he bragged, 'I've hep'ed Jon Murray's mama out a couple of times.'"

She wrinkled her forehead. "How did he know I'm Jon's mom?" Of course, Lamar was a far better detective than she, his skills honed by years of genealogical research.

"I pointed you out to him at the symphony last winter. Granddaddy and I both love symphonies, so for Christmas these past few years, Mama and Daddy have given us season tickets. Last February, we were a few rows behind you and another lady, so I pointed you out and told him you were Jon's mother, since he'd met Jon not long before. He never forgets a face, like me." His gaze slid over toward Hollis. She bent and picked up a speck off the floor.

Kenny went on smoothly. "So when he saw you at the history center, he recognized you right away. He called me later to ask whether you were staying out here all by yourself. He said he'd heard something that made him think your husband's out of town a lot. I said I thought he works up in Washington most of the time. Is that right?"

Katharine nodded reluctantly.

Kenny spoke in the tone of all youth when confronted with the foolish prejudices of their elders. "Granddaddy doesn't think a woman should live on her own."

"I'm used to it," she assured him. "And I have an excellent security system."

"And our family isn't far away," Hollis chimed in behind her. "Good night." There was no misinterpreting her tone.

Before Kenny left, he leaned close to Katharine and whispered, "I take it Hollis is dealing with her problem. That's good."

She had no idea what he meant, but she wasn't about to say so.

"Hollis is fine," she assured him.

"I'm sure glad to hear it." He looked over Katharine's shoulder and said louder than necessary, "I'll be going then. You all have a nice evening." He ran lightly down the steps.

"Ah'll be goin', then. Y'all have a nahse evenin'," Hollis mocked softly. She shifted her big shoulder bag and said, "I put the dishes in the dishwasher. I thought I ought to stick around while Kenny was here."

"Thanks. He seems nice enough, though."

Hollis shrugged. "You can't tell about people from how they seem. Good night."

Katharine grabbed her by the shoulder. "What aren't you saying?"

Hollis pulled away. "Nothing. I don't like him, that's all. We can't all like everybody." She also ran down the stairs to her car, but in Hollis's case, it looked like a bolt.

As Katharine carefully checked to be sure all her doors were locked, she admitted that the evening had disturbed her. What was it about Kenny that Hollis disliked so much? And how had he known who she was, to point her out to his grandfather?

She also disliked the fact that strangers had been discussing her staying home alone. She double-checked to be sure the security system was on, and even then she had a hard time settling down to doing anything constructive. Finally she pulled out the bills and spent an hour writing checks, but she had trouble concentrating and had to tear up one check after she wrote the amount on the date line. What had Kenny been referring to when he'd asked about Hollis? Girls at college seldom told their parents everything. What did Kenny know that she—and maybe Posey—didn't?

She felt so jumpy that when the phone rang at ten, she looked at it apprehensively. Nobody she knew except Tom called after nine, and he was at a late meeting that evening.

To her utter delight, it was Jon. "I got an e-mail from Kenny. He said he fixed your computer and stayed for dinner."

Katharine was pleased that Kenny would report on his evening to Jon. That raised him in her estimation again. "He did, but he wouldn't let me pay him."

Jon laughed. "He's making an indecent amount of money, and a home-cooked meal probably did him good."

When they hung up, Katharine missed her family so much she felt a physical ache. The house seemed enormous, full of dark corners. She carried the small cat up with her to bed, but at the top of the stairs, as she was about to switch off the downstairs-hall light, she changed her mind. For the first time since her children were small she left hall lights on, upstairs and down.

Chapter 14

About the time Katharine was going up to bed, Murdoch Payne was sitting beside her telephone dithering. Dithering was something Murdoch did well. Making a decision could be so difficult. She was far better at impulsive acts, committed on the spur of the moment without thinking things through. When she acted on impulse, she felt as if she were swimming with the current in a fast-moving stream. When she stopped to think, it was as if somebody had put huge boulders in the water of life.

Take her upcoming trip, for instance. She had dithered for weeks about whether to attend the reunion of her old college roommates in New England. Should she spend the money? Would she have any fun? They were all more accomplished than she, and married.

She had almost decided not to go, when she found a promising link that might connect Dolley Payne Madison to their branch of the Payne family tree. The next morning she had seen an ad in the paper for a cheap flight to Boston, called that very hour to make a plane reservation, got a good seat, and even got a good deal on a hotel. It was a bit far from campus, but surely her friends wouldn't mind transporting her. Why couldn't all of life be that simple?

Simple for Murdoch meant anything that gave Murdoch what she wanted.

What she wanted at the moment was not simple, however. People didn't gossip about Bara in her presence, but she'd heard enough to know Foley was trying to squeeze every penny he could out of their divorce, and in spite of what Bara had said the previous afternoon, it would be like her to give Foley the Dolley Payne Madison silver tea set in exchange for something she wanted more. That worried Murdoch to death.

Before she went out of town, she wanted Bara to solemnly promise she would not let that set go out of the family. She reached for the phone, then drew back. She had never persuaded Bara of anything before. Why should she think she could this time?

She was desperate enough to try.

Across Buckhead, Foley Weidenauer stood in the door and considered his wife in the light streaming from the hall. She lay in the library on a black leather couch with her eyes closed. Asleep? Or drunk? It was past eleven. How long had she lain there? He hadn't heard any sounds since he'd arrived home at eight.

Foley had been listening for sounds that she was going to bed. He wanted to prowl the house that evening to make sure she hadn't removed any of the things on their inventory. He also wanted to look for items he could replace with copies of lesser value. He had already commissioned a talented young artist to reproduce the Monet in the front hall. It ought to be finished in a week. Bara was attached to that painting, so she would be sure to want it, but having had it appraised recently, she'd be unlikely to look at it too closely anytime soon.

He looked around the familiar room—the room that used to be *his* library—and his eyes encountered those of Winston Arthur Holcomb staring at him from above the fireplace. Bara had taken the oil portrait from her father's closet the day they let her into the condo after he died, and asked a couple of gardeners to take down a perfectly good hunting scene and hang it up. Foley had thought about protesting, but had decided to wait until she'd recovered a little from her daddy's death. He hadn't expected that to take so long.

Once he had definitely decided on divorce, he had a better idea. He had brought in an art dealer he knew to evaluate the painting one afternoon while Bara was out. The man had recently been taken to the cleaners in a vicious divorce, so he was quite amenable to inflating the value. Bara had been happy to believe a portrait of her old man was worth that much, and Foley had included it in her share of the settlement.

"She's welcome to you," he told Winnie silently. He glided across the thick rug and stood looking down at her. She wore black silk pajamas with a matching robe and black velvet slippers. Her hair fell across the black arm of the couch in swirls of silver. She was still attractive when she let her face relax. Sleep—or alcoholic stupor—erased the lines of bitterness around her mouth and hid the anger in her eyes.

Her eyes were what had first attracted Foley. One of many CPAs in a large firm that handled the accounts of Holcomb & Associates, he had been invited to an office party Winnie Holcomb had thrown. Bored and about to leave, he had heard a laugh, looked across the room, and seen a woman with a cloud of black curls and dark, smoldering eyes—the kind of eyes you could jump into and drown. They flashed in his direction as somebody in her circle finished a joke, and she threw back her head and laughed again.

Foley, who measured his pleasure with the same precision he devoted to accounting, had been enchanted by the abandon of that laugh. He had noted that the drink in her glass was clear, so he crossed to the bar and asked the bartender if he knew what the woman in the emerald dress was drinking. The bartender looked where he was pointing. "Miss Bara? She only drinks water. It's water, all right. Never touches anything stronger."

"Then give me two waters on the rocks."

Carrying the drinks before him, Foley had worked his way through the crowd to her side. "I see your drink is almost gone. Care for another?"

She had started to refuse, but he leaned over and whispered, "It's water. Looks like gin or vodka, but it's not as likely to make us disgrace ourselves in front of the boss."

She had registered surprise, then delight, and said in a husky voice, "My beverage of choice."

He had stood beside her for nearly half an hour, charmed and charming. He knew he could be charming. Women had been telling him so for years. Foley, however, had been waiting for the woman who could help him up the ladder he was determined to climb.

He'd had no idea when he met her that Bara Branwell could be that woman. He figured she had to be somebody important in Winnie Holcomb's world, since that was the sort of party it was, but not having grown up in Atlanta, he had no idea she was Winnie's daughter. Still, she had intrigued him. She seemed young for her years, yet sophisticated as Foley could never be. Because Foley possessed at least the rudiments of a conscience, he would remind himself in years to come that he had liked her before he knew who she was; he had not married her for her money or her name.

Not entirely.

The night they met, after what he had considered enough chitchat, he asked her to dinner after the party. She had agreed, with one stipulation. "I'll come, but I'll drive my own car. It's a rule I observe."

Not until after they had met twice more for dinner and enjoyed a lot of good laughs together did somebody clap him on the shoulder in the Atlanta Athletic Club locker room one afternoon and say, "I hear you are squiring Bara Holcomb. Some folks have all the luck."

"Holcomb?" Foley had asked, bewildered. "I thought her name was Branwell."

"Bara Holcomb Branwell." The other man punched him lightly. "Don't try to pretend you didn't know."

"Know what?"

"That she's Winnie Holcomb's only living child, with enough in the bank to keep half of Atlanta for the rest of our natural lives. But you'd better be careful. Winnie is real protective where she's concerned."

Foley had done a lot of thinking while he walked the treadmill and rode the exercise bike that afternoon. He had considered their difference in age and what it would mean in years to come. He had balanced that against the probability of a position at Holcomb & Associates, a house in Buckhead, and entrée into Atlanta's highest circles. By the time he headed to the shower, he had made a decision. He would have that woman if it was the last thing he ever did.

It had taken him five months to persuade her to elope to Greece. After they got back, she had taken him to her daddy's office, flung out one arm, and said, "Here's my new husband, Winnie. He's been keeping accounts for you for years. Think you could find him a job in the firm?"

Winnie had been far from pleased about Foley, but he was glad to see Bara happy. Throughout the following year, Foley had worked to keep her happy—and to convince Winnie that he would be an asset to the firm. He had been, dammit! Look at how well he'd handled Winnie once he had the job. For months the big man had eyed him like a new rooster intruding on his coop, but Foley had set himself to charm Winnie as he had charmed Bara. He not only did excellent work for the firm, but he had also learned the great man's likes and dislikes—and challenged his opinion often enough to keep Winnie from seeing his son-in-law as a toady. Winnie never trusted men he could not respect.

Gradually Winnie had begun to rely on him, even if he never really liked him. When Foley saw that Winnie's liking was lacking, he had set out to charm the board. Winnie had objected to Foley's rise to chief financial officer, but by then Foley had had the votes. Some folks said Winnie had jumped off his balcony because of his grandson's death. Foley knew differently. It had happened the day Bara warned Winnie that the board intended to make Foley CEO when Winnie retired. Foley had made the mistake of boasting to her, not thinking she'd tell Winnie so soon. Winnie had called Foley and blistered his ears with his anger. He'd called a couple of board members as well. Before he could call more, he had died. Within two days the board had called an emergency meeting, and Foley had been elected.

He again met the eyes of the man in the portrait over the fireplace. "Not bad for a boy with a whore for a mother and a john for a dad, eh? But you should never have said what you did to me that last afternoon."

Winnie's gaze held his. Foley flushed and looked away.

Bara stirred, drawing his attention. He had Winnie's company and he had Winnie's daughter. The question now was, what was he going to do with *her*?

The Arabs wouldn't wait forever. They'd find another company more amenable to their wooing. If Bara didn't soon agree to a divorce and a fair division of their joint assets—from the day they married, Foley had considered everything she owned their "joint assets"—another solution would have to be found.

He had never imagined she'd be so set against divorce. She was no longer madly in love with him, but the idea that he would leave her for a younger woman made her livid. Had she really thought he'd stick around while she withered? These past couple of years, they had rattled around in their big house like strangers.

Strangers. Foley ran that word by what passed for his conscience and found it calmed the puny thing considerably. Strangers weren't the same as family. If Bara didn't sign those contracts soon, Foley might consider a contract of a very different kind.

The phone startled him. He started backing out of the room, but Bara opened her eyes before he could disappear. "Hi," she said drowsily, apparently forgetting the hostilities between them for an instant. Then she swung her legs off the couch and demanded, in the voice he had grown accustomed to, "How did you get in here? What do you want?"

Foley had no intention of telling her about the back-door key he'd had duplicated before his lawyer turned over his keys to Scotty—especially since Carlene had used it so disastrously the day before. But Foley had known he would need a key, had known the bitch would be nasty enough to demand his keys and put a deadbolt on the inside door to the basement.

Instead of answering, he looked around to see where she'd left the cordless phone. Bara could never be bothered to replace phones on their chargers. He found it on a small table across the room. The table was covered with dust. She never cleaned between visits from the service.

"Hello?"

"I–I–I wanted Bara." Good old Murdoch. Never could talk to a man without stammering.

Foley held out the phone. "It's your charming cousin." Let Murdoch make of that what she would.

Bara took the receiver. "Hello?" She was still only half awake—or drunk. Foley considered her, wondering which.

He had been astonished when she'd started drinking a few months before, and even more astonished at how unsurprised other people were. However, if she wanted to drink herself to death rather than divorce him, Foley was willing to help. Once he had determined her drink of choice, he made sure to keep some hidden in his basement bathroom. He also kept a record of how much she took. That could come in handy in court.

The other thing that surprised him was a rumor he'd heard that week: that her first husband had beaten her and that Bara—feisty, independent Bara—had been terrified of him. Foley had tucked that piece of information away in case he needed it. The woman was not invincible.

He eased across the large foyer and into the dining room, where he propped himself against the table to eavesdrop. Her voice carried. Who knew what she might say to Murdoch that could be of use to him?

She didn't say a word for a while. Instead, she took a deep breath and waited like she did when she wasn't going to answer and wanted somebody to stew in his or her own juices. Winnie used to do that, too. It was one of the first things that had infuriated Foley about them both.

Murdoch sounded upset about something. Foley could hear the tinny sound of her voice all the way out in the hall. Bara let her run down, then spoke wearily. "I don't need your advice on how to take care of my things." She stopped.

"I don't see that what I do is any business of yours," she said a moment later.

What was she talking about? Even Murdoch wouldn't be foolish enough to advise Bara on what do to with her father's company.

The house? It had belonged to Murdoch's grandparents, too. Did she think that gave her a claim on it? She could think again. Bara's grandfather had deeded her the house when she married her first husband. Foley had made sure of that before he married her. And before their second month of marriage he had persuaded her to put his name on the deed as well as on her bank accounts. "That way, if anything were to happen to you, I'd have the right and means to take care of you and our children." Not that he had ever really considered that the brats had anything to do with him.

Bara had hesitated, but in those days he had known how to get her to do almost anything he wanted. When had he lost that touch?

Murdoch's excited chatter reached him where he stood.

Bara huffed. "That's nonsense and you know it. Nana gave it to *me*. By name."

Not the house, then. Her grandfather gave that to her. Foley took a mental inventory of its contents. He'd never been clear on what else Bara had inherited from whom. Living in the place was like living in a family museum. What on earth could Murdoch be that desperate about?

He chewed his lip, thinking. He ought to take every portable valuable they had to a vault, some day when Bara went out, to be sure they were still around to be counted in the settlement. Bara was so sneaky, she might think of doing the same thing if he didn't beat her to it.

Foley had spent several happy evenings going down his appraiser's list. He looked appreciatively around the dining room. Just the silver he could see was worth a considerable fortune.

An unfamiliar gleam caught his eye and held it. A gun, on the table. He started to pick it up, caught himself in time.

So his dear wife had a gun?

Foley smiled, but he stepped toward the foyer so he wouldn't be near the gun when she got off the phone. No need to remind her she'd left it there.

Bara spotted the motion. "Look," she said quickly, "I can't talk right now. I've got a rat in the house. Call me when you get back." She laid the phone down on

the foyer table beside a crystal heron that was a commissioned, one-of-a-kind piece by Hans Godo Fräbel.
It was both valuable and lovely, and Foley was determined to have it. So what if some group had given it
to Bara in appreciation of something she had done for
them? As he kept reminding her, sentiment has no
place in divorce.

"What did you want?" she demanded.

"What did Murdoch want?" he countered, striving
to make his voice jovial.

Bara waved the question away as unimportant.
"Nothing to do with you."

"I might disagree with that assessment if I knew all
the facts, but that's not what I wanted to talk about right
now. I have a deal for you. Sit down." He motioned her
to a chair beside the table where she had laid down the
phone.

To his surprise, she sat. He stood, to keep the
advantage, and paced on the Bokhara rug that warmed
the marble floor.

"I have changed my mind. I won't ask for all your
daddy's shares, only for enough of them to give me a
slight majority of the company. As an officer, I've got
some shares of my own, you know."

"I thought they were *ours*," she said with heavy
emphasis. "Everything else seems to be."

"I never put you on that account. Listen. Here's the deal: I'll let you keep this house, I'll take the lake house, and we'll split our investment portfolio fifty-fifty—if you will agree to give me enough shares to guarantee the sale. Once the sale goes through, you'll benefit like all the other shareholders."

She opened her mouth to protest, but he held up one hand for silence. "Hear me out. If we don't sell, what will happen to the firm? You know as well as I do that there isn't another architect at Holcomb & Associates who could touch your daddy for style and business acumen."

Acumen. Foley was proud of that word. He'd searched the thesaurus for a term he could use to describe Winnie that would touch Bara's heart. Was she impressed? She was fiddling with the tie to her robe. Was she considering his offer?

"That's my final offer," he said when she didn't respond. "If you turn this down, so help me, it's gonna be all-out war."

She got up and went to the library door, stood looking toward the picture over the mantelpiece.

"Your daddy's not here to protect you any longer."

She reached into her pocket. He froze. Did she carry a second gun?

She brought out cigarettes.

"When did you start smoking? You called it a filthy stinking habit." Besides, she knew good and well that he detested the smell and taste of tobacco on a woman. It reminded him of his mother, whom he had spent most of his life trying to forget.

She brought out a big silver lighter that looked like it ought to belong to a man. Probably another of Winnie's artifacts. She was surrounding herself with them lately. Didn't she realize how pathetic that was?

Bara lit up with practiced ease, lifted her face to him, and blew smoke his way.

"I have a deal for you," she replied. "Why don't you proceed straight to hell without passing GO? I am not giving you any of Winnie's shares. If you can give me good reasons why we ought to sell, and if the new owners agree to retain the name of the firm in Atlanta, I might consider voting my shares to sell." She held up a warning finger. "Might, mind you. But you can live in that basement until you rot before I'll give you a single share in the company besides those you've wangled out of the board over the years. Or the lake house. Or any of the money my family has worked so hard to accumulate. If we go to court, I'll fight you until neither of us has a penny left, and I'll raise a stink like you cannot imagine. Or maybe I ought to shoot you now and save myself a lot of trouble."

She swept past him and ascended the curved marble staircase. She liked to have the last word.

Foley picked up the portable phone. Sure enough, she hadn't remembered to disconnect. That used to irritate the hell out of him.

Hearing Murdoch's excited breath, he smiled. "Murdoch? I'm sorry. Bara forgot to disconnect again. Good night." He rang off and laid the phone back on the foyer table. If the batteries ran down, that was Bara's problem.

But he was elated. Mason could subpoena Murdoch to testify that he'd made Bara a more than decent offer, and she had not only spurned him, she had threatened him.

He wasn't through. No woman since his mother had threatened him and gotten away with it. He ascended the stairs and caught his wife's elbow before she reached her door. He swung her around and punched her in the stomach, hard.

She doubled over, unable to breathe. He shoved her into her room. She stumbled and fell, still clutching her stomach. Her dark eyes blazed with anger, but he saw the flicker of fear.

He stood over her and growled, "That's a taste of what you'll get if you ever threaten me again. Do you understand?"

She slammed the door behind him. He heard the key in the lock. "You will get controlling shares in that company over my dead body!" she yelled.

He paused in his journey down the hall to call back, "If necessary, my dear, that is precisely how I will get them."

Chapter 15

Wednesday

Bara was dreaming she was a child, drawing in a corner of Winnie's library while he worked. He sometimes took her drawings to his office downtown and posted them on his bulletin board. "She draws far better than I did at that age," he often boasted. "Of course, she's known since she was five that she wants to be an architect. I didn't decide until I was grown." The horror of bombing beautiful buildings had driven him to spend his life replacing them.

Bara had wanted to be an architect until her junior year in high school, when her school guidance counselor and Nettie's incessant hammering finally persuaded her that women had no business being architects, that she would be far happier and fulfilled if she attended a good women's college, married well, bred children, and served on charitable boards. If Winnie had been disappointed, he had never let her know. But although Bara had done her duty to society, she had never gotten the raw thrill even from breeding her children that she used to get from drawing a building exactly right.

In her dream, Bara was drawing a house. She wanted it to be perfect for Winnie, but the proportions were wrong. Again and again she erased and tried again, but she could not get them right. And why didn't Winnie answer his phone?

She rolled over and felt a pain in her gut. Awareness swept her like a riptide. Foley had hit her. Winnie was dead. Her life, not her drawing, was all wrong. And it was *her* phone that was ringing.

She fumbled for the receiver and managed a slurred "Hello?"

"Hi, it's Katharine Murray. I've been doing your research, and I found a friend of my son's who knows something about medals. He says the army gives a citation with each one. Your dad probably kept them somewhere."

Bara struggled to come awake. She sat up in bed, wincing as her sore midriff protested. "Citations? You mean on paper?"

"I presume so."

Bara reached for the bottle beside her bed. There were still a couple of drinks left. One sip and her mind cleared. Two, and the pain was dulled. Whiskey was a panacea for everything that ailed you.

"I can look in his files," she told Katharine. "If I find them, how about if I bring them over to your place and we can match the citations with the medals?"

"If you can get here by ten. I have to go out at eleven. And if we can figure out which bomber group your dad was with, Kenny—Jon's friend—said that a lot of military groups have their own Web sites with stories and memoirs on them. Some even have pictures."

As she dressed, Bara felt more excitement than she had in months. She dragged on black linen slacks and a black-and-white top, slid her feet into black sandals, and went to the bathroom for the sketchiest of ablutions. As she washed her face, however, the sight of her ragged, chewed nails repulsed her. She ought to look through a few more boxes and see if she could find more of Winnie's fifties. She desperately needed a manicure.

Down in the kitchen, she bypassed breakfast but went to the fridge for the gin and Bloody Mary mix. Bloody Marys were good for you. Full of vitamin C. She drank one and put a second into an insulated cup that looked like coffee.

Before she left, she ran down to the basement. As she had hoped, Foley had put more bottles of *Rare Breed* under his sink. As she refilled her flask, she wondered if he knew she was helping herself to his liquor. Probably not. He didn't know she drank.

She grabbed her purse and the flask and hurried to her car. Not until she was halfway to the storage company did she remember she had forgotten once again to set the alarm.

"What difference does it make?" she asked, lifting her cup to her lips. "If somebody comes in and takes everything there, I won't have much less than I have right now."

On the way to the storage company she watched to be sure she wasn't followed, and she strode toward her unit with a bounce in her step. She was going to spend the entire day doing something she wanted to do. The citations would explain everything she needed to know. When she and Katharine finished, she would take the medals to a framer her family had used for years and he would help her, as he always had, to select the best way to display them. After that, she would buy a scrapbook and put the citations in it for Chip.

Chip was too young to appreciate the gift yet, but in a few years Bara would read the citations to him. She could picture his awe when he learned what a hero his great-granddaddy had been. Somewhere she had a photograph of Winnie in uniform. She could put that in the front of the scrapbook, with the citations. If she could find a Web site with pictures, she might locate pictures of Winnie with his men, or pictures of planes like the ones he flew. She could download those and print them for the scrapbook, too. She couldn't remember the last time she had been so pleased with her plans for a day.

Winnie, like many creative people, had worked best in an atmosphere of cheerful clutter, so his library often looked like it had been visited by a friendly whirlwind. His files, however, he had kept in perfect order. Bara found the citations in a file labeled MILITARY MATTERS. She didn't bother to read them, just yanked the file out from the others.

The next file, a fat one, caught her eye and made her smile. It was labeled MUNIFICENT MATTERS. Her father used to hand out their allowance each week with the words, "Here's your munificent sum." Her eyes widened as she opened the file and found five stacks of hundred dollar bills, bound by rubber bands.

"Thank you, Winnie!" she breathed as she stuffed them into her purse.

"I told you he was organized where it mattered," she informed her mother as she resealed the box of files and locked the unit. Nettie had often deplored the state of her husband's library, had made him shut the wide double doors when they had guests.

"I used to be like Winnie," Bara informed the world as she started for the car. "My rooms might be a bit cluttered, but my drawers and files were all in order—before my whole life fell apart. They *were*," she insisted, although nobody had contradicted her but her conscience.

Lordy, Katharine was perky in the morning! She greeted Bara looking fresh and pert in sage-green linen pants and a creamy shirt, with her hair shining and her lipstick fresh. Bara felt a hundred and two.

She noted with approval that Katharine was barefoot, and kicked off her own shoes. Katharine smiled. "I hate shoes, don't you?"

"I've always thought I must have been born in Micronesia in all my former incarnations," Bara replied.

"I've spread out the medals on the breakfast-room table. Let's work in there," Katharine suggested.

The breakfast room must be the woman's favorite place in the house. She had a perfectly good dining-room table a lot closer. Oh—the chairs were missing. Bara hoped she could make it to the breakfast room. She felt a bit wobbly. Must be the heat. The weatherman had predicted that the thermometer would reach a hundred by noon.

Katharine not only had the medals spread out on the table, she had made neat little paper tents to identify each one. Bara leaned both arms on the table to steady herself while she read the labels aloud: "Presidential Unit Citation, Air Medal, Medal of Honor, Bronze Star, World War II medal, Purple Hearts. Very organized."

"Thanks. I thought that might help you know which citation went with which medal. I printed up something on the bombing of Ploesti, too, since his whole group earned the Presidential Unit Citation for that. My son's friend was very impressed with your father, by the way. Would you like a cup of tea?"

"Nothing for me but ice water," Bara said virtuously. "I don't need all that caffeine." She collapsed into the nearest chair, riffled through Winnie's file, and was puzzled. "There are more medals than citations. I only have six citations and there are eight medals."

Katharine set a glass of water before her. Bara wished she'd thought to stick her flask in her purse before she came in, so she'd have something to add to the water. She took a sip and felt nausea sweep over her.

"Maybe some of the medals didn't come with citations," Katharine suggested. "Have you read them?"

Bara shook her head. "I came straight here as soon as I found them."

"Browse through them while I give some instructions to my maid? I'll be right back."

Bara gave her ten points for tact.

The first citation was for Art's Purple Heart. She knew how her big brother had died, but something clutched at her throat as she read it in black-and-white. She gulped down the whole glass of water and got herself another before she could go on.

She also fetched the box of tissues from the countertop. This might be harder than she had thought. She wiped her eyes as she picked up one Purple Heart and laid it on top of the citation. "One down, seven to go."

The second citation was for Art's Bronze Star. She laid it down on that citation. She would read it later.

The third belonged to her father's Air Medal, earned November 1, 1944, after flying thirty missions with the Fifteenth Air Force. She picked the medal up and admired it. She didn't remember it from her childhood exploration of the box.

The fourth she paired with another Purple Heart. Winnie had earned it for a flak wound in the shoulder during a bombing raid over Germany during May 1944. That shoulder had pained him whenever it rained.

The fifth was for the Presidential Unit Citation that her father's unit had earned for raids on Ploesti, Romania, during the autumn of 1943. She laid the citation on top of Katharine's printout, promising herself she would read it, too, after all the medals were identified.

The sixth citation went with another Purple Heart. Winnie had received it for a wound he'd received flying a mission over the Mediterranean in January 1943. That must have been the great red scar on his back. She had only seen it once, when she'd mistakenly walked in on him as he was getting ready to shower.

Those were all the citations in the file, but two medals remained: one with a rather garish ribbon attached to it and the words WORLD WAR II across it—in case somebody forgot which war they fought in?—and the gold star that was her favorite, which Katharine had labeled MEDAL OF HONOR.

When Katharine returned, Bara told her, "I don't have anything about the Medal of Honor and this other medal."

Katharine picked up the bigger medal first. "This is a Victory Medal, given to everybody who served in the war. Maybe it didn't come with a citation. But Kenny—Jon's friend—printed out the citation your dad got with the Medal of Honor. They are so important, all those particular citations are available online." She took it from the countertop and handed it to Bara. "It's the highest award the military gives. I understand that even enlisted men who earn it get saluted by officers."

Bara took the sheet and began to scan the page. Her hands trembled with excitement. "This must have been the battle where Winnie lost his leg. I've never known exactly how that happened. He would never talk about it. All he'd say was that he got wounded and sent home."

"Why don't I leave you to read it to yourself?" Katharine offered.

"No, stay. I need you here." To her surprise, Bara discovered it was true. She hadn't made a new friend in years, but she was coming to like this competent woman Tom Murray had married. How had she missed knowing her all these years?

She took an unsteady breath and began to read. She read silently, but her lips began forming the words until she finally murmured aloud, "'. . . thinking only of saving his crewman, continued to fly.'" She could read no more.

"'Something stupid that other folks thought very brave.' That's what he told me he did."

"He must have been in enormous pain."

Bara thrust the page at Katharine. "You read the rest."

"Are you sure?"

"Yes. I can't."

Katharine found the place. Her voice trembled as the story unfolded, and when she got to the place where Winnie's death was reported, they both had tears in their eyes.

Bara was the first to recover. "But like Mark Twain said, the rumors of Winnie's death were greatly exaggerated."

Katharine laughed unsteadily. "That's exactly what my niece said last night."

"How much more is there?"

"Just a paragraph." Katharine read on.

At the end, Bara held up a hand to stop her. "That can't be right."

"What?"

"February 15, 1945. He had to have come home earlier than that." She silently counted on her fingers. "I was born September fifth in New York City, where Winnie was studying architecture. He, Nettie, and Art moved up there that summer and Winnie started at Columbia in the fall. I was born up there, which made me a Yankee—a fact my elementary classmates never let me forget."

Katharine grew very still. "Oh." In the silence, Bara could tell she was also counting months. "Maybe you were premature."

"Two and a half months? Not likely, given that I once heard Nettie rehearsing with close friends the difficulties she went through with Art's birth. She wouldn't have missed that chance to brag about my coming so early."

Katharine rose. "I left my computer on. Let me see what else I can find out about Blechhammer. Maybe they got the year wrong." She left like one fleeing.

"On a Medal of Honor citation?" Bara called after her. She was talking to air. She could already hear Katharine tap-tapping at her computer.

Bara had never needed a drink worse. Her body shook. A flash of heat swept over her as if she were in a burning plane. Her mind was addled.

Could the government make that kind of mistake? She doubted it. But Winnie could not have been in Italy until the middle of February. He couldn't have!

Bara craned her head and made sure she could still hear the gentle *thump, thump* of Katharine's fingers on the keyboard. On tiptoe she approached the pantry and, with one watchful eye on the door to the hall, checked inside. No liquor. In the refrigerator, an open bottle of gin sat on the lower shelf. She dumped the water from her glass and refilled it with gin. Drank half the gin and filled it again. Now the bottle was empty.

She filled the bottle with water to what she hoped was the former mark. With luck, Katharine didn't drink gin, or would think it had gone flat.

But for once in Bara's life, alcohol failed her. She could still remember what she was trying to forget: If Winnie had been in Italy until the middle of February, she could not be his daughter. And her mother—prim, self-righteous Nettie—

It was unbelievable. Unthinkable.

Hurrying to the table, she snatched up the citation Katharine had printed out and read the last line again.

Panic consumed her. She shoved all the citations back into their folder, the Medal of Honor printout on top. She grabbed the medals and flung them into the cigar box. She tucked them under her arm, snatched up her purse, and strode toward the front door.

Katharine looked up from her computer. "The dates for the battle are right," she called. "Are you leaving?"

"You bet I am." Bara thrust her feet angrily into her sandals. "I'm going to find somebody who can tell me what the hell this is all about."

Chapter 16

Bara roared down the Murrays' drive so fast she took out half a hydrangea when her car veered off the asphalt. She careened through Buckhead with one question circling her mind: If she wasn't Winnie Holcomb's daughter, who was she?

Even in Bara's wildest days, crazy from her beloved grandmother's death and railing against her mother and all the senseless, stuffy restrictions she despised, the knowledge that she was Winnie's daughter had been her anchor. It had restrained her from removing all her clothes in the fountain, tempered her foot on the gas pedal as she drag-raced down Peachtree Street, kept her insouciant in the Fulton County Jail. She knew Winnie would arrive with her bail. Knew she would still have his love even if, temporarily, she lost his approval.

He'd had a wild streak of his own. He and Oscar Anderson had taken flying lessons in high school against their parents' wishes. In their senior year, they "borrowed" (without permission) two small planes belonging to friends of their fathers and raced them to Jacksonville on a dare. Scrapes they had gotten into during college sent them into roars of laughter sixty years later. It was because Winnie could already fly that he'd become a bomber pilot when the war began. For a time, he'd been a flying instructor out in Oklahoma.

But if he had not gotten home from Italy until February, her mother would have been well and truly pregnant by then. Would he have stood for that? Stuck with Nettie? Probably. Winnie was an honorable man and an Episcopalian. They didn't get divorces back then.

Like many children, Bara had always regarded her parents' courtship and early years of marriage—even Art's birth—as a mere prelude to her own appearance. She vaguely knew they had gotten engaged the year Nettie made her debut, married after Winnie graduated—ending Nettie's college education after her sophomore year. "Education is not as important as good breeding, for women," Nettie was fond of saying, smoothing her skirt over her well-bred knees. Art had been born in 1941, while Winnie was at Emory Law

School. The war had interrupted Winnie's law studies. Nettie and Art had moved back in with her parents during the war, into the house Bara now owned. Nettie was ostensibly awaiting Winnie's return.

What had she really been doing?

When Winnie came home and decided to pursue architecture instead of law, had he chosen Columbia and moved to New York in June instead of waiting for fall because his wife was growing visibly pregnant and they didn't want people to know?

Nana Payne must have known. Was that why she was so kind to Bara? Had her kindness been pity, not love?

Bara had to pull off the road, shaking with terror. Winnie and Nana Payne had been the pillars of her life. If they crumbled, what did she have left?

Memories stirred in Bara's sluggish mind, oddities from her childhood.

She had been a slow child, slow to speak and slow to understand what others said to her. One of her earliest memories was of Winnie holding her on his lap and trying to talk about a doll she held. She had clutched the doll, afraid he would take it, but she could make no sense of what he was saying. Had her being slow made it easier for them to keep people from counting months and knowing how old she was?

They had moved to Atlanta the summer before she turned five. Her mother had taken her to nursery school the week after her fifth birthday and tried to tell Miss Collins that Bara was four. Bara had raised indignant eyes and said, "No. I had my birthday, remember? I am five!"

Her mother had laughed in that fake way she did when she was embarrassed. "I guess you are. I forgot."

"Shouldn't she go to kindergarten?" Miss Collins had whispered.

"Not this year," her mother had whispered back. "Don't mention how old she is to the other children. Pretend she is four."

"But she is so tall."

"Yes, but we feel it better to hold her back a year."

"You were always holding me back," Bara muttered. The hot August sun poured down on the Jag, but she drove aimlessly with her windows down, chilled to the soul.

During her entire school career, Nettie had told her to tell people she was a year younger than she was, although Bara had towered over her classmates until adolescence. Her entire school experience had been colored by the fact that she knew she was older than the others, but nobody else knew. She had excelled in school, but had accepted that it was because she was older—that she must be, in some way, less intelligent than people her own age.

And yet, she'd always made better grades than Art, and her test scores were higher in high school, as well. When Winnie urged him to study harder, or when he and Bara quarreled—which was often, since he tended to ignore Bara and she followed him like a shadow until he got angry and sent her away—Art would shout things like, "Life was better before you ruined it!" Or "Why did you have to come and mess everything up?" He would have been four when she was born. Had he been aware of the stress that preceded her birth?

Nettie never put candles on Bara's birthday cakes. Art had candles, but Bara's cakes were elaborately decorated instead. Nettie would explain, "I didn't want to ruin the pretty icing with candles." Because the cakes were so beautiful, Bara had felt that cakes with candles were inferior. But had Nettie simply been protecting her own Buckhead reputation?

Nettie and Winnie had quarreled when Bara wanted to get a driver's license the week of her sixteenth birthday. "It's time to stop this silliness," Winnie had shouted.

"We don't want the boys in her class to know she's older than they are," Nettie replied, "and none of them can drive yet. Do you want her driving boys all over town?"

Winnie had given in and stomped off to his library—increasingly his refuge from the tantrums Nettie threw at home but never in public. Nettie had warned Bara, "Don't ever tell boys you are older, honey. Men don't like older women."

"Men don't like _____ " One of the unvarying tenets of her mother's universe. The other was "You'll never get married if you _____ " Marriage was the end-all and be-all of a girl's life.

"Your marriage wasn't so hot," Bara stormed as she prowled the streets of Buckhead. "But what man, besides Winnie, liked you? Who was he, dammit?"

Who would be likely to know?

Rita Louise had been Nettie's best friend. She would know. But would she tell what she knew after a lifetime of covering up? Better save her for later.

Uncle Scotty ought to know. He was Nettie's brother, and he hadn't left Atlanta during the war. He had spent the war down at Fort Gillem, helping direct supplies to troops from the quartermaster depot.

He hadn't left Atlanta.

That's what she was looking for, wasn't it? A man who had been home while Winnie was overseas. But not Uncle Scotty. Not his own sister.

What about Father John? Or Oscar Anderson?

Gall rose in Bara's throat as she considered Oscar. Nettie had known him all her life, but if Oscar were Bara's father, he'd be Payne's grandfather, as well as Hamilton's. Surely Oscar would never have let them marry and produce Chip if that were the case.

If he had known.

Nettie was a private person. Had she told the father of her child that she was pregnant?

Bara felt nauseated just thinking those thoughts. Her thoughts rattled along like a car with poor shocks on a red dirt road. Hadn't Oscar done something in the war? Seemed like he had. He was a Quaker and didn't fight, but wasn't he in the ambulance corps? Bara remembered several times when he'd flown off to some sort of reunion. She wasn't clear what the corps was, or where and when Oscar might have been part of it, but Ann Rose or Hamilton might know.

What about Father John? Bara didn't know whether he'd been in the war or stayed to serve his congregation. He'd had dark eyes, like hers, and hair like wet tar. He wasn't any taller than she, but Nettie had been tall. That could be where her height had come from.

"Don't be silly," she told herself. "John Phipps was a priest. Surely Mother—"

The thought revolted her. Yet Nettie had been very religious. And there were dozens if not hundreds of stories about women who fell in love with their minister or priest—especially when the women were particularly lonely and vulnerable.

Father John had been a charismatic man. Could he have been lonely, too? Of course he could, married to the original ice maiden. Nobody in Buckhead had been surprised that Rita Louise had no children. Virgin births happen so seldom.

So Father John was a definite possibility, and Oscar could be. If not them, then who?

Her tanned arm resting on the steering wheel sent her thoughts jolting along in another direction. What if her father had been black? She tanned much darker than either of her parents. Her mother would never have willingly slept with a black man, but what if she had been raped? Those were wild days in Atlanta. Was that the cause of her mother's extreme racism in later years? And the reason for her apparent dislike of her daughter? It would certainly explain Winnie's hustling Nettie out of town.

If that were so, Bara would probably never know who her father was. She needed to know *something*.

She checked her watch. It was nearly noon. Uncle Scotty visited Aunt Eloise each morning after a round of golf. He would probably still be at the nursing home. She'd take him to lunch on some of Winnie's money. Scotty wouldn't get a nap this afternoon until Bara had tried to make him tell her what she wanted to know.

She pulled into the parking lot of the nursing home and opened her door before she switched off the car. With long, quick strides she hurried into the building and scrawled her name on the sign-in sheet at the desk.

She didn't visit often, but she was known to the aides who had been there awhile. One of them gave her a bright smile and said, "We are feeling pretty good today!"

Bara gave her a withering look. "I'm glad you are and hope Aunt Eloise is. I personally feel like hell. Is she still in the same room?"

The aide tossed her head. "Of course." As Bara hurried away, she heard the aide say to another, "We certainly are snotty today, aren't we?"

Bara checked her step for an instant, but the remark wasn't worth a detour in her agenda. She strode down the hall and into her aunt's room.

One glance showed her that Scotty was not there. Another glance revealed that Eloise was sneaking chocolate behind her hand. Eloise was diabetic. Scotty knew she wasn't supposed to have candy, but he brought a bar in from time to time because he knew she loved it.

Bara was backing out to inform a nurse when Eloise looked up and exclaimed, "A visitor. How nice!"

Eloise had never been a pretty woman. She had a plump, pink face with a round little chin stuck on like an afterthought, and her hair was constantly either too tight from a new perm or bedraggled like it needed one. No hairdresser had ever gotten Eloise Payne's hair styled well. But she was a fluttery, soft woman, the opposite of Nettie's stout rigidity. She had been a great success as a first-grade teacher, and Bara, as a child, had found her a lot more comforting than her mother. As an adult, Bara was still fond of her.

"Hello, Aunt Eloise. It's a gorgeous day outside."

Eloise had a private room with a view. Winnie had seen to that. Her chair was by the window, and if she had chosen to look, she could have seen the Atlanta skyline softened by smog. Instead, her attention was on the television news.

Since she was having a good day, only a tenseness in her posture and an anxious shadow behind her eyes betrayed her knowledge that something was terribly wrong with her and she was not sure what it was. On bad days, her eyes were vague and bewildered.

She gestured to the other chair. "Have a seat, dear. How nice of you to come."

It was obvious she didn't have a clue who Bara might be or where either one of them was, but one of the unfathomable twists of her dementia was that although memory had gone, her courtesy remained.

Do you know who my daddy was? Bara wanted to beg, but she bit back the words and forced herself to take a deep breath before speaking. No point in upsetting the poor woman. She would only retreat into confusion. Bara smiled and tried to put some enthusiasm into her words. "Aunt Eloise, it's Bara. Nettie's daughter."

"I know who you are, dear."

Was that true? Early in her Alzheimer's, Aunt Eloise had learned to lie convincingly.

Bara considered.

Eloise's memory of the distant past was generally better than her memory of anything in the past twenty years, and she and Scotty had been married before the war. Murdoch was a much-delayed (and, in Bara's opinion, a most dubious) blessing in their marriage. Could a kernel of memory lurking in Eloise's distressed mind be dredged up by conversation?

"You've known me all my life. That's why I came to see you." Bara put one hand on Eloise's soft, plump one. "I've found something of Winnie's that puzzles me. A war medal."

Eloise picked at her blue robe nervously, required to take a test she had not prepared for. "The war's over, isn't it, dear? I don't know why everybody still goes on about it." Eloise had always regretted the way Atlanta forgot Scotty's contribution to the war effort and lionized Winnie's.

"I don't want to go on about the war," Bara assured her, "but I would like to know about Winnie's medals. I want to frame them for Chip."

"Chip?" Eloise's memory had stopped processing new data before Chip's birth. At the moment, she was more interested in a commercial featuring bears bragging on toilet paper.

"My grandson." Bara moved quickly to what she wanted to know. "I read the citation that came with one of Winnie's medals, and it said Winnie came home from the war in February. Do you remember exactly when he came home?"

When Eloise paused, Bara thought it was hopeless. Eloise, however, had only been waiting until the bears had finished touting their toilet paper. She nodded. "Oh my, yes. George Washington's Birthday. Nettie had planned a big do to welcome him home, and all her decorations and desserts had a cherry theme. But it turned out to be a terrible day."

"A terrible day because he came home?"

"Oh no, dear, because of the ice storm. Ice everywhere. All the wires were down, the roads impossible. Poor Nettie, all her food spoiled."

So the date on the citation was right. Bara almost didn't dare ask the next question.

"I was born the next September. Was I a premature baby? Do you remember?"

Eloise's hands plucked her robe. "Murdoch was premature. A month early. I wasn't at all prepared. Didn't even have sheets for her crib. Nettie had given hers away. I had to lay the baby on one of our sheets, folded up, until Scotty could get to a store." She gave Bara a delighted smile. "Murdoch is my daughter. She's going to Boston Thursday."

"I know." Bara never got accustomed to Eloise's sudden swings into the present, could never figure out what triggered them. "But was I a premature baby, like Murdoch?"

Eloise's eyes clouded. "Who did you say you are again, dear?"

"Bara. Nettie's daughter."

Eloise shook her head. "Nettie didn't want the daughter. Just her son. She never wanted the daughter."

Even though she had suspected that all along, hearing it stated as casual fact took Bara's breath away.

"Why didn't she want her daughter?"

Eloise's brow furrowed in thought. Bara had an instant of hope that she would get the truth, but the effort was too much. Eloise's memory slid away. Their interview was over.

Bara drove from the nursing home to the house where Scotty lived. A one-story brick painted white with black shutters, it sat on a small lot with a detached one-car garage at the end of the drive. Eloise had been fond of gardening and had planted beds of perennials around the massive oaks, but neither Scotty nor Murdoch cared to garden, and the lawn service Scotty used did little more than rake and mow. Foot-high oak volunteers sprouted in beds of ivy. Weeds crowded out flowers. Once shapely shrubs branched out in all directions.

Scotty's Mercedes hunkered down as usual in the drive, for Murdoch used the garage. Bara pulled close behind it and set her brake. She had never trusted that driveway since she had come out one afternoon to find that her car had rolled halfway across the street.

Scotty never locked the door if he was home, so she walked straight in, wondering as she always did whether Scotty minded that his whole house would fit into a quarter of one floor in the one he grew up in. He was eating lunch—a sandwich and a beer—in the minuscule dining room, the sports section of the paper open beside him.

"To what do I owe the pleasure?" he inquired without getting up. "Did you bring a check?"

"No, I've brought some questions." She pulled out a chair uninvited. He chomped his way through his sandwich without inviting her to make one, although pastrami, Havarti cheese, rye bread, and jars of pickles sat beside mustard and mayonnaise in plain view on the kitchen counter ten feet away. When her stomach growled, she remembered she hadn't eaten all day. No wonder she felt giddy.

"I've been reading the citations that went with Winnie's war medals." She rose and went to the kitchen. The smell of the food almost turned her stomach, but she resolutely slapped mayonnaise on two slices of bread and united them with cheese and pastrami. She opened a Coors from the fridge and brought the food back to the table on a paper-towel plate. "I've found something I don't understand. I was reading his Medal of Honor citation, about how he landed a plane that was almost destroyed, even with his leg badly wounded—"

"Stupid thing to do. Should have parachuted out with the crew."

"He'd have been abandoning a man whose parachute had burned up."

Scotty shrugged. "It was war. People died."

She forced a little laugh. "Winnie told me he got that medal for doing something stupid that people later thought was very brave."

"Yeah, he did, and he never let people forget it."

"He never talked about it," she protested.

"He limped. That was a constant reminder he was better than the rest of us." Scotty resumed his avid perusal of the sports section.

Bara ate her sandwich and considered the best approach to get what she wanted. "I didn't come here to fight. I came to find out what happened after that. The citation said he came home in February. Aunt Eloise says—"

"You talked to Eloise? When?" Suddenly she had Scotty's full attention.

"Just now."

"You know you can't count on anything she says." He had a guarded look in his eyes.

"She was having a good day. She remembered there was an ice storm the weekend Winnie was supposed to come home, and all Mama's food got spoiled."

He relaxed and grunted, "Good for Eloise! There *was* a storm. I'd forgotten that. We were freezing up here while Winnie lounged around a pool in Miami. He always did get the breaks. Their plane couldn't land with the ice storm, so they got diverted to Florida. We didn't have power for three days."

"And Mama's party food got spoiled?"

He shrugged. "Is that what Eloise said? I guess it's true. But what would you expect? It took another week for Winnie to get home. Nettie was real put out. She had announced a big do in his honor, but by then people had other plans. I told her Winnie wouldn't want a welcome-home party, the condition he was in and with the war still going on. Hell, he was on crutches and in a lot of pain."

"But are you sure he didn't get home until February?" Bara pressed. "I was born the fifth of September, you know."

His gaze slid to the window. "I can't keep track of my *own* birthday, girl. How do you expect me to remember yours? You needn't expect a present unless I get paid."

She couldn't keep impatience out of her voice. "You've never bought me a present in your life. What I want to know is how I got born so soon after my daddy got home."

"How should I know? I don't pay attention to things like that."

"You'd know if I was so premature that they worried about me."

"Nobody worried about you that year," he said bluntly. "That came later. Poor Nettie. I don't know why she put up with it." He put both hands on the table and used them to lever himself to his feet. "I'm tired. Played nine holes this morning and pulled a shoulder.

Had to quit. I need a nap. Don't bother me with all this. It's done. Finished."

"Did Mama—?"

Before she could finish, he slammed a fist on the table. "My sister may not have been perfect, but she put up with you all those years. She was a blessed saint!"

They glared at each other.

"She was no saint." Bara blazed, snatching up her purse. "You and she fought all the time, she and Winnie fought all the time, and she and Nana—"

"Get out!" He waved one hand angrily. "Don't come in here saying things about poor Nettie. You'll never know all she went through for you!"

"What? What did she go through? That's all I want to know."

"You must have a very short memory. Drunken brawls, dancing in your underwear—what didn't she put up with? But what's done is done. Go home. Get drunk. Eventually you'll forget. I have." He lumbered toward his bedroom.

"I'm going," Bara called after him, "but I may be back."

She was a mile away before she remembered she had meant to get his key to her house.

Chapter 17

B ara's sandwich only reminded her stomach how little she had fed it in the past two days. She decided to stop by her house and make a quick omelet before tackling Rita Louise. On the way she finished the bourbon in her flask.

In the kitchen she made a Bloody Mary, then pulled out eggs, butter, and milk. She found no ham, cheese, tomatoes, or mushrooms, but it didn't matter. She'd already had cheese and wasn't real fond of vegetables, anyway. She could eat a plain omelet with her Bloody Mary.

She sipped it while she pulled down a cast-iron skillet from a rack near the ceiling, put the pan on the stove, and turned the gas on high. Katharine had turned her electric stove to medium, but Bara was in a hurry.

She took another sip before she broke the eggs into a bowl and added milk. Oops, too much milk. Oh well, milk was good for you. She beat the eggs and poured them into the pan. Saw the butter sitting on the counter and remembered she should have put it in first. Couldn't be helped. She finished her drink and added a large dollop of butter to the eggs. Salted and peppered the thick yellow mixture and added a few drops of hot sauce. She ought to tell Katharine about hot sauce. It pepped up scrambled eggs.

She fetched bread and made toast. Fixed another Bloody Mary. Found a plate, some silverware, and wondered where the hell her cook had kept the napkins.

As she yanked off a paper towel to use instead, she smelled smoke, and looked around to see the eggs sending up signals over the stove. She snatched up the iron frying pan and blistered her palm on the handle. Dropped the skillet on the floor, cracking a ceramic tile. "Damn and blast it!" she shouted. The eggs remained firmly in the pan.

Leaving the mess on the floor and the gas on high, she downed the Bloody Mary in three gulps, put ice on her burn, and headed out to find some decent food.

When she saw a Starbucks, she pulled in and bought a cup of coffee. It was a lot stronger than she.

It practically walked from the counter to her table. Her limbs felt like string.

She stared into the cup and thought of days when she had eaten delicious meals without a thought for what went into preparing them, when she had spent twenties as casually as if they were pennies. Now she counted pennies as if they were dollars and nobody cared if she starved.

She felt tears of self-pity welling in her eyes, but blinked them away. She would not cry. Foley would not make her cry.

Wait! She still had Winnie's cash in her pocketbook. How could she have forgotten?

She went to the counter to get a big blueberry muffin, but when she tried to pay with a hundred-dollar bill, the cashier shook her head. "Honey, I can't change that. Haven't you got anything smaller?"

Bara found enough change for one piece of biscotti. She dipped the hard pastry in her coffee and wished she had eaten more at Scotty's. Wished she had watched more carefully when Katharine was making that omelet. Wished somebody she knew would come in, so she could hit them up for change or a muffin. Wished she had refilled the flask and brought it in with her.

That was what she really wished.

She drained her cup and pulled herself to her feet. She would go see if Ann Rose or Nettie's other friends knew anything, then she might as well see Rita Louise and get it over with.

However, Rita Louise was not a woman she liked to confront on an empty stomach. She would need a drink before she went over. Maybe two. She stopped at a liquor store and bought an entire case of her favorite brand of bourbon. "Having a party," she explained, even though they hadn't asked. Sensible people, they had no problem with hundred-dollar bills.

Two hours later, exhausted, she drove into the dark private garage that was part of Rita Louise's condominium. She pulled her Jag into a far corner, and unscrewed the cap off one of her new bottles. She needed a drink before she went upstairs. Maybe two. In the end, she drank half a bottle. She needed to work up her courage before she entered the lion's den.

Rita Louise's condominium faced west, over the treetops of Buckhead. "Look," she said to Bara, pointing from her terrace. "Those trees are in the yard of the house where I grew up."

Buckhead was covered in trees, and they all looked alike to Bara. Besides, the height of the terrace was making her dizzy.

"I need to talk to you," she said, her tongue thick and unruly. "Inside. It's too hot to sit out here today."

Rita Louise's nostrils flared in distaste, but she led the way through French doors to her exquisite living room. It was small but elegant, decorated in gray, cream, and rose, to complement Rita Louise's silver hair, pink cheeks, and blue eyes.

Bara stumbled as she followed, caught an armchair to steady herself. Since the chair was there, she sat. No point in walking farther than she had to.

Rita Louise, pretty in a pink pantsuit, sat on her rose brocade sofa.

Bara, in her black pantsuit, felt like a crow. Or a buzzard.

When Bara didn't immediately speak, Rita Louise leaned forward and said gently, "I understand you are having some"—she paused delicately, for the subject was not one that ladies discuss—"a little financial difficulty lately, dear."

Bara barked a laugh. "You might say that, considering that Foley has screwed me to the wall and locked up every asset I own." She thought, wonder of wonders, that Rita Louise was going to pry open her frozen purse strings and offer her a loan.

Rita Louise's voice dropped further, so that Bara could barely hear. "I would be willing to buy that Louis

Tiffany lamp, Bara. For your sake and in memory of
your dear mother."

Bara stared. "I don't want to sell my lamp. It was
Nana's. Besides, Foley has put it on the inventory. I
can't sell a thing in the house until we get this divorce
mess sorted out."

"Have you had the lamp appraised?"

"Everything in the house has been appraised except
me. I'm the only worthless thing there." She tried
another laugh, but it caught in her throat.

"Would Foley notice if one lamp was missing?"

"Foley would notice if one grain of sugar was missing. I think he prowls the house counting up the dollars
while I'm asleep."

"Well, if you could agree to sell the lamp . . ."

"We can't agree on a blessed thing right now, and
I'm not selling anything Nana left me. They are all I
have of her, and the most precious things I own."

With obvious disappointment Rita Louise sat back
against her cushions and contemplated Bara with distaste. When she frowned at Bara's nails, Bara clenched
her hands in her lap.

"I came to talk to you about Mother. I discovered
something this morning that has upset me considerably. I hope you might be able to clear it up for me."

Rita Louise sat, a queen granting an audience, waiting for Bara to complete her petition.

Bara explained about finding the medals, taking them to Katharine's, and reading the citation that went with her father's Medal of Honor. She knew she was taking a long time with the story. Some of the words tied up her tongue. A few times Rita Louise made a slight motion of impatience. But Bara was having a hard time making herself come to the point. Finally she blurted out her problem.

"If Daddy didn't get home until February, then either I came awfully early, or—"

Rita Louise's eyes were chips of flint. "What are you suggesting?"

"That Winnie wasn't my father. How could he have been?"

Rita Louise drew herself even more erect. "That is not a thing you ought to question."

"I have to question it, unless I was born far too early. Was I? Is that why I was slow?"

"You were never slow, dear. You were very bright."

"I had to stay back a year. Was that because I was born early?"

Rita Louise pursed her lips like a drawstring purse. "You weren't born in Atlanta. Your parents were living in New York. Besides, we did not discuss things like that back then. People had a sense of decency, and privacy."

"Bull!" Bara said bluntly. "She told you all about Art's birth one afternoon. How he wouldn't turn and she was in agony for hours—"

"Eavesdropping, Bara?" Ice dripped from every word.

"No, reading behind the couch when you all came in. Please help me, Aunt Rita Louise." The childhood name came out unbidden and desperate. "If Winnie came home in February—"

Rita Louise leaned over and patted her hand. "It was a long time ago, dear. It's all over and done with now."

The pat, both gentle and patronizing, raised Bara's temper to the flash point. "It's not over and done with! I'm still here, and I deserve to know the truth. Who was my father? Who was Nettie sleeping with while Winnie was at war?"

Those words were the dam that had held back the tears. They gushed down her cheeks and scalded the burned hand she held up to conceal them. Sobs of frustration shook her—frustration with Rita Louise, with Eloise, with Scotty, with the eggs, with Starbucks, with Katharine for discovering the truth, and most of all with Winnie and Nettie for keeping such a horrendous secret between them. "I have to know," she sobbed over and over. "I have to know."

Rita Louse sat like a stone. Her maid came to the door, but Rita Louise gave an imperious wave, and she melted back into the recesses of the condo. Bara scarcely noticed. She was consumed by grief.

When Bara's sobs subsided, Rita Louise said, "You never appreciated your mother. She was a fine person and did much good in this city. But all your life you quarreled with her, rebelled against her, and broke her heart with your shenanigans. Now you come here speaking slurs against her good name after she sacrificed more for you than you will ever know."

"I *want* to know." Bara raised her ravaged face. "I need to know. What did she sacrifice for me? Was Winnie my father?"

"Of course he was your father. He raised you, supported you—now stop slandering your mother's good name and leave, please. I want you to go." Rita Louise reached for her cane and maneuvered herself into a standing position.

Bara stood, too, none too steady on her feet. "I am not trying to slander Mother's name. I am trying to find out who I am."

"You are who you make yourself." Rita Louise inclined her head toward the door.

"Was it Father John?" Bara barked. "Or don't you know?"

Rita Louise raised a hand and slapped her. One of her rings left a long scratch on Bara's cheek. "Get out of my house!" She lifted the cane to point, lost her balance, and sank to the sofa, so pale that her lipstick looked like a swipe of blood on her face. "Get out!"

Bara headed to the door. "I've been thrown out of better places than this. And you aren't done with me. I'm going to tear this town apart until I find out what I want to know."

Bara took the slowest elevator in creation down to the parking garage and lunged for her car. Inside, she twisted the top off the half-empty bottle and lifted it to her lips. When she finished that one, she opened another. Next thing she knew, she was slumped in the front seat of her car and the parking garage was lit by soft orange lights. She started the car and checked the clock on the dash. Ten o'clock? Where had the day gone? She was losing a lot of hours lately.

Two empty bottles lay on the carpet with one half-empty one. She got back out and lugged the case of liquor to the trunk. It was a crime to drive with open liquor in your car, and she couldn't afford to get arrested.

Chapter 18

Katharine had been startled but relieved by Bara's abrupt departure. She had done what she had agreed to do. Bara could handle the rest of her problems. Katharine had problems of her own—starting with the fact that she had to spend the rest of the day shopping.

By the time Hollis arrived, she had reached a decision. "I will not waste a lot of money on stuff I don't really want. Let's hit Goodwill and the Salvation Army."

"Works for me." One of Posey's complaints about her youngest daughter was that Hollis bought most of her clothes and a good bit of her décor at thrift stores. "When she has perfectly good credit cards at Bloomingdale's, Nordstrom, and Neiman Marcus."

Hollis held out two sheets of paper. "This is a list of surfaces that need something on them."

Katharine stared in dismay. "Alternatively, why don't we call Bloomingdale's, have them deliver every knickknack in stock, and spend our day by the pool?"

"Very funny. This is for downstairs, of course. I thought for upstairs we'd buy small frames for family pictures and set them around. For now, anyway. You do still have some pictures, don't you?"

"Photographs." Katharine's eyes went automatically to the dining-room arch. From the front hall she used to be able to see oil portraits of Jon and Susan when they were very small. They had been slashed to ribbons by her vandals. That loss was still her keenest.

"Don't grieve for the portraits, Aunt Kat. Susan and Jon both hated those pictures." Hollis seemed to think that was a consoling thought. "I'd throw out the one Mom had painted of me, except she'd kill me."

"Very likely. We didn't get them painted for you kids, we had them painted to suggest to strangers that you were once sweet and lovable. Let me get my purse, and I'm ready to go." Katharine needed a moment to compose her face.

Hollis must have realized she had blundered, for she called after her, "I'll be lovable the rest of the day. I'm lovable when I'm shopping. And I'll drive. I'm in my rental car and get unlimited mileage."

Katharine agreed, until she saw the car Hollis was driving. "That thing looks like an upholstered roller skate. We'll take my car. I also have a rental with unlimited mileage. And I've had a brilliant idea." She picked up several CDs from the countertop. "How about if we head up I–575 to Jasper, Ellijay, and Blue Ridge, and browse some of the little antique shops we were talking about last night? Some of them have pretty reasonable prices, and we'll get a jaunt out of town."

Hollis eyed her aunt suspiciously. "You aren't planning on trying to find Kenny's old home place, are you?"

"I don't have a clue where that might be."

"Then it's a dynamite idea. I'll bet we can find some great stuff."

Katharine drove and Hollis fed the CD player. Not until they were past the Woodstock exit did Katharine get around to the question that had bothered her the evening before. "Why, exactly, don't you like Kenny? He seemed nice enough to me."

"Would you drop that subject?" Hollis blazed. "There's bad chemistry between us. Can't you let it go at that?"

"Subject dropped," Katharine assured her.

A few minutes later, Hollis brought it up again. "Don't you think he seems a little phony? I mean, I know other kids from North Georgia, and they don't spout sentences like 'the old log cabin up home' or 'the floor of our shack.'"

As Katharine remembered it, Kenny had used that phrase in a sarcastic reply to something Hollis had said, but she had to agree with Hollis's next words.

"Maybe he thinks it's cute to put on that hillbilly act, but I'll bet he lives in a neat brick house on an ordinary street in Canton, or even around here somewhere." She indicated the suburban sprawl that was inching north as Atlanta stretched into the hills. "I'll also bet the only antiques his mother has are dishes her mother left her. He was trying to impress you, that's all."

Katharine thought that over. "Maybe so, but he was right about our hall table and the dining-room rug. On the other hand, his grandfather looks like he rode his Harley down from a mobile home. The man wears black T-shirts and boots that have been scuffed by hard work, and he has a ponytail, an earring, and tattoos on both biceps."

Hollis grinned. "Sounds like my kind of guy. Too bad Kenny isn't more like him."

"Where did you all meet, again?"

Hollis screwed up her face, like she was trying to remember. "I think he was in the car one time when Jon gave me a ride."

Katharine had known Hollis too long to be fooled. She knew there was more to the story.

"That's it? You hadn't seen him but once until yesterday?" That didn't explain the antipathy between them. Or Kenny's reference to Hollis's "problem."

Hollis lifted her chin and gave Katharine the icy face she usually reserved for her mother. "If you intend to spend the afternoon discussing Kenny Todd, I'd as soon go home."

She did not speak again until they pulled into the first parking lot.

Katharine would not look back on the afternoon as one of her best that disturbing summer. Hollis handed her the list and forgot it while she drifted off in each store to examine embroidered linen hand towels and cutwork tablecloths. Katharine, meanwhile, wandered the aisles and recognized half the "antiques" as things she had grown up with.

Only the knowledge that if she didn't finish Hollis's list that afternoon she'd have to spend yet another day shopping kept her doggedly buying figurines, porcelain plates, and other bric-a-brac that had absolutely no meaning in her life. Some of it she liked well enough to live with awhile. Most of it she would box up and give away as soon as the party was over. Her only comfort was that it was cheaper than Bloomingdale's.

The last shop had a set of twin bedspreads she actually thought quite pretty. "How about getting these for the upstairs bedroom? I can take back the ones we already bought, and we wouldn't have to repaint."

Hollis wrinkled her nose. "Eeew. Boring *and* ugly, and not old enough to be cool. I'll bet you had some just like them in high school."

Katharine took a second, startled look and recognized them. She hadn't had any like them, but the most popular girl in her high-school class did. Katharine had wished she could have them instead of the practical corded spreads her mother ordered from Sears. Boring and ugly, indeed! She headed to the car reflecting that maybe she'd take some of her new bric-a-brac out to the patio after the party and smash it. It would be cheaper than a psychiatrist.

It was past ten before they got back to Katharine's and unloaded their purchases. Hollis promised to come the next morning to hang pictures and help place things. Disgruntled and exhausted, Katharine looked forward to bed with a good book. The end of the day had to be better than the rest.

That's what she thought until she listened to her voice mail messages.

Posey, bewildered: "Bara just left. She's dead drunk and telling some rambling story about how you figured out Winnie wasn't her father. She wanted to know if Daddy was in Atlanta during the war. Can you imagine? Call me and fill me in on what's going on."

Murdoch Payne, whiny: "Katharine, I wish you hadn't offered to help Bara with those medals. She has been over to the nursing home upsetting Mama. Daddy is furious. I can't reach Bara, but when you see her again, tell her not to bother them while I'm away."

Ann Rose: "Kat, do you know what is going on with Bara? She stopped by a few minutes ago demanding to know where Oscar was during the war. From something she said, I gather you had suggested Winnie wasn't really her dad. Is that true? If you have time, give me a call."

Payne Anderson, distraught: "Katharine, please give me a call. I don't know what you told Mama today, but she has gone plumb crazy!"

Rita Louise, proper and staid: "Katharine, I don't know why you stirred Bara up like this, but you did her no service. If she asks you to do more research for her, I urge you to decline."

Katharine decided to make herself a gin and tonic and carry it up to bed. It had been that kind of day.

When she took her first sip, she was puzzled. After her second, she was furious. Bara Weidenauer owed her half a bottle of gin.

Chapter 19

Thursday

Bara had the old dream again, the one that used to terrify her as a child.

She roamed her house, looking for Mother, but Mother was gone. Nobody would tell her where. She begged and cried, but they put her in a dark place. "Until you stop crying," a woman warned. Then two men came, enormous and black against sunlight streaming behind them in the door. "They have come for the child," the woman said. Bara turned and ran into a back room, screaming. Another man—someone she ought to recognize but didn't—tugged her by the arm and drew her back to one of the strangers, who knelt and picked her up. She screamed and tried to get away, but he pressed her head against his shoulder and would not let her go. She was terrified she would smother. Finally she collapsed, sobbing, and he carried her away. The only difference this time was that she wore a huge heart-shaped locket that thump, thump, thumped against her chest and made it ache.

The dream had come often when she was small. She would scream and scream until Winnie came and held her. She had continued to have it during times of stress all her life, and she had dreamed it often since Winnie's death.

Her therapist suggested that it represented her fear of the unknown, the loss of her maternal side because of her anger against Nettie, and the child within that she had allowed others to steal. Bara knew only that it still had the power to terrify.

She awoke Thursday morning shaking and confused. Every bone ached. Her cheek rested on something scratchy and wet. She heard the phone and waited for someone to answer.

It kept ringing. Why didn't the servants get it?

She lifted her head to see where she was. That was a mistake. The entire world whirled while a hammer pounded her skull steadily from behind.

She dropped her head and identified the dampness beneath her cheek as drool. Disgusted, she would have moved, but didn't dare. At least the drool was warm.

After a couple more rings the phone stopped. But where was she?

After two futile tries, she summoned the skill to open one eye.

Legs. Furniture legs. She blinked, looked again, and recognized the sleek ebony table in her foyer. By moving her head the tiniest fraction of an inch she saw she was lying on her hall rug. The thick wool Bokhara was bright red with medallions picked out in black and cream. The medallions seemed to be dancing. She couldn't remember them ever dancing before, not since she and Ray brought the rug back from their trip to Pakistan.

"*My* trip to Pakistan," she muttered. "Ray was too drunk to know where he was."

She knew where she was, but what was she doing on the floor?

Gradually pieces of the previous day descended like buzzards to pick her spirit to shreds.

Katharine and her dreadful printout. Scotty. Rita Louise throwing her out of her house. Had there been others?

She could not remember. She was as bad as Ray.

Fat tears squeezed between her closed eyelids. "I am so ashamed," she whimpered an apology to anybody she had offended. "So ashamed."

Also nauseated. The world seemed to be moving in a slow whirl.

She couldn't remember driving home or how she had gotten as far as the rug. How long had she been lying there?

She squinted toward the sidelights and saw sunlight streaming in. Lordy! Had she slept on the floor all night? No wonder she was so stiff. The Bokhara was thick, but not thick enough to compensate for the marble beneath.

"I must be a princess," she muttered. "I feel every vein in that marble."

You're no princess. You are sixty-two, too old to sleep on the floor.

"Cut me some slack, Nettie." She rolled over and dragged herself to her feet, but when she tried to stand she stumbled and crashed into the table, sending the Fräbel heron crashing to the floor. With a cry of dismay she reeled, embraced a potted ficus, and fell with it to the floor.

She lay amid dirt and shredded fronds and contemplated the mess. Any minute Foley would dash upstairs and cut off her head with a crystal shard. When she heard nothing, she squinted and checked her watch. Already ten? Foley would be at work. She must have lain on the floor for hours and hours. No wonder she was stiff. And sick. So sick—

She barely made it to the powder room before she lost everything she had eaten for the last twenty years.

She scooped water onto her face, splashing it all down her front. "Why on earth did you drink so much?" she asked the hideous woman in the mirror. "You know it makes you sick and revolting."

She staggered toward the nearest phone. Sinking into a chair, she called Maria.

Maria did not live in Buckhead. She never attended fancy parties. Yet she was possibly the best friend Bara had. With Maria she never needed to pretend.

"Maria? It's Bara."

"*¡Querida!* I haven't seen you for nearly three weeks. Have you been traveling?"

"No, I've been, um, dealing with stuff around here."

"Are you off the wagon?" Bara heard worry in Maria's voice, not criticism. In the background she also heard children's voices. Maria ran a day-care home for two of her grandchildren and several other children. It was the only way she had to pay her bills.

Bara hated to keep Maria from the kids, but she needed to talk to her.

"Yeah. More and more stuff kept coming down, and I fell off. Now I'm sick as a dog. I think I'm going to die."

"You are not going to die. You are too tough to die. You *are* going to stop drinking. You can do it. You've done it before. But you must come to the meetings. And pray. You cannot do this alone."

"I don't think I can do it at all. Things have never been this bad, and I can't pray since Winnie died."

"Your father was not God. I keep telling you, but you do not hear me. He was a man, like other men. Smart, maybe. Rich, certainly. But still, only a man."

Bara's voice came out in a whisper. "He may not have even been my daddy. Yesterday, I learned something. . . ."

"Whoever he was, he cannot help you now. Ask God to help you."

"Nobody can help me. You don't know—"

"Don't give me that. I do know, and if I can do it, you can do it. It's only for today, remember? One day at a time."

"It's harder this time. Last time it was for the kids."

That was what had drawn her to Maria Ortiz in the first place.

They had met twenty-five years before, at the first Alcoholics Anonymous meeting Bara ever attended.

Externally, they had little in common: Bara, rangy and sleek in a black turtleneck and black jeans she had donned as the least conspicuous clothes in her wardrobe; Maria, short and curvy, wearing a cheap red blouse and the new jeans that were the best she had.

Nor was Maria's story Bara's story. Maria had been born in Mexico and as a child, regularly crossed the border with her migrant-worker parents. From ten she had been used and abused by a series of men. When she was twelve one of them had introduced her to alcohol. In it she had found solace from the hell that was her life. "Drunk out of my mind, I had four children by four different men, none of whom ever provided a penny of child support," she had told the group, "so for years I supported my family with my only marketable skill, the world's oldest profession."

Then she had said the words that caught Bara's attention: "Two months ago, I looked at my kids and said, 'Maria, for the sake of your kids, you have to stop drinking. They did not ask to be brought into this world, but they deserve the best you can give them.' I have been sober two months today. With the help of God and those in this room, I intend to stay that way."

The previous day, Bara had sat, sick as a dog, on the side of her bed and looked into two-year-old Payne's bewildered eyes. "Mommie sick?"

"Mommie's sick." Bara headed to the toilet.

Later that morning, her doctor had confirmed her suspicions: She was pregnant with her second child. "You need to stop drinking," he told her. "Alcohol does permanent damage to unborn children."

She had gotten home from the doctor to find Ray drunk and screaming at Payne while the nanny cowered in a corner. Bara sent Ray off to play golf, calmed the nanny, reassured Payne, and confronted her own face in the mirror. "You have got to stop drinking for the sake of your children. They deserve at least one sober parent." She called AA that morning.

Maria had walked beside her during the pregnancy and for twenty-five years since. Bara thought of Maria as a secret jewel she kept hidden from other friends. She had no idea what Maria thought of her.

"Promise me you will not drink today and you will come to the meeting tonight. You need us."

"I won't drink today. Well, maybe one. The hair of the dog. But after that—"

"That's what we say. Just one more. You are an alcoholic, Bara. Say it."

"I am not an alcoholic. I can quit any time I want to."

"So quit right this minute." When Bara didn't answer, Maria spoke in a gentler tone. "You cannot do it by yourself. Come spend the day with me and the children."

Bara shuddered. "I am not a sight for children's eyes."

"Do I need to come over there? I can ask a neighbor to watch the children and get somebody to bring me."

That told Bara how worried she was. Maria had never come to her house, and had no car.

"You don't have to come. I'll be all right."

"Will I see you at the meeting tonight?"

"I don't know if I can come tonight. I've got some stuff I have to figure out. But I will not drink today."

"Vow it on your mother's grave."

"My mother would roll in her grave if I swore on it."

"It's your own grave, if you keep drinking. Remember that. Now promise me you will come tonight."

"I will come." It was to make that promise that Bara had called in the first place.

The level of noise behind Maria had been steadily rising. "I gotta go before Luis kills Conchita for the last doughnut. See you tonight."

"See you tonight." Bara hung up and felt a better person already.

Back in the hall, she looked at the mess. She ought to get a broom and sweep up the glass and dirt, but she didn't know where the broom was kept. Or how to use it, for that matter, but how hard could it be? She'd buy one next time she was out. She was going to take control of her life again.

She went to the powder room and looked the woman in the mirror straight in the eye. "You will not let the bastards get you down. Not Foley, not Nettie, not even Winnie."

But the new loss of Winnie was too much for her to bear. She collapsed on the powder-room floor, sobbing.

Chapter 20

Thursday morning, Katharine put off returning calls as long as possible. It wasn't hard. She was extremely busy. But she worried about Bara—and was puzzled by that.

She scarcely knew the woman and didn't particularly like her, so why should she worry so? She certainly felt no responsibility for Bara's erratic trail through Buckhead the day before. *I merely did what she asked me to do,* she reminded herself. Yet the disintegrating eccentric kept intruding on her thoughts.

At nine, Hollis came with Dalton. "Have you decided where you want your pictures?"

"Not yet. I was waiting for you."

"Procrastinating again?"

"I wasn't procrastinating, I was delaying the decision."

"Like there's a difference."

"There is," Katharine assured her. "Delay is putting something off until you need to do it. Procrastination is putting it off past the time it needs to be done. I was delaying until you got here, because I knew you'd have firm opinions about the matter."

"Good distinction," Dalton said. They were the only two words she heard him utter.

She and Hollis spent half an hour deciding where each picture should go. Dalton spent the next two hours on a ladder, taking orders from Hollis. While they were working, Katharine washed the things they had bought in the mountains. She tried calling the Weidenauer home several times, but got only voice mail. She didn't feel she knew Bara well enough to ask her to call back, and couldn't think of a tactful way to ask on a machine if she was all right, so she didn't leave messages.

At ten she called the upholsterer to see when she should expect the furniture.

His accent was as country as Kenny's, but with the broader tones of South Georgia. "I'm sorry, Miz Murray, we're running a tad behind, but I may be able to bring some of it out Monday. I'll have the rest for sure by the middle of next week."

"You promised it for today," Katharine reminded him.

"I know I did, but my mother-in-law got sick and we had to run down to Valdosta for a few days, then one of my workers up and had a baby. That's put us pretty far behind."

Katharine itched to remind him that he'd had several months to get in a substitute to cope with the new mother's leave of absence, but she dared not be rude to a man who held all her furniture hostage.

"Your dining-room chairs are done, the two plaid chairs are done, the couches are nearly finished, and I'm fixing to start on the living-room chairs this very morning," he boasted.

"*Start?*" Katharine heard Aunt Sara Claire's disapproval in her tone of voice. She took a deep breath and said, as levelly as she could, "I'm very sorry about your mother-in-law. Is she doing better?"

"She's gonna be fine. But like I said, that and the new baby's put me a little behind."

"But you do remember that I have to have that furniture early next week, right? I'm having a party here, and need couches and chairs."

She didn't mention that the party wasn't until Saturday and would be held outdoors even in the unlikely case of rain. Tom had ordered a tent with transparent sides and sufficient chairs and small tables to accommodate the guests. A firm that was already behind and had absolutely promised delivery for Thursday ought to be able to deliver by the following Tuesday.

"Wednesday at the very latest," he assured her as if reading her thoughts.

She wished she believed him.

Tom called at noon and said in a rush, "I've got bad news, hon."

She steeled herself to hear that he'd have to stay in Washington all weekend. She'd had that kind of disappointment before.

The news wasn't that bad. "I probably won't be able to fly out today. It's raining frogs and newts up here and they are predicting things will get worse. That tropical depression has come up the East Coast and stalled out off Maryland, blanketing everything between here and New York with sheets of rain. I'll get home as soon as I can, and I have cleared the decks here to stay down there all next week, but it's unlikely planes will go out today."

When Katharine didn't speak immediately, he said, "Let me guess. You haven't read the paper or looked at television news since I left, so you didn't know about the tropical depression."

"I've been busy."

Tom, who was becoming more of a Washingtonian by the year, couldn't conceive of being too busy to keep up with news about the nation's capital. "Katharine! The country could be on a red terrorist alert and you wouldn't have a clue until terrorists came rolling up the drive."

"How much sooner would I need to know? There wouldn't be a dadgum thing I could do about it. But don't worry about coming in today. I've got things under control." How many times had she reassured him with those words in the past twenty-five years? As usual, it happened to be true. "Hollis is hanging pictures on our newly painted walls, and later we're going to place stuff we bought in antique stores yesterday."

"What kind of stuff?" Tom sounded wary. In his experience, antiques were pricey tables and rugs, and represented a major investment.

"Relax. We didn't break the bank. We just bought some little things to set around on tables and mantelpieces for the party. You can help me decide later what to keep and what to get rid of. Hollis claimed that without them the house looked like a developer's model home."

"It is a model home—to your efficiency and good taste."

"Hold your vote on my good taste until you see the stuff. But Hollis has done a marvelous job. She's been worth every penny."

"She's not really hanging pictures, is she? Should she be on ladders?"

"She's supervising. The work is being done by a silent young man named Dalton."

"Blue hair?"

"Purple streaks this time. Otherwise, very like the others."

"And the furniture comes today?"

"No, but the man says Wednesday, at the latest." She couldn't keep doubt from her voice.

"If it doesn't come, I'll head over there with a shotgun and sit on a stump watching while they finish it up. He will not mess up our party."

"Right. By the way, can we buy a car on Saturday? The rental is nice, but I'd like to get one of my own."

"No problem. See you when I can. I love you."

"Love you, too." As she hung up, she prayed, "Let that storm move north," then was instantly contrite. If New England flooded, she would feel very guilty. Her mother used to say that guilt was what women do best.

Speaking of guilt, she might as well deal with yesterday's calls.

She returned them in order of least likely to yell at her. Posey was at aerobics. Ann Rose was sympathetic and concerned for Bara. Rita Louise was chilly, Murdoch annoyed. To each she said basically the same thing: "I simply researched the medals. I cannot imagine what more I could do. I don't know Bara well enough to have any influence over her."

Finally she took a deep breath and called Bara's daughter.

Payne answered the phone with a wary, "Hello?" As soon as she recognized Katharine's voice, dismay and relief flowed out in a torrent. "Oh, Katharine, I'm so glad it's you. My phone has been ringing off the hook. Mama has gone crazy, and I don't mean maybe. After you dug up all that stuff about Granddaddy's medals, she visited everybody she knows, saying the most gosh-awful things about Nana. I doubt if Aunt Rita Louise will ever speak to either one of us again, and Murdoch called me this morning to remind me she's leaving town this evening and to tell me to keep Mama away from Aunt Eloise while she's gone. An aide at the nursing home told Uncle Scotty that Mama went to the nursing home and ranted like a banshee. Murdoch says he is livid. Can you calm Mama down?"

"I don't know what I can do," Katharine replied, when Payne paused for breath.

"You started it all." Payne sounded no older than Chip. "You have to *stop* her."

"All I did was identify your grandfather's medals and print out the citation for his Medal of Honor."

Katharine kept her voice reasonable, trying to interject some sanity into the conversation.

"That's what's got her so riled up. I must have had ten calls from irate women. Yesterday Mama went to see every close friend my grandmother ever had, claiming that she knows good and well Nana slept with somebody while Winnie was away at war, and she's going to find out who it was, so they might as well tell her. She has accused half the men in Buckhead who were in Winnie's generation. Their widows and sisters are furious. She even came over here this morning, asking Hamilton if his granddaddy went to the war or stayed home. When Hamilton realized she was asking whether *Dr. Oscar* could have been her daddy, he ordered her out of our house. You have to stop her, Katharine. You have to!"

"I don't know what I can do. I don't know your mother well—"

"Good thing. Otherwise, she'd be calling to accuse *your* granddaddy of being her daddy."

"It wouldn't do her any good. For one thing, it would have been my daddy. Daddy was forty-five when I was born. But he was also a New Yorker. He didn't move down south until after the war."

"Lucky you. If Miss Sara Claire were alive, poor Mr. Walter would have been a prime candidate. You don't reckon he could have been, do you?" Payne sounded hopeful.

Katharine could guess why. A dead adulterer with a dead wife was far better than an adulterer, dead or alive, with a wife Payne would have to encounter at future events.

Katharine almost hated to dash the young woman's hopes. "Not a chance. Uncle Walter had mumps right after they got married, which was before the war. They made him sterile."

When Katharine's mother had privately told her that fact when she was fourteen, Katharine had asked, "Was Aunt Sara Claire terribly disappointed? Is that why she is the way she is—all prickly and pruney?"

Her mother had laughed. "Heavens no. Sara Claire has always been fastidious. Children would have driven her wild. Now she doesn't have to put up with them and it's all Walter's fault. She couldn't have arranged it better herself."

Payne spent the next five minutes trying to persuade Katharine to calm her mother, but Katharine remained firm.

"I'm sorry. I wish I could help," she concluded. She knew her response was more manners than truth, but she hung up determined not to let Bara Weidenauer become her problem.

After all the pictures were hung, Hollis took a look around and asked, "What's still missing? Even when we place the stuff we bought yesterday, there's something—what did you used to have over there?" She pointed to a corner of the hall.

"A big ficus," Katharine told her. "They smashed all my plants."

"Of course. You had plants all over the place. Go to a nursery and buy some. I'll arrange the things we bought yesterday."

Katharine started to tell Hollis to go buy plants herself, that she'd like to arrange her own things, thank you very much, but she didn't want somebody else choosing her plants, either. She could move things if she didn't like where Hollis put them.

She spent a pleasant couple of hours wandering around the nursery, one of very few people there, since severe watering restrictions during the drought were discouraging most people from planting. She got home with her rental car full of ferns, hanging baskets, two topiaries, various small potted plants, and five African violets for the bay window in the breakfast room. She staggered into the kitchen with arms full of foliage and found Hollis eating a carton of yogurt at the breakfast table. "I don't suppose Dalton is still here?"

"Nope, he's been gone for ages." Hollis continued to eat her way through the yogurt while Katharine carried in plants.

"That's all?" Hollis asked. "I thought you were getting some trees. What are we going to put in the hall?"

Katharine took a moment to catch her breath. "The nursery will deliver five trees tomorrow morning. Here's a list of what they are bringing. Help me decide which goes where."

"First, I want you to see how great the stuff we bought looks, now that it's in place. Come on!"

Katharine admired Hollis's placement of their "stuff," and they discussed where the plants should go. She waited until Hollis left, then spent an hour rearranging her new possessions—trying not to regret the ones they were replacing and thinking up reasons to justify to Hollis the changes she was making. "Because it's my house and I can do what I want to," she finally said aloud.

As she moved around various rooms, exchanging a figurine for a plate, candlesticks with a pitcher, she remembered something her mother used to say as she went about the house tweaking things after guests had left: "I'm reclaiming my nest."

She had an evening meeting, and when she got home, she filled a big bowl with butter-pecan ice cream and carried it upstairs. It wasn't yet ten, but she deserved an early evening with ice cream and a good book.

From the landing she looked down with satisfaction. For the first time since the break-in, the house looked and felt like home. Even without tall plants and uphol-stered furniture, her nest felt reclaimed.

What will you do now?

The question settled around her in the stillness.

"Get on with my life," she answered aloud.

What life?

Whose voice was that? She suspected it was her own fears.

"I'm going to research my family history and find out about my grandparents and great-grandparents," she replied. "I'm going to construct my family tree and maybe Tom's, as well. Posey won't do theirs, and while Susan, Jon, and Posey's girls may not care now, they may later. And," she added as she went into her bedroom and placed a chair under her doorknob, "this weekend, after Tom gets home, we are going to buy me a car." She gave a happy little skip as she headed to bed.

She climbed under the sheet, ate ice cream, and enjoyed her book. Her world was once again in order.

She had no premonition it was about to fall apart.

Chapter 21

While Katharine was deciding where to hang pictures, arguing with the upholsterer, and wandering around the nursery, Bara was having a frustrating day.

She spent the morning making fruitless visits to more friends of her mother. All grew almost as icy as Rita Louise when she explained what she wanted. Some, forewarned, refused to let her in their homes. Others asked her in and heard her out, then requested her to leave. Only one, who had always been sharper than her mother's inner circle, was any help. She met Bara on her front porch and announced, "I don't have a thing to tell you, honey, but have you looked at your birth certificate? Maybe it will tell you what you want to know."

What a brilliant idea. Why hadn't she thought of that before?

Maybe because she couldn't recall ever having seen her birth certificate. Did she have a copy? She'd gotten her first passport when she was twelve, so Winnie or Nettie must have shown it to somebody—or had they? When she had gotten her driver's license, Nettie had taken her down and simply signed a paper stating that Bara was her daughter, born in New York on September 5, 1945. That was sufficient then if you were white and affluent. When Bara renewed her passport a few years later, her old passport and a driver's license had been identification enough. Things used to be so simple.

She had no idea how she had gotten her Social Security number. She had never seen a card, or needed one, since she had never worked. But the number appeared on her legal documents, so it had to have come from somewhere. Winnie took care of things like that.

Oh, Winnie! Her love for him was becoming mixed with anger, disgust, and bursts of hatred.

She spent an hour going through her files looking for a birth certificate, then wasted a couple more hours going through Winnie's papers in the storeroom, trying to find a copy. She found a little more money, but no certificate. By then, the storeroom was beginning to look as chaotic as her house, and sitting in Winnie's big chair surrounded by his possessions no longer felt comforting, as it used to. Her life had been irreparably split into Before and After.

In the parking lot she saw an employee, who said, "Hey, you aren't living here, are you? I keep seeing you around."

She said, "No, I keep needing things that are stored out here. Today I was looking for my birth certificate. Can't find the danged thing."

He said, "You can get a copy. Just call down to the state offices."

Why hadn't she known that?

She sat in the parking lot and wondered what other simple facts of daily living the rest of the world knew and she didn't. She called New York from her car. After speaking to half the citizens of the state, and having to plug in the cell phone and keep her motor running to keep from running down the phone battery, she eventually found someone who could give her information about what she'd have to do to obtain a duplicate birth certificate. As they hung up, the woman said, "You need to know that we're real backed up here, though. Go ahead and request it, but I wouldn't count on it reaching Georgia in your lifetime."

By that time it was nearly four, and Bara hadn't eaten all day. She hadn't had a drink, either. She considered stopping at a restaurant, but Winnie's money wouldn't last forever, and besides, she had all that food she'd bought. Ann Rose had sent Francie over with it late Monday,

That had been an enlightening experience. Francie had asked all sorts of questions, starting with, "Where do you want me to put these things?"

"Put everything in the refrigerator," Bara had told her with a wave of her hand.

"Everything doesn't go in the refrigerator, honey." Then Francie and she began a litany.

"Where is your fruit bowl?"

"I don't know."

"Do you keep your bread in the refrigerator?"

"I don't know."

"Do you want both the chicken and the pork chops in the freezer, or are you going to use one of them in the next day or two?"

"I have no idea."

Bara had never known food required so many decisions.

She had no idea where Francie had put most of the stuff, either, but she had seen the pork chops in the refrigerator that morning and remembered a cantaloupe on the counter. Surely she could grill a pork chop and slice a cantaloupe.

Feeling halfway competent at the notion of cooking a real meal, she remembered to lock the door between her house and garage and to arm the security system. She found a shelf of cookbooks and looked up pork chops, but the recipes were all a column long and used words like *braise* that she didn't understand. They also required things she didn't have or know where to find if she did have them. In a movie she'd watched as a kid, she had seen a cowboy throw a chop into a frying pan over an open fire and cook it. How hard could that be?

She picked up the iron skillet from the floor and tried to scrape out the dried egg. After a futile two minutes, she hurled the skillet into the trash compacter and reached for a stainless-steel one. She turned the gas on high and stood over the burner while the chop fried, flipping it every few seconds to be sure neither side burned. The meat was eventually hard on the outside and pink inside, but edible.

The cantaloupe, on the other hand, turned out to be full of slime and seeds. Annoyed at having wasted money on the rotten thing, she scraped out the disgusting part and tried the rest. It tasted exactly like it was supposed to. She ate dinner standing at the kitchen counter: the entire cantaloupe, her chop, and a glass of water. Not a bad supper.

Feeling virtuous, she tossed the dishes into a sink overflowing with glasses, mugs, bowls, and spoons, and cursed Foley for firing her staff.

Her eye lit on the case of liquor sitting on the counter. She couldn't remember putting it there. Had it miraculously appeared in her kitchen to tempt her?

She leaned against the counter and eyed it judiciously. Four thirty, and she had not had a drink all day. She felt euphoric. Healthy, even. She could lick this thing! She had done it before.

But she felt the liquor calling her. To distract herself, she picked up the old envelope she had found Monday morning. She couldn't remember bringing it into the house, or if she had opened it again since she'd found it. She dumped it out and pawed through the contents.

Her old report cards she set to one side to burn the next time she lit a fire. She browsed through her old letters and found that her worst fears were true. They were inane, often little more than a request for money. "I'm sorry I didn't write more often," she murmured to Winnie, wherever he was.

The clippings were mostly about her. Seven years old, dancing with Winnie at a ball. Ten years old, standing stiffly beside Nettie at some function, pouring tea. Gads, how she had hated that dress! At sixteen, winning a track meet. "I was as fast as the wind," she boasted aloud. Most of the others were pictures of Winnie with various committees. One—presumably the oldest, since it was yellow and brittle—pictured a foreigner who was missing in Atlanta. It asked readers with information about the man, to call the paper. Bara could not imagine why Winnie had kept it.

She shoved the clippings and letters back into the envelope and picked up Winnie's driver's licenses. Discarding those too old to have pictures on them, she held the most recent and looked at the dear, familiar face. It shimmered and shifted under the fluorescent light, and became the face of a man she no longer trusted.

"Why did I open that cigar box?" She slammed the license down on the counter. "Just like Pandora, I should have left well enough alone."

She was reaching for the locket when the telephone rang.

"I'm in the driveway," Foley announced. "We need to talk. Open the garage door and let me come in."

"Not by the hair on my chinny-chin-chin." The line from the "Three Little Pigs" came as an automatic response to his last words. She hadn't thought of it before, but Foley looked a lot like the Big Bad Wolf in a book she'd had as a kid.

"Seriously. I need to talk to you. Let me in."

"You hit me!"

"I know. I'm sorry. I got a little out of control. It won't happen again. Let me in."

She unlocked the back door, disarmed the security system, and pushed the button to raise his garage door. He parked his black Mercedes, climbed out, and followed her inside.

"Look," he said, setting his briefcase on the counter, "we got a call from the folks who want to buy the firm. We have to make a decision by tomorrow afternoon. I need your shares."

She crossed her arms over her chest. "Convince me to vote them the way you want."

"I don't want your vote, I want the shares. Then I'll move out this weekend and leave you everything—both houses, the investments, your precious car."

She was tempted. If she had been drinking she might have agreed. If Winnie hadn't raised her to look every business deal over carefully—every business deal except marriage, she thought ruefully—she might have agreed. But she was cold sober and she didn't like the look in Foley's eye.

"I'll have to think about it. I'll let you know in the morning."

He shook his head. "There's no time to think. I need you to sign them over to me now."

"No deal."

Before she saw it coming, he'd done a one-two punch to her face and her stomach, smack in the middle of her pork chop and cantaloupe. A rush of hot liquid spewed from her mouth and down his tailor-made suit.

He drew back, disgusted, and swore as he grabbed a paper towel and started wiping his jacket and silk tie.

While he was distracted, she grabbed a long knife from the butcher block on the counter. "Get out of here. Get out!" She could scarcely breathe and she hurt bad, but she would kill him if she had to. She would not be beaten up by another man.

He looked at the knife and at the mess down his once-immaculate front. "I warn you. This is all-out war. You needn't expect any sympathy from me after this." He picked up the briefcase he'd set on the counter and headed for the door to the basement.

"So what's new?" she shouted after him, then hurried to lock the deadbolt.

Back in the kitchen, the shiny bottles drew her like a magnet. She hurt so bad, and she was so thirsty! She felt physically pulled toward the nearest bottle. A longing. A yearning. A sick hollow in the pit of herself that only a drink could fill.

"I deserve a little one, after all I've been through," she informed an invisible jury. "I've been very good today."

Yet even as she poured half a glass of bourbon and threw it down her throat like unpleasant medicine, she was filled with self-loathing. "That's all I needed," she pleaded with the universe. "Just one. I'll go up now and have a little nap before AA."

As she headed for the stairs, she didn't notice she was carrying a bottle in each hand.

Her bedroom was on the front of the house, facing east, and a big oak grew outside the window. By late afternoon the room was dim. She switched on all the lights to cheer her spirits. It had been a hell of a day. A hell of a week. She sat on the side of her bed and looked at the bottles she had placed on her nightstand. "I overdid it yesterday, but right now, all I need is one more drink to help me relax. I need sleep so badly. Just a couple of hours, then I'll get up and go to the damned meeting."

She finished both bottles and fell across her bed, fully clothed.

Bara didn't know what woke her. She'd been having the dream again: two big men standing in her doorway, coming for her. She had been terrified. She had run and run, the big heart *thump, thump, thumping* against her chest, but then she heard a loud noise and froze. What was that?

A moment later she knew she was awake, but she was still terrified. Why?

She tried to turn over and drag the duvet over her head, but rolled off her bed onto the floor. Startled, she clutched the silky cover to pull herself up. The whole duvet slid off the bed and piled on top of her. That was good. The room was too bright anyway. Why were all the lights on? What time was it? She crimped her eyes and peered at the clock. Nine fifty. Morning or evening?

Beyond the windows, the sky was black. Evening, then. So why were her drapes open? The maid knew she liked her drapes drawn at dusk.

She pulled the thick cover over her head and lay surrounded by soft darkness, her cheek sinking into the carpet's deep pile. She was so comfortable. Maybe she would lie there until she died. How long would that take?

"I got nothing better to do." Her voice was slurred even to her own ears. "Got nothing better to do for the rest of my life than lie here and die."

She pulled her knees toward her chest in her favorite sleeping posture as a child.

Her stomach cramped. With the pain came memory—fuzzy, but memory. Foley had punched her. Hard. With the memory came rage. "Damn you, Foley!" she muttered, shifting one hand to press against her sore abdomen. "You could have busted my spleen. I could kill you. I could kill you!"

Rage fueled her muscles. She shook off the comforter like a dog shedding water. Pain throbbed in her stomach and face, and she realized she was seeing with only her right eye. She reached up to the left one. It was swollen shut.

"You've done it this time, buster!" she warned. "First thing in the morning, I'm calling the cops and swearing out a restraining order. I'll make them take pictures, too." All the things she had refused to do while married to Ray. Back then she had still thought it was all her fault.

She pulled herself to her knees by holding on to the rail of the bed. The room, full of unnecessary brightness, swam around and around. She closed her good eye and rested her cheek on the mattress until the dizziness lessened. She hauled herself to her feet and stood until she was steady, then staggered around switching off all the lights except her bedside lamp. She lurched into the bathroom and was royally sick in the toilet. After she rinsed her mouth, she pressed a cold washcloth to her brow. Only then did she dare confront the mirror.

"Hag!" She leaned near to examine the swollen, dark eye and to trace a red mark on her cheek with one forefinger.

If only her memory weren't so muddy.

"Old age," she muttered.

She remembered fixing supper and Foley coming in from work. They had talked. What had they talked about? She couldn't remember. He hit her. She remembered that. She just didn't remember why.

How had she gotten up the stairs to bed?

She stumbled back into the bedroom to check out the scene. Two fifths of bourbon stood on her night stand, empty. *Rare Breed*, the kind Foley bought. Had she taken it? Was that why he'd hit her?

She couldn't remember. "I musta needed a little something to forget," she consoled herself.

What was that noise? Thumps. Sounded like it came from downstairs.

Had she locked the doors and armed the security system before she came up?

"Everybody in town has a key. I gotta set the security system." She headed for the hall.

At the top of the stairs she saw that the front door wasn't even shut. Had somebody already gotten in? Where was that gun? Had she left it on the dining-room table? Could she reach it before somebody else did?

The next day, she would not be able to remember.

Katharine flipped on the television at eleven to watch the rest of the news in case something had happened that Tom would mention later and think she ought to know.

In the middle of a report that Tropical Storm Auguste was pounding the Northeast with strong winds and torrential rain, the anchor's face appeared. "We interrupt the weather to bring you a tragic breaking story. Foley Weidenauer, CEO of Holcomb and Associates, has been shot and killed this evening in his Buckhead home. Bara Weidenauer, his wife, has been rushed to Piedmont Hospital with severe injuries. We'll have more on this story as information becomes available. Stay tuned."

Katharine sank into her pillows, scarcely able to breathe. Surely this had nothing to do with Bara's medals. How could it?

She watched until the news was over, but the only additional information was that the houses were too far apart for neighbors to have heard or seen anything. Katharine could have told them that.

What she could not have told anyone was why she felt so guilty.

Chapter 22

Friday

Katharine's night was full of uneasy dreams interspersed with wakeful periods during which she worried about and prayed for Bara. She told herself repeatedly the tragedy had nothing to do with the medals, but guilt hovers close in the dark. Not until dawn did she sink into a dreamless sleep. When the phone rang, she grabbed the receiver with an absolute conviction that any caller at that hour had dreadful news about some member of her family.

"Yeah?" she managed through frozen vocal cords. She eyed the clock. Eight o'clock. Her muzzy brain sorted through the days of the week and came up with Friday.

Posey was immediately contrite. "Did I wake you? I'm sorry. I wanted to tell you something I heard on the news. Foley Weidenauer has been shot and Bara is at—"

"Piedmont. I know." Katharine stifled a yawn. "I heard it on the TV last night. It is awful. You're right." In spite of that, she yearned to cocoon herself in her sheets and sleep another couple of hours.

"Why didn't you call me as soon as you heard?" Posey demanded.

"I didn't want to wake *you* up."

Sarcasm rolled off Posey like oil off Teflon. "Next time, do."

Katharine considered saying Foley wouldn't have a next time and she hoped Bara wouldn't, either, but it was easier to say, "I will. Do they know who did it?"

"Not yet. They said the usual stuff about anybody having information please call the police. Maybe you ought to call them."

"I don't have any information."

"Payne called Lolly yesterday and said lots of women are no longer speaking to Bara—and probably not to Payne, either—because of what you said. Maybe one of them killed Foley."

Indignation shot through Katharine and jolted her awake. "I didn't say a thing. All I did was print out a citation her daddy got with his Medal of Honor." Irritated out of sleep, she sat up and shoved back the cover.

"We ought to go over to the hospital for at least a little while. Lolly won't be able to go until she gets the twins off to school."

"You go. I scarcely know Payne, and she'll have lots of friends there, I'm sure."

Posey ignored the last half of the sentence. "Of course you know her. She and Lolly roomed together at Vanderbilt, and they're both Tri-Delts, remember?"

Posey was a Tri-Delt, her mother had been a Tri-Delt, her grandmother had probably been a Tri-Delt. In the South, the sorority is practically a family legacy. It also forges a mystical bond among women of all generations. Posey's mother used to tell how, in the thirties, as a college student she had been traveling in England and lost her return ticket. On the wharf, panicked, she had seen a Tri-Delt pin on an elderly woman's collar. "I put out my hand and said, 'Brenau.' She said, 'Ole Miss,' and she bought me a ticket home."

"I can see why you ought to go over," Katharine agreed, "but I'm not a Tri-Delt and I scarcely know Payne, so I can't see one reason why I ought to go. Besides, if she blames me for what happened, I'm the last person she'll want to see."

"She doesn't blame you, exactly. And you could apologize."

"Apologize for what?" Hours spent reminding herself that she had no reason to feel guilty erupted into frustration. "You were the one who insisted I research those medals. You were the one who told Bara I could find out what her father earned them for. That's exactly what I did and all I did. Maybe you ought to apologize."

"What I heard at aerobics yesterday afternoon was that you told Bara that Nettie was sleeping with half the men in Buckhead while Winnie was at war."

"I said no such thing! I printed out one citation from the Internet, the one for Winnie's Medal of Honor. It said that he was wounded in December 1944 and sent home in February 1945. Since Bara was born in September 1945, she herself concluded that Winnie could not have been her birth father."

"That's all you did?"

"That's all."

Posey paused again to mull that over. "Maybe he flew home for some quick R&R. He was a pilot. Or maybe one of his pals flew Nettie over there. You're sure you didn't imply that poor Nettie . . ."

"I didn't imply a thing. But the soldiers were fighting a war, Posey, not flitting across the Atlantic for conjugal visits."

"Oh. Then it almost had to be Nettie and somebody around here, didn't it? I wonder who?"

After Bara's histrionics, Katharine suspected a lot of other people were wondering the same thing. "I can't see what any of this has to do with Bara getting shot, can you?"

"She wasn't shot, she was beaten up. Why did you think she was shot?"

"Last night's news said Foley had been shot and she was taken to the hospital with severe injuries. I presumed . . ."

"No, he was shot and she was beaten. They think somebody came in and beat her up, Foley interrupted him, and whoever it was shot him."

"And you think Bara upset someone badly enough these past two days for them to want to beat her? That's ridiculous. Any candidate for her birth father would have to be well over eighty. I have a hard time seeing anybody that age waltzing in at ten o'clock at night to beat her, don't you?"

Even as she said it, Katharine remembered that during the summer she had encountered two other men well up in years who had still been capable of inflicting violence on others. Surely they were the exceptions.

Posey didn't think so. "They could if they were upset enough. But I don't really think the killer was anybody from Buckhead. Those kinds of people don't live in our neighborhood. Probably somebody on drugs or something. And I still think we need to go sit with Payne, at least for a little while."

"You go. She won't want to see me."

"I've got a little problem." Posey hesitated, then spoke in a rush. "I was on my way to aerobics when I heard the news, and I got so upset, I went a tad fast around a corner, ran off the curb, and hit a tree. My front fender has a teeny little dent and the engine is making a funny *clunk clunk*, so I don't think I ought to drive it, do you? I've called Triple A to come tow it to the dealer's, but could you come get me? I'll take you to breakfast at the OK Café afterward. Don't tell Tom if you talk to him, though—he'd tell Wrens, and I'd hate for Wrens to worry."

Katharine had known Posey long enough to translate all that. "You don't want Wrens to know you've wrecked your car."

"I didn't wreck it, exactly. I got a dent. Can you come? And bring your charge card. I'll need a little loan."

It was Posey's habit, when she had an expenditure that she didn't want Wrens to question, to ask Katharine to put it on her charge card and to write Katharine a check. Katharine sometimes wondered what Wrens thought about the fact that his wife wrote her sister-in-law so many checks. Did he suspect Tom wasn't adequately providing for his wife? Or simply that Katharine was a spendthrift and a sponge?

Posey's "teeny little dent" was actually a crushed right front fender with the headlight dangling like a damaged eye from a socket and the wheel bent in like a turned foot. The poor convertible was definitely not in driving condition.

"You're so lucky you get to keep your family's books," Posey said as Katharine handed the tow-truck driver her charge card. "You can charge anything and write all the checks you want to, and Tom never knows."

Katharine signed the charge, but she wasn't sure *lucky* was the appropriate word.

They had to follow the convertible to the dealer, of course, where Posey explained carefully (and several times) that they should call Katharine when the car was ready. While she was making those arrangements, Katharine wandered around the showroom, but saw nothing that caught her eye.

She was starving by the time they got to her rental car. "OK Café?" she inquired.

"Yes, but first, I think we need to run by and see Payne. Just for a minute. I want to offer to keep little

Chip a day or two this week, if she needs me to." Posey took a lipstick out of her bag and freshened her lips while Katharine pulled into traffic. She knew good and well that in the end, Posey would either ask Julia, her housekeeper, to entertain the child or persuade Lolly to add Chip to her household, but Posey's motive sounded more altruistic than the one that propelled Katharine toward Piedmont Hospital. She was simply curious.

"You look better than I do," Posey said when her mouth was made up to her satisfaction. "Is that a new outfit? Celery suits you. But I just threw this old thing on to drive to the gym. Do you reckon Payne will mind? Maybe we ought to stop by the house so I can change."

Posey's house was in the other direction and she looked enchanting in a rose cotton jogging suit that Katharine knew for a fact was less than a year old. She had no problem saying, "You look fine for a hospital waiting room. If they give prizes for appropriate clothing, you're sure to win."

Bara was in the ICU. They found Payne in the family waiting room, surrounded by friends, but there was no sign of Scotty or Murdoch. Payne looked wan and exhausted. Her jeans and T-shirt had obviously been slept in. Her dark eyes were circled with darker rings, and her curls were more tousled than fashionable. When she saw Posey, she stumbled into her arms and clutched her without a word.

"How is she?" Posey asked when Payne let her go.

"Not good. She's in a coma, she's covered with bruises, and she's got lots of broken bones: her left shoulder and wrist, a couple of ribs, her right tibia, and at least one skull fracture. They've put in a tube to drain fluid off her brain, but they say they can't set anything until tomorrow, after the swelling goes down. Oh, Posey, she looks pitiful!" Payne's voice wobbled like a top that is slowly winding down. "She's black, blue, and green all over her arms, her head, her stomach, her face—I can't believe anybody would do that to her! But thank you both for coming."

"Have you eaten breakfast?" Posey asked.

Payne shook her head. "I couldn't keep anything down. I'm too worried."

"You'll have to eat," Posey chided her. "Keep your strength up. Your mother is going to need you. Where are Hamilton and Chip?"

"At Ann Rose's. Hamilton took Chip over last night, then came back here. He went on rounds this morning and said he'd have breakfast with them afterward, because we think Chip needs to see one of us. He's terribly worried about—"

She broke off as a police officer came into the waiting room and called softly, "Family of Bara Weidenauer?" Payne excused herself and joined him. He looked younger than she, and miserable at what he had to tell her. As he spoke, her eyes widened and she started to sway. He put out an arm to steady her.

Posey flew across the room and supported her before she crumpled. As she led Payne to a nearby vacant chair and gently lowered her into it, she demanded, "What did you say to her?"

The policeman remained polite, even when confronted by a Fury in a jogging suit. "I'm sorry, ma'am, but I had to explain that we're putting an officer outside her mother's door."

Payne looked from Posey to Katharine, her expression wild. "When Mama's well enough, they may charge her with Foley's murder!"

Chapter 23

Payne's words carried. Her friends clustered around her. Other families in the waiting room faced toward the officer and glared. A lot of solidarity can be built up among people who suffer together through an entire night.

The man in the chair next to Payne rose and offered Posey his seat. Posey put an arm around Payne's waist and held her close. "Is that true?" she demanded of the officer. "Are you fixing to charge Bara with killing Foley?"

"Not me personally." He held up both hands to deny the accusation. "I'm just the messenger, here. But her prints were the only ones on the murder weapon and there was no sign that the door had been forced."

Payne fell forward, head on her knees, shaking with sobs. "Mama wouldn't shoot anybody! She wouldn't!"

Katharine couldn't help remembering Bara's declaration that if Foley Weidenauer were found dead, she would have done it. Had shooting been included among her preferred methods of execution? Katharine couldn't remember.

"Did you test her hands for gunshot residue?" demanded one of Payne's friends.

The officer was polite but stern. "You've been watching too many police shows on television, ma'am. Residue doesn't last but a few hours, and they didn't think to do it before the hospital cleaned her up after she got here." He added, to Payne, "If you have the clothes she was wearing, we might get something from them."

Payne shook her head. "The emergency room cut them off her, so they were ruined. I told Hamilton to put them in his mother's garbage. I couldn't stand to see them again. And the garbage was picked up early this morning."

Katharine had a question. "How did the police hear about the murder?"

"We got a nine-one-one call from the house. Whoever placed it didn't speak, just laid the phone down on a table. It could have been her, it could have been somebody else. When we got there, the front door was standing open."

That was the first hopeful thing they had heard so far.

Payne lifted her head long enough to point out another. "There isn't a phone in the dining room."

"She wasn't found in the dining room. Mr. Weidenauer was in there, but she was in the front hall, not far from the table where the portable phone was lying."

Posey frowned up at him. "Payne says Bara is black and blue, so either Foley beat the tar out of her or somebody else did. She wasn't making any calls."

Posey might be sitting and the officer standing, she might be five-foot-two to his six-feet-plus, but he backed up a step. "I understand, ma'am, but she could have called before she passed out. She was able to put a pillow under her head. Look, I was simply told to inform the family we'd be stationing somebody at the door. I'd call Mrs. Weidenauer's lawyer, if I were you."

He fled.

"Don't call your Uncle Scotty. Have Hamilton call somebody else," Posey directed Payne. "Have his mother call Oscar and Jeffers, too. You need the whole family here. And get somebody in to take pictures of Bara's bruises today, while they are still fresh. Some of them could disappear in a day or two."

In spite of her fluffy look, Posey could be shrewd.

Payne nodded and grew calmer now that she had tasks to think about. "I didn't even know Mama had a gun," she said after a couple of sniffs. "If I had, I'd have taken it away. She hadn't been . . ." She hesitated as if searching for a word.

Sober was the one that came to Katharine's mind, but Payne finished, ". . . very well lately. Still, I don't know where she would have gotten a gun." She broke down again.

Posey sat beside her and held her while she cried. Eventually, Payne lifted wet eyes to Katharine. "I know this must have something to do with what you told Mama. Can't you do anything to help?"

Katharine's protest that she hadn't done a thing except print out one citation from the Internet fell on deaf ears. "Mama went plumb crazy after you talked to her," Payne insisted, "and she made a lot of people mad. Maybe one of them—I don't know, got out of control. You could at least talk to people or something. After all, you started it."

"**You did** start it," Posey repeated as they walked toward the parking lot.

"I did not start it. If we have to assign blame here, you started it, by telling Bara I could research those medals. Why don't you go talk to all those women? You've known them longer than I have."

"We'll both go, but first let's go to the OK Café."

"It's all the way across Buckhead. We're a lot closer to several other good places."

"Yeah, but I'm needing comfort food right now."

The OK Café is located at the corner of Northside Drive and West Pace's Ferry Road—which, with typical Atlanta logic, continues west as plain old Pace's Ferry Road. For decades the big diner has been a Buckhead institution. Teens stop there at the end of weekend dates. Executives meet for power breakfasts. Friends stop by for coffee and pastry. From early morning until late evening, OK Café's friendly staff dispenses down-to-earth food at reasonable prices.

Katharine pulled in at ten, by which time she was ready to breakfast on her fingers, one by one.

"Payne has a point," Posey said when they were seated in a booth. "This probably does have something to do with what you told Bara." Without taking a breath, she looked up at the waitress and said, "I'll have orange juice, waffles, and bacon."

Katharine seconded Posey's order, then said, "I still have a hard time picturing any of Buckhead's octogenarians showing up at Bara's past ten P.M., giving a good reason to be there at that hour, shooting Foley, and beating Bara. Don't you?"

"Shhh," Posey cautioned. "Don't talk so loud. Maybe it was her real daddy."

Katharine leaned across the table and lowered her voice. "Get real, Posey. In that case, why shoot Foley instead of Bara? Besides, if her 'real' daddy"—Katharine sketched quotes with her fingers—"exists, all he has to do is sit tight and say nothing. I mean, what's Bara going to do—run DNA tests on all the old men in Buckhead, or their children? You heard her talking about the way Foley has been treating her lately. Chances are good they got in a fight, he beat her, and she shot him."

They became aware of the waitress standing there with two juices and eyes bigger than oranges.

"A book we're writing together," Posey said with an airy wave.

"I hope Payne remembers to get pictures of those bruises," she said when the waitress had gone. She reached for her cell phone. "That can make a difference to a jury, and in another day or two, some of them could disappear." She punched in one digit.

"Who are you calling?"

"Lolly. She's a good photographer. I'll tell her to take the pictures while she's there."

By the time she and Lolly finished talking over the situation, the waffles had come.

"So we're agreed we have to do something, right?" Posey asked as she tucked in. "Otherwise, the police are going to arrest Bara."

"I wouldn't know where to start."

"Sure you do. We'll talk to the people Bara talked to and see if any of them can tell us anything."

"That's real specific. You go. You're the one who wants to know."

"I don't have a car. Drop me off so I can change, then pick me up in, say, an hour? We can go talk to people."

Wrens always said that Posey's best talent was running other peoples' lives.

Katharine acquiesced only because arguing with Posey in that mood was worse than driving around Atlanta talking to people, and for the first day in weeks, she didn't have anything pressing to do.

After she dropped off Posey, Katharine decided to swing by St. Philip's Cathedral. She and Tom were members of Trinity Presbyterian, but she had promised Ann Rose she'd see if they could use one of St. Philip's rooms to train tutors. Her errand only took a few minutes. Ann Rose and Jeffers were such pillars of the congregation that Katharine left the office with the sense that if Ann Rose requested the sanctuary for a rain dance, the church would order umbrellas.

As she left, she decided a few minutes spent praying for Bara might do more good than any conversations she and Posey were likely to have with Nettie Payne's old friends. As she slipped into the back pew, she saw only one other person in the holy space: a small, thin woman with her head covered by a gray scarf, kneeling near the front.

As Katharine sank to her knees and folded her hands, she reflected that there was something fitting about kneeling when praying for others.

Gradually she became aware of a whisper penetrating the silence. "I have sinned! I have most grievously sinned!"

Katharine peeped between her fingers and saw Rita Louise approaching up the aisle with her hands clasped before her and eyes on the carpet, like a woman on a pilgrimage. She had not yet noticed Katharine.

Katharine was torn between slipping out and asking if she could help. As Rita Louise drew nearer, Katharine could see that her cheeks were wet and stained with tears.

"Can I help you?" Katharine asked softly.

Rita Louise stopped, startled, then flapped a lace-edged peach handkerchief in distress. "Don't speak to me, Katharine. I have done a most despicable thing!"

She rushed out.

Chapter 24

"A despicable thing?" Anybody but Posey would have had a deep wrinkle between her waxed brows. Katharine knew Posey didn't have a wrinkle. She'd spent too much on Botox and plastic surgery to permit wrinkles to form. Posey let tone of voice convey her distress. "You are sure that's what Rita Louise said? She did a despicable thing?"

"A *most* despicable thing." Katharine wondered if she'd made a mistake by calling Posey on her way home. She had sworn Posey to secrecy, so she didn't fear that Posey would blurt out the story during a beauty-parlor fest of "sharing heartfelt concern for other women," but Posey was worrying Rita Louise's words like a cat with a string.

"I'll bet *she* shot Foley, don't you? She found him beating the tar out of Bara, and—" Posey came to a stop.

"And what? Whipped a trusty gun out of her pocketbook and drilled him neatly between the eyes? Pressed Bara's fingers to the gun and left without being able to say goodbye to her hostess? Don't be silly. Whatever Rita Louise has done, I don't think she shot Foley. For one thing, she's too frail. Any gun has some kick, doesn't it? But even a little kick, and Rita Louise would have been knocked off her feet, and been found lying beside Bara with a broken hip. Besides, everybody knows she's in bed by nine."

Posey heaved a deep sigh. "I'd rather it was her than Bara. Wouldn't you?"

"I'm glad that's a choice I don't have to make."

"What do you think she's done if she didn't kill Foley?"

"I have no idea, and she made it clear she doesn't want to talk about it."

"She might talk if you went alone, you being Sara Claire's niece, and all. I mean, you're practically family."

"Think again. She once informed me that my mother was a wild political renegade who abandoned Buckhead, taught her daughter none of the social graces, then sent the child back to foist herself on polite society."

"She didn't!"

"She certainly did. Granted, that was back when I was in my early twenties and more outspoken than

I am now. I had asked her why they didn't take the money they were spending on a black-tie ball and give it directly to the poor, and while it is a question that often deserves to be asked, Rita Louise was heading up that particular function. She has never forgotten—and definitely does not consider me family."

"So how soon can you come over so we can go talk to other people?"

Katharine spoke magic words to thrill Posey's romantic soul: "I need to go home. Tom may have gotten there while we were out."

"Oh. Well, you all spend some time together, then call me. Have fun."

Tom wasn't home. Katharine swiped a couple of chocolate-chip cookies from the round belly of her cookie-jar pig, and while she munched them with a glass of tea, she considered what she and Posey might accomplish by running all over town talking to people Bara had already talked to in the past two days. Nothing. Solving the murder had to be left to the police. She and Posey had no right or reason to poke around in the mystery of Bara's parentage without Bara's permission. She had just come to that comforting conclusion right when Payne called again. "I hate to bother you, but Mama's awake and asking for you. Could you come back?"

Payne had freshened up since Katharine's earlier visit. Her hair was combed, her lipstick bright. She had even changed clothes, and her face wore an expression Katharine recognized from her own days in ICU waiting rooms. Payne had gone from frantic to resigned—the only two states of being in a place like that.

She greeted Katharine like an old friend. "I am so glad you would come. She's awake but very agitated, and she keeps asking for you."

"Will they let me in?"

"I told them you are her sister."

From strangers to bosom buddies to sisters in less than a week. Katharine couldn't ever remember a relationship developing so quickly. Given how well Bara was known in Atlanta, she doubted if the hospital staff was fooled, but if her visit could help calm Bara, she'd play along.

Payne walked her to the doors of the unit. "She doesn't remember a thing. Says she came home yesterday afternoon and had supper. That's all she remembers. Not a thing between suppertime and waking up in the hospital a little while ago."

Katharine couldn't ever remember visiting a patient with a police officer at the door. She wondered if she'd be frisked before entering, but the man simply gave her a nod as she passed.

Even though Katharine knew about Bara's injuries, she was unprepared for the rainbow of green, purple, and gray that covered the left side of her face and the instant aging process the accident had wreaked. In a faded hospital gown and a nest of pillows and blankets, Bara looked shrunken and ancient.

When Katharine came close to the bed, Bara grabbed her with a hand that felt like a talon. "Find out," she rasped. "Find—" The word ended in a burst of coughing.

"The police are doing all they can," Katharine assured her. "They will find whoever did this." She winged a silent prayer that it was so.

Bara tried to shift her position in the bed and winced with pain. She clutched Katharine tighter. "Find . . . my daddy. Need to know! And envelope . . . in kitchen. Lock . . ." Again she was racked by a cough, then the hand clutching Katharine's tightened to a vise. "Bring." The raspy voice grew weak. "Promise?"

"I promise," said Katharine.

Bara turned her head into her pillow and closed her eyes.

The scene was so like a movie death scene, Katharine was terrified. She summoned a passing nurse. The nurse eyed Bara with an experienced eye, took a quick pulse, and checked monitors over the bed. "Sleeping. She comes and goes. I suggest you come back in an hour."

Katharine had no intention of coming back that weekend. She left the unit wondering how on earth she had gotten involved in that mess. Tom was coming home. They had a huge party to prepare for. She wanted to buy a car. She had no time to fetch envelopes from Bara's kitchen or track down Bara's purported birth father—if such a person existed beyond the realm of Bara's alcohol-sodden imagination. Besides, she scarcely knew the woman. She would tell Payne about the envelope and go home.

She found Payne talking with a police officer. "I don't know if I could bear it." When she saw Katharine, she reached out and clutched her much as Bara had clutched her minutes before. "They want me to go walk through Mama's house to see if anything is missing. I can't go in there by myself. Could you go with me? It won't take long."

Katharine had never been inside, but she had seen the house. Walking through would not be a quick proposition.

If Susan were ever in a similar situation . . . That had to be her mother.

How could Susan be in a similar situation? Katharine protested silently.

If Susan ever needed a friend, wouldn't you hope somebody would step to the plate?

Besides, added the waspish voice of Sara Claire, *you did promise you'd get that envelope.*

"Your mother wants an envelope she left in the kitchen," Katharine told Payne. "I could go with you if we leave right now."

"The sooner the better," the officer told them.

"That was all Mother wanted to see you about?" Payne asked as Katharine followed the cruiser toward Bara's house. "An envelope?"

Katharine had long ago concluded that an inconvenient truth is wiser in the long run than a kinder lie. "No, she still wants me to try and find out who her birth father was, but I think that's something you ought to pursue, not me."

"I can't leave her right now for a wild-goose chase. They think she killed Foley!"

When Katharine didn't reply, Payne added, "The officer we are following was over at the house this morning. He says the place is a mess, with glass and dirt all over the floor of the front hall. They think Mama and Foley were fighting and she shot him. I told him Mama doesn't have a gun, but he said hers were the only fingerprints on it and they have no record of who it belongs to. I cannot believe Mama had a gun and I never knew it. Besides, if she'd been going to shoot anybody, she'd have shot Daddy years ago. I don't believe she let Foley beat her, either. After living with Daddy, she would never have stood for that."

It was precisely Bara's not standing for it that could be the problem, but Katharine didn't point out the fact.

In another moment, Payne burst out, "I'm sure all those questions she was asking must have something to do with this. That's why I wish you would see what you can find out about . . . you know. Won't you?"

"I don't see how I can. It would look like nothing but blatant curiosity on my part."

"You could tell folks I sent you."

"Sorry. I don't think it's something I can do."

Annoyance flitted across Payne's face. Katharine pulled to a stop with relief. "We're here."

The vans and paraphernalia of a crime scene/media event crowded into the circular drive. News reporters recognized Payne and came rushing toward the car with cameras. "I don't know a thing!" she protested, covering her face.

Katharine and the police officer hustled her inside.

A man in a business suit met them just inside the door. "Detective Swale." He extended a hand to Payne. "Homicide." Obviously a man of few words. He had a rumpled look, like he either hadn't slept or kept his clothes in a wad by his bed.

"Have you figured out what happened?" Payne demanded. "Have you found any clue to who came in and did this thing?"

"Not yet." He jingled the change in his pocket. Katharine suspected it was a nervous habit he wasn't even aware of. Uncle Walter used to do that when perturbed.

Payne didn't seem to notice. "But you know it couldn't have been Mama, right? I mean, she was unconscious, the front door was standing open. . . ."

"She could have gotten to the phone, tried to leave the house, realized she was too weak, and gone back in before she collapsed."

"Or somebody else could have beaten her unconscious, Foley came in and surprised him, he shot Foley and put Mama's prints on the gun."

"That's one possibility. But it's hard to believe somebody that vicious would have taken the time to put a pillow under her head. It's more likely that Mrs. Weidenauer and her husband had an altercation—"

What a civilized word for an uncivilized act, Katharine thought.

"—and she shot him, then was able to stagger to the phone and grab a pillow before she passed out from her injuries."

"It wasn't my mother. Somebody must have broken in."

"There's no evidence of a break-in, and Mr. Weidenauer had a key to the back door in his pocket."

"That rat! Mama's lawyer made him give back all his keys. He must have made a duplicate."

"It did look new," the detective agreed. He didn't add, or need to, that if Foley had come into the house uninvited, that could have provoked the "altercation" that led to his death.

Payne had been so focused on the detective, she hadn't looked at the foyer until that moment. She gave such a cry that Katharine thought she had hurt herself until she fell on her knees and picked up a scrap of crystal. "Mama's Fräbel!" She held out what looked like a piece of wing. "Mama got an Otto Godo Fräbel piece for her work with the elderly. A heron. It must have gotten broken." Her throat was clogged with tears.

Katharine was having trouble breathing herself. Seeing the glass and dirt on the floor gave her a flashback of standing in her own home two months before and seeing all her precious things ruined. Her knees wobbled. She knew exactly how Payne felt—and why she was weeping over the heron. It wasn't its monetary value. It represented the entire mess.

Speaking of mess, dirt littered the floor. Seeking the source, Katharine saw a large potted ficus lying on its side. "That tree needs water," she said to the detective, "and to be repotted soon if it's to survive. It's been without water too long."

"Is that right?" He looked at it curiously.

"That's right," she snapped. "Couldn't somebody set it back in its pot and water it?"

"Sorry, ma'am. This is a crime scene, not a nursery. The dirt is evidence. See? It's been tracked all over, even up the stairs."

She peered at the dirt nearest her feet. "This has been here longer than twelve hours. Look how dry it is. And that big a tree wouldn't have wilted in that short of a time."

"Are you a horticulturalist?"

"No, but I grow plants."

"We'll check it out."

She had little faith that he would, but he immediately motioned one of the techs to join him near the tree and said something she could not hear.

"Do you notice anything missing here?" the officer who had brought them asked.

Payne swiped tears off her face and climbed to her feet. "A valuable painting from over the foyer table," she said when she had looked around. "It was a Monet."

Katharine looked about as well. She remembered Bara saying the house had been built to outshine the old governor's mansion. In that it might have succeeded, but while it was elegant, it was heavy and showy. Quantities of Georgia marble had been quarried for the floor of the foyer. The banisters of the large curving staircase looked like ebony, and its treads were also marble. Red carpet ran down the center of the stairs like a river of blood.

Katharine suspected the airy drapes and modern furnishings had been Bara's, not her grandfather's. They displayed better taste than the house itself.

Shards of glass crunched underfoot as they walked toward the dining room. "Watch your shoes," called a tech. "That glass is sharp."

Payne stopped in the doorway and pressed one hand to her cheek. "The Dolley Madison tea set!" she whispered. "Murdoch is going to kill us!"

The officer poised his pen over his notebook. "A tea set. What was included?"

"A large tray, a coffeepot, a teapot, a sugar bowl, a creamer, and"—Payne colored delicately—"I don't know the official name for it. Mama called it the slop

jar. It was where people poured out cold coffee or tea
before they refilled their cup." She moved toward the
buffet like a woman dazed.

"How valuable was this set? Was it insured?"

"It was insured, but it's priceless. It was a gift from
President Madison and his wife to one of her cousins.
Their names were engraved on it." Payne stroked the
top of the buffet as if she were rubbing a magic lamp
for a genie who could return the set.

Having wept over losing her own grandmother's
silver service in her break-in, Katharine thought she
understood Payne's stricken look until she heard the
repeated whisper. "Murdoch is going to kill us!"

"This Murdoch," said the officer, pencil poised.
"Who is he?"

"She. She's Mama's first cousin, and obsessed with
family history."

"Could she have taken the service?"

Payne shook her head. "She's in Boston. She called
today from up there, begging me to have Mama put
that tea set in a safe place. She was worried Foley would
try to take it in the divorce." Payne's voice faltered. "I
had to tell her he's dead." She whirled to ask Katharine,
"Will we have to plan his funeral? I don't think I could
stand that."

"Don't worry about it right now," she advised.

"Anything else missing?" the officer inquired.

His brisk tone helped Payne recover. She peered around. "Silver candlesticks used to be on the mantelpiece. There were silver trays and a pitcher on that shelf of the china cabinet." She pulled open a drawer. "All the flatware is here." She looked around again, then pointed to a round table between two front windows. "A Tiffany lamp sat on that table."

The officer made a note. "Would you check the other rooms, please?"

They roamed the entire house, but nothing else seemed to be missing until they got to her mother's room.

"What happened here?" Payne demanded of the crew inside. All the covers were on the floor, the duvet dragged nearly to the door.

A woman shook her head. "We don't know. We're trying to work it out."

All the terror of the past hours caught up with Payne in the doorway. She started to shake and then to sob, pressing her face into her hands. "Whoever it was found Mama here! He must have killed Foley first, then dragged her—beat her—who knows what he did to her?" She fell to her knees, sobbing.

Katharine put her arms around Payne's shoulders and spoke in her most soothing voice. "Calm down, now. We don't know what happened. We need to wait until Bara is better. Calm down. Calm down." Gradually Payne's hysterics subsided and she let Katharine lead her down the stairs. Katharine wondered if Payne had seen the empty bourbon bottles on the nightstand.

The kitchen was their last stop. Payne wrinkled her nose and sniffed. "This place is a mess and it stinks." She spoke in the grumpy voice of somebody who regrets losing control and is willing to take her frustration out on the next irritant that comes along. "Foley fired the staff and hired a cleaning service to come once a week. I don't know which service he was using, or what day they are supposed to come, but I suppose we can't get them out here anyway until the police are done." She noticed a skillet full of burned eggs sitting in a box on the counter. "What is that?"

"Evidence," the officer told her. "We found it in the trash compactor."

"And you think what?" she demanded with a brittle laugh. "That Foley beat Mama because she burned his eggs? She never cooked."

"Her fingerprints are on the skillet, ma'am. Excuse me, I need to make a call." He stepped into the hall and closed the swinging door, leaving them alone.

Payne stared into the skillet as if it were a magic mirror that could tell her who the murderer was.

Katharine spied a large manila envelope on the countertop with a locket lying beside it. *Locket,* not *lock.* That's what Bara had been trying to say.

"This is what she wanted me to get—the envelope and the locket."

Payne peered into the envelope. "Looks like old newspaper clippings and stuff." She slid a fingernail into the locket. "And this is just an old picture of Mother. Maybe the locket was Nana's." She put the locket in the envelope, slid the envelope sideways into the front of her pants, and pulled her shirt low over it. "Can you see it?"

Katharine heard something outside in the hall: the jingle of coins. She motioned for Payne to be quiet. Payne shivered. "I don't like being here, do you? Let's go."

Katharine was nervous about Payne walking out of the kitchen with what might be considered evidence. "Do you think you ought to?" she whispered. "It's illegal to remove something from a crime scene."

"If Mama wants it, I'm taking it." Payne's mouth was set in a line very like her mother's.

Change was still jingling faintly in the hall.

Katharine spoke louder. "If there's nothing missing in here, I need to be going. I have other things I have to do today." Payne was rustling as she walked, so Katharine added, "I guess you don't look forward to telling Murdoch about that tea set, do you? When does she get back?"

"Too soon." Payne took her cue and spoke loudly, too. "It took all the tact I had to keep her from getting on the first plane and coming home. The best I could do was persuade her to stay until Monday evening. I wish she'd stay up there all week. Mama doesn't want Murdoch hovering over her. She says Murdoch reminds her of fingernails on a blackboard."

Katharine wished she hadn't heard that. It was so apt, it would be hard to forget.

As they went out the swinging door, the detective pushed away from the wall. "Mrs. Anderson? May I have a word?"

He looked at Katharine, obviously waiting for her to disappear.

She was going to oblige, but Payne grabbed her elbow. "I want her to stay. Have you found evidence to clear Mama?"

"No, ma'am, but I have just gotten a report on a second gun we found in a drawer in the dining room. It was one reported stolen by Winston Holcomb three years before his death."

"You think Mama stole a gun from Winnie? She doesn't even like guns."

"We don't think anything at the moment. I wanted to keep you abreast of developments." His change jingled merrily. "We're having some tests run on it. Are you finished in the house?"

His eyes flickered toward the kitchen door, but he didn't open it.

In the car on the way back to the hospital, Payne pulled out the envelope and peered inside. She pulled out a political button that read I LIKE IKE. "Odd," she said. "Winnie voted Democrat."

"He fought in Europe," Katharine reminded her. "Maybe he liked Eisenhower even if he didn't vote for him."

"Or he liked the button." Payne tucked the flap inside the envelope. "It looks like a lot of junk, frankly."

"Your mother wanted it, though."

Payne reached behind her and laid the envelope on Katharine's backseat. "She doesn't have any place to keep it right now, and I'll lose it if I take it. Keep it for a day or two and bring it to her when she gets her own hospital room."

As Katharine drove home after dropping Payne off, she wondered how and when she had become Bara Weidenauer's personal assistant.

Chapter 25

P osey called before Katharine got home. "Are you
on your way to my house?"

"No, I'm on my way home from the hospital. Bara
is conscious and wanted to see me about something."

"What?" Posey had no problem with blatant curiosity.

"There was an envelope at her house she wanted
me to check on."

"Okay. We can do it on our way to talk to the
women."

"I got it. I went with Payne to walk through the
house to see if anything was missing."

"Oh." Katharine could tell Posey was miffed at being
left out. "And . . . ?" Posey hinted.

"The only things Payne noticed missing were a
painting and some silver, including a tea set Murdoch

was telling me about on Monday. Oh, and a Tiffany lamp."

"Well, come get me. It's almost one. If we're going to see any people—"

"I don't want to go see people. I want to get home and check my to-do list."

"You promised we'd go to lunch."

"We didn't eat breakfast until ten."

"I know, but I've gotten dressed. We can get a salad or something and you can tell me about Bara. I don't like you talking on the phone while you're driving."

Katharine turned at the next corner, willing to visit over a light lunch.

She was halfway to Posey's before she remembered that her sister-in-law had called *her*.

She found Hollis alone in the kitchen, wearing black shorts and a black tank top, eating yogurt. "Mama's upstairs fixing her face and Uncle Tom called a few minutes ago. He said he couldn't get you on your cell phone."

That must have been while she was talking to Posey. "Was he still in Washington?"

Hollis brushed a dollop of yogurt from her flat chest before she answered. "No, he said he was going up to the lake house, and to call him."

Katharine punched in his number. The lake house? The lake house was three hours away. Why should he be going there when they had so much to do?

He probably wasn't outside the metro area yet. Maybe she could persuade him to turn around.

"Sorry, hon," he told her, "but we've sprung a major water leak in the yard, and with the water restrictions, the county is threatening to levy enormous fines and turn off our water for months if we don't get up there and see about it. They left a message on the machine. I picked it up when I came in. Where were you?"

"Visiting Bara Weidenauer."

"Again? I told you she was going to consume you."

"If I hadn't been with Bara, I'd have been home to take the call about the leak, then I'd have been consumed by that. Besides, Bara's not consuming me, she's in the hospital and just wanted to tell me something." Enough of that subject. She had far more important issues at the moment. "When will you be home?"

"Heaven only knows. I will be running on PST—plumber standard time. I've called somebody, but he said he can't get out until tomorrow morning."

"Which could mean afternoon or even Monday. I guess this wipes out shopping for a car tomorrow, then." She didn't mean to sound cranky, but she was not only disappointed, she was tired of being disappointed.

"Afraid so. We can look next week. I've been wondering if we ought to lease you one instead of buying it."

"My dad always said leasing a car is like renting a house. You pay off somebody else's loan and wind up with nothing in the end."

"Yeah, but they'd take care of maintenance. You wouldn't have to worry about it."

"I'm used to car maintenance." She heard her tone of voice and wondered, *Why are we having this conversation? Cars weren't important at the moment.* "Why don't I keep the rental until after the party? We don't need to be thinking about cars with everything else we have to do, and you sure don't need this discussion while you're driving up I–85."

He was agreeable. "Okay. But hey, why don't you come up for the weekend? I bought a case of drinking water, we can swim to keep clean, and I'll fill buckets for toilet flushing before I cut off the water."

She almost agreed. That was what she usually did. But if she went up, Tom would expect her to deal with the plumber. That's what he usually did.

"We've got people coming next weekend," she reminded him. "I've got things to do."

"Then I guess I'll see you when I get back."

"Have fun."

He would have fun. Tom loved nothing so much as a lazy couple of days to read and swim. It sounded so tempting that Katharine almost reconsidered. She had her finger on the redial button when Posey came down the stairs calling brightly, "I'm ready for lunch. Let's go!"

As Katharine headed down the Buitons' drive, Posey fanned herself with a piece of paper she'd brought along. "Turn up the air conditioner. I'm having a menopausal moment."

She didn't look menopausal, she looked gorgeous. She'd put on a suit of peacock blue with a wisp of a skirt and peacock-blue heels to match. She even had a little boa around her neck.

"You're a lot more dressed up than I am." Katharine was still wearing the celery pants and top she had put on in a hurry after Posey called.

"I know, but I just got this suit and I wanted to break it in. Did Hollis tell you what she was doing this morning while you and I were with Payne?"

"Sleeping?" Katharine was well acquainted with the younger generation's topsy-turvy schedules.

"No, she was visiting Oriental rug dealers looking for a part-time job." Posey was as upset as if Hollis had been enlisting in the army. "I reminded her she is already designing and making costumes for two theaters, which keeps her up half the night, she is still working for you, and she has promised to help Marsha Montague redecorate her house when yours is done. And heaven knows, Marsha's needs it, although I don't know if she will like a single thing Hollis suggests, and I don't want Hollis offending one of my very best friends—"

"Hollis has excellent taste," Katharine assured her as she pulled out between the high pillars that supported the Buitons' wrought-iron gates.

She still wished she knew what problem Kenny had been referring to. He'd sounded like Hollis had an ongoing problem, not a one-time mistake in judgment, and there were some very serious problems young adults could have in this generation. AIDS, other sexually transmitted diseases, addictions, and alcoholism came to mind. Katharine hoped her niece wasn't concealing something and trying to carry a heavy burden alone.

From the passenger seat, Posey's lament rolled on. ". . . said she has hired two women to come to her place to sew costumes and your house is finished and Marsha's won't take all her time, and she realized this week that she doesn't know enough about Oriental rugs to make recommendations about them, so she wants to work in a store for a while to learn what she can. A store!" Posey made it sound like a brothel.

"She really ought to know about rugs if she plans to recommend them."

"I don't see why. All she has to do is go somewhere and pick one with colors that match the room. Besides, I don't like the idea of strange women coming into our house to sew."

Hollis lived in four rooms above the Buitons' garage in a renovated apartment once designed for a chauffeur. "They won't come inside your house. Her stairs go up through the garage. And they might not be strange."

"Get real. If they are Hollis's friends, they will be strange."

That was true enough. "Speaking of Hollis, do you know if she had any serious problems in college?"

Posey gave a genteel snort. "The child *is* a problem. Nothing but one problem after another since she was born. I swear, if I hadn't been awake for her birth—"

"—you would think she was a changeling. I know. Relax. You're frowning."

Posey's face reverted to the wide-eyed look her plastic surgeon had created. "You always stick up for her. But why should you think she had problems?"

"Somebody asked me recently if she was dealing with her 'problem.' I wondered what he meant."

"Beats me. As far as I was concerned, the years Hollis was down in Savannah were the most peaceful years I've had since her birth. But you know kids today. They never tell us anything. She could have been on drugs, had annual abortions, and eloped with an alien from Mars without our knowing a thing about it. All we knew was that she got good grades, called whenever she needed money, and seemed the same at holidays— dreadfully the same, dragging a parade of the most awful boys home to meet us."

Katharine hid a smile. She was convinced Hollis mostly brought the young men home to shock her mother. She had never seen any indication that Hollis gave a flip for any of them. "She got that national award for the textile she designed," Katharine pointed out. "And didn't she make better grades than either Lolly or Molly?"

"What did I say? You always take up for her. But speaking of trouble, do you know what else Foley Weidenauer has done?"

Katharine was startled. "Since he got shot?"

"No, two days ago. I called Payne just before I came downstairs, and she was distraught. When she got back to the hospital a little while ago, they informed her that Foley canceled Bara's health insurance! They admitted her last night with the information she used a month or so ago when she had a little face-lift, but when they checked with the insurance company this morning, they found that Foley had taken her off his policy! I tell you, if that man hadn't been killed, I'd go over and kill him myself. He was lower than a basement leak."

"So what's happening with Bara?"

"They were talking about moving her down to Grady. Payne was frantic! Bara's money isn't accessible, Winnie's estate hasn't been probated yet, and she and Hamilton have put most of what Ray left Payne into their house, Hamilton's retirement account, and a college fund for Chip that they aren't supposed to touch. I told her to stop worrying, we'll manage to pay the bills somehow."

Posey sounded like she and Wrens would be down to their last nickel if they helped with Bara's bills, but Katharine knew that wasn't true, no matter how high the bill might go. Still, it was a generous thing they were doing. She couldn't imagine Bara in the county hospital.

"You shouldn't have to pay it all."

"We won't. I'll call people and ask them to chip in. How much could you and Tom come up with?"

Katharine didn't mind frowning, wrinkles or no wrinkles. "I haven't taken that woman to raise! I'll talk to Tom, but I keep telling you, I don't really know her."

Posey ignored her. "Can you imagine being that low-down dirty? I swear—"

Katharine inserted a CD. "Maybe this will take your mind off him for a few minutes."

Posey listened to the mellow, blended voices and shook her head. "Low-class, trashy music. How you can stand that country-western stuff is beyond me."

"It's not country western, it's a bluegrass group Tom heard in Washington, and it's not low class or trashy. Tom likes it, I like it, Hollis likes it, even Bara liked it when she came by to bring her daddy's medals. Listen to how well those voices blend."

Music wasn't one of Posey's interests. "Speaking of Bara, I don't think I'd better make anybody mad right now—do you? Since I'm calling around to ask folks for help with her hospital bills. So I think you'll have to go in and ask questions by yourself. I'll wait in the car. Then we can stop by the Swan Coach House for a late lunch."

"I am not going to ask anybody any questions. We're only going to lunch, remember? I told Payne at the hospital I have no reason whatsoever to be asking people if they know who Bara's daddy was."

Posey looked at her watch. "But it's hardly one, and we ate breakfast at ten. You could at least go see the people Bara upset the most in these past two days. All you have to ask is whether they have any idea why somebody would want to beat her up."

"From what Payne said, every one of them wanted to beat her up. Most of them are, however, too genteel to do so."

"So they sent somebody to do it for them. The thug beat Bara, Foley surprised them, and they killed him."

"How many elderly people around here know how to hire a thug? Be serious, Posey."

"You might be surprised. All you have to do is watch to see if anybody looks guilty."

"The police could do a better job of that."

"They won't. They think Foley beat up Bara, and she shot him."

"Which is the most likely scenario."

"Nonsense. She hasn't been sober enough in the past few weeks to shoot straight." Posey held up a small sheet of paper. "While Payne was on the phone, I asked her for a list of the women who were most upset after Bara was there. It's only six people. Won't you at least talk to them—if you won't go see Rita Louise?"

"I am not going to talk with Rita Louise. That is final."

"Okay, then turn right. You might as well start with the closest house."

Katharine felt like she had been run over by a small, blond steamroller.

She drove from one home to another, citing Payne's request and Posey's reason for her being there, and feeling more and more foolish. Every woman she visited was horrified at what had happened to Foley and Bara, but still miffed by her earlier visit and glad to pour their irritation into Katharine's lap.

Posey polluted the environment and wasted gas keeping cool in the car while Katharine trekked from embarrassing interviews to mortifying ones. She was not a happy camper as she climbed in the car after the fourth visit. "Okay, is that everybody on your list?"

"Everybody except Ann Rose and Rita Louise. And I'm starving."

Katharine checked her watch. It was two thirty. "I am willing to talk with Ann Rose, but after that, I am going home. I know you and Payne think I have nothing to do with my life but traipse all over Atlanta trying to do the police's job, but I do have other things to do."

"What about lunch?"

"I'll stop by a filling station and get you a candy bar."

Posey decided to go in at Ann Rose's. "I'd like to make sure Chip is okay."

"He's with a doting grandmother," Katharine pointed out.

"Yeah, but his other grandmother got beat up, and I'm sort of his third grandmother. I want to make sure he's all right."

Chip, however, was not in evidence when Ann Rose opened the door. She shoved a pair of red-rimmed reading glasses onto the top of her head and stepped back to let them in. "Come on in. Chip is napping and I was putting together the tutor training workshop for next week." She didn't apologize for her faded denim skirt, short-sleeved oxford-cloth shirt, or scuffed brown loafers. Like Katharine, Ann Rose preferred comfort to elegance for a casual day at home.

She motioned for them to follow her. "Let's go to the conservatory. The front of the house is too gloomy to visit in at this time of day." In the breakfast room, which she had claimed as her office, stacks of books and papers filled the table, spilled onto the floor, and crept toward the door. "I keep meaning to get that stuff organized," she apologized, "but one project seems to lead to another before I get around to clearing up the first one."

"It was cleared for the luncheon," Posey reminded her.

"Only because Francie put everything in brown paper bags in the garage. When I dumped them back out, the stuff was more disorganized than ever. Come on out here. Can I get you something to drink?"

"I'd love some tea," Posey told her. "Katharine was supposed to take me to lunch, but she reneged."

"I didn't renege, I got kidnapped," Katharine retorted.

Ann Rose stepped into the kitchen to speak to Francie, then joined them in the conservatory. As always, it was humid, but Katharine's spirit had been chilled by the day's events. It felt pleasant to be amid tropical plants she had grown up with. When she praised the orchids, Ann Rose gently touched one of the most spectacular ones, a huge white-and-purple cattleya of the sort Katharine had worn to her senior prom. "I'm sorry Oscar isn't here to see this. He propagated it himself, and this is its first year to bloom."

Soon after they settled themselves on bright cushions in white wicker chairs, Francie brought out a tray holding iced tea, lemon, and a plate of small sandwiches and éclairs.

Katharine was mortified. "You didn't need to fix us lunch."

"I'm glad you did." Posey was already reaching for one.

Ann Rose waved away Katharine's protests. "They are left over from the literacy meeting. You don't want me eating them until Jeffers gets back, do you? Now, what can I do for you?"

"Katharine wanted to ask you some questions," Posey said promptly.

Ann Rose waited expectantly. Katharine swallowed a bite of sandwich and wiped her mouth with the small linen napkin. "I didn't," she told Ann Rose. "Posey and Payne have the bright idea that we ought to talk to everybody Bara visited this week asking about her mother. They seem to think that had something to do with her getting beaten and Foley getting shot. I think they even hope somebody will fling up her hands and exclaim, 'I did it. Arrest me!' However, I've talked to most of them already today, and so far, nobody has."

Ann Rose flung up her hands. "I did it. Arrest me!" She lowered her hands with a small, embarrassed smile. "Shame on me for making light of this terrible thing. Of course I didn't do it, and neither would any of the other women Bara went to see. All she wanted to know was whether any of us knew who her father could have been. Who would have beaten her for asking about that after all these years?" She bent to set her empty glass on the table. "Frankly, I don't believe Nettie had an affair, either. It wasn't like her. She was almost pathetically attached to Winnie. Remember how jealous she was if another woman so much as laughed with him at a party? She wouldn't have jeopardized her marriage that way. I also cannot believe that such a secret could have been kept for so long, especially once Winnie and Nettie were both dead. When Bara roared into the house with all those accusations, I figured she had gotten something very wrong. She wasn't coherent, anyway. She was what my mother used to delicately call 'under the weather.'"

"Drunk," said Posey bluntly. "I sure hope her time in the hospital will get her back on the wagon."

"I do, too," Ann Rose agreed, "but I don't know what her incentive will be to quit. Last time it was her children. She was so afraid Ray would hurt them, or that she'd be drunk and couldn't take care of them. But what incentive does she have now?"

"Her own self-respect?" Katharine suggested.

Ann Rose shook her head. "It takes more than that. There needs to be a reason why not drinking is worth the agony of quitting. I hope she finds that reason. And I wish I could help you, but I can't."

Later, however, as she showed them to the door, she glanced into the library and stopped so suddenly that Katharine bumped into her. "Sorry. I've had an idea. Oscar is great about putting pictures in albums as soon as he gets them—much better than Jeffers or I.

We're leaving Hamilton and Payne a mismatched set of shoeboxes filled with unidentified pictures, but Oscar has photo albums going back to his childhood. I'll look through them tonight and see if I can find anything to shed light on this."

"Have you called Oscar and Jeffers to come home?" Posey asked. "I think Bara would like to have Oscar here right now, and I'm sure Payne and Hamilton would like to have both of them."

Ann Rose shook her head again. "I can't call them. They're busy, and it's not possible to take calls. And even if they could, Bara's in no danger, and I'm sure they would think what they are doing more important than hanging around watching her heal. So do I. They've looked forward to this trip for years, and it's not as if they could do anything here. Still, they touch base every few days. I'll tell them about it when they call."

"I don't see how you can stand having Jeffers gone so long," Posey told her.

Ann Rose's eyes twinkled. "I'll bet Katharine knows. Francie and I are enjoying having the house to ourselves. We eat in the kitchen, I go to bed when I want to and get up when I want to—two nights ago I read an entire book in bed without worrying I was keeping Jeffers up when he had to be up early for morning rounds. I've spread projects out all over the back rooms, and Francie and I have reached an agreement: I don't mess up the front of the house and she doesn't mess with my projects at the back. I'm not advocating divorce or widowhood, but it is very nice to have some time on your own."

Posey looked unconvinced.

"Shall we go see Eloise and Scotty next?" she asked Katharine as they got in the car.

"I'm done with this. It's pointless."

"Don't fuss at me," Posey protested. "This mess isn't my fault."

"It most certainly is. You were the one who told Bara I could research those medals. If I hadn't done that—by the way, have you registered for that tutor training yet?"

"Not yet. I'll get around to it."

"You'd better. You owe me big time, lady."

"I owe you? You owe me lunch at the Swan Coach House." Posey gave Katharine a defiant look, then nibbled her lower lip. "I didn't mean to let you in for all this, you know."

Katharine's anger evaporated. "I know. Things snowball. I'll tell you what. You take the tutor training, and I'll take you to lunch at the Coach House to celebrate when you're done."

When Posey got out at her front door, she asked, "Has Tom gotten back, do you think?"

"Back and gone again. He had to go up to the lake house. We've sprung a water leak."

"Does he know how to cope with a water leak?"

"He will after this weekend."

Chapter 26

Katharine was halfway up her driveway when she noticed a forest on her veranda.

"Damn!" She only swore in times of great distress, but this was such a time. She had completely forgotten that the nursery had promised to deliver five large potted plants for her house that morning. How was she ever going to get them inside?

She pulled into the garage and laid her head on her steering wheel. If she had been there when Tom arrived, they could have managed together. If Tom had noticed the plants, he could have taken them in by himself. Instead, once again she faced a problem that would require all her ingenuity to solve. Why, oh why, had she permitted Jon to head to China? Since he was twelve, he'd been her muscle man. "I need to buy me a dolly," she decided. But not that afternoon. She'd have to think of something else.

As she climbed out of the car, she saw dirt and the glint of glass on her front seat carpet. She and Payne must have tracked it from Bara's front hall. She fetched the small vacuum and cleaned it up. When she went to hang up the vacuum, she noticed Bara's envelope on her backseat. Would she be invading Bara's privacy by looking at its contents?

What the heck? Bara was invading her schedule with a vengeance, and there must be something in that envelope that Bara considered important, since she'd made Katharine drive all the way to Piedmont Hospital and begged her to get it.

She dumped it out onto her breakfast-room table to sort through the contents. The locket bounced on the countertop, then clattered onto the ceramic-tile floor. Katharine picked it up and checked to be sure it hadn't been dented. It hadn't, but it was already a battered thing, black with tarnish and ornately decorated with a raised rosebud surrounded by three leaves. It looked not so much old as old-fashioned.

She slid a fingernail inside the crack and popped the two halves open. As Payne had said, the picture inside was of Bara in her early twenties, dressed in a vintage dress from the thirties or forties. Perhaps for a party?

Whose locket had it been? Katharine couldn't imagine Nettie wearing it—or wearing Bara's picture around her neck. Not only was Nettie not the sentimental type, but the locket would have been too large and ornate for her austere taste.

Katharine flipped it over and traced script initials engraved on the back. "*A.M.*"

She had no idea who that could have been. Bara might know. If she didn't, Murdoch would be certain to.

Winnie's old driver's licenses told her nothing she didn't know except his birthday.

Katharine smiled at Bara's excellent report cards, which contained recurring teacher comments: *Bara talks too much. Bara distracts other students with her antics.* Nothing had changed on that front.

A pile of letters turned out to be all from Bara to Winnie: trivial chatter about a college girl's days. If any of them contained something pertinent to Bara's current situation, Katharine couldn't detect it. Still, she suspected that the letters and report cards were what Bara didn't want to lose.

She picked up the locket again. Had Bara mentioned the locket at any point before the hospital conversation? If so, she could not remember when.

She idly read the clippings. They were the kind you save in a private envelope if you are a modest man proud of your child, as Winnie had been. Some extolled his various activities in Atlanta, including his work on the Olympic committee, but most were about Bara—not only social pictures of various functions, but of Bara winning track meets all through high school.

Only one clipping was not about the family. Older than the rest, yellowed and faded, it pictured a middle-aged man with a drooping mustache and sad eyes. The story reported that a family in Ohio was asking for information about the whereabouts of Anton Molnar, from Velenje, Yugoslavia. A defector, he was known to have arrived in Atlanta the previous Friday for business of a personal nature, but should have reached their home by the following Tuesday. He had never shown up. Anyone having information about Mr. Molnar was asked to contact the newspaper.

Why would Winnie have kept that clipping?

That was the kind of puzzle Katharine enjoyed. As she made herself a sandwich, she wondered if anybody had ever located Mr. Molnar and where he had been found. While she ate, she read the clipping again. It gave no clue to the date of the paper, but on the back she read a paragraph about progress on the construction of "the new Lenox Square Mall."

Online, she searched for "history of Lenox Square Mall, Atlanta." She learned that the mall—at that time the largest in the Southeast—had opened in 1959. She checked her watch. The Atlanta History Center library would still be open. She checked her to-do list, decided she had nothing pressing that afternoon, and drove to the center to peruse back issues of the *Atlanta Constitution* from 1959. She'd think about what to do with the plants when she got home.

She found what she was looking for in a June edition of the paper. The article had appeared on a Friday. The following Sunday, the paper had announced that the body of an unidentified white man, discovered the prior Monday in the parking lot of O'Keefe High School, north of Georgia Tech, had been identified as Anton Molnar, defector from Yugoslavia. He had been shot through the head, apparently the victim of robbery and murder while visiting the city. An editorial deplored the fact that tourists and "those seeking freedom from oppression" were not safe while visiting Atlanta, and urged the city to become a more tourist-friendly place.

Katharine searched for Molnar's name in subsequent issues of the paper, but found nothing.

As she drove home, she wondered about his family in Yugoslavia. Had they ever learned what happened to him? Had his parents died thinking he had not cared enough to try and communicate once he reached the United States?

At home, she checked out Velenje on the Internet. It was a city located in the Alps of Slovenia, which used to be the northwest lobe of Yugoslavia. While she was online, she looked up Slovenia. A small country, not as large as the state of Georgia, it sounded like a lovely place to visit the next time Tom had to be in Eastern Europe. She bookmarked the site.

She shut off her computer with the determination that, except for featuring prominently in her prayers for the next week or so, Bara Weidenauer had consumed all the time she was likely to get.

She called Hollis. "Do you have any strong male friends who can help me get some plants inside?"

"Dalton is at my place right this minute, discussing sets for a play. Shall I bring him over?"

"If you would, I'll buy you both a pizza."

As she waited for them to come, Katharine mused that if Hollis ever moved out of town, she really would be in a pickle.

The phone rang at nine. She reached for it with reluctance. The day had begun with Posey's call about Bara. Was this someone with more bad news?

The voice on the other end was cheerful enough. "Miz Murray? This is Kenny. Kenny Todd? I'm sorry for calling so late, and I don't want to bother you or anything, but you said you'd like to hear

Mama sing? Well, I came up home this evening and learned they've got a gig Sunday morning to close out a revival. It's up in Ellijay, not far from our house, and everybody is getting together at Granddaddy's afterward for bar-be-cue. You don't have to come, of course, but Granddaddy says if you and your husband would like to join us, we'd be proud to have you."

"Tom's not here this weekend." Katharine disliked using Tom as a tactful reason to decline, but couldn't think of a better one at the moment. "He's up at our lake house, waiting on a plumber."

"You can come by yourself, if you want. We'd be glad to have you."

She opened her mouth to turn down the invitation and was surprised to find herself saying instead, "I'd enjoy that. Maybe Hollis could come instead of Tom."

"I don't know about Hollis."

Katharine was embarrassed. She wasn't in the habit of inviting people to other people's parties. "Of course not. I'll come alone."

She had misinterpreted Kenny's hesitation. "Oh, you can ask Hollis, no problem. I just don't know if she'll *want* to. I doubt if bluegrass music and bar-be-cue are much her style."

"You might be surprised. But it's all right. I'll come alone."

"Oh no, ma'am, go ahead and ask her. She can come even if your husband comes. There'll be plenty of food, and we can find her a seat. You don't know if she likes to ride horses, do you?"

"She loves to ride. Do you have a horse?"

"We got a couple. Tell her to bring riding clothes, if she comes. You, too, if you like."

"Not for me, thanks. I've never had a speaking acquaintance with horses."

Kenny laughed. "They can be right nice to talk to." His voice grew anxious again. "Tell Hollis we'd be glad to have her, but she doesn't have to come if she doesn't want to—not that she would. I'll come down and fetch you, if you like."

"Let me drive. That way you can stay later with your folks." And Katharine could leave when she wanted to.

"If you're sure you don't mind. Like I said, I'm already up home now, and I'm sure Granddaddy would like having me around here to he'p out a little. He's roasting a pig." He gave directions to the church, then advised, "I'd leave by nine. It'll take you a good hour and a half to get here, and you'll want to come a little early. The church may fill up fast."

Katharine hung up wondering what she had gotten herself into. "A country church revival," she muttered to Phebe, who was weaving in and out around her ankles. "It may not even be air conditioned. Then I have to listen to a program of heaven only knows what quality of music, and spend several more hours with people I do not know and have little or nothing in common with. Whatever possessed me?"

She mulled that over as she got ready for bed. Why had she accepted Kenny's invitation when she'd meant to decline? What had nudged her to get so involved with Bara that past week?

Like her mother, Katharine believed we are given certain people at certain times for purposes we don't fathom at the time. She had experienced how nudges and seeming coincidences could be woven together and move inexorably toward an unexpected end. Look at how she had been led from Aunt Lucy's boxes of personal junk to solve an old Atlanta murder, prove a convicted man's innocence, and expose vicious hypocrisy. Look at how she and Dr. Flo Gadney had been drawn by an isolated grave down on the coast into a web of deceit spanning several generations.

Even if Posey had been the agent who thrust Bara into Katharine's life, was Bara part of a similar pattern? Were the medals simply a means to a greater end?

She considered a series of coincidences that past week. Bara found the medals the morning before Ann Rose's meeting, which Posey attended only because Katharine needed a ride. Posey persuaded Katharine to investigate the medals. Tom brought home a bluegrass CD because he'd gone to a concert on a night when he didn't have a meeting, Katharine selected the CD at random to wash dishes by, and Bara liked it because she'd had a North Georgia nanny. Kenny came to fix the computer and "happened" to be knowledgeable about military medals. Katharine switched on the CD to calm a stormy atmosphere, and Kenny had noticed it because his mother sometimes sang bluegrass. Less than a week later, his mother "happened" to be singing to close out a revival. Were those coincidences? An archbishop of Canterbury once said, "When I pray, coincidences happen."

"I haven't been praying for anything more on my plate," Katharine protested. But was it possible that Kenny's granddaddy could shed some light on Bara's problem? He was a serious genealogist. Did he know how to track a biological father? Maybe Sunday would help to end Bara's quest.

Or not.

Maybe Sunday had nothing to do with Bara. Maybe Katharine had made a stupid remark over supper on Tuesday and would spend Sunday paying for it.

"I have no clue why I'm going," she told Phebe as she lifted the little cat into her lap. "Maybe I need a break. But what does one wear to church when there's a barbecue at Granddaddy's to follow?"

She punched in Hollis's number. Hollis would still be up, and Hollis would know.

To her utter surprise—and contrary to Kenny's prediction—Hollis accepted the invitation. "I want to see what kind of house he lives in. If it's not an ordinary house near a town, I'll buy you dinner."

She had one question when she heard about the horses. "Western or English saddles?"

"I have no idea. You'll probably be trotting around a pasture, so what difference does it make?"

"I'll wear jeans. But they'd better not be broken-down nags usually used to plow a field."

Even with Hollis's reservations, Katharine would be glad to have her company, whether Tom got home in time to go or not. Hollis would be a lot more fun to talk with about the event afterward. "What do you think we ought to wear?"

"You wear black slacks and a white cotton top with that stunning turquoise necklace Uncle Tom brought back from Arizona last month. And take your embroidered cotton jacket for church and in case the afternoon is cool."

"Nothing is cool right now," Katharine reminded her. "The whole country is having a heat wave." But the jacket was a good idea. It would dress up the slacks for church but wasn't too dressy if the rest of the women were in polyester dresses. She'd stick a scarf in her purse in case the necklace was too dressy for the barbecue. Maybe the day would be fun. At least she wouldn't be sitting home alone if Tom stayed at the lake.

Chapter 27

Saturday

He did.

He called Saturday morning to report, "The plumber got here, but when he dug out that leaking pipe, it was so old that part of it crumbled in his hand. He says he's going to have to replace the entire system from the road to the house and may have to replace some of the pipes inside. It sounds like a long, drawn-out process to me."

Tom, who could negotiate with a roomful of senators and get them to agree, sounded baffled. He had never in their married life had to cope with a plumbing crisis. They had all happened while he was out of town.

Katharine was about to sympathize when he added, "I'm thinking I'll tell him to leave it for now. We can call him in a week or two, when the party is over. Then I can come on home now."

If he left the lake house now, Katharine would have to deal with the plumbing crisis later.

"Don't let him leave," she told him. "If you do, we'll have a dickens of a time getting him back. Ask exactly how long he thinks the whole job will take."

Tom spoke to someone nearby, then came back to the phone. "He says at least until Monday evening."

"Then stay up there and see it through. You have stuff to read, don't you?"

"I have plenty of books, but you're having to deal with all the party stuff."

On a scale of things she didn't want to deal with, plumbing ranked far above the party.

"The party is under control. Go ahead and get the plumbing fixed while the man is there."

"I could come on home and tell him to do the work and bill us."

"Heavens, no. Things crop up in plumbing you don't expect. You have to be available to make decisions. Otherwise, he'll stop when he gets to a new problem and leave with the job half-finished. We might never see him again. Or he'll do stuff we didn't want or need. Tell him you can only stay until Monday night, so he needs to be done by then."

"I think you ought to come up here. You know how to handle these things."

He probably meant it as a compliment. Three months earlier, Katharine would have canceled her plans with Kenny, driven to the mountains, and dealt with the plumbing problem. Taking care of people was what she did. On her forty-sixth birthday, when she'd realized her children were all through college, her elderly relatives were all dead, and nobody really needed her, she'd had a few moments of panic. What would she do with the rest of her life?

Since then, however, she had discovered it had never been her life; it had been somebody else's. She didn't regret a moment she had spent caring for people, but this was the season for her to find out who she was and was meant to be, and it was past time for her husband and children to learn to care for themselves.

"No." She firmly pushed down tendrils of guilt sprouting around the edges of her resolve. "I've made plans for tomorrow and have things I need to do down here today."

"But you know how to talk to these people better than I do. You've got more experience." That was the closest Tom Murray—competent, capable Tom Murray—would ever come to a whine.

She took a deep, steadying breath. "Consider it a learning curve." That's what he said when she faced some new challenge while he was away. "I've already mastered learning curves for dealing with repair people, caring for children, caring for the elderly, and coping with break-ins and vandalism. It's time you mastered some of them, too."

Silence.

" I don't want you so helpless that you have to stop off on your way home from my funeral to get yourself another wife." She hoped to make him laugh.

Silence.

"Tom, it's your house as much as mine. Deal with it."

He sighed. "Okay. Can I call you if I run into something I can't answer?"

"Of course. And honey? I love you."

He sighed. "Love you, too, but I gotta go. The man is waiting for my answer."

Katharine sank into the nearest chair and pumped air with one fist. She was as worn out as if she had run a marathon or swum a mile, but she had won. She had won!

Payne called at noon. "Mama is feeling better today, and really wants to see that envelope. Do you think you could bring it over?"

Katharine felt she ought to take something to Kenny's family on Sunday, and decided on a plant. On her way to the florist's, she could drop the envelope by the hospital.

Instead, in the waiting room Payne suggested, "Why don't you visit her this hour instead of me? I'll run down and get something to eat."

Katharine nodded briefly to the officer at Bara's door and wondered if the nurses were used to him by now. Probably so. Human beings can get accustomed to the most outrageous things.

Bara looked worse than the day before. Her bruises had turned yellow and purple with green edges. She wore a bandage on her head, had a cast on her left wrist, and her right leg was in traction. Her mind was clear, however, and she was feeling garrulous.

"I'm not at my best," she greeted Katharine in a murmur. "Half my bones are broken and my face is a mess."

"It really is." Katharine saw no reason for subterfuge. The woman had a mirror in her bed table. She laid the envelope on the covers. "I brought your envelope and the locket."

"Would you take out the locket and try to open it? I'm a little handicapped here." Bara gestured to her arm cast.

Katharine opened it with a fingernail and held it where Bara could see it. "It doesn't have anything in it except your picture." Or did it? She hadn't pried out the picture to see if anything was behind it.

Bara peered through bleary eyes. "That's not me. I never wore my hair like that. It must be my grandmother Payne. She had dark eyes like mine." She again peered at the picture. "You think I look like her?"

"Very much."

Bara grabbed the locket and clasped it in one fist. Tears squeezed between her lids. "I miss her so much. She was a wonderful grandmother. I used to go over to her house when I was small and we'd make biscuits. We'd roll them out, then she'd let me cut them out with a bottle top. They made the cutest little biscuits you ever saw." She dropped the locket back into the envelope. "You'll need to take all this back with you. I don't have space to keep anything here. I'll get it later."

"Why don't I leave them with Payne?"

Bara echoed what Payne had said the day before. "She has enough on her mind right now. She might lose it. Besides," —Bara's face lit with a flicker of a grin that made her look more like her old self— "my old report cards are in there. No point giving her more ammunition against me than she's already got. Would you hand me my water?" She motioned toward a big cup on her nightstand. "They keep putting it where I can't reach it." When she had slaked her thirst, she confided, "I'm in a bigger mess than I look. Have you heard they think I shot Foley?"

"I heard." Katharine kept her voice noncommittal.

"The disgusting thing is, I can't remember. Doesn't that take the cake? I may have killed the bum and can't remember doing it. Can't remember a thing after I came home Thursday afternoon. I remember going to the storage unit to look for something—I don't know what it was—and I remember driving home and cooking supper. I made a pork chop and a cantaloupe." She said it as proudly as if she had prepared a six-course meal. "The cantaloupe was rotten though. The middle was all full of slimy stuff and seeds."

"They all have that in them. You have to scrape it out."

"Really? That's what I did." Bara's husky laugh rang through the unit. A curious nurse looked their way and smiled. "I must be a better cook than I thought. I thought it was rotten, but I ate it anyway and it tasted great. The pork chop was a bit dry, though. What do you do to make them moist?"

"Get well and come over to my house, and I'll show you." Katharine couldn't believe she had said that. Was she offering to teach Bara Weidenauer to cook?

"Okay, but I'm gonna be out of commission for a while. After here, I have to go to rehab. Not rehab like drunks go to," she added quickly, "but the kind where they make you walk on a track and swim and stuff."

"You'll be home before you know it." Katharine was trying to cheer her up, but Bara looked gloomier.

"If they convict me of killing Foley, I may go to jail. Wouldn't it be the funniest thing you ever heard if I have to go to jail for killing the louse when I can't remember doing it?"

"Surely they have other suspects."

"Not that I've heard. I had a detective in here all morning asking questions like 'Who else besides you has been in the dining room recently?' I told him the whole world may have keys to my front door, but the only people I can remember are Foley, Scotty, Murdoch, and Carlene, Foley's bimbo. She was in the house when I got home Wednesday, and so were Scotty and Murdoch. Carlene was stealing my jewelry upstairs, Murdoch was checking that I hadn't hocked the Dolley Madison tea set, and Scotty was wanting part of his fee for doing nothing about my divorce. He suggested I sell the tea set and pretend it had gotten stolen—even offered to find me a buyer on the QT—but he's out of the running for suspect. He was playing poker Thursday night like he always does, and Murdoch was on her way to Boston." Bara gave a wry smile. "Looks like the only real suspects are me and

Foley, but nobody thinks he killed himself, even me. Besides, he was shot with my gun, which I admit leaving on the dining-room table. I don't remember shooting him, though, even if the detective does think I'm faking."

Katharine picked up what sounded like the weakest link in that chain of evidence. "Why would you have left the gun lying around on the table?"

Bara shrugged. "I didn't know what else to do with it at the time."

Katharine thought that over. Things did look black for Bara.

Bara broke the silence and echoed her thoughts. "It doesn't look real good, does it? I was the only one with a motive to murder Foley, my prints are on the gun, no stranger had been in the house, and I've even admitted it was my gun. Winnie gave it to me back when I was in college."

"What does your lawyer say?"

Bara gave a short, blunt laugh. "I can't afford a lawyer. Until this mess is cleared up, I still can't get to my bank accounts. Hamilton wanted to hire one and pay for it himself, but I told him no way. I am not going to be beholden to my kids. One good bit of news, though. Mason Benefield was in this morning. He was representing Foley in the divorce, but now that Foley's dead, he's slinking back with his tail between his legs, wanting to be my friend again. He said he's uncovered evidence that Foley was squirreling money away in offshore accounts. If I manage to stay out of jail, I may inherit all of that as Foley's next of kin. How about them apples?" She leaned against her pillow with a smug smile. "Foley tries to do me out of everything I have, and instead winds up murdered and making me richer. There is a God."

"There is a God, but I don't think he's in the business of murder to make folks richer," Katharine cautioned.

"Justice," Bara murmured, her voice growing weaker. "In the business of justice. Speaking of justice, do you think they've got enough to convict me?"

"I have no idea." But Katharine had to admit, the case looked grim. Like Bara said, there wasn't another suspect.

"If I don't go to jail, I'm not going back to that house." Bara's voice was drowsy, as if medication was taking effect. "It was never a happy house. I'm gonna sell it and get something smaller. Something like yours, maybe."

Katharine managed not to wince. Bara hadn't meant it for an insult. After living in her mansion, six bedrooms *would* be "something smaller."

"Or a condo," Bara mused. "Like Winnie—"

She broke off abruptly to stare out the window at the Atlanta skyline. "Winnie wasn't my daddy. Did I tell you that, before I" —she struggled to find the right words— "came here?" Her voice was growing weaker with every word.

"You told me." Katharine reached out and smoothed a wrinkle in her blanket. "But you know, a daddy isn't simply the man who helps create you. A daddy is somebody who is there for you all your life. I think Winnie was definitely your daddy."

Bara grabbed her hand and held it. "He loved me. I know he loved me." Her face begged for comfort.

"Everybody knew he loved you. You were the pride of his life." Katharine held out the envelope. "This is full of clippings about you."

Bara took a deep breath and roused a bit. "No matter who Nettie slept with, Winnie loved me. He was my *daddy*."

"He sure was."

Katharine was ready to leave, but Bara still held her hand. "I don't think I shot Foley," she said with a frown. "I think I would remember that, don't you?" She looked away, toward the window, and muttered under her breath, "I sure as hell remember killing Winnie."

Katharine was startled. Had the policeman outside the door heard? If so, he gave no sign.

Before she could think of a reply, Bara was saying, "Oh! I remember Foley hitting me, too! He punched me in the stomach." Her lips twisted in a wry grin.

"I spewed all over him. I'd just eaten supper. Served him right." She removed her hand from Katharine's and gingerly touched her ribs. "He musta busted something. It's funny, but I don't think he hit me in the ribs and I know he didn't hit me this hard." Her hand swept from her head toward her toes sticking out from the cast.

"Do you remember anything else?"

"He went down to the basement. I remember that. I yelled at him, and locked the door. That's the last thing I remember. I lost a whole day. Have you ever lost a day of your life, Katharine?" Her voice was scarcely audible. "As old as I am, I can't afford to go around losing days. If I did, the day I killed Foley isn't one I'd want to lose. I'd want to remember that."

A nurse stepped in. "There's someone else to see you, Mrs. Weidenauer. A woman named Maria Ortiz. Do you feel up to another quick visit?" She slewed her eyes toward Katharine on the last two words and Katharine knew her time was up.

"Maria." Bara lingered on the word like it was chocolate. "I wonder how she knew I was here. Let her come in."

The nurse headed to the waiting room and Katharine said her goodbyes. On her way out she passed a short, stocky woman with a swarthy complexion, black hair grizzled with gray, and a bright green shirt. The woman didn't notice her. She was trotting toward Bara's cubicle like a horse heading to the barn. "*¡Querida!*" Katharine heard her cry out.

Payne sat in the waiting room with Scotty beside her. Legs stretched out before him, he was snoozing. Payne wore a puzzled expression. "Did you meet somebody named Maria in Mama's room?" she asked Katharine.

"No, but I think we passed on my way out."

"I wonder who she is. She showed up here a few minutes ago and insisted she had to see my mother. I told her I'd ask the nurse, thinking they'd say no, but the nurse said Mama wanted to see her."

"Bara sounded delighted she had come."

Payne shrugged. "Maybe she's one of the maids Foley fired. Mama used to know the names of all their kids and husbands, and used to sit in the kitchen with them drinking coffee and talking all morning sometimes. It drove Foley crazy."

"She seemed better today, I thought."

"A little better. They were able to set her leg and her wrist. They don't set ribs or collarbones. She's still in pain, but she's more coherent than she was."

Their voices roused Scotty. He blinked and struggled to his feet in a half-awake show of manners. "Good to see you, Katharine. Good of you to come."

He rubbed his florid face to get the sleep out of his eyes, then stuck out his hand. His palm was hot, damp, and revolting. "I must have been dozing. Seem to be doing a lot of that lately. Fell asleep on the couch last evening and almost missed my weekly poker game. Didn't get there until nearly ten. Isn't this some to-do?" He seemed oblivious that his booming voice might be disturbing other families. "Who could have done such a terrible thing to our Bara?"

Katharine had never liked Scotty, but she pitied him. What she pitied was his inability to live up to the illustrious Atlanta reputation his family had achieved in nearly two centuries. In another pond, among other frogs, Scotty might have been modestly successful at a number of things. In Buckhead he was the incompetent who had failed to live up to his family. What Katharine disliked was his façade of bonhomie and success that forced others to pretend along with him. She and Tom sometimes wondered how Scotty paid Buckhead taxes and kept up his membership in the Ansley Park Golf Club.

"Do the police have any more ideas who it could have been?" she asked Payne.

Scotty answered. "Not a clue. I don't know what we pay them for. By now they should have had those fellas by the scruff of the neck."

"What fellows?" Again Katharine addressed Payne, and again, Scotty answered.

"Those ruffians who broke in there, robbed the place, and did this to Bara."

Katharine persisted in trying to talk to Payne. "Bara said they still think she shot Foley."

"Fools!" The words burst from Scotty like a minor explosion. "They think he beat her and she shot him. I keep telling them she doesn't know a thing about guns, but they say her prints were on it. Any fool who watches television knows you can put somebody's prints on a gun and make it look like they shot it."

Katharine wondered if it was really that simple. Wouldn't it be hard to get somebody else's hand to hold the gun in the right position without smudging the prints or getting your own on the gun as well?

"I don't think they're as sure about Mama as they were." Payne seized the crack in her great-uncle's tirade and slid softly into the conversation. "Not since they've learned about the missing silver and painting."

"Including a tea set that has been in our family for two hundred years," Scotty said in a blend of boast and chagrin. "Should have been mine. I was older than Nettie." He didn't actually say, "Then it wouldn't have gotten stolen," but the implication was clear.

"Grandmother Payne left it directly to Mama," Payne told him sharply, "and told her to leave it to her oldest daughter. Besides, the tea service wasn't the only thing stolen. They took several trays, a vase, a pitcher, a set of candelabra, the Monet from the hall, and the Louis Tiffany lamp by the window. Anything that was easy to grab in the dining room. They also knocked over a plant and shattered that crystal heron in the front hall."

Scotty shoved one hand through his gray curls. "Murdoch is gonna kill me when she finds out about that tea set. She must have told me fifty times before she left town to call Bara and make her take it to the bank for safekeeping. It was the last thing she said as she climbed in the cab to the airport, and she even called from Boston last night—in the middle of the best hand I had all evening—to see if I'd talked to Bara." He rubbed his face. "I meant to, I just hadn't gotten around to it." He gave a blunt, not-funny laugh. "All Murdoch was worried about was that Foley might get his hands on that tea service. She never imagined it would get stolen. She is flat-out gonna kill us all."

Katharine felt there were more serious issues at stake than Murdoch's wrath.

"Do the police actually know anything more than they did yesterday?" she asked.

Payne shook her head. "Not much. I told them they ought to check out the woman Foley was seeing, but I don't know her name. Mama would never share something like that with me. Do you know who she was, Uncle Scotty?"

Scotty didn't seem to have been listening. "Who?"

"The woman Foley was seeing. Do you know her name?"

"With a figure like that, who needs a name?" Then he caught the look Payne and Katharine exchanged and muttered, "Carmen or something like that. I don't know her last name."

"That reminds me," Katharine told Payne. "Your mother had rented a storage shed for your grandfather's things from his condo and office. You might ask her about it and go over to check it out, to make sure somebody didn't steal the key and raid the unit, as well."

"I will." Payne blinked and suddenly looked very young. "There's so much to deal with."

"I know." Katharine almost added, "If there's anything I can do—" but for once she swallowed twenty years of training at her mother's knee. It nearly choked her.

Scotty checked his watch. "I'd better be going." He added, to Katharine, "Shall I walk you to your car? I just came to hang out with Payne and keep her company."

Remembering how she had found him, Katharine had trouble keeping a straight face. When she caught

Payne's eye, Payne turned away and gave a cough that sounded suspiciously like a cover-up for a snort.

In the parking lot, Scotty stopped by a silver Mercedes convertible parked in a handicapped space.

Katharine gave him a swift, appraising look. "I didn't realize you had a health problem."

"I don't. I got the tag for Eloise, but since she doesn't need it any longer . . ." He let the sentence trail off, obviously expecting Katharine to concur that it would be a shame to let the tag go to waste.

She frowned at him. "I drove my mother and two aunts for years, and they badly needed those handicapped spaces." When he didn't reply, she added, "Be careful. If God sees you, you may wind up needing one." To take the sting out, she added, "How *is* Eloise?"

He unlocked his door like a man who didn't want to stick around if he wasn't being admired. "About the same. Good days and bad days. Today is a bad day. I haven't told her about Bara, so don't tell her if you go over."

Katharine had never visited Eloise Holcomb. She scarcely knew the woman. That made it real easy to promise, "I won't say a word."

Chapter 28

Sunday

When Katharine and Hollis got to the mountain church on Sunday morning, they found not a small white-frame building out in the country with a cemetery beside it, but a large, corrugated-steel building with a brick front and a huge parking lot full of cars. The people heading toward the doors in a steady stream were dressed not in what Katharine thought of as Sunday clothes but in jeans and running shoes. The teens wore shorts. Neither men nor women wore jackets. Hoping the building would not be overly air conditioned, Katharine left hers in the car.

She saw Kenny before he saw them. Standing on the top step, he was more formally dressed than the other men, wearing a blue oxford-cloth shirt the same color as his eyes and khaki slacks with a sharp crease. He peered around the crowd with a look both nervous and hopeful. When he glimpsed them, his face lit for a second, then went completely rigid. Katharine wondered if she had imagined that lightning second of joy.

"I'm glad you could come," he greeted them formally. "Granddaddy is saving us seats up front." He was wearing a spicy aftershave. Katharine had no doubts about which of them he had dressed up for when his glance darted to Hollis before he said to her aunt, "You look real nice."

Hollis did look prettier than usual. She had put on a pale yellow cotton top instead of her standard black, and wore simple hoops instead of the dangling earrings she usually favored.

The sanctuary was enormous, with a soaring ceiling, chairs instead of pews, and huge colorful banners in lieu of windows. It seethed with people greeting one another, hugging, kissing, and talking at a pitch that seemed likely to raise the roof. Kenny led them down to the third row from the front, where his grandfather, Lamar Franklin, had saved three seats by putting shiny black loafers on two and his wallet on the third. He stood in sock feet and stuck out a calloused hand.

"Hey, Miz Murray. I'm real glad you all could come today."

He sounded like they were old friends, although Katharine had only met him three times before: twice at the Atlanta History Center and once when he'd dropped a book by her house and stayed for cookies and tea with Katharine and a friend. He had been very helpful with two genealogy searches she had done, though, and she had discovered she liked the old coot.

He had spruced up for church. His gray ponytail lay in a freshly washed ringlet down his back, and not only had he worn the polished loafers instead of scuffed work boots, he had managed to clean all the roofing tar from the creases of his hands. As usual he wore black jeans and a black T-shirt, but Katharine supposed this was his Sunday shirt, for the message across his chest admonished, A CLEAR CONSCIENCE IS USUALLY THE SIGN OF A POOR MEMORY.

He gave Hollis a penetrating look. "You must be Hollis. I'm Lamar Franklin, Kenny's grandpa. You doing all right?" His voice was full of concern.

"I'm doing fine." Hollis shot Kenny a look Katharine was glad she could not read. Kenny turned bright pink and bent to collect his grandfather's possessions from the chair. Lamar slipped his feet into his loafers and motioned Katharine toward the chair on his right. "Let's all sit down. They're gonna be starting in a minute." Sure enough, the melee was beginning to organize itself as people filed into rows and others climbed onto what looked like a stage.

Accustomed to a hushed sanctuary with a pulpit, a communion table, and a choir loft up front, Katharine was bewildered by several mikes, kitchen stools, a proliferation of power cords, and some initial confusion as ten musicians connected with six electric guitars, two keyboards, a basket of percussion instruments, and a drum set. A miked voice boomed over the crowd. "Welcome, y'all. Are you ready to worship God?" She had to look closely at the musicians to see that it was the man with the black electric guitar speaking.

"Yeah!" voices roared back.

He struck a chord, the drummer rattled the snares, and the whole crowd rushed to its feet. Katharine wondered why they had bothered to sit.

She found the music jarring—too loud and too repetitive, more like a pep rally than a worship service. Unable to think, much less worship, in all that noise, she considered the three women musicians and decided Kenny's mother must be the tambourine player, the one with flowing brown hair, full breasts under a skin-tight red top, and a fixed look of ecstasy on her face. She didn't look at all like Kenny, but the blond at one keyboard and the redhead on drums were far too young.

No wonder Kenny was embarrassed by her singing. She tended to bawl the words out with an abandon Katharine found embarrassing, too. She looked at Hollis to see how she was reacting, but Hollis had her eyes closed and was swaying with the music, apparently caught up in the celebration. Beyond her, Kenny had his head bowed and eyes closed, but he wasn't singing.

Katharine endured.

After a while, Lamar Franklin leaned over to ask, "Would you like to sit down? My legs get tired about now." He sank to his chair and she gratefully followed suit. She checked her watch. They had been standing for fifteen minutes. Nobody under forty seemed to mind.

He leaned close again. "Hang in there. It gets better in a minute. This is for the young folks."

"I don't think I was ever that young when I *was* that young," Katharine told him. He grinned and nodded.

As he had promised, the worship leader gradually led the congregation from their boisterous beginning into softer, gentler songs. Now that she could hear the music, she learned that Lamar had a surprisingly sweet tenor. Kenny finally joined in, too, but he seemed on a dedicated journey to find the right note in the right key.

Again Lamar leaned close. "The kid can do a lot of things, but sing isn't one of them. The best to be said is that he makes a joyful noise."

When the music ended, Hollis dropped into the chair beside her with her face shining. Kenny gave her a quick, puzzled look, but seemed to like what he saw. When she glanced his way, though, he looked away.

The keyboard played softly and the congregation sat in prayerful silence while the musicians quietly removed everything except five mikes, four stools, and one keyboard from the stage. When they had finished, a man in a bright green shirt and tan slacks came to the central mike, and what Katharine thought of as God's pep rally resumed.

With a broad smile, he raised both hands into the air and shouted, "We've had a great week of services, haven't we?"

The crowd broke into applause.

"We've discovered that the Christian faith is not something you believe, it's something you do!"

"Yeah!"

"It's not something to ram down people's throats. It's got to be contagious or it's nothing at all."

"Yeah!"

His voice grew quieter. "We've learned that God blesses us not by giving us stuff, making us better or richer than other people, or taking away all our troubles. God blesses us by walking with us through the troubles of life, and uses the way we walk through those troubles to show other folks what this faith is all about. Is that right?"

"That's right," the congregation called back softly.

"Well, nothing lives and grows without being fed, so we're gonna wrap up this week with a time of feeding our spirits. Sit back, close your eyes, and let God speak to you through Mama and the Aunts!"

Katharine and Hollis stared at each other in delight. But then Katharine noticed Kenny. He sat hunched in his seat, looking at the floor and rubbing his palms together as if he were trying to light a fire.

As the room burst into applause, Hollis hissed fiercely, "Your mother is one of *them*?"

He nodded as if confessing to a crime.

"Why didn't you tell us?"

Kenny shrugged.

"You said they were 'just okay.'"

He hunched deeper, as pink as a baby's bottom. "I didn't know what else to say."

Lamar leaned over and told Hollis, "It embarrasses him to death when his mama sings in public. He's always been that way."

Katharine studied the five women coming onstage. Two carried guitars, one a mandolin. One seated herself behind a plucked dulcimer and another took her place at the keyboard. They all had masses of blond curls and wore denim outfits with cowgirl boots. They were gorgeous and obviously professional.

Katharine leaned over and whispered, "None of them looks old enough to be your mother." She meant it for a compliment, but Kenny looked even more miserable.

Then the dulcimer struck the first simple chord and she forgot Kenny.

The women made the music seem effortless, yet the harmonies were intricate and the arrangements complicated. For the next hour Katharine gave herself up to what was not only one of the most professional musical performances she'd ever attended, but one of the deepest worship experiences. At the end, she felt as refreshed as if she'd stood under a cool waterfall on a hot summer day.

When the music ended and the preacher climbed back on the stage, Lamar said, "I'm gonna duck out. I need to get things ready up home."

"Do you want any help?"

"No, the fellas have been cooking while we were here. They've probably got most of it under control. See you in a little while." He stood and worked his way down the aisle, shaking hands and accepting hugs all the way.

"**You'd better** follow me," Kenny said after the service. "It's kinda hard to tell folks how to get there." He had avoided discussing his mother and her sisters after the service, replying to their questions with, "We can talk about that later. We ought to be getting up to Granddaddy's now, ahead of the crowd."

As Katharine followed his Mustang, she saw why he wanted to lead them in. They wound their way onto progressively smaller roads and eventually turned onto a gravel road marked only by six mailboxes perched on one long board. That road wandered up a mountain around several hairpin bends. Not a single house was visible in the hardwood forest on each side.

At the top of the ridge she had to slow to a creep, because she could not see where the road went after the crest of the hill. It could end in a sheer drop, for all she could tell.

"He could be taking us back in these hills to murder us," Hollis warned.

Katharine braked to descend the mountain. "I hope there's a place to turn around at the end. There's no way I'm backing out." Fortunately, Kenny had slowed ahead to wait for her.

Around the next bend, Hollis gasped in surprise. Katharine took her eyes off the road now and then to look down into a small horseshoe cove with a stream running through it and what looked like a sampling of houses from a builders' convention scattered along the stream. One was large and brick, the kind you saw on expensive lots in any American suburb—except this one had enough acreage around it to make it look grand rather than cramped. One was white and square like a cotton plantation home, with fat columns holding up the porch roof in front. A third was contemporary, lots of glass and a cantilevered deck overlooking the hills. One was a sprawling white farmhouse with wide porches and a red barn behind it. In a pasture at the back, three sleek horses grazed. The fifth house was built of Georgia granite but resembled a Tuscan villa, complete with grapevines rising on terraced land above it and a small orchard of young apple trees to one side.

At the head of the cove stood a small weathered farmhouse that had never seen a coat of paint. A waterfall fell from a cliff at its back and made a rainbow over its rusty tin roof. Two chimneys peeked through trees that towered over the house and shaded its broad front porch. Rockers filled the porch. Long tables covered in white marched across the front lawn and a cloud of smoke rose from the side yard. Katharine rolled down her window. They could smell roasting meat over the scent of dust from the road. She had the feeling she'd like to pull up one of those rockers and stay forever.

"I don't see an ordinary brick house on a street in town," she told Hollis.

Hollis didn't say a word. She wore the balky look of somebody who knew she ought to apologize but was determined to resist as long as possible.

Katharine rubbed salt in the wound. "Those look like pretty nice horses, too."

"Don't you say a word about what I said," Hollis warned.

"I won't if you'll treat Kenny nice, just for today."

"Just for today." Hollis looked away, but Katharine was certain she had seen a smile.

Kenny pulled into the circular drive in front of the Tara look-alike. Two red-and-white spaniels bounded out to meet the car. Three cats sunned on the front steps. Kenny bent to stroke the cats and fondle the dogs' ears before he addressed Katharine.

"Mama said to bring you to her house in case you'd like to freshen up. Granddaddy's facilities are a bit primitive." He still seemed embarrassed as he led the way to the porch and into a large front hall. "You can use the front bedroom and bathroom upstairs, if you'd like."

Hollis took one look at the rug in the vast front hall and turned deep rose. It was an Aubusson at least as old as the one on Katharine's dining-room floor.

The entire house was furnished in antiques. Hollis lightly fingered a tapestry hanging in the stairwell, and in the upstairs bedroom she looked in awe at the canopy over the mahogany bed. "That has to be two hundred years old! Isn't it fantastic?"

It was, but Katharine agreed with Kenny's remark the first evening he'd come to her house: The house was more like a museum than a home. Where did the family kick off their shoes and relax?

When she and Hollis went back downstairs, they found Kenny sitting on the porch steps holding a knotted cloth while one of the dogs playfully tried to take it away. "Grrr!" Kenny growled. "Grrr!"

"You make a good dog," Hollis informed him.

He grinned. "I ought to. I grew up with dogs instead of children—except for Wanda, and she didn't count."

Katharine indicated the other houses. "Are these all your relatives?"

"Yep. Vik and Janie have the rock house—he grows grapes and hopes to grow apples one of these days."

"I thought you said he was a mechanic," said Hollis.

"Whaddya know? You *were* paying attention. He's a mechanic by profession, but he grows grapes as a hobby. He and Beau share the orchard." He pointed to the farmhouse. "Flossie and Beau live there. It's their horses we'll be riding. Did you bring some other clothes?" He eyed her slacks dubiously.

"Jeans. They're in the car."

"You might want to put them on."

"Are you sure you ought to ride?" Katharine asked, suddenly anxious. She didn't want Hollis pulling something loose from her healing wound. "I mean, if you have to jerk the reins or something . . ."

Hollis gave her a look of disdain. "You control the horse with your legs, not your arms. I'll need a mounting block or something to get up, but I'll be fine after that." She looked down at Kenny's church clothes. "Are you planning to ride in that?"

"No, my stuff is down at Granddaddy's. I'll change when we get there."

While Hollis fetched her duffle bag from the car, Kenny continued his verbal tour of the cove. "The modern place across the stream belongs to Wanda and Floyd. Bessie and Buddy are next door in the brick place and Granddaddy's down at the end. Most of the uncles work with Granddaddy, so they built the houses together."

"Where did you live before here?" Hollis asked as she came up the porch steps.

Kenny either wasn't listening or pretended not to hear. Katharine suspected it was the latter, from the way he flushed as he peered at a couple of cars cresting the rise into the valley. "Hurry and get dressed. We ought to be getting on over to Granddaddy's. Looks like everybody's finally here."

Chapter 29

Katharine presumed lunch would be Kenny's family, herself, and Hollis. Instead, before the musicians arrived, dozens of other people showed up bearing potato salad, congealed salads, slaw, casseroles, baked beans, Brunswick stew, and a variety of home-made cakes and pies.

While Kenny went to change, Lamar took Katharine and Hollis around the group, introducing them as "Miz Murray, another genealogist, and her niece, Hollis, Kenny's friend."

"I am not Kenny's friend," Hollis whispered fiercely to Katharine.

"It's okay. I'm not a genealogist, either," Katharine whispered back.

"You're more of a genealogist than I am Kenny's friend."

But when Kenny appeared in jeans and a T-shirt, Hollis abandoned his grandfather and went to help him put ice in tall cups for soft drinks and tea.

Katharine noticed at least fifteen cats of varying ages and sizes weaving in and out among the guests, and remembered Kenny's comment about having a few up in the barn.

She also saw the plaque Kenny had mentioned:

> WARNING! EXPLOSIVES! IN CASE OF FIRE,
> THIS PROPERTY WILL NOT BE PROTECTED
> BY THE FIRE DEPARTMENT.
> THE FIRE MARSHALL

Knowing Lamar, she didn't know if it was official or a joke.

"Oh, it's real, all right," he told her. "I got a basement full of old cannonballs and ammunition from the War of Secession that we've dug up at various building sites over the years, and the fire department says they can't endanger their fire fighters. I figure we're so far from the station, we'd burn down before they got here, anyway, so I don't let that keep me awake at night." Lamar put a hand at Katharine's back and steered her toward the smoking pit. "These no-good ugly men standing around doing nothing are my daughters' husbands."

The men had lifted the pig and were carving it onto huge platters with sweat streaming down their heat-reddened faces. Each man wore a bright T-shirt with a message across the front.

"I dressed them up for the occasion," Lamar boasted. He clapped the nearest man on the shoulder. "This here's Buddy. He's married to Bessie, and he's both an electrician and an army-trained demolition expert. His shirt is no joke."

Buddy was tall, broad, balding, and nearly forty. His blue shirt read, I AM A BOMB TECHNICIAN. IF YOU SEE ME RUNNING, TRY TO KEEP UP.

Lamar moved on to a man up to his elbows in greasy pig. He looked almost as young as Kenny. He was handsome in an Elvis sort of way, with lean muscles and a black curl falling over his forehead. "This is Floyd, married to Wanda, my youngest. He's a pretty good carpenter when he keeps his mind off NASCAR races." Yellow letters on Floyd's green shirt warned, IF EVERYTHING IS COMING YOUR WAY, YOU ARE IN THE WRONG LANE.

A man in a purple shirt held up greasy hands. "Sorry I can't shake right now. I'm Jake, Kenny's daddy. He thinks a heap of your son." His shirt read, KEEP STARING. I MIGHT DO A TRICK.

"Jake's got the same sense of humor as Pop, here," Floyd told her with a snicker.

The next man had a shock of white hair. His muscles looked hard, his hands calloused. He wore a red

T-shirt that announced, I USED TO HAVE AN OPEN MIND, BUT MY BRAINS KEPT FALLING OUT, and he was shadowed by a miniature of himself who looked about five.

He grinned. "Hey, Katharine. Beau Wendell. Long time no see."

Katharine barely managed not to gasp. She and Tom had known Beau years before. A banker, he and his wife moved in the Murrays' extended social circle and attended their church. Their daughter had gone to preschool with Susan. Katharine had lost touch with them years before, but she was darned sure that the wife she had known wasn't one of Lamar Franklin's singing daughters.

"Good to see you again," she murmured. "Is this your grandson?" His daughter must have married young.

Floyd snickered again.

"No, this is my son, Joe."

Katharine's face flamed, but it had been an honest mistake. Beau was older than Tom—probably no more than ten years younger than Lamar. To hide her chagrin, she bent down to extend a hand to the child. "Hello, Joe. Good to meet you."

"You're a purty lady," he said in a broad North Georgia accent.

As she bid the men goodbye and moved on with Lamar, she couldn't help wondering: would Tom leave her one day, marry again, and have more children? She repressed a shudder.

Two hours later Katharine sat on a rocker on Lamar's wide front porch wishing Tom were there. The food and the company were gone. Hollis and Kenny had finished eating and ridden up the side of the mountain. The family was busy putting away food and dousing the fire, but they had refused her offers of help. They treated her like a special guest, but she felt very much the outsider. The only living creature paying her any attention was a black cat that had claimed her lap and was making the hot day even hotter.

She was still having trouble telling Kenny's aunts apart, for they had come home and changed their costumes for ordinary clothes. Kenny's mother wore a flowing, flowery dress. Wanda, the youngest, was in short cut-offs and flip-flops and looked as young as Hollis. Katharine thought it was Flossie who was pregnant, but she couldn't remember who Flossie was married to. And was it Bessie or Janie in the denim jumper directing the others as they carried in leftovers? Whichever she was, in bare feet and with her hair pulled back with a scrunchy, she didn't look like anybody who would have sung for a president.

"That's Janie." Lamar ended Katharine's quandary as he took the rocker at her side and bent to pick up a gray tabby. "She's the one in charge of the kitchen. You having trouble keeping the girls and their husbands straight?"

"A bit," Katharine confessed.

He chuckled. "They're like those logic puzzles Kenny used to bring home from school. The folks in the brick house do not grow grapes. The ones in the modern house do not have a child. The one who plays drums lives in the farmhouse. I made a little chart to help you sort us out." He handed Katharine a sheet of paper.

Katharine scanned the table and grinned. At the top, Lamar had written, *Smartest and handsomest, Lamar Franklin. His daughters and their worthless husbands:*

Name	Lives in . . .	Plays . . .	Husband	His job . . .
Melinda	Plantation house	Lead guitar	Jake	Mason
Bessie	Brick house	Dulcimer, backup guitar	Buddy	Electrician
Janie	Stone house	Banjo, mandolin	Viktor	Mechanic
Flossie	Farm-house	Percussion	Beau	Plumber
Wanda	Modern house	Keyboard	Floyd	Carpenter

Lamar pointed and explained. "Melinda and Bessie are the oldest, Wanda is the baby—"

"—and I'm the best-adjusted, poorly treated middle child." Janie sank into the rocker on the other side. "Whew! We've got most of the stuff in the freezer and the refrigerator and the others are washing up, but you're gonna have to make sure the men douse that fire good, Daddy, as dry as it is. And don't let them sit down until they've put all the tables in the trucks to take back to the church later. I plan on sitting here with Katharine and resting awhile."

Lamar got up with a huff and handed Janie his cat. "This is the one who bosses me around like her mother used to. I need me a wife who can take her in hand." He ambled toward the men at the smoking pit.

"It's a good thing you've got a husband," Janie said with laughter in her voice, "or I think Daddy would be making eyes at you. He thinks you hung the moon." Her face was flushed and damp, and she fanned with one hand. "It sure is hot today, isn't it?" But she didn't seem to mind the cat on her lap.

Katharine was glad she didn't have to reply to Janie's first remarks. "It sure is." She peered down at the chart Lamar had left with her. "Do all your husbands work for your daddy?"

That made Janie laugh aloud. "I only got one, and he works for himself. The other husbands don't work *for*

Daddy, but *with* him. He's both a roofer and a general contractor, and they all have their own businesses with their own crews. But I'm the only daughter who dared marry a man Daddy couldn't hire. Of course, Beau—Flossie's husband—wasn't a plumber to begin with. He was a banker down in Atlanta."

Katharine started to tell her she already knew that, but decided not to bring Beau's past into the conversation.

Janie had no such inhibitions. "He and his first wife fixed up a big old house down there, so he learned to be real handy, but then they got divorced and she got the house, so he bought a condo down there and a cabin not far from here, to live in on weekends. Ten years ago he hired Daddy to put a new roof on the cabin, and he hired Buddy to rewire the place. Flossie helped Buddy with the wiring. She might not look it, but she's a good electrician. Daddy made all of us learn some phase of building. Anyway, back to Beau and Flossie: Even though he was more 'n twenty years older than her, they fell in love and decided to get married. She didn't want to live down in Atlanta away from the rest of us, though, and Beau was tired of being a banker, so he decided to retire and move up here full time. Daddy didn't have a good plumber and Beau liked plumbing, so he got his license and put together a crew. Once he got his business started, he helped Buddy and Jake set up theirs better. He insisted they all hire somebody to keep the books, too, and suggested we hire her to keep books for the music side of the business. Melinda had been doing that, but she was glad to give it up. Having Beau in the family has been good for everybody."

Katharine's gaze wandered to the yard, where Beau was playing Frisbee with Joe. The little boy chortled with pleasure when he flipped it back and his daddy missed it. She had to admit that Beau looked very content.

"Beau and Flossie are the ones with the farmhouse and horses?"

"Yeah. He says he'd always wanted to farm a little, keep horses, and have a passel of young'uns, but his first wife wanted one child and hated the country. The baby Flossie's having in January will be their fourth."

"How many children are in the family besides Kenny?" Katharine had seen a lot of children around during dinner, but except for the little boy, they seemed to have disappeared.

"Six right now—all girls except Joe. We tend to run to girls in the family, as you might have noticed. Bessie's Rena is eleven. She's spending the weekend with a friend. I have a couple and Flossie has a couple, but they are all under five, so they're inside napping right now. Kenny was the only bud on the bush for years. Once he went off to college, we all sort of blossomed. I wouldn't be surprised if Wanda didn't start a family pretty soon."

"Melinda doesn't look old enough to have a son who has graduated from college." Katharine's younger child had just graduated, too, and Melinda looked years younger than she.

Janie made a wry face. "She's not. She and Jake ran off and got married when she wasn't but sixteen, and Kenny was born seven months later. Mama and Daddy were fit to be tied. Wanda, Mama's youngest, was barely two. But Kenny was such a sweetheart, none of us ever regretted his coming, and Jake and Melinda have lived down everybody's dire predictions that they'd never make it. They're as happy now as they were back then."

"So Kenny and Wanda grew up together."

"I'm not sure that's the way Kenny would put it. Wanda has always kept him reminded she is the aunt and he's only the nephew. Besides, she's been working since she was six."

"But Kenny doesn't sing." Katharine didn't bother to make it a question. Anybody who had heard him knew that.

"No, but he has lots of other talents. He started working with Daddy on houses when he was about nine, and he worked with Jake on our house when he wasn't but fifteen. Jake's a mason, and he and Kenny did all the stonework. Kenny worked the next couple of summers with Viktor, my husband, and Viktor says he'd make a fine mechanic, especially since cars have computers in them nowadays." Janie sounded as proud as if she, not Melinda, were Kenny's mother.

"Is it you or Viktor who grows the grapes?"

"Viktor. He's from Yugoslavia—Slovenia, it is now. His family has a vineyard there."

Katharine felt disparate parts of her week start moving toward one another like tectonic plates. "I was reading about Slovenia last night. It sounds like a lovely place."

"It is. We go back every year for a visit and so he can do research. He's a nut about genealogy, like Daddy. Don't get either one of them—" She pressed a hand to her mouth. "I'm sorry. I forgot you do genealogy, too."

"Not as much as your daddy does."

"Viktor is worse. He's traced his family back nearly two thousand years. Can you imagine? They've had a vineyard for two hundred. His oldest brother owns it since their daddy died, and their second brother works for him, but Viktor was crazy about cars, so he learned to be a mechanic and came over here to work on imports. I met him when I took my BMW in for a checkup seven years ago."

A short man with eyes like black olives and a shock of black curly hair came up the steps and dropped a kiss on Janie's head. "Are you talking about me?"

"I'm telling Katharine you love cars."

"I do. See?" He held his arms wide so Katharine could read the message on his bright orange shirt: I GOT A NEW CAR FOR MY WIFE. BEST TRADE I EVER MADE.

"Don't believe him," Janie told Katharine. "He adores me."

"I adore her cooking." Viktor patted his ample paunch. "Janie's the only one in the bunch who can cook." He sat on the floor and leaned his curly head against her legs.

"Mama did the cooking," Janie explained. "Even after the girls got married, everybody ate here at night after work. And since I didn't get married until five years ago—four years after Flossie, even—and since Wanda is hopeless in a kitchen, I was the one who helped Mama. After she died, it fell to me to do the cooking. We still pretty much eat at Daddy's every night."

"Is a good family," Viktor said. "Everybody lives near and helps one another."

"Who cooks when Mama and the Aunts are on tour?" Katharine wondered.

"We men *can* cook," Viktor reminded her. "Today the women went to church and we stayed home slaving over a hot pit."

"For which we are all grateful." Janie tugged his curls fondly.

"Where did you live before you built your houses?" Katharine didn't see a sign of earlier habitations, but the small farmhouse surely wasn't large enough for all the daughters and their husbands.

"Daddy gave each daughter a piece of land when we got married. Melinda and Bessie put trailers on theirs—Daddy can get them cheap from people who are replacing them with houses."

"Mobile homes," Viktor said in a voice rich with disgust. "The state house of Georgia. I come to visit Janie's family the first time and what do I see? A family of builders and not one of them has a proper home. Daddy in this old pile, two of them in trailers, and Flossie and Beau in a little cabin in the woods. I say to Janie, 'I will not marry you until we build something worthy of you, to hold your precious things.' She had them in storage. Can you imagine? She and her sisters would go to the storage place to admire their furniture."

Janie nodded. "It's true. We'd all started collecting antiques years ago, but we had no place to put them.

We planned to build someday, but if it hadn't been for Viktor, I don't know if someday would have ever come." Again she stroked his head. "He got the others busy and they built our house while he planted his vineyard and orchard."

Viktor waved toward the houses up the cove. "Once her sisters saw Janie's fine house, they all insisted on houses. Five houses in five years, to suit the owners. Now people come to visit and look!" His hand swept out to encompass the cove. "They see what the men can do, and everybody gets more business. Much better, right?"

"Much better," Katharine agreed. But if the houses had all been built in the past five years, Kenny had grown up in a mobile home. Did that explain his flushed reluctance to tell Hollis where he used to live? Katharine wished she knew how to tell him not to be ashamed of his past, that a close family is a rare and precious thing.

"I was helping Katharine sort out the family," Janie said. "Don't interrupt, Viktor. You distract me."

He stroked her ankle and gave Katharine a wink. "That is what I do best. But I can tell you about the family. Here is how I learned them apart. Melinda is the oldest and the prettiest. Bessie is the most serious. My Janie is the sweetest. The three of them, they fell down the staircase. Boom, boom, boom." His hand made stairs in the air.

"We are like stair steps," Janie corrected him, "one year apart."

"They were so much trouble, Mama waited eight years to have Flossie. She was such a handful, poor Mama waited another five years to have Wanda. Wanda is the baby, and spoiled rotten. After her, Mama gave up." His grin was so impish, Katharine smiled back.

"When did you all start singing together?" she asked Janie.

"About the time I got born. We always sang at home, and Mama and Daddy sang duets in churches around here. Bessie and Melinda started singing with them when they were four and five. The next year I joined them, and gradually we girls started getting asked to sing by ourselves. By the time we were in middle school, we were singing all over the South, even up into Kentucky. Flossie started singing with us when she was eight, not long after Kenny was born."

"But they were not Mama and the Aunts," Viktor interrupted. "They were the Sunshine Sisters. Even Wanda sang."

Janie nodded. "We added Wanda when she was six, but poor Kenny couldn't carry a tune. Nobody can understand it. I guess he takes after Jake."

"He is too embarrassed," Viktor declared. "When his Mama sings in public, he goes all pink and wishes he could sink into the earth."

"And he's mortified by our name," Janie added, "especially since it was all his fault. One day when he was four, we were rehearsing and Kenny was coloring out in the auditorium—like he had to do a lot, poor thing. A man came up to him and said, 'Aren't they really hot?' and Kenny heaved this tremendous sigh and said, 'They're not so hot. They're just Mama and the aunts.' The man turned out to be an agent scouting us, and he loved the name, so that's who we became. He took us international, so poor Kenny spent his whole life being dragged from one gig to another. We home schooled him—or on-the-road schooled him, I guess would be more accurate—until high school, when he pitched a fit and said he wanted a normal life for a change. He moved in with Daddy and Mama and he's lived here ever since. Won't even sleep over at Melinda and Jake's. Says it feels like it's a museum."

"Kenny has not suffered," Vik protested. "Some boys spend their childhood wondering where they will get their next meal. When I grew up—"

"Katharine was reading up on Slovenia last night," Janie interrupted.

"It sounds lovely." Katharine agreed with Janie that the afternoon was too peaceful for a recital of sad childhoods. "I think I'd like to visit."

"It is wonderful," he agreed. "The Alps in the north, the Adriatic to the southwest, and beautiful vineyards and orchards in between. You would like it there."

"Do you know the town of . . ." Katharine struggled to remember where Anton Molnar had come from. "Something like 'Valentine'?"

"Velenje? My family's home city, up in the Alps. Famous for coal mining. I still have cousins there, but our branch of the family moved down to more fertile soil and started a vineyard a while ago." He sounded as if it had happened in his childhood, not two hundred years before.

"Would you be able to locate the family of a man who came from there to America back in 1959?"

"A defector." Viktor said it fiercely and did not make it a question.

Katharine remembered that he had been born in Yugoslavia during the Communist years, and appreciated the patriotism that kept him loyal to the country he still loved. "I'm afraid so, but he was killed in Atlanta before he could enjoy his freedom. I found the story last night in some old clippings, and wondered whether his family ever knew what happened to him. His name was Anton Molnar."

Viktor drew his bushy brows together. "Why does the name sound familiar? He is not part of our family, I don't think. Perhaps he is from a branch family for one of my many cousins. Write down his name and I will try to find out about him. I have several cousins in Velenje with whom I correspond by e-mail."

She found a pen in her purse, but not paper. He reached in his pants pocket and pulled out two business cards. "Write his name and your e-mail on the back of one and keep the other. Ellijay is not so far from Atlanta. If you get yourself a good European car, bring it to me to fix. I do not work on anything else."

She pocketed the card. "I'll keep that in mind. I need to buy one soon. What kind would you recommend?"

He frowned at her rental. "What is the matter with that one?"

"It belongs to Enterprise. My car got totaled last month."

"Ah." He sounded relieved. "As a mechanic, I would recommend a Saab. They are wonderful to drive and"—he winked—"they often need repairs. However, if I were your husband, I would buy you a Volvo, for they are very safe. And if I were your lover? I would recommend that you drive several cars until you feel about one the way you feel about me. But as a new friend? Let me think."

As if drawn by a magnet, Kenny's uncles and Lamar came up on the porch to join in the automobile discussion. Even the aunts perched on the steps and added comments and objections. Buddy and Jake were in a heated discussion about American versus Japanese when they heard galloping hooves. Hollis raced across the pasture, followed by Kenny shouting something at her.

"Don't look like a friendly race to me," Floyd said. They watched Hollis kick her feet free from the stirrups, lie sideways across her saddle, and slide to the ground.

"Odd way to dismount," said Floyd.

"She got shot in the chest a month back," Lamar told him. Katharine wondered what else Kenny might have told his grandfather about their family.

"Smart way to get down, then, " said Beau.

They all watched Hollis lead her horse toward the barn while Kenny slid to a stop behind her, still shouting.

Lamar pulled himself to his feet from where he'd been perched on the top step, playing with the ears of one of the red-and-white spaniels. "Maybe I ought to go check on them."

Katharine stood, too. "I'll drive you down. It's time we were going, anyway."

Beau joined them. "I'll rub down Hollis's horse so you can be getting on your way. Traffic gets heavy heading into town if you wait much longer."

"I will check on Anton Molnar and let you know," Vik called after Katharine.

They pulled up in front of the barn in time to hear Hollis yell over her shoulder, "I don't care, you don't need to talk like trailer trash!"

Kenny pulled his horse into the barn after her, his voice high and strident. "I may be trailer trash, but I'm not a drunk or a drug addict!"

"Whoa boy, whoa boy!" Lamar crossed the space from car to barn quicker than Katharine would have believed, and laid a hand on Kenny's shoulder. "You got no call to talk that way to a guest."

Kenny grew red and froze up. Hollis rubbed her horse furiously.

Beau took the curry comb. "Let me do that. Don't want you rubbing a hole in my horse."

"Sorry," Hollis muttered. "She's a wonderful horse."

"Come ride her anytime, but I think your aunt is ready to go now. I'll finish up for you."

"Thanks." Katharine gave Beau a grateful smile.

He grinned back. "Tell Tom I said hello. My invitation is for you all, too. Come back anytime. We'd love to have you."

"You know him?" Hollis asked as they got in their car.

"Years ago. He used to live in Buckhead." Katharine pulled onto the gravel road. Gravel crunched under their tires as she headed uphill toward the ridge.

"Really? Weird." Hollis looked over her shoulder at the cove they were leaving. "It's a weird family."

"Maybe so, but what on earth—?"

Hollis held up one hand. "I do not want to discuss it. In fact, I do not want to hear Kenny Todd's name again in my lifetime. Is that understood? If not, I'll get out right here and walk to Atlanta."

Her eyes were bright and she looked feverish, but Katharine knew it was anger, not drugs or alcohol. Hollis seldom drank, and since middle school she had been vociferous about the stupidity of using drugs. Nor had Katharine seen any of the signs parents are taught to look for that Hollis was a closet alcoholic or addict. Was that the "problem" Kenny had referred to? What had given him that idea?

As darkness shut down around them, she decided to ask. "That was a weird thing he-who-shall-not-be-named yelled at you this afternoon—that he isn't an alcoholic or a drug addict. Had you said he was?"

"Um, no."

"Had he said you were?"

Hollis didn't reply for so long that Katharine thought she was being snubbed. Then, out of the darkness, Hollis asked in a small voice, "Did you ever do one really dumb thing that haunted you for the rest of your entire life?"

Katharine thought it over, in order to answer honestly. The first that came to mind was breaking off with a boy she had really loved in high school over a stupid quarrel on graduation night. She had refused his calls, returned his letters, and driven him away before she had realized what a mistake that was. When she had met Tom, she'd thought that was behind her—until she had run into Hobart Hastings again at the Atlanta History Center the previous June. They were currently trying to work out what it might mean to be friends after all that history.

However, Hollis had seen them lunching together that same day and had worried ever since that Hasty might be replacing Tom in her aunt's affections. He wasn't—they had become two different people since high school—but Katharine decided that wasn't the example she was looking for. Hasty was up in Michigan visiting his estranged wife and daughter. She had no desire to drag him into the current conversation.

"I've done my share of dumb things," she said, "but most of them eventually got worked out. You know what your Uncle Tom says, don't you? 'Nothing becomes too big to handle if you deal with it when it's small enough to contain.' Or something like that."

"Yeah, but some things get big real fast." Hollis rode for another half mile in silence, then admitted, "One time when I was back in Atlanta during college, I went to a party with Jon and some of his friends. Kenny was there, too. We kind of enjoyed each other, even though I thought he talked weird and dressed funny. The party, though, was duller than dishwater, so when some guys I knew from high school asked us to go to another party, I said 'great!' Kenny said he thought it would be rude to leave one party to go to another. I said that was silly, we could go wherever we liked, and I went without him. At the other party somebody handed me a drink, but you know I don't like to drink, so I only drank a few sips and then poured the rest down a potted palm. Still, I began to feel odd, and when I saw some of the girls passing out, I realized somebody might be putting date-rape drugs in the drinks. I was looking for a glass of water when a guy I sort of knew came over with some punch and said, "This is mild." It tasted like lemonade. I drank two glasses and was feeling woozy when I heard one of the guys bragging to another that chemistry majors had made the punch with hundred-proof alcohol. By then I could hardly walk, but I knew I needed to get out of there. Guys were dragging girls to back rooms all the time. I staggered out to the street and called Jon, because we had a deal that if either of us ever got drunk, we'd call to be picked up."

Katharine didn't have time to process that. Hollis was already moving ahead.

"I sat down next to a tree and waited for Jon to come, but he had loaned somebody his car, so Kenny brought him. By the time they got there, I was sick as a dog. I threw up all over both of them and Kenny's car. Kenny was utterly disgusted. I don't know how he ever got the smell out of his upholstery, and Jon said later that Kenny asked several times about his 'weird druggie cousin.' That's all he'll ever see when he looks at me."

"I'm not sure that's true," Katharine said cautiously. "He looked pretty happy to see you this morning. Have you ever told him what really happened?"

"I hadn't seen him again until your house. I thought about telling him this afternoon, we were having such a good time. The view was gorgeous from up on top of the ridge, and those horses were wonderful. He's a good rider, too. I never knew he liked to ride. But he has no idea how to take a compliment. When I told him he was a better rider than I am, he said you learn to ride, growing up in a barn. I was so tired of him acting like a hayseed when he isn't one that I said some things I shouldn't have, then he said some really spiteful things back. I don't care if I never speak to him again!"

They had arrived at her house by that time. Hollis got out and slammed the car door so hard that Katharine hoped she hadn't done permanent damage to the rental vehicle.

Chapter 30

Monday

Ann Rose called early Monday morning. "I went through Oscar's albums, and I've found something interesting about Bara that you need to see. Can you come over?"

Katharine consulted the to-do list on her counter, decided it was still in the "delay" stage rather than the "procrastination" zone, and agreed she could be there in fifteen minutes. On the way over, however, she reflected that one week earlier, she had scarcely known Bara Weidenauer. Since then, the woman and her problems had co-opted her life.

Ann Rose led her directly to Oscar's library at the back of the house, a comfortable, cluttered room with shelves overflowing with books and a large leather desk chair shaped to fit Oscar's considerable bulk.

"Look." Ann Rose lifted a brown cardboard album covered to look like leather—very like those Katharine's Aunt Lucy had filled back in the thirties and forties. Ann Rose opened it across the desk. "This one is mostly Oscar's high school and college days, but it includes the war years. I don't think they could get much film, because there aren't many pictures from then. Here he and Winnie are in high school."

Katharine peered down at a small sepia picture with scalloped edges, in which two boys in leather helmets and jackets clowned for the camera next to a small plane. No one would have predicted that the lanky boy on the right would grow into a prosperous architect, or that the skinny one on the left would become a stout doctor.

Ann Rose flipped over two pages, hunting for a particular picture. "Here! This is the one I was looking for. See?"

A man and a woman stood beside a large bush. She was handing him a round hydrangea blossom while he faced directly into the camera. Katharine had no trouble recognizing Nettie and Winnie Holcomb. Winnie was already striking, if not traditionally handsome, and Nettie already had the look of a bad-tempered but highly bred horse, which grew more pronounced over the years. Beneath the picture was written in block letters, FAREWELL NETTIE AND WINNIE, HAVE FUN IN NEW YORK!

"If Oscar wrote that, he writes better than most doctors I know," Katharine commented.

"He went to Tech to study engineering. He didn't decide to become a doctor until he served in the ambulance corps. He and Winnie both changed professions as a result of the war. But what do you notice about the picture?"

Katharine studied the picture carefully. "It had to have been taken in summertime. The hydrangea is in full bloom."

"Right. And this is the section of pictures Oscar took in 1945, after he got home from Europe."

"But Nettie—" Katharine peered down in surprise at the slender woman standing with her side to the camera. "She doesn't look the least bit pregnant!"

"That's what I noticed, too. If Bara was born in September . . ."

"She must have been adopted." Katharine was so surprised, she sat in the nearest chair. "I wonder why they never told her."

"People didn't, back then. They kept it a deep, dark secret so children wouldn't get traumatized."

Ann Rose sounded as angry with Winnie and Nettie as Katharine felt.

"So instead, she gets traumatized when it's too late to ask the questions she'd like to ask."

Ann Rose closed the album and rested her hand on it. "Do you think we should tell Bara? Or show her this and let her draw her own conclusions?"

"I don't know. She's not in the best shape right now to get hit with it, but maybe it would cheer her to know Nettie wasn't her blood kin."

They sat in silence for a few minutes, neither wiser than the other about what to do with what they knew.

"Can you ask Oscar the next time he calls?"

"Yes, but that will be a while. I spoke with Jeffers Saturday and told him about Bara."

"Rita Louise knows something, but I don't know if she'd tell what she knows." Katharine related what had happened at the cathedral.

"Eloise might tell us something, as well. She's two daisies short of a bouquet where the present is concerned, but she sometimes talks quite clearly about the past."

How like Ann Rose, Katharine thought, *with all she has to do, to still take time to visit a woman who won't remember she's been there.*

One word caught her attention. "You said 'us.' Would you talk to Rita Louise and Eloise for Bara?"

"No, but I will go with you," Ann Rose consulted her watch, "if we go now. Chip won't get back until nearly noon. I think I must go, don't you? After all, I was the one who found the picture, and it was at my house that Bara first asked you to look into these medals. You shouldn't have to shoulder this alone."

I shouldn't have to shoulder it at all, Katharine mused while Francie helped Ann Rose figure out where she had dropped her purse when she last came in the house.

"She's having a better day today," the aide said as they signed in at the desk. "Her sugar was so out of whack yesterday, we were afraid we'd have to call the doctor. We finally got it under control, but we think her husband has been sneaking her sweets again."

"Is she diabetic?" Katharine asked Ann Rose as they walked down the long hall to Eloise's room.

"Apparently so. I didn't know." Ann Rose looked ruefully at a bag Francie had sent, filled with petit fours and éclairs left over from the party. "I think we'll leave these at the nurses' station, don't you?"

Eloise Payne sat beside the window, looking up at the sky. Katharine wondered what she was seeing. If Eloise had lowered her gaze she could have seen trees and shrubs on the nursing-home grounds with the smudge of Atlanta's skyline on the horizon. Instead, since the sky was a gray heat haze, she seemed mesmerized by nothing.

Katharine was grateful that her parents had not outlived their minds.

"Hello." Eloise welcomed them with a smile. "How nice of you to come." She was neat and pretty, her hair freshly set and her nails manicured. Only if you looked into her eyes did you see that there was nobody home.

Eloise peered at Ann Rose and asked, puzzled, "Are you my sister?"

Ann Rose sat beside her and took one hand. "No, we're your friends. I'm Ann Rose Anderson and this is Katharine Murray. Oscar Anderson is my father-in-law. You know Oscar. He went to school with Scotty and Winnie. We want to talk to you about the war."

Since there were only two chairs, Katharine sat on the edge of the bed and let Ann Rose steer the conversation.

Eloise looked puzzled. "Are we at war?"

"I meant World War Two, when Scotty was in the army and Winnie was a pilot. Over in Europe. You and Nettie stayed home with little Art."

"Scotty was in Atlanta. Were you in the war?" Eloise waited for Ann Rose to fill the gaps in her memory.

"No. But do you remember Bara, Art's little sister?"

Eloise puzzled that over. "The girl."

Ann Rose nodded encouragingly. "Little Bara."

Eloise watched her fingers pluck the throw and spoke as if to herself, her words scarcely audible. "Scotty thought her ugly and skinny, but I liked her. She had very expressive eyes, even before she could understand what we were saying."

"Did Nettie and Winnie adopt her in New York?" Ann Rose slid the blunt question in like butter.

Eloise looked up, suddenly angry. "Nettie! She made him do it, you know. He didn't want to. But Nettie insisted. He had nightmares for weeks, after. Terrible dreams." She plucked at the soft pink throw covering her knees, eager for them to understand.

"Nettie wanted to adopt the child but Winnie didn't?" Ann Rose asked, puzzled.

Eloise stared like a pupil who doesn't understand the question. "In New York," Ann Rose prompted her.

Eloise nodded. "Scotty doesn't, but I do. I like seeing all the people. Murdoch likes to go, too." She turned to Katharine. "I'm glad you finally decided to come see me. My own sister, and you never come. Nobody ever comes. Nobody!" Her voice rose. "I sit in this stinking place day after day and they don't feed me, don't bathe me. . . . I'm not leaving you a penny! Not one red cent. You never come!"

An aide rushed in and began to talk softly. "It's okay, Miss Eloise. You need to rest. Let me help you to your bed. You need to rest." She waved toward the door and spoke softly to Ann Rose and Katharine, "I'm sorry, you need to leave now. She gets like this sometimes."

As they walked to the car, Ann Rose asked, "Did you get anything from that?"

"Not much, except Nettie wanted to adopt the child and Winnie didn't—which is odd, considering the way they treated her later. He adored Bara, and she him."

Ann Rose nodded soberly. "He was Bara's god. She has never been the same since Winnie . . ."

Katharine almost confessed right then what Bara had told her, but she couldn't bring herself to repeat it aloud, even to Ann Rose. Surely Bara had been confused from drugs.

Ann Rose was still mulling over what Eloise had said. "I wonder why Winnie didn't want the child. I mean, he had such a heart for children. Look at how much he contributed every year to various charities for children."

"And you would think adoption would be something a couple ought to agree on before they do it."

Ann Rose's face grew grave. "Nettie and Winnie agreed on very few things, from what I understood." She checked her watch. "I think we have time to swing by Rita Louise's."

Katharine grimaced. "The shorter our visit, the better, as far as I am concerned."

"But I think we ought to call before we arrive on her doorstep, don't you?" Ann Rose pulled her cell phone from her capacious bag.

"Don't tell her I'm with you," Katharine warned, "or she might suspect what we want."

"Come in, dear," Rita Louise welcomed Ann Rose dressed in a powder blue linen dress and low gray heels, every hair in place.

Her cordiality dropped several degrees when she glimpsed Katharine, and plummeted as her gaze traveled down Katharine's clothes. Rita Louise belonged to the school of ladies who manage to drag themselves to the beauty parlor every week long after they get too frail for other functions, and who rise and dress for company every day whether they expect guests or not. Katharine's Aunt Sara Claire had been the same.

Ann Rose's classic khaki skirt, starched striped blouse, and polished flats with stockings passed muster, but Rita Louise's expression made it clear that the turquoise cotton T, cropped khaki pants, and turquoise leather flip-flops Katharine had put on for a casual day at home were not acceptable for a morning call.

If Rita Louise remembered her tearful confession to Katharine at the cathedral, she gave no sign. Feeling like an urchin dragged in off the street, Katharine decided to let Ann Rose do the talking.

"We've come on a sort of delicate matter," Ann Rose began when they were seated with cups of steaming coffee before them. "I think you know that Bara asked Katharine, here, to help her identify a box of medals she found among Winnie's things, and in the process they came across a citation stating that Winnie didn't get home from the war until February of 1945."

Rita Louise gave a chilly nod.

"Do you also know that the police may suspect Bara of shooting Foley?"

"Yes." Rita Louise didn't indicate whether she agreed or disagreed with that theory.

Katharine gave Ann Rose high marks for plowing on through rising ice. "Now they have discovered that some valuables are missing, so they are beginning to wonder if someone came in from the outside and beat up Bara, Foley interrupted them, and the intruder shot him. Payne wonders whether the intrusion had anything to do with all the visits Bara made last week."

"Payne wonders whether one of *us* killed Foley and beat Bara?"

Rita Louise's power bills must be low in the summer, Katharine reflected. The woman could chill the air with a look. Even Ann Rose was nonplussed.

Katharine decided it was time to pull her share of the sled. "Payne asked me to at least talk to the people Bara talked to, to see if they have any inkling of what kind of hornet's nest Bara may have stirred up."

Rita Louise lowered her face to her coffee cup so they could not see her expression. "Bara spoke and acted rashly, before she thought. Nettie did her best to civilize the child, but—"

"Bara was adopted, wasn't she?" Ann Rose asked.

When Rita Louise looked like she was about to deny it, Ann Rose added quickly, "I found a picture in Oscar's album showing Nettie three months before Bara was born. Nettie wasn't pregnant." She put one hand on the gnarled bejeweled ones. "If you know something, Rita Louise, you need to tell it. For Bara's sake."

"Everything in the world has been done for Bara's sake! What has she given in return? She despised the woman who raised her. She flouted the society that nurtured her. She brought disgrace on the family name."

Katharine would have argued Bara's case. After all, the woman and her eccentricity had raised more money for charity in Atlanta than Rita Louise. She had survived two dreadful marriages and managed to raise decent children. She had stayed sober for twenty-five years. But before she could defend Bara, Ann Rose chose a simpler and more effective way.

"For truth's sake, then," Ann Rose said gently. "Because it is truth that sets us free."

Rita Louise did a moment of private battle before she sagged. Her shoulders slumped. Her spine curved. Her chin quivered. She had to set down her coffee cup because her hands trembled too much to hold it. To Katharine, it was like watching a spring thaw after a particularly severe winter.

Rita Louise spoke only to Ann Rose. Katharine felt uneasy, like she was eavesdropping on a confessional. "I don't know what to do. Promises are sacred. I have believed that. I do believe it."

"You made a promise to somebody you aren't sure you should keep?"

Rita Louise twisted her hands in her lap. "Yes. Years ago, a good friend asked me to share her burden. In great distress she told me a secret and asked me never to reveal it to anyone. I promised, even though . . ." She broke off and said hoarsely, "I gave my word, but sometimes I wonder if I was wrong. I kept my promise, though. I never even told John."

"Did the secret concern Bara?"

Rita Louise hesitated. "Yes."

"Nettie is gone and Bara still here. I'm not asking you to tell us, but you could tell Bara if you know anything about her birth parents."

Rita Louise grew cross. "I don't know what good it does to rake that up now."

"Maybe you have carried Nettie's burden long enough."

Rita Louise reached for her coffee and took a sip, and made a slight face. Katharine's was still warm. Had Rita Louise's chilled from contact with her lips?

Rita Louise set the cup back on its saucer and said, "When Nettie and Winnie moved back down here after Winnie finished at Columbia, they brought Bara with them. Nettie pretended the child had been born while they were up there. She even tried to make people think Bara was younger than she actually was, though the girl was tall and precocious. Nettie told me privately that she had adopted Bara when the child was three, but it was difficult for her."

"Do you know why Winnie would have objected?" Katharine asked.

"Winnie objected?" That clearly puzzled Rita Louise. "It was Nettie who objected. She did not want another child. Art was a lovely boy, no trouble at all, but his birth was difficult. She could not have more children. They had both accepted that, but then Winnie foisted that child on poor Nettie, in spite of her strenuous objections. No woman would gladly do what she did. Take in another woman's child and raise

it as your own. Look at it every single day and watch
the other mother's face grow clearer and clearer before
you. Nettie was a saint!"

The ice was rising again. Rita Louise clasped her
hands before her.

"Do you feel you did wrong by concealing from
Bara that Nettie was not her birth mother?" Ann Rose
probed the old woman's conscience as delicately as a
surgeon.

"Why, no. Nettie did not want that known. I would
not go against her wishes simply because Bara stormed
in here drunk, demanding to know the truth. The
truth? The truth would destroy her. She worshipped
Winnie."

"Winnie was her father," Katharine reminded her.
"He raised her and adored her. That's what makes a
father."

Rita Louise's laugh was harsh. "Oh, yes, Winnie was
her father. But he was never worth her worship. He
drove poor Nettie . . ." She took a deep breath. "I made
a promise and I will keep it. You tell Bara that Winnie
was her father and Nettie was her mother. That is all
she needs to know. Now, I need for you to leave. I am
weary."

Back in the car, Ann Rose gave Katharine a rueful
smile. "I don't know which of them is crazier, Eloise

or Rita Louise. Do we know a single thing we didn't know before?"

Katharine considered the two stories. "They remember the adoption very differently. I wonder which of them we should believe."

She replayed the conversations over in her mind while she drove home from Ann Rose's and realized something she had not picked up at the time. When Rita Louise spoke of telling Bara that she was adopted, she had not spoken of keeping or breaking promises. She had spoken of honoring Nettie's wishes. It was when she spoke of "what Winnie drove poor Nettie to do" that she had mentioned the promise again. What promise could Rita Louise have made that was eating up her very soul?

Chapter 31

Viktor's e-mail arrived late Monday afternoon:

Anton Molnar was a hero during the world war. He was active in the resistance movement and did some amazing things. You can find articles about him on the Internet, telling how he hid out in barns, moved invisibly through battles, and saved countless lives. A couple of the articles are in English. I will translate the others, if you like, but I don't know how true they are. Some stories get exaggerated over the years. Speaking of exaggeration, according to my cousin, Anton defected to the US in the late fifties and was brutally gunned down on Atlanta's dangerous streets. I can't get my cousin to visit me. He thinks everybody in Georgia carries a gun. He doesn't think Anton has any family left. His twin sister died in forty-seven of tuberculosis, and his parents had died before he left home.

Katharine mulled over the e-mail and checked Anton Molnar's story through the English articles online, kicking herself for looking up Slovenia on Friday, but not Molnar. How young did you have to be to turn automatically to the Internet when you had a question?

A paragraph in one story held her attention: "Anton Molnar is credited with saving more American lives than any other member of the Yugoslavian resistance. Men forced to bail out of damaged planes were brought to him, and Molnar smuggled them to Allied troops, often taking them through actual skirmishes safely. He was known as the Gray Ghost for his ability to pass invisibly through the lines."

She thought that over a few minutes, then found Kenny's card and called his office.

"Why, hey, Miz Murray. I was fixing to call and ask if I could come up to your place tonight or later this week to drop off Hollis's clothes. She left them at Mama's after she changed into her riding things."

"You could take them by her house," Katharine suggested.

"I know the way to your place. Besides, she probably won't ever want to see me again."

He sounded forlorn and very young. Katharine wished she could reassure him, but she had no data to contradict him. "I'll be here all evening. You might want to wait until the traffic lets up and come later."

"I'll work a little late, then, grab a bite of supper, and come around seven thirty. Will that be all right?"

"That will be fine."

She was about to hang up when he asked, "Did you want something else? I mean, since you called and all."

Katharine wondered if senility was setting in early. "Yes, I did. What was that Web site you used to find the citation for Bara Weidenauer's father's Medal of Honor?"

He rattled it off so quickly she missed half of it.

"Try it again slowly, please."

"Sorry."

He repeated it and she copied it carefully: www .army.mil. Then she read it back to him, to be sure she'd gotten it right.

"That's it. Did you get Uncle Vik's e-mail? He said he'd found out about somebody for you."

"Yes, and I think it's going to be real helpful. I'll write and thank him."

"Okay. I'll see you tonight."

She found Winnie's citation and read it again. He had been rescued in Yugoslavia and smuggled to Allied forces. Had Anton Molnar done the smuggling? Was it Winnie he had come to see in Atlanta?

Was it Winnie who had shot him? Did Nettie know, and Winnie make her promise not to tell? Was that what Rita Louise knew?

Katharine was still sitting at the computer thinking that over when she heard Tom call from the kitchen. "Hello? Anybody home?"

She went with pleasure to meet him. "You're home earlier than I expected. Did the plumbing go all right?"

"Not bad." He set his duffle on the countertop and went to open a beer. She set the duffle on the floor and he frowned. "Sorry. I keep forgetting about germs."

"Germs don't forget about you. How much work did he have to do?"

"Enough to deal with the problem. Mostly outside. Sometime in the coming months we'll have to replumb most of the house, but he and I agreed that could wait until you can go up there and stay awhile."

"Thanks a lot." But Katharine didn't really mind. She'd take lots of books and escape to the lake house in the autumn, when the leaves were turning and geese were flying over. Maybe she'd ask Ann Rose and

Posey to each come up for a couple of days to enjoy the solitude. The older she got, the more she appreciated close women friends.

When the doorbell rang, Tom and Katharine were sitting in his library enjoying a rare weekday evening at home. The sunlight was slanting through the French doors leading out to the sunroom and they were both reading, with the added pleasure of being able to look up occasionally and smile at each other.

He got reluctantly to his feet. "Who could that be?"

"It's probably Kenny Todd, Jon's friend. He said he'd stop by to drop off some clothes Hollis left at their place on Sunday. Come meet him. I think you'll like him." Katharine had already told Tom about their Sunday afternoon, including its abrupt ending.

They answered the door together, and she introduced the men. Kenny stood as tall as he could and stuck out his hand. "It's a real honor to meet you, sir. Jon has told me about what you do and how good you are at it."

Tom accepted the compliment with his usual modest grace, then asked, "Did he also tell you I was seldom home for any of the important events in his life?"

Kenny hesitated. Tom clapped him on the shoulder. "Didn't mean to embarrass you. I wanted to point out that I know there are two sides to any story. Speaking of that, Katharine here says you and Hollis had a bit of a dustup on Sunday."

Katharine was startled, but not really surprised. It was in line with Tom's conviction that small issues become big issues only if they aren't confronted and defused before they grow too large to be contained.

Kenny cleared his throat. "We had a disagreement, yes sir. She lives in a very different world than I do."

"Nonsense." Tom kept his arm around Kenny's shoulder and led him into the hall, then looked around, bewildered. "Is there any place for three people to sit in this house?"

"Just the breakfast room," Katharine told him. "Or out by the pool."

"Let's go out by the pool. It's nice at this time of day. Do you have time for a little visit, Ken?"

"It's Kenny, sir. I never took to 'Ken.' And yes, I'm free this evening."

They stopped in the kitchen long enough for the men to grab cold beer and Katharine to fix herself a glass of tea, then wandered out into the soft light of the closing day.

When they were all seated, Tom leaned toward Kenny and said, "Now tell me about these two different worlds you and Hollis inhabit. I sort of thought we all lived in the same world."

Kenny looked around him. "I have to differ, sir. Hollis grew up in a place like this—a big house in the city. She's like a butterfly or something. I grew up in the mountains in a—ah—very simple home. My people work hard for their living. I don't mean you don't work hard, or anything, but—"

"I understand. You mean they come home tired, sweaty, and dirty at the end of the day."

"Well, yessir."

"Do you? Come home sweaty and dirty, I mean. I understood you work with computers."

"Well, yessir, I do. And I don't get dirty, but I do work hard. I expect you do, too."

"Some days. But talking about houses, Katharine tells me your parents live in a house that looks like *Gone with the Wind*."

"Well, yessir, they built it a couple of years ago, but they don't know what to do with it. Mama has filled it up with so many antiques, the only comfortable place to sit is the kitchen. And she never cooks or cleans like a real mother. She's all the time off singing somewhere."

"I heard Mama and the Aunts sing in Washington. They are a wonderful group."

"Well, yessir, I guess they are if you like that kind of thing."

"I do. They bring joy to a lot of people. And I want to let you in on a secret. Hollis's mama never cooks or cleans, either. And Hollis hates her parents' big fancy house. She lives in four rooms over their garage—by choice, not because they kicked her out. And she works very hard for her living. She sews costumes for theaters until late at night, and she has helped Katharine redecorate this entire house after a break-in—"

"—and she's about to work mornings for an Oriental rug dealer, learning the trade," Katharine interrupted. She added with a smile, "I think she doesn't want you knowing more about rugs than she does."

A smile flitted across Kenny's face before he grew solemn again.

"Now, I don't need to know details about the disagreement you had," Tom continued, "but I don't want you thinking that you and Hollis are all that different."

Kenny's face had gone stone hard again. "Well, I don't like to speak ill of your relative, sir, but she is a bit of a snob."

Tom laughed. "We're all snobs, Kenny. Every one of us has some things we think are a lot better than others. I'm a snob where music is concerned. I won't let you run down your mother's music when I know it is excellent. You are a snob where your mother's house is concerned. You think she isn't quite good enough for it."

Kenny's mouth dropped open. "I never said that."

"Not in so many words, but yes, you did. I'm a snob, you're a snob—even Katharine is a snob." He leaned close and said softly, but loud enough for her to hear, "She thinks SUVs turn people into bullies and are bad for the environment. She won't hear of me buying her another one. So tell me," he went on in a natural voice, "how is Hollis a snob?"

"She doesn't like the way I talk. She says I talk like trailer trash. Well, sir, I am trailer trash, and proud of it!" His face was flushed and he blazed with anger.

Tom thought that over. "You think people who live in trailers—modular homes, I believe they are called now—are trash, Kenny?"

"No sir. I know some fine people who live in mobile homes. But Hollis doesn't."

"I wonder." Tom pulled out his cell phone and punched one number. "Hello, Hollis? This is Uncle Tom. I have a question for you. As a representative of the young adults of America, what do you think about people who live in modular homes, mobile homes, whatever you want to call them?" He held out his phone so the others could hear her answer.

"Is this for a Senate investigation or something?" she asked.

"It's for an investigation, yes."

"Well, I think they need to set standards to make modular homes safer. Just because some people don't make as much as your fat-cat legislators doesn't mean they don't deserve decent housing. People should be safe in their homes, not likely to be blown away by tornadoes or hurricanes."

"What about the people themselves? What do you think about them?"

"What's to think? They're just like the rest of us. Modular homes make a lot of sense for single moms, young couples, and elderly people who don't have big incomes or don't want to spend all their time keeping house."

"I understand you recently used the term 'trailer trash.' Would you define that for me?"

"What's this really about?" She sounded suspicious.

"I'm trying to get the full picture of people who live in mobile homes. You worked with some of them down in Savannah, didn't you?"

"Yes, but there was nothing trashy about them. They were poor and couldn't afford anything better, but they were as smart, as ambitious, as deserving . . ." She ran out of adjectives.

"So trailer trash would be . . . ?"

"Folks who don't care about themselves, don't try to better themselves, and spread garbage around for other people to pick up."

"Thank you. I have that duly noted as the opinion of the young adults of America. And listen, I'll be home all this week. If you want to come over some evening to visit, I'd love to see you and thank you for the work you've done on the house."

"You owe me a check, too—a fat one. I've worked my buns off on that house."

"It shows. Thanks." He closed the phone and put it in his pocket. "Hollis is never shy about giving me an opinion from the young adults of America. I check in with her from time to time to keep abreast of things."

Kenny scratched the side of his face. "That's different from what she said on Sunday."

"She said you didn't need to talk like trailer trash," Katharine reminded him. "At least that's what I heard."

"Is that right?" Tom asked. When Kenny nodded, he said, "What do you suppose she meant by trailer trash?"

"Folks who don't bother to learn how to talk educated?"

"But you *are* educated. Is it possible that Hollis doesn't understand how educated people from the north Georgia mountains talk? Maybe you need to educate *her.*"

Kenny shook his head. "I don't reckon she'd want to learn."

"You won't know unless you try. Now tell me how you think Tech football is shaping up for the season. Is that new quarterback any good?"

They drifted from football to computers, and sat chatting until nearly nine. As Kenny stood on the front veranda saying his goodbyes, Tom said casually, "You might give Hollis a call sometime. I know she's missing Jon, and she could use a friend who doesn't have purple hair."

Again a smile flickered on Kenny's face, but all he said was, "Thanks for a great evening."

Not until he had driven down the drive did Katharine remember the original reason for his visit. "He forgot to give us Hollis's clothes."

"Good. Maybe he'll deliver them in person. Hollis could do a lot worse than that young man, Kat. And think about it—we could have Mama and the Aunts in the family!"

"Don't marry them off yet," she suggested. "They still aren't speaking."

Chapter 32

Tuesday

Tuesday morning Katharine called the upholsterer and was told the furniture would be delivered after four. Since Tom was making important calls from his library at home, she decided she might as well run errands for the party. Seeing a shoe sale, she stopped and bought a new pair. When she passed Piedmont Hospital on her way home, she decided to stop and see how Bara was doing, and remembering Rita Louise's icy looks the day before, replaced her sandals with the new shoes before going in.

That was a mistake. By the time she walked to the ICU, the little toe on her left foot was tingling. There, she was told, "Mrs. Weidenauer has gone into a private room." That entailed another long walk. By the time she got to Bara's hall, the toe was burning like fire.

At least the room was easy to spot. It was the only one with a police officer at the door.

Katharine cautiously peeped in. Bara had not been given a view—another building of Piedmont's burgeoning complex was right outside her window—but the room was as bright as a carnival, full of flowers, fruit baskets, and cards. Even suspected of murder, Bara Weidenauer was a favorite in Buckhead.

Payne and the small, dark woman Katharine had glimpsed on Saturday afternoon occupied Bara's two visitor chairs.

"I thought you'd deserted me," Bara greeted her. "Haven't seen you for days."

"I need to talk with Katharine a minute." Payne rose and dragged Katharine into the hall. "Can you stay a little while? I'd like to run down and get some breakfast, but I don't want to leave Mama alone."

"I hadn't planned on staying long, but she has another visitor."

"Yeah, but I don't know that woman, and I'm afraid—" Payne bit her lip and glanced back into the room. "Look, you probably know Mama has a drinking problem. I don't want anybody sneaking her in some liquor."

"Nobody's getting liquor through that door," the police officer assured her.

Payne gave him a withering look. "You have no idea how persuasive my mama can be."

Katharine knew how persuasive Bara could be. Why else was she standing in that hospital when she'd scarcely known the woman eight days before? However, her experience in keeping a determined alcoholic away from liquor was minimal. "I can stay until you get back from breakfast," she agreed, "but I don't know how much good I can do. If somebody comes in and tries to hand her a bottle, shall I wrestle them to the ground?"

Payne ignored her flippancy. "Your being here will do her good. She really likes you."

Katharine felt a flush of pleasure, mixed with surprise. In spite of herself, she was becoming fond of Bara, too.

"Mrs. Anderson? I'm glad I caught you."

They hadn't noticed the detective coming toward them, but Katharine should have been alerted. He was jingling the coins in his pocket.

"I wanted to let you know we got more information on that second gun we found, the one in your mother's drawer that was reported stolen by Winston Holcomb. Turns out it fired the bullet found in the skull of Mr. Holcomb."

"Mama had the gun that killed Winnie?" Payne sounded like she was having trouble taking it in. "She must have found it in his condo."

"No, ma'am. We went over that condo at the time of death. Mr. Holcomb's death was officially closed as a suicide, but this opens that case again."

Finally Payne understood. "You can't think Mama killed Winnie! That's impossible! She worshiped him." She looked to Katharine for assent.

Remembering Bara's confession, Katharine said nothing.

"Most murders are committed by somebody close to the victim, ma'am. But Mr. Weidenauer also lived in that house. Maybe he killed Mr. Holcomb and Mrs. Weidenauer found out."

He didn't bother to complete the thought. Katharine saw her own conclusion dawn in Payne's eyes: this gave Bara a far stronger motive for murder than self-defense.

Payne clutched Katharine's elbow. "Go stay with Mama. I've got to call Hamilton. She's got to have a lawyer, no matter what she says!"

As soon as Katharine went back in the room, Bara growled, "Was Payne telling you to keep me off the sauce? No, you don't have to answer. She's alerting everybody who comes in. She's a better watchdog than a pit bull. But she doesn't need to worry. I've got Maria." She gestured to the woman who had risen to give Katharine the chair by the bed. "Maria, this is my new friend, Katharine Murray. Katharine, this is my long-time friend and AA sponsor, Maria Ortiz. Maria will do a lot more than Payne ever could to keep me on the straight and narrow, now that I've climbed back on the wagon. She's worse than two pit bulls. But dammit, Maria, I need a drink!"

"She's on pain killers," Maria told Katharine. "It makes her mean, but not dangerous. And she knows mixing liquor and drugs can kill her."

"How are you feeling?" Katharine asked Bara. She accepted the chair Maria had offered and, with relief, slipped both feet from the confining shoes and relaxed them on the cool floor.

Maria moved to the chair on the other side of the bed, playing the hospital visitation version of musical chairs.

"Lousy," said Bara. "The people who moved me up here must be accustomed to moving furniture. They shoved me around like a couch or something. And the food is terrible."

"She had a delicious breakfast and ate every bite. Her daughter spoils her rotten, her friends bring her fruit and flowers—" Maria gave a deep chuckle, but one filled with sympathy. "She is grumpy because she cannot have the one thing she craves, which she knows will kill her if she does not give it up. I know," she added humbly. "I have been there myself. She will make it, but it will not be easy."

"Maria saved my life," Bara told Katharine. "She was the one who called nine-one-one."

"Don't tell her!" Maria said sharply.

Katharine was already asking, "Have you told the police?"

"I cannot tell the police. They will not believe me. They will think we beat Bara and killed her husband."

"We?" Was that simply Maria's grasp of English pronouns?

"She was with a friend," Bara explained. "Somebody else from AA. I'd promised to attend a meeting." She asked the building outside her window, "Why didn't I keep that promise? None of this would have happened if I had." She continued her explanation. "Bert, the guy who drove her to my place, has a record for robbery and assault. We can't drag him into this mess. He's gone straight since he stopped drinking."

"But if they knew he was in that house . . ." Maria's eyes were wide with fright. "Please tell no one!"

"You'll have to tell your lawyer," Katharine told Bara. "This could be very important."

"I told you, I'm not getting a lawyer. I can't afford to pay one. I'll tell my own story and hope they believe me."

Was Bara really that brave? Or was she counting on her family's membership in the Good Old Boys' network to save her? Katharine would leave it to Payne to tell her mother they were hiring a lawyer over her protests, but she did want to impress Maria with how serious her testimony could be.

"They think Bara called nine-one-one. They think she shot Foley, made the call, and fainted."

"But she was unconscious! I tried and tried and could not wake her."

"Tell Katharine what you told me," Bara instructed.

Reluctantly, Maria complied. "I went to see why she did not come to the meeting like she promised. My friend drove me to her house, for I have no car. Such a big house! I never imagined. When we got there, the only lights were upstairs but the front door was open, so I rang the bell and peeped into the hall. I know how easy it is to drink too much and forget to close your door. I think maybe Bara is getting ready for bed upstairs and will hear the bell, but she does not come, so we tiptoe into the front hall. I step on broken glass. *This is strange,* I think. *Surely such a grand house has servants to sweep.* My friend, he thinks we should get out of there, but I am worried for Bara. 'Get your flashlight,' I tell him. 'I do not want to turn on a light, but I want to make sure she is okay.' When we shine the flashlight in the front hall—a very grand hall!—we see Bara lying at the foot of the stairs, all in a heap. I think she has gotten drunk and fallen down the stairs. I try to waken her, but she will not wake up. And while I am trying, my friend sees a man lying in the dining room, and he is shot through the head. We were terrified! Whoever has shot the man must have hurt Bara, as well, and he may still be in the house! My friend insists we leave. I do not want to go without Bara, but I know it could be dangerous to move her. My friend pulls my arm. He says he must not be found there. Back when he was still drinking, he was a thief and once he beat a man. He cannot give the police a reason they will believe for why he is in that house. So I fetch a pillow from the living room and put it beneath Bara's head—"

"You put the pillow under her head?" Katharine interrupted. "That's one reason they think Bara shot Foley. They think she was conscious long enough to call nine-one-one and get a pillow."

"Oh, no, she was deeply unconscious. I could not wake her. Because I knew we should not move her, I did the only thing I could think of to make her comfortable. My friend is urging me to get out of there, pronto! But before we go, I call nine-one-one on a phone lying on the table. I do like I read once in a mystery book, where someone calls and does not speak, but leaves the telephone on so the police can trace the call and know where to go. We drive down the block and wait. Soon we see the police and emergency vehicles come, so we know someone will take care of Bara."

"She saved my dadgum life," Bara repeated.

"Do you remember anything more about what happened?" Katharine asked her.

Bara shook her head, then pressed one hand to it as if it ached. "Not a thing. I know I fixed supper and ate it, and Foley came in and tried again to make me give him Winnie's shares." She grinned. "I do remember something else. I pulled a knife on him. Nearly scared him to death."

"Don't tell the police that," Katharine warned.

"I won't. But if I'd stabbed him, none of the rest would have happened, would it?"

"If you'd stabbed him and remembered it, you'd be in a worse fix than you are. You don't remember a thing about being downstairs later, though?"

"Not a thing."

"She was in an alcoholic blackout," Maria said with conviction.

"I'm getting old, and I have a concussion," Bara insisted.

"You were in an alcoholic blackout," Maria repeated. "But that will not save you. No jury or judge will permit that as an excuse for murder."

"Maybe you could tell about coming to the house without involving your friend," Katharine suggested to Maria. "At least tell them Bara was deeply unconscious and the door was wide open."

Bara immediately disagreed. "Maria has a record of her own. Besides, they'd be sure to find out she doesn't drive, and under cross-examination, they'd crucify her. She'd have to tell about Bert, and they might even try to implicate her. She can't testify. It's enough that I know she saved my life." She turned back to Maria. "Katharine is helping me figure out who my daddy was." To Katharine, again, "Have you had any more luck with that?" She clearly wanted to change the subject.

"Not exactly." Katharine wondered how much to tell her.

"Lean on Rita Louise. She ought to know something, but she wouldn't tell me."

"Can you picture me or anybody else leaning on Rita Louise? But I did speak with her."

"And?"

"Ann Rose and I went over because she found a picture of your parents in one of Oscar's albums—"

"Let's talk plain here. You mean Nettie and her husband?"

If Bara wanted plain talking, she would get it. "Of Nettie and Winnie, taken in June of forty-five. Nettie wasn't pregnant."

"She wasn't? She had to have been."

"She wasn't. So Ann Rose asked Rita Louise point-blank if you were adopted. Rita Louise said yes, they adopted you while they lived in New York."

"Adopted me?" Bara said it slowly, taking it in. "Neither of them were my parents?"

Maria spoke sharply. "Both of them were your parents. They raised you just as I raised Farah after my friend Sonja was killed by her pimp. I am Farah's mother as much as I am the mother of the children I gave birth to. Birth only takes nine months, *querida*. Parenting takes a lifetime."

"I know." Bara spoke slowly, processing as she went. "Winnie *was* my daddy. He was a great dad. But even if she'd birthed me, Nettie wasn't much of a mother."

"She was still your mother." Maria stood up. "I must get home. I will come tomorrow. You will be fine until then." It sounded more like a command than a statement.

"I will be fine until then," Bara concurred, "but I still want a drink. I need one, bad!" Her body shook with intensity, and she gave an involuntary groan of pain.

Maria kissed her cheek. "Poor dear, you hurt, yes. And you wish you could take away all the pain of what has happened. But liquor will only add to your pain, and wanting and needing are two different things. You want a drink, but you need to give it up. *Hasta luego.*"

"There goes my real mother," Bara told Katharine when Maria had gone. "She's a good ten years younger than me, but she's raised me." She pulled her good arm out from the covers and peered at it. "Maybe I'm really Hispanic, like Maria. Maybe I was the illegitimate child of Latino teenagers from New York. Maybe that's why I am so dark."

"I don't think Rita Louise knows anything about that—or even Eloise."

Bara laughed. "Eloise doesn't know her own name. You went to see her?"

"Ann Rose and I did. She was muddy about the present, but remembered several things about the past. She seemed to know you were adopted, but she didn't tell us anything more than that." Katharine saw no point in giving Bara the conflicting stories about which of her parents insisted on adopting her and which one protested.

Bara closed her eyes and seemed to be taking it in. "Then I have no clue who I really am. That is the weirdest thing about this whole setup. Why didn't they tell me?"

"People didn't always, back then." Katharine repeated what Ann Rose had said. "Perhaps they didn't want to upset you."

"Still, Winnie was a good daddy. The best." Bara spoke the words as if tasting each one. "Now I know why Nettie didn't want people to know when I was born. And what Art used to mean when he'd say things like, 'Before you came.' Winnie never made a distinction between Art and me, though, like Nettie did. He was my real daddy, and I killed him. I killed him as surely as if I'd pulled the trigger."

With her eyes closed, she could have been talking to herself. "I went to his place and told him the board was going to make Foley CEO as soon as he retired. Foley had just called to tell me. Winnie said that would happen over his dead body, that he would make some calls and get it stopped. I told him I knew that's what he would say, but that I had come to tell him I thought Foley deserved it, that he had worked hard for the company all those years, and that he—Winnie—shouldn't try to stop the board. So help me, God, I believed it.

I never knew what Foley had in mind. But Winnie knew what a low-down snake Foley was. After I left, he made some calls. I know at least two men he spoke with. They told me later he'd asked them not to vote for Foley. Both told him they'd think it over, but neither promised. Later that afternoon Winnie went out on his balcony and . . ." Her voice grew thick and she looked away.

Was Bara sincere? Or was she preparing Katharine for a time when she might be called to the witness stand to testify, if the murder of Winnie was added to the charge of murdering Foley?

When Katharine didn't speak, Bara said roughly, "I know some people think somebody else came in and shot him, but I never will. I think Winnie saw everything he had worked for going up in smoke, and me taking Foley's side. I killed my daddy!" Tears rolled unchecked down her cheeks.

Katharine wanted a direct answer to a direct question. "You didn't literally shoot him?"

"Not literally."

"They've found the gun that did it."

Bara's eyes flew open. "Where?"

"In a drawer in your dining room."

"Oh. That gun." Her excitement vanished as suddenly as it had come. "It wasn't in a drawer, it was lying near me, with my fingerprints all over it. But that was a gun Winnie gave me in college. It couldn't have been used to kill him. It had been in my attic for forty years. Nobody knew I had it except Winnie. I'd brought it down one day last week and left it on the dining-room table, fool that I am. Whoever used it just had to pick it up and fire."

"I'm not talking about the gun that killed Foley. This was another one. The detective said they found it in a drawer. Didn't Payne tell you?"

"Payne doesn't tell me a dadgum thing. She keeps saying, 'Don't worry, Mama, rest.' How am I supposed to rest when I may have shot and killed a man and can't remember doing it? I mean, Foley was a rat and he wanted killing, but I cannot believe I would have actually done it—or that I could have if I'd wanted to. I'm a lousy shot." She looked at her hand. "Unless alcohol improves your aim. Do you reckon?"

"I doubt it. But the gun I was talking about, the one that killed Winnie, was a second gun they found in a drawer in your dining room."

"No way! I'd been through every one of those drawers the Monday before, hoping I might have left money or liquor in one of them. There wasn't a gun in there. Who was it registered to?"

"Winnie. He had reported it stolen three years before he died. The detective told Payne on Saturday that they'd found it and traced it to Winnie. While we were out in the hall a minute ago, he said they've matched it to the bullet that killed your dad."

"He was murdered? Oh, God!" It was a sigh of a prayer, followed by a wince of pain. Bara said nothing for several minutes. At last she said, "I never had it. Did they say my prints were on it, too?"

"No prints. It had been wiped."

Bara pulled the covers over her head, as if this was one thing too many to know. Katharine wondered if Payne was right, and she should not have been told.

Bara had gone to earth to think. In a moment she said, as if working it out as she went, "I did not put it in my drawer and it wasn't there last Monday. That morning I looked everywhere I could think of for money to buy groceries, and finally went to the storage unit. That's when I found the medals. This gets weirder and weirder, Katharine. Could somebody want me in jail? I don't mean to sound paranoid or anything, but somebody has planted two guns on me and left me next to Foley's body. Who could hate me that much? Have I offended someone to that extent?"

Katharine couldn't answer that, but she could ask some pertinent questions. The problem was, the most pertinent one was also impertinent, the one a lady never asks. Since Bara wanted plain speaking, Katharine asked it anyway. "Who benefits from your death?"

Bara wasn't offended, but her laugh was harsh. "Nobody, until all this mess is cleared up. Foley froze my accounts, remember? But if we ever get through this without it all going to the lawyers, then Payne gets everything. As soon as Foley started talking about wanting a divorce, I went to our lawyer and changed the will so that Payne would get everything if I died either during or after a divorce. I'm not utterly dumb. I knew it would be easier for Foley to hire somebody to kill me than to divorce me, and I wanted to make sure he wouldn't get more than half no matter what happened. It's a shame Foley got shot. He'd be such a good suspect."

"Nobody else benefits? Not Scotty, or Murdoch?" Katharine hated bringing them into the discussion, but if Bara was right, somebody had to have a motive for all this.

Bara shook her head. "Scotty poor-mouths about needing money all the time, but I didn't leave either of them a penny. Why should I? They're taken care of for life, and Murdoch's too old to have kids. Besides, they have no claim to my money. Most of mine was Winnie's or Ray's. My share of our grandparents' estate was the house, some silver, a Monet painting

I liked, and a Tiffany lamp Nana always kept in the front window and I loved as a child. It doesn't go with a thing I own, but I still keep it in the window."

Katharine didn't tell her the tea set, painting, and lamp were stolen. If Payne was shielding her mother from as much as possible, she would honor that.

She heard Payne's voice in the hall and rose to leave. But before Payne got through the door, Murdoch burst into the room screeching, "You poor darling! You look absolutely awful!"

Chapter 33

I t's good to see you, too." Bara put up one cheek
with the air of one who wishes she didn't have to.
Murdoch kissed her as if she wished she didn't have to,
either. "So glad you came to cheer me up. I thought you
were in Boston for the week. I hope you didn't hurry
home on my account."

"Of course I did." Murdoch set her big purse on
Bara's uninjured foot. Payne moved it to the floor.
Murdoch tugged down the jacket of a green polyester pantsuit that made her look like a chubby frog and
patted her dreary hair. "When Payne called Saturday,
I'd have come right away, but changing tickets is so
expensive, especially for the same day. A cousin doesn't
count for those bereavement tickets, like a member of
your immediate family."

Bara didn't try to conceal a yawn. "I think they are called compassion tickets and are for when somebody dies. You could have counted Foley, I suppose, if you could have drummed up some compassion for him. No, I don't mean that. He was a weasel, but he's a dead weasel and deserves some respect, even from me. Did you get in last night?"

"No, I had my car at the airport and came straight here. I'd have been here sooner, but there was a wreck on the connector and I had to sit there half an hour." She went closer to the head of the bed and peered down. "You look terrible."

"You don't look so good yourself, but I'm getting better each day. Hope to be out of here and to a rehab center—the exercise kind—soon. Maybe by then they'll know who did all this."

Murdoch looked confused. "Didn't you shoot Foley? I heard you tell him you would."

Bara forgot her injuries long enough to rear up as far as she could. "You what?" She collapsed against her pillows, groaning.

"Tuesday night, when I called to tell you to put the Dolley Payne Madison tea set in the bank—remember?" Murdoch sounded so put out with Bara that Katharine wanted to smack her.

"Vaguely," said Bara.

Murdoch sighed. "And see? It got stolen, just like I said."

"Stolen?" Bara looked from Murdoch to Payne. "What got stolen?"

Payne glared at Murdoch. "I wasn't going to tell her." She said to her mother, "Some silver and stuff."

"What stuff?"

"The Monet in the hall, a lot of your silver, and the Tiffany lamp."

"Oh!" Bara arched her neck and screwed her eyes shut like she'd gotten a new physical blow. "I was just telling Katharine about that lamp and picture. Anything else?"

Payne shook her head. "Not that I saw, but you'd know better than I would. I don't know why they didn't take the flatware. It was in a drawer right under the Madison tea set."

Murdoch leaned closer to Bara and spoke in what Katharine presumed she thought was a consoling tone. "Losing the tea set doesn't matter as much as it could have. The only two George Paynes I've found in our family so far were born a hundred years too late. I'll bet somebody in our family bought the tea set at an auction or estate sale because of the name. Alas, so far, I cannot find any connection between Dolley Payne Madison's family and ours."

Katharine noticed that even so, Murdoch still gave the president's wife her full name. To keep the possibility of a connection alive?

"The set is priceless, nevertheless," Payne pointed out.

"Yes, but it isn't as if it belonged to the family." Murdoch looked around for confirmation, but got none. Miffed, she said waspishly, "You forgot to hang up the phone, Bara. Before Foley found it, I heard you tell him you were going to shoot him and get it over with."

"Don't you ever repeat that!" Payne said fiercely.

"If they ask me, I'll have to. I can't lie in court."

And you'll enjoy every second of it, thought Katharine.

There's something lovable about every human creature, her mother reminded her. *You just have to look for it.*

I'm pretty sure Murdoch is the exception that proves that rule.

"I didn't say I was going to shoot him," Bara corrected Murdoch. "I may have said something like, 'I might as well shoot you and get it over with,' but that was two days before he died, and I didn't shoot him—at least I don't think I did. I don't remember doing it."

"Daddy said you had a concussion and can't remember anything about that night. But I'm sure you had a good reason to shoot him, even if he was bending over backward to give you a good deal." Seeing blank stares from everybody in the room, Murdoch elaborated. "I heard Foley tell Bara he'd give her the Buckhead house and just take the lake house, and he'd split all their money. All she had to do was give him enough shares of Uncle Winnie's company so he could vote to sell. He *was* being reasonable," she said to Bara.

"He was never reasonable," Bara snapped. "Payne, get her out of here. She makes me hurt all over."

Payne shot Katharine a pleading look. Reluctantly, Katharine shoved her feet back into her new shoes and tried not to wince as she stood. "I was about to leave. Bara needs to rest. Want to walk with me to the parking lot, Murdoch?"

Payne called as they reached the door, "Don't you say a word to anybody about—you know."

"I couldn't lie, Payne," Murdoch said, loud enough for the policeman outside the door to hear her. "If somebody asks me, I'll have to tell them."

Murdoch's rubber soled shoes squeaked on the vinyl tiles as they walked down the hall. When they were out of earshot of Bara's room, she complained,

"I knew they would try to make me lie. As soon as I heard what had happened, I told myself, 'They aren't going to want me telling what I heard.' But I did hear it. She said, 'I ought to shoot you and get it over with.'"

"It's the kind of thing people say in an argument. It doesn't mean she was going to do it."

"She was furious. And Foley *was* being kind. He truly was. I know some people didn't like him, but he was always a gentleman to me. He'd ask about Mother and how she was, or he'd make little jokes like, 'Still climbing the family tree, Murdoch?'" She tittered. "He had such a great sense of humor. I found him charming. Bara never really appreciated him."

"He could be charming," Katharine agreed. "I liked him at the few functions where we met. But he lost his charm for me as soon as I heard he hit Bara hard enough to break bones."

She was having trouble concentrating on the conversation. She could feel a blister forming as they walked. She contemplated the long hobble to her car with dread.

"He didn't!"

Katharine had to think a second to remember what Murdoch was referring to. "He or somebody did. You saw her. Broken shoulder, broken wrist, a couple of ribs, her right leg, and at least one skull fracture. Not to mention the bruises on her face and the concussion."

"Why should they think Foley did all that? She could have fallen downstairs."

It was an idea. Katharine remembered the curving marble staircase, ending at a marble foyer. And how was it Maria had described Bara when she found her? Lying in a heap at the bottom, as if she had gotten drunk and fallen down? Would a fall down a marble staircase result in the injuries Bara had? Looked like it would have killed her. But it was carpeted. . . .

Katharine would have to think about that later. At the moment her whole attention was on a spot on her little toe smaller than a dime.

To distract her thoughts while they waited at the elevator, she said, "Both your daddy and Payne thought you'd be a lot more upset about the tea set."

"I would have been devastated if it had been connected to our family, but since it isn't—there's no use crying over spilt milk."

Especially if the milk belongs to your cousin.

In the elevator, Murdoch was full of her research. "I got a lot of work done yesterday. I found all sorts of relatives I didn't know we had! I even found a George Payne of the right age, married to Ellen, and he probably was a cousin of Dolley Payne Madison, but I couldn't find any connection between his family and ours. Of course, his was up in New England, and ours was down in Georgia."

"That might have had something to do with it."

Sarcasm was wasted on Murdoch. All she seemed to want was an audience. "But who knows? When I go to England in October, maybe I'll find we are related after all. If I do, I am going to be so angry about that tea set. I warned Bara she needed to put it somewhere safe!"

Katharine regarded her curiously. Postponed anger was a new concept. But she felt confined in the elevator. It was too small for the two of them and Murdoch's obsession. She was glad when they reached the bottom.

Murdoch turned one way and Katharine the other. "The garage is this way," Murdoch called after her.

"Mine isn't. I came from that direction."

"Are you limping?"

Katharine gave her a rueful smile and held up her foot, ridiculously grateful for the first interest Murdoch had ever shown in her. "New shoes. I didn't know I'd have so far to walk."

"Would you like a lift? I've got a really close space. I'm lucky that way. Parking spaces open up for me."

"Lucky for both of us." Katharine accepted the offer gladly.

Murdoch's daddy might drive a Mercedes, but she drove a white Buick several years old—her mother's old car. A purple suitcase sat on the backseat. Seeing Katharine's glance, Murdoch said, "I wanted a color that didn't look like everybody else's on the carousel."

"But why didn't you put it in the trunk?"

Murdoch hesitated—to ask herself the same question? "I was only going to be in there a minute, and besides, the hospital ought to have good security."

Katharine didn't point out a sign directly above the hood stating that the garage was not responsible for items stolen from cars.

As Murdoch continued to chatter about her research while she drove, Katharine wondered: Do people get self-centered from living alone, or do people wind up alone because they are so self-centered?

That was followed by a scary thought. *When Tom has been gone awhile, do I do that to people? Hang on to them and bore them to death with my own obsessions?*

At least I don't make an idol of family, she comforted herself.

Family idolatry seemed rampant in the Payne family. All her life Bara had idolized a living relative, while Murdoch idolized the dead ones.

Surreptitiously Katharine slid off her painful shoe
and rubbed her foot on the carpet. She felt a prick from
something on the bottom of her foot, but savored the
relief of her unconfined toe. Dare she walk barefoot to
her car?

"I appreciate the lift. I can get out here. The elevator is right there." Katharine slid her foot back into her
shoe and felt a sharper prick. Great. Now she had two
wounds instead of one. She could hardly wait to get to
her car.

She tried not to limp the short distance to the elevator and then to her car, but as soon as she sat down
she jerked off the shoe and peered at her foot. Even in
the dim lights of the parking garage, she could see that
the blistering toe was red and angry, while a tiny spot
of blood swelled from her sole. Something must have
clung to her bare foot from Bara's floor and worked its
way in while she walked. Heaven only knew how many
germs it had carried in with it.

She used a tissue to stanch the blood and wished she
had a flashlight so she could see the spot more clearly.
In the dimness of the garage she saw nothing—except
dirt. She was glad she hadn't examined the foot in
Murdoch's presence. Her sole was filthy. Accustomed
to going barefoot around her house and even out onto
the patio, she must have forgotten to wash her feet
before sliding them into her sandals.

She scratched the wound gently and felt something sharp. She had no tweezers, but didn't Tom keep Scotch tape in his armrest? But she wasn't in his car—she was in the rental. Drat!

She dampened a bit of tissue with spit and stuck it to the wound to stanch the blood. That would have to do until she got home.

As she drove, she mulled over Bara's situation, trying various scenarios.

Scenario one: A thief came to rob the house. Bara heard the intruder, came down to confront him, and got beaten up. Foley heard the beating and came up. The intruder grabbed the convenient gun and shot him, then put Bara's prints on the gun—to make it look like she had killed Foley—and escaped with the loot. Surely that was plausible enough for a good attorney to instill reasonable doubt in the minds of a jury?

Unfortunately, scenario two was more likely: Foley was lifting the family silver and Bara heard him after he'd removed most of what he was after. She went down to confront him, he beat her, she snatched the gun from the table and shot him, then collapsed to the floor.

What happened to the silver, the lamp, and the Monet? Whether it was her father's voice or her own, Katharine knew it was his legal mind at work.

Maybe Foley's mistress took the loot. Maybe they conspired together and were putting things in her car when Bara surprised them. After—or while—Bara shot Foley, the woman fled.

Had the police asked Bara for the woman's name? Would Bara remember it? Might it stimulate her poor brain to remember more about that dreadful evening?

Katharine's own brain was stimulated to recall something Bara *had* remembered: Scotty had been at her house the week before, asking for money. That opened up a whole new avenue of thought. Scotty, playing the amiable fool, but knowing that Foley was likely to get away with treasures that had been in his family for years. Scotty, who might feel he had a justifiable excuse to take back the treasures. Scotty, who had "fallen asleep" and been late for his Thursday poker game. Scotty, who could have carried all the stuff to his house and had days to dispose of it, with Murdoch away. Scotty, who knew somebody who could sell Bara's tea service—and possibly the other items?—on the QT. Scotty, who had a key to Bara's house, because he grew up there.

Did Bara hear him from upstairs and come down to investigate? Or had he come to her room to argue with her, and. . . ?

That's where Katharine's imagination shut down. She could imagine Scotty shooting Foley on the spur of the moment if interrupted in looting the house, but where did Bara fit into the scenario? Katharine could not imagine Scotty beating Bara.

But if Scotty knew Bara was adopted, would that make a difference to him?

Katharine was a firm believer that an adopted child is completely a member of his or her adoptive family, but the witnesses agreed that Nettie Holcomb hadn't felt that way. Nettie had preferred Art and never warmed up to Bara. Scotty was a better actor than Nettie—years of bonhomie proved that. But had he secretly resented Bara, too? Enough to beat her if she came upon him robbing her house? Enough to frame her for Foley's murder?

Katharine couldn't investigate Foley's girlfriend, and she wasn't willing to believe Bara had killed him, but she decided she would like to ask Eloise a few questions.

Since Posey's was on the way to the nursing home, she stopped by, hoping Posey could go with her. She preferred to question Eloise in front of a witness.

Posey was at aerobics, but Julia, her housekeeper, was puttering in the red, black, and white kitchen. "Are you limping, Miss Kat?"

"I've got a blister and a splinter in my foot," Katharine admitted.

"Come on into this here powder room and let me have a look." After she'd examined the foot, Julia fetched a large bowl, tweezers, Band-aids, antibiotic cream, and a soft wash cloth. She filled the bowl with warm soapy water. "Put your foot in there a minute. This may hurt a little, but I'll fix you right up."

Feeling younger than Hollis, Katharine sat on the lid of the toilet and let Julia wash her foot, wincing when the blister sank into hot water and again when the wash cloth passed over the splinter in her sole.

Julia noticed the second wince and reached for the tweezers. "Let's see what you got in there." In an instant she held up something that glittered in the light. "That's no splinter. You picked up a little piece of glass." It was a tiny spike, perhaps a quarter of an inch long. "What you been doing to those poor feet? That's a bad blister on that toe, too." She applied antibiotic cream liberally to the wound and sore toe. Katharine wasn't sure why the cream was needed on the blister, but it felt heavenly to have Julia's strong fingers massage her feet.

Julia stuck on a Band-aid and heaved herself to her feet. "You go straight home and put that foot up a while," she instructed. "Tell Tom to order in a pizza or something for dinner."

"In a little while," Katharine hedged. "I have one short errand to run for Bara Weidenauer first."

Julia filled a glass with ice and poured in tea to the brim. As she handed it to Katharine, she demanded, "When you gonna learn not to take on everybody else's troubles? Sometimes that can be more trouble than it's worth."

Within an hour, Katharine would heartily echo those sentiments.

Chapter 34

Much refreshed, Katharine drove to visit Eloise. She found Eloise by her window again, looking up at the hazy sky. Did that suit her hazy thoughts?

"Hello, Miss Eloise. It's Katharine Murray, Ann Rose's friend."

"I know who you are, dear. It is so good to see you." Eloise gave her a welcoming smile. "I don't know if I have any cookies in the jar in my kitchen, but I can at least make us some coffee. It is good of you to stop by." She attempted to rise, but straps fastened her arms to the arms of the chair.

Katharine laid a hand on one shoulder. "I don't need coffee this morning, but thank you, anyway. How are you feeling?" She took the visitor's chair.

Eloise settled into her seat. "I'm fine. Nothing the matter whatsoever. And you? Were you limping?"

Imagine her noticing. "Just a little. I have a blister." Katharine tried to think how to get from a blister to what she wanted to ask. "I got it walking from the hospital parking lot to Bara's room. Did you know she's in Piedmont?"

"Bara? What's the matter with the child? She is never ill. Art has a weak throat and Murdoch gets a dreadful cold every winter, but Bara is strong as a horse. Strange, considering."

"She—uh—fell down some stairs a couple of days ago." Perhaps it was true.

"Oh, dear. Will she be all right? Nobody ever tells me anything. Nobody ever comes—"

"I came," Katharine said quickly. She didn't want Eloise veering off into anger. "I want to ask you a question about Scotty."

Eloise peered at her. "Are you from the newspaper, dear? I never speak to reporters."

"No," Katharine assured her. "I am Ann Rose's friend."

"How is dear Ann Rose? I haven't seen her for ages. Such a charming girl. I knew her mother, you know. She made me laugh."

"Ann is fine. She and I came earlier, to ask you about Nettie."

The name made Eloise widen her nostrils and shy
back. "Nettie made him do it. He's not a bad man. She
insisted!"

"Do what?" Conversing with Eloise was like walking on ball bearings.

"You know, dear. About the man."

Before Katharine could react, Eloise was chirping
on like a canary whose cover had been taken off. "He
didn't want to do it. He really didn't. But Nettie made
him. That man showed up and wanted to talk to Bara,
and Nettie was afraid people might find out about"
—she peered toward the door with an anxious frown,
and her voice dropped—"you know. She couldn't stand
that. And Winnie was out of town. She didn't know
what to do about the man."

Katharine hazarded a guess. "The man from
Yugoslavia?"

"Some foreign place. Coming to the house like that,
demanding to see Bara."

"Was he Bara's father?"

Eloise gave her a puzzled look. "Winnie was Bara's
father."

"But Bara was adopted. Didn't you know that?"

Eloise peered toward the door and the window, then
lowered her voice to a whisper. "Winnie went and got
her, but we never speak about it. Nettie doesn't want
people to know. She's so ashamed. That's why . . ."

Eloise broke off, her face puckered in distress. "Scotty is not a bad man. He's not! He's just weak. It was Nettie who made him do it!"

She was getting excited again. Katharine stroked her arm and murmured, "I know."

"What are you all talking about?" Murdoch stood in the doorway. How much had she heard?

A nurse came in behind her with a syringe on a tray. "It's time for your mother's insulin." Murdoch took the tray. "I'll give it to her."

When the nurse had left, Murdoch repeated, "What were you talking about?"

Katharine thought quickly. "I was asking your mother if they knew Bara was adopted." That wasn't going to be a secret much longer, anyway.

"Sure." Murdoch set the syringe tray on a table beside Eloise. "They adopted her in New York. I didn't know, though, until last week. All these years, they never told me. But we had been over at Bara's—I wanted a good look at the silver service before I went to Boston—and on the way home Daddy started talking about how it was a shame she got Nana's things, because she wasn't really part of the family." Murdoch's face grew pink. "Nana had no cause to bypass Aunt Nettie and me and leave the most valuable things in the family to Bara!" Murdoch had rocketed from calm straight to the screeching stage. Katharine wondered if she was in the early stages of her mother's condition.

Afraid they would disturb the other residents, Katharine lowered her voice, but felt compelled to protest. "Adopted children belong as much as birth children do. Once they are adopted, they are family."

"But Bara always was her favorite." The perennial whine of younger children.

Katharine stood. "Well, since you've arrived, I'll let you two have a visit. It's good to see you, Eloise."

She meant to hurry past, but Murdoch caught her arm. "Why were you asking her questions about Daddy?"

So she had overheard part of the conversation.

Did she know what her father had done?

"Bara asked me to try and find out who her birth parents were." Katharine tugged, trying to gently disengage her arm. "I had hoped your mother knew."

Murdoch's grip tightened. "I think it's more than that. You like solving mysteries, don't you? And murders. Genealogy isn't serious for you. It's just a pretext for sticking your nose into other people's business." Her eyes glittered, and a drop of moisture formed at the end of her nose. "Bara should never have had that tea set! And the Monet? Do you know how much that thing is worth? Millions! But she hung it right in her front hall, like it was no more valuable than something in a scruffy motel."

Katharine doubted that Bara had any acquaintance with pictures in scruffy motels, but this wasn't the time to think about that. Murdoch was so close she could smell coffee on her breath, and her eyes glittered. How far would she go to protect her father?

In a quick gesture, Murdoch grabbed the syringe and held it aloft. Katharine frantically tried to remember what she knew about insulin. Couldn't it be deadly, injected into a person without diabetes? In another instant, Murdoch would jab the syringe into Katharine's arm.

Katharine summoned more energy than she knew she possessed and wrenched away. Screaming, she dashed for the door. "Help! Help!" She pelted down the hall.

"Stop, thief!" Murdoch cried behind her.

An orderly ran after Katharine. "Stop her!" Katharine gasped at him. Her sandals slipped on the tile floor. "She's trying to kill me!"

She heard him pause, but any second Murdoch and her murderous syringe could be upon her. She kicked off her sandals and darted for the front door. Ignoring the gravel that bruised her feet, she ran to her car. Murdoch's Buick was backed into the adjoining space, its bumper scraping the low white concrete wall in spite of several signs in the lot reading PLEASE DO NOT BACK IN.

Katharine slid into her seat and locked the door with no seconds to spare. Murdoch pounded on her window. "Don't you go spreading stories about Daddy, you hear me! If you do, we'll sue you for slander. Bara didn't deserve all that! She doesn't need the money. And she doesn't even like the tea service. It shouldn't have gone to Bara. She isn't part of our family! She doesn't love it like I do. To her, it's something on a sideboard. She never sat at Nana's imagining Dolley Payne Madison drinking tea from that pot. And the Monet! Fifteen million dollars, and Foley wanted half. He'd have gotten it, too. Everybody said so."

Katharine started her engine. If she had to, she'd back out and take Murdoch with her. When her car started to roll, Murdoch jumped back, still shouting.

Katharine looked over her right shoulder to make sure she was clear on that side, and glimpsed the luggage on the backseat of the Buick. Two more pieces of the puzzle fell into place, rearranging her conclusions. Instead of backing straight, she turned so that her car blocked Murdoch's in front. The concrete wall blocked it behind.

She stopped and lowered her window a crack. "It

wasn't Scotty," she called. "It was you! You didn't fly to Boston Thursday night. You couldn't. They were socked in by the storm. Tom couldn't come home that night."

Clear as a memory, she could see Murdoch dithering in the congested Atlanta airport, uncertain whether it was better to stay and hope for a flight or go home and sleep in her own bed. Worrying about the silver service and whether Bara could keep it safe for another week. Deciding to go to her house and tackle her, remove it forcibly if necessary, knowing that Bara would probably be drunk.

"Also, you took a cab to the airport. Your dad said so. But with all that time to waste, you decided to go get your car and drive to Bara's to get the things, didn't you? Scotty was playing poker. Did he even know you'd been home? I'm surprised he didn't report your car stolen."

"I park in the garage."

As soon as she said that, Murdoch turned an unlovely shade of red. But she quickly recovered and lifted her chin. "You can't prove a bit of it." She headed to her car.

Katharine cracked her passenger window and called, "Your hotel will know when you arrived in Boston. And I picked up a splinter of glass somewhere. Was it from the floor of your car when you gave me a ride?"

But even as she spoke, Katharine knew Murdoch was right. Without Bara's stolen items, why should the police take her accusations seriously? Murdoch had a reason for her prints to be at Bara's, and who in the Atlanta airport would have noticed if she'd slipped out for a couple of hours? Murdoch was so easy to overlook.

Katharine shifted her foot and felt the sore place where the glass shard had been. Perhaps, even if Murdoch vacuumed, the police could find traces of dirt and glass on the floor of her car that matched the debris in Bara's front hall. Somewhere in Atlanta there might be a cabby who remembered picking her up at the airport or at a MARTA station and taking her home. Maybe an airport car park would have a record of when she came in or went out. But what would persuade the police to put in the man-hours or run the tests required to prove any of that? Only the silver, the lamp, and the Monet.

Oh God, what do I do now? Katharine was baffled.

Murdoch sneered over the roof of the Buick. "That's the silliest thing I ever heard of. Move your car. I'm going home."

Katharine almost left. But some prayers are answered in the oddest ways.

Murdoch pressed the automatic button to open the door. Instead, her trunk lid flew up. Inside was a pile of lumpy blankets with what looked like a wrapped painting on top.

With a scream of fury, Murdoch slammed the trunk and jumped in her car. She started her engine, pressed down on the gas. Her car hit Katharine's with enough force to whiplash her neck and jar her teeth. The side door caved and the air bags deployed.

Fighting her air bag, Katharine grabbed her cell phone and punched 911. Before they answered, Murdoch had backed up as far as the car could go, then rammed her again. Katharine couldn't find the steering wheel, so she held onto the armrest with one hand while she held the phone with the other. "A madwoman is attacking my car, and I think she's committed a murder. Come quickly!" She gave the address and hung up.

Again and again Murdoch slammed her. Katharine clutched the armrest with both hands, feeling like she had fallen into a blender. Between blows, she considered jumping out, but she felt safer in the car.

The next time Murdoch hit Katharine, she gunned her engine until it roared. Did she think she could push a car sideways? Katharine was afraid she could. She stepped on the emergency brake and prayed for help.

Chapter 35

W hy didn't you call me?" Tom demanded. He was looking in dismay at the condition of her rental car.

Katharine collapsed against the soft leather of the Lexus passenger seat. "It never occurred to me. You aren't usually here to call." She closed her eyes as he started the engine. "Before we go home, I ought to stop by the hospital and tell Bara what's happened."

"How about if I drop you off and run over to Enterprise to tell them about their car? I don't know Bara very well."

"I will be delighted to let you deal with the car." She could get used to having him at home.

When she got to Bara's room, she found Payne propped in the windowsill, Ann Rose in one visitor's chair, and Oscar Anderson in the other. The normal bags under Oscar's eyes had doubled in size and darkened from his exhausting trip, but he still rose with gallant courtesy to offer Katharine his chair. "Hamilton tracked me down and told me to come home, that Bara needed me." He gave Katharine a sharp look. "You don't look well, either."

"I don't feel real well. I've just spent the last half hour in a cocktail shaker." She stumbled to the chair he'd offered and sat down. "It was Murdoch," she told Bara. "She went to take the things—for safekeeping, she says—and Foley surprised her. He had a gun—the one they found in your buffet—"

"The one that killed Winnie?" Bara's voice was a croak. She looked away. "He killed him. The bastard killed him. I should have known. Oh, Winnie!"

Katharine was too weary to give Bara time to grieve. She could grieve later. "When Murdoch saw Foley's gun, she grabbed up the one on your table and shot him."

"Murdoch always acts before she thinks." Bara was pale under her bruises, but her wry sense of humor remained. "She'll probably tell the judge it was my fault for leaving the gun on the table. Was she wanting the silver service?"

"I think it was the Monet. She told me how much it is worth, and on the way over here I remembered that last Monday at Ann Rose's, she said she hoped to take a trip to England if she could get the money, but in the car this afternoon, she said, 'when I go to England.' I think it was the money she wanted as much as the silver service. She also told the police she tried to make it look like you had killed Foley because you have more money to pay lawyers than she does. And by the way, all the stuff was in her trunk."

Bara shook her head. "Good old Murdoch. And she's right—I do have more money than she does right now, but I sure didn't that night." Bara waved a listless hand. "So none of that had anything to do with finding my father?"

Oscar leaned toward the bed. "Your father?" He wheezed when he bent over, so he stood erect again.

Bara huffed. "Come off it, Oscar. You had to know I was adopted. But Murdoch didn't know."

"Yes she did," Katharine corrected her. "Scotty told her, to rub salt in the wound that you had the tea set. That's the reason she used to justify going to get it—that you weren't entitled to it because you aren't . . ."

". . . in her precious bloodline?" Bara finished for her. "Grandmother Payne left it to me by name. Not to 'my granddaughter,' but 'to my beloved Bara Halcomb.' She left it to me."

"You weren't adopted," Oscar said bluntly.

"Yes I was. We found out this week. Rita Louise said they adopted me in New York."

"Horse feathers! That may be what Nettie told Rita Louise and the rest of her cronies, but I went with Winnie myself, all the way to Yugoslavia, to get you. Your mother had died, and your uncle had gotten word to Winnie that he couldn't keep you and his mother was old, so Winnie and I flew over and smuggled you out of the country. We hitched a ride over with some of his old army buddies. The whole continent was still pretty chaotic in those days, so it was a heck of a lot easier than it would be now. We went to the house where you were living with your uncle and—"

Bara stared at him. She pressed a hand to her mouth and her eyes grew wide. "The men in the door! I was so scared!"

"You were terrified. You were barely three and had recently lost your mother to tuberculosis, and here were two big men you didn't know coming to take you away. You kicked and screamed and tried to run away, but Winnie picked you up and held you until you calmed down a bit. When we got back, since I was in med school, I could finagle you a Georgia birth certificate, but Winnie didn't need to adopt you. You were his daughter."

Bara struggled up on her pillows. "I was?"

Oscar nodded. "He should have told you himself, but Nettie made him promise. She only agreed to take you if he never admitted to anybody he'd had an affair with somebody else."

"Who?"

"A nurse who took care of him when he was shot down over Yugoslavia. Ana Molnar. She and her twin brother were active in the resistance, and hid Winnie for several weeks before smuggling him back to U.S. forces."

"Anton Molnar!" Katharine exclaimed. "The man who got killed."

A nurse came in and fiddled with Bara's IV bag. "She's due for more pain medication," she explained. Everybody waited to speak again until she left.

Oscar answered Katharine. "Winnie promised Anton while we were there that if he ever wanted to leave Yugoslavia, he'd support him until he could find work. An outfit in Ohio that helped defectors managed to get him out of the country, but Winnie was out of town the weekend he must have arrived in Atlanta. The first Winnie knew Anton had come was when he saw his picture in the paper with an article saying he was missing in Atlanta. He gave me a call and we tried everything we knew to track him down, but next thing we knew, an unidentified body from the prior week turned out to be Anton. He'd been shot in a street robbery soon after he arrived, apparently."

Katharine took a quick reading on her conscience and decided to withhold what she knew about that for the moment. Bara was having enough shocks for one day.

Ann Rose seemed to read her thoughts. "I'll bet that's what's haunting Rita Louise. I'll bet Nettie told Rita Louise about Winnie's little fling and who Bara was, and when the man came to the house and talked to Nettie, I'll bet Nettie told Rita Louise that too, but made her promise not to tell. When Rita Louise realized he had been killed—"

Katharine nodded. "But she had given her word not to tell." She looked at Bara to see if she was listening.

"A grave sin of omission," Ann Rose said soberly.

Bara wasn't interested in Rita Louise's soul. She was still back in Yugoslavia, mulling over her own existence. "Winnie had lost a leg and was in awful shape. How . . ."

"The leg wound wasn't originally too bad," Oscar informed her. "It was healing nicely until he and Anton started south, but they got caught in the middle of a skirmish and had to bed down in a barn for three nights. Winnie's wound got infected. By the time they got help, it was too late to save it. He told me the Messerschmitt didn't cost him a leg, it was manure."

"The locket," Bara said to Katharine.

"Do you still have that thing?" Oscar exclaimed. "Great big silver heart? You had it around your neck when we fetched you, with your mother's picture in one side and Winnie's in the other. It was much too big for such a little neck, but you wouldn't take it off, even to sleep. We had a fine flight home, I can tell you that. You didn't understand a word we said, Winnie only understood a few words you said, and you were hysterical most of the time." His eyes twinkled to take away the sting of his next words. "There were minutes when I'd gladly have pitched you out the door, but Winnie held you the entire way."

Bara smiled. "He was my daddy." A shadow creased her forehead. "Poor Nettie. No wonder she didn't like me. I look so much like my mother, it must have been hard on her. . . ." She closed her eyes, growing sleepy. "She put up with it better than I would have."

Oscar stood. "We'll go and let you rest. You've got a lot to think about. Don't try to process it all today."

"I won't." She opened her eyes slightly. "Where's Murdoch?"

"The police have taken her away," Katharine told her.

Bara closed her eyes again, as if tired of the subject. "Tell her I'll pay her legal fees."

"You won't!" Payne objected. "Not after all she's done."

"I will. Life is about choices, Payne. I've made more than my quota of bad ones—your daddy and Foley, to name two. But some good came out of that." She reached for her daughter's hand and squeezed it. "You, and Win . . ." her voice faltered. She pressed her lips together and took a deep breath through her nose, then went on with determination. "Anyway, my life isn't over yet, so while I have some choices left, I want to make a few good ones. I've already decided to sober up again, and get rid of my house."

"Your house?" Payne's voice rose in protest.

"It has never been a happy house, not since Nana died, and I don't need all that space. I'm also going to vote Winnie's shares the way he—no, the way *I* think they ought to be voted. It's time I took seriously the responsibilities he left me. I may even see if I can get a place on the board. And I want to pay Murdoch's lawyer."

"She tried to kill you!" Payne reminded her.

Bara squeezed her hand again. "No she didn't, honey, she killed Foley. And I have no doubt whatsoever that he would have killed her for trying to take those things if she had not shot first. He was getting real violent." She gingerly touched her discolored cheek. "I'll testify, if she wants to plead self-defense, and I want to pay her lawyer. I don't want Murdoch spending the rest of her mother's life in jail."

"Granddaddy wouldn't have," Payne muttered.

"Winnie was a man, not God," Bara said drowsily. "He made mistakes, like the rest of us." Her mouth curved in the old impish grin. "But I'll bet even Winnie would pay Murdoch for ridding my house of vermin."

Chapter 36

Katharine and Tom arrived home to find two burly men and a truck in their front drive. "We got your sofas and chairs," one announced cheerfully.

"Bring them in," Katharine ordered. "I need to go freshen up."

Upstairs, she washed her feet again, put on more antibiotic cream and Band-aids, and slipped into soft slippers. She sat for a moment on the side of her bed, feeling the soreness in her neck and shoulders. She wished she could crawl in and sleep for a day, but she couldn't leave Tom to do all the work downstairs. She padded down to find him in the living room, directing the men to place two blue-plaid chairs beside the peach living-room sofas.

"Those chairs belong in the den," Katharine told him.

He frowned. "Are you sure? They look okay in here."

"They belong in the den down the hall," she told the men.

"The den already has chairs," Tom protested.

"Then they must be the ones that belong in here."

They weren't. The chairs in the den were small red wing chairs Katharine had never seen before. "Those aren't our chairs! Our chairs are large and upholstered in blue and peach, with one matching ottoman."

The smaller of the two men scratched his head. "I didn't see any pink and blue chairs. Did you, Willie?"

Willie wiped sweat off his forehead in a practiced gesture with a forearm that recently had been pressed against Katharine's new upholstery. "Naw, Pete. I sure didn't. Others, neither. Only them checky chairs she don't like in the living room, and these here red ones. The red ones look nice in here," he told Katharine in a pleading tone.

"They look nice but they aren't my chairs." She headed to the phone.

The upholsterer apologized profusely. He didn't know how such a mistake had been made. He alluded again to his sick mother-in-law and the woman employee who'd had the gall to have a baby in the midst of their busiest month all year. He admitted that the red chairs belonged to a woman out in Ansley Park, who had expected them a couple of weeks back. He finally confessed that he hadn't started on Katharine's flowered living-room chairs. He also confessed that he wasn't speaking to her from his shop, but from his wife's parents' condo down at Panama City Beach. "We thought, now that her mother is better, that we'd all have a little vacation to celebrate."

"But what about my chairs?"

"I'll get on them first thing we get back," he promised.

"I've got a hundred and fifty people coming on Saturday. I need those chairs!"

"A hundred and fifty people can't sit on two chairs, ma'am. Now you calm down. I'm doing the best I can, see? I told you I'll get right on them when we get back, and that's the best I can do. Of course, if you want the men to bring them back to you this afternoon, they can, but they're all to pieces."

Katharine pictured her living room with two naked chairs, stuffing spilling all over the carpet. "No, do them next week. But I expect a discount, do you understand? They are already a week overdue—"

"I know, but my mother-in-law got sick, and then one of my best workers up and had a baby."

She hung up. She'd heard that song before.

"We won't get the chairs until after the party," she informed Tom.

"It's a shame we can't keep the red ones. They wouldn't look bad with the couches and the rug."

"That's brilliant! Willie?"

Willie was in the process of heaving one of the red chairs onto his broad back. "Yessum?"

"Bring the red chairs to the living room. We'll keep them until ours arrive."

"But ma'am! If they ain't your chairs—"

"They are for now. Put them in the living room."

"I doan' know what Mister Hammond is gonna say."

"Mister Hammond is gonna say his mother-in-law got sick and somebody had a baby. I'm saying I have to have chairs for Saturday. You can come get them Monday morning, if you like. But if somebody spills something on them at my party, you all will re-cover them for the other lady free of charge. Do you understand?"

"Yessum. I understand. But Mister Hammond ain't gonna like it."

"Mister Hammond is in Panama City Beach. How is he going to know?"

A broad grin split his face. "Right. Pete? Come help me move these here chairs."

When they had gone, Katharine collapsed onto the newly covered sofa and reached for the gin and tonic Tom handed her. She took a long cold swallow. "Thanks, hon. I needed that."

He took a swig of beer. "I can't believe they brought the wrong chairs."

She set down her glass and rubbed both cheeks with her palms to massage away the past several weeks. "They brought the wrong chairs. The glazier had to order glass for the kitchen cabinets twice because he measured wrong. One of the bedrooms upstairs is the wrong color of blue."

"FedEx left boxes of china and silver outside by the front door." Tom continued the litany as he sat down beside her.

"And did you see the trees on the front veranda Friday when you got home?"

"Yeah. I thought they looked a little strange."

"They were for indoors. I had to call Hollis to find muscles to move them in. I don't mean to complain, but this gives you a taste of what my summer has been like."

He pulled her head to his shoulder. "Poor hon. Shall I take you out to dinner?"

"You'd better, if you plan to eat."

He checked his watch. "Shall we go car hunting before we eat? I've been thinking, and I really do think we need another Escalade. They are big and safe, and . . ." He paused to take another gulp of beer.

"It's not about you."

He was so startled he choked. When he'd recovered, he said, "I beg your pardon?" He obviously thought she was joking.

Katharine wasn't smiling. "We're talking about my car. It's not about you, or what *you* want. It's about me and what *I* want. You picked the Lexus. I want a car that gets good gas mileage and doesn't cost more than a lot of families make in a year. One that is easy on the environment—things I value. And I want to go sit in cars and get the feel of them. Find one I fall in love with. I've got some models in mind, but I need to spend time with each of them before I decide."

He blinked. "Do you have any idea how long that could take?"

"It doesn't matter. I'll get another rental until the party is over, then next week I'll start looking."

"I won't be here next week."

"You don't have to be here for me to pick it out. I promise not to sign anything until you get home."

"You don't know a thing about cars."

"Do you? Really?"

He thought that over. "Not really, I guess. I know what I like, and what has good ratings. But picking cars is supposed to be a guy thing."

"I spent last Sunday afternoon with a bunch of guys who know cars the way you know senators. They gave me tips about what to look for and avoid, and they suggested three models they'd recommend. I really want to do this, Tom."

He draped one arm over her shoulder. "If you want to do it, do it." He leaned closer and whispered in her ear, "And I like your style, lady, but could you tell me one thing? What have you done with my wife?"

HARPER(LUXE)

THE NEW LUXURY IN READING

We hope you enjoyed reading
our new, comfortable print size and found it
an experience you would like to repeat.

Well — you're in luck!

HarperLuxe offers the finest in fiction and
nonfiction books in this same larger print size and
paperback format. Light and easy to read, HarperLuxe
paperbacks are for book lovers who want to see
what they are reading without the strain.

For a full listing of titles and
new releases to come, please visit our website:

www.HarperLuxe.com